The Hotel Avocado

BOB MORTIMER

The Hotel Avocado

GALLERY BOOKS UK

First published in Great Britain by Simon & Schuster UK Ltd, 2024

3 5 7 9 10 8 6 4

Simon & Schuster UK Ltd
1st Floor
222 Gray's Inn Road
London WC1X 8HB

Simon & Schuster: Celebrating 100 Years of Publishing in 2024

www.simonandschuster.co.uk
www.simonandschuster.com.au
www.simonandschuster.co.in

Simon & Schuster Australia, Sydney
Simon & Schuster India, New Delhi

A CIP catalogue record for this book is available from the British Library

Hardback ISBN: 978-1-3985-2962-5
Trade paperback ISBN: 978-1-3985-3702-6
eBook ISBN: 978-1-3985-2963-2

Typeset in Bembo Std by Palimpsest Book Production Ltd, Falkirk, Stirlingshire

Printed and Bound in the UK using 100% Renewable Electricity at
CPI Group (UK) Ltd

For my wife Lisa
In recognition of her revised and updated systems

1

If you've never heard of the Hotel Avocado, then you are way behind me. Miles back, in fact. If you have heard of it, then well done you, but don't go getting all pumped up about it because I've actually *seen* it. I see it most days. Sometimes from the pavement as I walk past, sometimes from the bus stop opposite when I'm having my lunch. To be honest, I'll take any vantage point I can. I'm not fussy like some people. There is a chance that you're someone that *has* seen it for yourself, in which case we are #equals. Better still, of course, you might be someone who has been inside or even *stayed* at the hotel. If that's the case, then I have to concede that you are an Avocado scholar compared to me. Yes, I've glanced through the front door and some of its windows (so I'd want credit for that), but I've never set a foot over its threshold. That would be the dream. Maybe one day.

For those who are coming to it all ignorant and innocent, let me add some paint to the picture. The hotel is second from the end of a long terrace of hotels and apartment buildings directly facing the sea on the promenade of my town called Brighton on the south coast of England.

It's a big five-storey Victorian stuccoed building painted a yellowy magnolia and nestled between two identically designed buildings: the Royal Hotel to the left and the Hove View Apartments on the end plot to the right. I doubt you'll have heard of either of these places. I hardly ever give them a second look. If you have heard of them or, better still, have an association with either of them, perhaps you could tell them to apply a lick of paint and get the windows cleaned. If they do that, I might give them a second chance. (Probably won't though.)

The Royal has a light box above its front door illuminating the hotel name and the boast that it has a three-crown rating from the people who enjoy giving out crowns to hoteliers. From what I've heard three crowns isn't all that. Apparently you get the first crown just for having a front door and a bed in every room. (The Avocado hasn't got any crowns. Doesn't need them. One look and you should be smitten.) The Royal has an air of neglect about it; the guttering and window frames are rotting and an inch or so of dead flies have laid themselves to rest on the inside of the light box. If I worked for the company that likes giving out the stars, I'd remove one star just for the fly cemetery and be confident my bosses would back me up come any kickback from the hotel owner.

The Hove View Apartments have seen better days somewhere along the way but I wasn't around to see them. If you ever saw them in their prime, then what a lovely memory that must be for you – have a fish taco on me and take a cream horn for your pudding while you're at it. At the top of the steps to the entrance of the apartments are two banks of intercoms with little paper inserts that announce the names of the people that live in each of the flats. I went and had a look at the names once, but they didn't mean anything to me. In fact, there is something about the building that makes me think those names don't mean anything to anyone else in the world, apart from the occupants of course. The very top buzzer had a little drawing of a crocodile and a duck next to it. I doubt that a crocodile actually resides in the flat. A duck, maybe, but not a crocodile. Not in this shitty climate.

You can forget those two places as far as I'm concerned; it's the Avocado that steals the show. For one, its windows are always clean, but listen to this (and apologies if you are one of the people who has seen the place): on the front of the hotel is a huge (five metres tall), sliced in half, fibreglass avocado hanging from the old flagpole above the fancy columned entrance. It's the star of the show and was the talk of the town when it was first raised into position. I heard a rumour that it was originally designed for a movie about a group of allotment owners up north who saved the local community from an American oil company that wanted to frack for gas in their area. The movie apparently had a lot of momentum behind it until some executive in the production office had the sudden realization that the idea was shit. If I was making a movie, the first thing I would do was make sure that the script was excellent. It seems madness to me that this detail is so often overlooked. (If you are in the movie industry or aligned with it in any way, you might like to pass this on. It's up to you.)

The actual name of the hotel is nowhere to be seen on the front of the building. The fruity visual does the job just fine on its own. (I know some people think the avocado is a vegetable, but if you're one of those people then I'm sorry but you are wrong. It's as much a fruit as a juicy satsuma, and if that upsets you then you're in for a surprise when I tell you about the aubergine.) At night a couple of spotlights drench the pale green wonder in light and fabulous shadows. I could stare at it for hours, and often do. The place is impressive enough during the day with its immaculate paintwork and polished tile steps, but at night? Wow! It could be a theatre or a museum or a dance hall with an excellent and well-established reputation. I think you could say I love this place.

The owner of the hotel is called Emily, and she took it over about six months ago. It's down to her that the place is looking so spruced up and enticing. Before she moved in, it was called The Honeymoon and it looked like a brothel or an all-you-can-eat Chinese restaurant. What a transformation. What a pleasure to behold. Emily is very pretty and full of energy and smiles. She has dark brown hair shaped into a long bob with a perfectly horizontal fringe. Medium build, medium height and if I was a bogus medium I would take a chance and predict that one day she will be the face of a new range of headphones or perhaps the poster girl for a scintillating toothpaste. I have never spoken to her but see her most days popping in and out of the hotel and getting on with business. My best friend Gary is her boyfriend and it's a joy whenever I see them strolling along the promenade together.

I know Gary very well. He's a nice bloke, short with a big nose, always friendly and always happy to have a chat. If you have a Gary in your life then I'm pleased for you. I doubt you're as close to your Gary as I am to mine but, nevertheless, well done, have a bar of fancy soap on me.

Anyway, one early evening I arrived at my usual spot on the bus-stop bench opposite the Avocado to find it wasn't the usual uplifting scene. The blue lights of police cars and an ambulance were giving the area an ominous vibe and a crowd had gathered on the promenade beside me to stare at the goings-on. *Where were they when nothing was occurring?* I asked myself. None of them were regulars like me, just part-timers looking for a buzz and hoping for a story they can tell to make them feel interesting for twenty seconds. *Would they welcome me if something gossip-worthy was occurring in their locality?* I very much doubt it.

Everyone was hushed as they watched a couple of paramedics run in and out of the hotel barking the occasional order to each other. There was a mumbling suggesting that a workman had suffered a heart attack or a fall, but something told me that it was more sinister than that. Three or four police cars were parked up and one of the officers was busy cordoning off the area in front of the hotel from the general public. I could sense there was something skew-whiff in the air. I've got a good nose for when things are off-kilter and fear and danger are on the cards and I'm usually right. In fact I'm always right. You can believe in this sixth sense of mine or not, it's up to you, but

5

remember: fear can be a terrible thing if you choose not to trust it.

The mumbling in the crowd increased in volume as a gurney emerged through the hotel doors and was danced down the steps towards an ambulance parked on the street. The paramedics in attendance didn't seem to be engaged in any life-saving activity. I was sure that this journey would be the patient's final taxi, a free ride to a place somewhere beyond the sun where the flowers never fade and the dogs don't bite.

Once the ambulance doors were closed, the crowd began to disperse. I stayed put. I wanted to see the place return to normal before I made my way home to bed. There were only three or four people left when I looked up to the roofline of the hotel and saw the figure of a small, slender man crawl through an angled skylight in the roof of the hotel. He turned himself around so that his stomach was pressed against the tiling and gingerly slid down the six or so feet to the roof edge. He stood up, placed his head in his hands and stared down at the street below. At a distance it appeared he was crying but, then again, maybe his body was twitching with laughter. He slowly lowered his arms and clasped his hands together in prayer. I suspected he was about to jump. I got a big extra dollop serving of the off-kilter feeling in my stomach and departed. That was not something to which I wanted to bear witness. If you want to call me a coward for leaving the scene then that's up to you, but remember: we can all throw a hook out and hope it catches some hurt. Thankfully, most of us have far better things to do with our lives.

You're going to find out from my best friend Gary that this evening was the start of the end of this story rather than the beginning of your journey, so I'll hand you over to him to pick up from wherever he wishes. A word of warning: Gary lacks a bit of confidence and gets very needy when he's under pressure. That's usually where I come in. Truth is, he'd be lost without me.

2

GARY

The last time you heard from me was six months ago, in 2010, when I was sat on a seafront bench in Brighton with my girl-friend Emily, my grumpy next-door neighbour Grace and her sheepdog-ish dog Lassoo. I was fending off their suggestion that we all move to Brighton together and help Emily run her recently deceased father's hotel. As you know I'm something of a shithouse, so the prospect of abandoning my legal career and moving away from Peckham filled me with dread, panic and anxiety.

Emily was committed to giving hotel ownership a bash, whether I joined her or not, and had already moved out of our Peckham flat to live in the top-floor apartment of the hotel which had previously been her family home. Grace, of course, loved to pretend she wanted to move to Brighton as well, but that was something we all knew she would never do. She was sixty-six years old and remained the most contrary and single-minded woman I had ever met. I wouldn't put anything past her but, come the crunch, I didn't think there was a crowbar anywhere in the world big enough to prise her away from her comfy flat in Peckham and the memories it held.

I was still living next door to Grace, in my one-bedroomed, third-floor, walkway-accessed local authority flat behind Peckham High Street in south London. My work as a legal assistant was as dull and predictable as ever, which suited me fine. After all the trouble with the corrupt south London police officers and the murderous Private Investigator John McCoy, I was glad to have normality back in my life. Ordinary, worry-free days are my favourite days of all the days that come to pass. McCoy and his police associates were all safely locked away on remand in prison awaiting trial. I would be summoned, as a prosecution witness at the trial, and that would be manageable. I work in the courts most days of the week so nothing really to fear there.

You might not be familiar with the case, so it's probably best I fill you in. In a nutshell, a computer dongle came into my possession which contained statements and video footage proving that a hard core of police officers based at Lewisham Police Station were as corrupt as they come; everything from witness intimidation to the planting of evidence and even the murder of the bloke who had given me the incriminating dongle. They were bad men, really bad, and I had got myself into very deep shit. Eventually my skin was saved by a certain DS Marks from the Met's anti-corruption unit. Unbeknown to me, he had been leading a longstanding investigation into the Lewisham coppers and came to my rescue just as it seemed they were going to dispose of me for good.

I owed my life to DS Marks and was determined to help him out by giving my evidence in court. He had worked on the case for many years and a guilty verdict would be his ultimate reward.

After Emily made the move full-time to Brighton, I would spend most of my weekends with her at the hotel. Some of these weekends we would just nest up in the apartment, eat junk food and watch TV. Sometimes I would help her complete a little project, like sanding and varnishing a banister or removing old bathroom fittings from one of the bedrooms. Sometimes we would get out and about and meander around the lanes and streets of Brighton and its outskirts. Emily liked to walk and once she started it was very hard to get her to stop, turn around and head for home. Her hip had been damaged by a bullet fired from the gun of her thug of an ex-boyfriend Tommy Briggs just before he turned the gun on himself. She had made a remarkable recovery and only got the odd twinge of pain first thing in the morning or last thing at night. 'Use it or lose it' was her motto and she stuck to it like a fanatic.

When it came to our weekend walks, Emily often preferred not to have a destination in mind; a general direction or vague purpose was enough. '*I need an orange hat*' or '*I want a kebab and I want to eat it in a small park*' or '*I've heard Peacehaven is a shithole, let's go and take a look*'. Because of this approach, I never really knew how many miles of striding my soft white lawyer's thighs would be subjected to. If she wore her jeans and Doc Martens boots, then I knew the walk would be casual in length, but if she wore her lime green jogging top, black stretchy jogging pants and luminous orange training shoes, I knew my pale, weak legs were in for a battering. If she tied her hair back into a ponytail, then, in a word, I was fucked. Whatever the weather I would wear jeans and my dark green puffa jacket. Lightweight and breathable, it's a really flexible bit of kit.

'When do you reckon we'll be back?' I would tentatively ask.

'Why does it matter?' she would reply.

'It doesn't. I was just wondering, you know, so we can plan the day.'

'Why do you need a plan? Are you pretending we're in the army or something?'

'So do you think we'll be back for lunch?'

'Who cares? We can grab something while we're out if need be.'

'Probably not back for lunch, then?'

'I don't know, Gary, I just don't know. As incredible as it might seem to you, I'm just going to see how it pans out and roll with it. Are you with me or against me?'

I would know by the tone of her voice that the conversation was over. Often she would emphasize/celebrate its passing with a brief flurry of shadow boxing or by lifting her foot onto my shoulder and shouting, 'Viva tomatoes!'

I guessed my weekend visits were a useful diversion for Emily from the anxiety and stress of getting the hotel ready for business. She would use me as a sounding board for her ideas and I tried my best to advise and encourage. I had an open invite to come and join her in Brighton, but it was something that we rarely discussed. She sensed it was a difficult decision for someone as cautious as me and never put me under any real pressure. It wasn't in Emily's nature to twist my arm. She was too proud and doggedly self-sufficient for that. The other interpretation, of course, was that she was ambivalent about me joining her in her new life. I didn't believe this was the case, but I had logged the possibility in the back of my mind so that if it proved to be true the impact wouldn't be as catastrophic on its arrival. My more pressing worry was that if things stayed as they were we would drift apart or, worse still, she would meet someone else. This is what had happened with all my previous relationships. I was going to have to make a decision sooner rather than later. Perhaps I was just waiting for something to happen that would force my decision one way or the other. Perhaps deep down I wanted to sabotage the whole thing and just wallow in the safety and dullness of my ordinary life in Peckham.

There was one time when the issue raised its head out of the blue and caused me unease. I had taken Grace and her dog Lassoo down to Brighton with me on one of my weekend stays. Emily wanted Grace to see the progress she had made refurbishing the rooms and sprucing the place up. On the Sunday evening, before Grace and I left for home, we all sat down on Emily's bench again for a farewell chat and an ice cream. Emily began talking about her staffing plans.

'I'm going to need a housekeeper, a cleaner, maybe a receptionist, maybe an assistant manager—'

'No, you don't,' Grace interrupted. 'This chump here can be

your assistant. You would have to buy him a new suit, of course, and some lifts for his shoes so he can reach the keys behind reception.'

'I'm a lawyer, Grace,' I replied with a slightly haughty curl on my lip. 'Emily needs somebody who knows the hotel business and is a people person, not a—'

'No, she doesn't!' interrupted Grace again. 'She knows the business inside out herself. She was brought up in the bloody hotel. What she needs is someone to support her and look after her and share the ups and downs with her – not some stranger who's just in it for a wage packet and a skive. Mind you, having said that, I bet you've got a good skive in you given half a chance.'

'What do you think?' I asked Emily, hoping her response would be light and non-committal.

'It's up to you. The job's yours if you want it, but you'll have to be quick.'

It was the perfect response to keep me in my comfort zone and I was happy to continue the conversation without undue anxiety.

'You don't really think that I could be of any use around the hotel, do you?' I asked.

'I might be able to train you up. Better the devil you know and all that.'

'Yeah, but what about "don't mix business and pleasure" and all that and everything?'

Grace let out an exaggerated groan and held her head in her hands as she barked out: 'Stop with the remarks, Gary.

Christ's sake, give yourself a boot up the arse and just see where you land for once.'

'We've been through this many times, Grace. I would have to give up my flat, which would cost a big chunk.'

'Oh, leave it out!' said Grace with full-on cockney contempt. 'You're the only big chunk in this situation. Just keep the flat on for a while. It's not like Emily is going to charge you effing rent, although I would if I was her.'

'And my job . . . I have to give three months' notice . . .'

Grace stood up and interrupted my jabbering once again.

'You could have given your notice in three months ago if you'd had the balls. I can't listen to this anymore. I'll be at the car.'

She gave Emily a hug. 'Good luck, darling. The hotel looks amazing. You're going to smash it,' she whispered into Emily's ear. Then, louder, with her face turned towards me: 'I'll smoke him out of his flat if need be then he'll have to get off his arse.'

And off she strode with Lassoo, who kept turning his head to keep an eye on Emily until they turned the corner out of sight.

'You'd better catch her up,' said Emily. 'Don't worry about things. We'll both be fine either way. Maybe in the not too distant you could get a legal job here in Brighton? You don't have to work at the hotel. It would be nice if we could spend more time together, that's all really. See you next weekend.'

She gave me a kiss on the cheek and turned and walked away. I think she might have had a tear in her eye but wasn't sure. I wasn't going to make a fuss. Emily didn't like fussing. As I watched her go, however, I felt a familiar little wave of worthlessness spread through me.

3

GARY

On the drive back to Peckham, Grace was unusually silent. I sensed a sulk. Lassoo seemed to be doing his best to back her up by lying stock still across the rear seats and letting out a foul odour at what seemed like pre-set intervals. '*Hurt Grace and I hurt you*' seemed to be his message. I turned on the radio. Grace turned it off. I turned up the heater. Grace lowered her window. I opened a pack of crisps. Grace snatched them off me, ate a few and then crushed the pack into her coat pocket. She knew I wouldn't dare pull her up on it. A couple of miles outside Lewes, on the A26, I broke the silence.

'What's got you all narked up?' I asked her outright.

'You.'

'Why? What have I done?'

'Nothing, just like you always do.'

'Is that a remark?'

'Don't get clever with me, and stop talking unless you've got something to say that's worth responding to.'

More silence. I pulled the car over onto the kerbside and turned off the engine.

'If you've got something to say, just say it,' I said.

In response, Grace got out of the car, shut the door and stood outside with her back towards me. Lassoo started to scratch at the rear window. Grace opened the door and let him out. Lassoo sat on the pavement with his back to me. It started to rain. They both got back in the car. I turned on the windscreen wipers, which immediately began to squeak and shudder. I turned them off. Grace turned them back on.

'Why did you do that?' I asked.

'Because I'd rather listen to them than you.'

'We're next-door neighbours, Grace. It works much better if we speak.'

'Not for me, it doesn't. Just drive on, please. Let's get this journey over and done with.'

'You trying to break my heart, Grace?'

'You haven't got one.'

'Yes, I have, I can feel it breaking as we speak.'

'Well, don't panic, you can still get a beat out of a broken heart. I should know.'

That rapped me on my knuckles and shut me up. She was of course referring to the heartbreak she lived with every day, triggered by the estrangement from her daughter Mary and her granddaughter Lizzie. It was now over four years since she had seen them and the pain seemed to be getting worse rather than better ever since Emily had suddenly stepped into her life and reminded her of what she was missing. She blamed herself. You can't reduce a person's life to one single moment, but if you could it would be that moment Grace made the call to go to the shops and leave Lizzie in her flat on her own. The rest is history: her daughter stopped all contact and the few friends she had on the estate collectively decided to shun her. I was working hard on her behalf to get her access to her grand-daughter either through mediation or the courts, but it was a slow and emotionally draining process. Grace wasn't the easiest of clients. She desperately wanted to see Lizzie but at the same time was stubbornly reluctant to talk about the issues involved.

I drove away. Grace started to let out the occasional theatrical sigh and got herself all fidgety and huffy in her seat. Then, out of the blue, she fired up.

'Do you expect that beautiful young girl to take on that great big hotel all on her own? Cos if you do then you can't think much of her.'

I didn't know how to respond. Lassoo stood up on the back seat so that I could see him in the rearview mirror. I would swear that he shook his head at me.

When we arrived back at our block of flats, she went on ahead, leaving me to deal with Lassoo. I let him off his lead and he ran straight to the play area where the see-saw used to be. At that moment, my squirrel friend appeared next to me at the base of a beech tree.

'Alright, mate,' I whispered to myself. 'You've got a sparkle in your eyes and a good high tail. Seems like things are going your way.'

'Thanks, Gary,' I replied on his behalf. 'I've met a new lady and that always puts a spring in my step. There's nothing like a new romance to put lotion on your bones. Have you thought around that as much as you maybe should?'

'I'm sorted, thanks.'

'Long-distance love, though, isn't it. Never easy. Maybe you should pack your bags, move in with her and seal the deal. Have you thought around that as sufficiently as you should?'

'Don't you start. So how did you meet this new lady of yours?' I asked.

'At a talent competition. She was stood balancing on top of a nut with just one leg while she sang a song about a ferry route or a fitness centre, something like that – it was hard to pick out the words because she had another couple of nuts wedged in her cheeks. But, boy, she had a tail on her – wide, plump and heavily curved. I'm seeing her later today over by the bins. Will be a fresh start for me and that's a good thing to be happening. You're looking a bit dreary, mate. Maybe you should think around a new beginning and how that might re-invigorate you.'

'Maybe I will,' I replied. 'Good luck with your date.'

And off he ran with his tail lofted in the air like a great big parting question mark.

By the time I arrived outside Grace's flat, the door was shut. I knocked cheerfully and she eventually opened it, but not enough to reveal herself. Lassoo slid in through the gap, pausing for a second to give me a look that said, '*You've bitten off more than you can chew here, mate.*' Then Grace shut the door on me and left me outside on the walkway.

Back in my flat, I sat on my old sofa and poured myself a beer. I always missed Emily the hardest for those first few hours after returning home from a visit. I think we had reached the status of being a serious couple, but this wasn't something I dared to presume (let alone mention). Her experiences with her previous boyfriend Tommy Briggs had been miserable, and I felt that if I appeared too keen, too clingy, she might run a mile. I had never asked her how she felt about 'us'. I don't know why. Maybe I feared the answer she might give.

I wanted to phone Emily, just to hear her voice as much as anything. We don't tend to speak much over the phone. She says she's too busy to have my waffle dulling up her mind and, anyway, she also says, we need to save up the chit chat for the weekends. She doesn't like phones – says she prefers real life. Sometimes when I phone her, she answers with a tart 'Yes, what is it?' I immediately think she's angry with me and that gets on her nerves and I apologize and she gets frustrated and I wish I'd never bothered phoning. Instead, I sent her a text message that read, 'Viva tomatoes X'. I didn't expect her to respond, but hoped it might put a smile on her face.

Why am I hedging my bets and not moving down to Brighton? I asked myself. What would a decent person do in this situation? Who cares? Why do I get so fixated on wanting people to think I'm a decent person? Who are these people who sit in judgement of me? Why don't they just fuck off to some prairie and harvest horseshit instead?

The choice to have a few more beers and watch TV was much easier than contemplating the one that really mattered.

By the time I went to bed, I'd managed to put the Brighton dilemma out of my mind and replaced it with a train of thought about what outfit I would like to be wearing when I'm laid out to rest in my coffin. I plumped for my shitty grey work suit, red cowboy boots and full tiger face paint. That would gain me a big slab of respect for the journey into the unknown, I thought.

4

GARY

It took a while to get back in favour with Grace, nearly a week as I recall. It was a memorable week because it included the day that I first met Mr Sequence. I should tell you about that.

On the Monday after Grace took her strop, I set off for work five minutes early so that I had time to check in on her. No surprise that she didn't answer the door when I knocked, so I bent down and peered through the letterbox to see if she was up and about. I could see the last few inches of Lassoo's nose sticking out beyond the jamb of the bedroom door. He was holding it perfectly still as if playing a game of musical statues.

'Hi, Lassoo,' I whispered.

The whiskers on his nose twitched ever so slightly, as if a ladybird had landed on them.

'I can see you, Lassoo.'

Another twitch and a brief dilation of his nostril, as if the ladybird had given him a tiny punch on his nose.

'Grace!' I shouted. 'Are you okay?'

There was no reply, but I noticed that Lassoo's nose was

slowly disappearing, millimetre by millimetre, back into the bedroom. When it was fully withdrawn, the bedroom door slammed shut.

'Go away!' shouted Grace. Lassoo added a bark for good measure.

It was going to take a large, good-quality meat pie to pull her out of this grump.

My first appointment was at 10am with a new client called Clive Sequence. (Sequins?) (The receptionist had just written it down as heard.) A glance at the appointments book simply stated that he required 'legal advice'. These generic, unspecific enquiries always landed on my desk. I finished my mid-morning cup of tea and slice of Battenberg cake and went downstairs to the reception to collect him. He was sat in the waiting area slouched on a chair with his skinny legs stretched out in front of him. He was slightly taller than me and was wearing a black puffa jacket with an integrated bright orange hood. He looked to be in his mid-fifties and had the thickest, most bouffant hairstyle I had seen on a man of that age for some time. Dark brown with a few wisps of grey, it was parted down the centre and had enough height either side of the parting to conceal a couple of sausage rolls. It then rolled down over his ears and formed a thick neck pelmet dense enough to provide cover for a nervous mouse. I wanted to touch it from the moment I saw it. When I introduced myself, he replied with a flat Northern accent – probably somewhere like Mansfield, but don't take my word for it.

'You're four minutes late,' he said.

'Yeah, sorry about that, my last appointment ran over slightly,' I lied.

'Oh yeah? I didn't see anyone leave just now.'

'Yeah, you wouldn't have, it was an online consultation.'

'What was the person's name?'

'I can't tell you that, it's confidential,' I said with minimal conviction and a slight squeaky break in my voice. This bloke seemed to know that I was bluffing. He must have a nose for it. He didn't let it drop. I was beginning to regret my deceit.

'Oh, confidential, is it? That's a horrible answer. So, what was his problem?'

'Honestly, Mr Sequence [Seaprince?], I can't talk about other clients' cases.'

'If you ask me you're acting a bit slippery, son.'

'I don't mean to be . . .'

His face suddenly broke out into a broad, insincere smile as he got up out of the seat and shook my hand.

'I'm only joshing with you, lad. Pleased to meet you, Mr Thorn. One thing, though: I can spot bullshit a mile off, so best leave that out of your repertoire when you're with me.'

I received his watery handshake and beckoned him to follow me upstairs to my office.

I took off my suit jacket and sat down behind my desk as he surveyed the office and then fixed his stare on the plate of cake crumbs next to my mug of tea.

'Was it a nice bit of cake?'

'Yeah, nice bit of Battenberg.'

'Ladies' cake, that is.'

'Either way, it's a classic.'

'You should try a man's cake.'

'What's a man's cake?'

'Date and walnut, as long as it's not iced.'

We paused for a moment. He sat down on the opposite side of the desk. Unlike his exotic hairstyle, his face was nondescript – long, pale and thin with a sharp, pointy nose. I'm moon-faced and big-nosed and I wondered if it was that contrast that made me suddenly feel cold towards him. I didn't want him to like me, and that rarely happens when I meet a new face.

'How can I help you, Mr Sequence?' I asked, before clarifying: 'Have I got that right? Sequence?'

'Yes, that's about right,' he replied.

I made a mental note to get the correct spelling of his name before he left.

'I need a little bit of legal advice,' he said.

'Well, you've come to the right place.'

He switched his gaze away from me for a second and ran his tongue along his lower lip before smacking his lips together.

'Good to know, that's really good to know,' he said as he removed a large vaping machine from his pocket and sucked on its nozzle with great passion, as if trying to suck the stone out of a hard green Spanish olive. With his eyes closed he let the cloud of vapour spill slowly through his fixed rictus smile, evidently savouring the stench of its smoky essence. The room was soon filled with the scent of apple and launderette. 'Lovely,' he announced and then opened his eyes wide and suddenly alert.

'I'm not in trouble as such,' he said, 'but I'm the type of person that likes to make informed decisions, wise decisions, decisions that won't come back and bite me on the neck. Do you know what I mean? Is that an approach you can sympathize with?'

'Yes, as a lawyer, very much so. I should have asked: would you like a cup of tea or anything?'

'Would you like to make me one?'

'I'm happy to make you one if a cup of tea appeals.'

'That's good to know but I'm okay for the moment.'

'Okay then, how can I help to inform you?'

He looked me up and down for a moment and I sensed a slight smirk within his attitude, probably caused by the cheapness of my suit.

'In a nutshell,' he said, 'I'm soon to appear as a witness for the police in a very serious criminal case involving some very nasty individuals whose reputation for violence is very real and very present. It might well suit me to fail to attend at the trial so as to avoid any repercussions.'

'Have you spoken to the police liaison officer in the case and expressed your worries to them?'

'No, I have not. I don't want my eventual actions regarding this to be misinterpreted unfairly in the light of any previous conversations with the police. Truth is, I'm beginning to feel a bit vulnerable. That's an awful way to feel, wouldn't you agree, Mr Thorn?'

'You can call me Gary and, yes, I agree.'

'That's good to know, Gary. I'm thinking maybe I should

move my address, and that way I can avoid being served the summons to appear in court and should they, the police, come looking for me, I'll be nowhere to be found.'

'It's very hard to hide from the police,' I said with the gravity of an actor playing the father in a coming-of-age movie.

'It is, Gary. Almost impossible for most people, but not for me, I think. You see, I'm a very selfish and resourceful individual and the thought of suffering violence against my person is a great motivator for me.'

'I can't advise you to break the law.' (Teacher in a civil rights movie.) 'If you fail to appear when summoned or fail to tell them of a change of address, then you will be in contempt of court. If your evidence is vital to the prosecution case, the court would more than likely adjourn the case anyway and you'll be no further forward.'

I noticed that he seemed to have very little interest in my advice (other than to sniff at it) and began to wonder why he was even here in the office.

'The only circumstance under which you would be excused,' I continued, 'is if you're suffering from severe physical or mental illness, and that doesn't seem to be the case with you.'

He relaxed back into his chair, brushed his fingers through his hair and opened his legs up unpleasantly wide. He took another long suck on his vape and blew the smoke directly towards me. I got a hint of vanilla but the main note was still the launderette – by the dryers, not the washing machines.

'What if I was to get a mate of mine to stab me in the arse the day before the trial? Might that do the trick?' he asked.

I laughed. He didn't.

'What would you do, Gary, if you were in my situation?' he asked.

'Well, I can answer you that, Mr Sequence. [Ceefax?] Because I am in a similar position – perhaps even worse, because the defendants in my case are policemen and, as you say, it's near-on impossible to hide from the police. I'm a bit worried about appearing in court – that's only natural – but it's not going to stop me from doing the right thing. I'm a good boy, you see?'

'Ah, and that's the rub, because you see, Gary, I'm not a good boy. In fact, some would say I'm a very bad boy. What if they offered you ten thousand pounds?'

'Nope.'

'A hundred thousand pounds?'

I laughed. 'That's not going to happen.'

'But what if it did?'

'It would still be a no.'

'What if they threatened you or someone close to you?'

'Then I would go to the police, and that's the advice I would give you. I hope I've made the situation clear. Is there anything else I can help you with?'

'Yes, but, in the meantime, might I take that cup of tea now, please?'

I left him in my office, went upstairs to the little cubbyhole kitchen and brewed him a cuppa. When I returned, Mr Sequence (Frequent?) was gone. My wallet was on my desk and I couldn't recall whether that was where I had left it. I had a quick rifle through and nothing appeared to be missing. I ran downstairs to reception but he was long gone.

I hadn't taken any contact details for him and I didn't believe for one moment that his name was Sequence. (I know his real name now, of course, but it is not a name I like to speak unless my hand is forced.)

5

GARY

I felt slightly nauseated by the lingering launderette stench of Mr Sequence around my office and was glad to get out and have my lunch down the road at Wayne's café. On my walk there I conjured up a daydream to lift my spirits. I imagined that I was walking along the road with the largest box of washing powder that had ever existed. It was six foot high but its weight was no problem for me. I carried it effortlessly on my shoulder like a powerful mayor. As I strode victorious down the street, startled onlookers gasped and waved. Children gazed in wonder and several pensioners fainted into the arms of their loved ones. Passing cars slowed down to observe the wonder, pulling down their windows to laud me.

'Wow, Gary, you're making that look effortless.'

'What you are doing is nothing short of magnificent!'

'There's not many men could lift that amount of detergent.'

'Hey, Gary, can I get a selfie with you and the powder?'

'That's incredible lifting power. Well done, son.'

It put a smile on my face for a moment and made me feel a bit brighter regarding my prospects.

Wayne was an occasional client of mine whenever he had legal problems and was a good connection I had made via my daily visits to his café. I don't know whether he viewed me any differently from his other regulars, but I liked to think he looked forward to my visits. We had an easy way between us and could create a sunny atmosphere for each other.

When I went in, Wayne was behind the counter polishing his new espresso machine with a dirty cloth. He no longer favoured the skinny parsnip-legged denim jeans, having moved on to what I would describe as a very basic safari suit brought up to date by being black and slightly baggy. His dad was sat in the window seat wearing his favourite brown pin-striped suit with a pale yellow shirt and blue floral tie. Immaculate, classy and not looking an inch of his sixty-plus years.

'Alright, Wayne, regular campachoochoo, please.'

'What roast do you want?' he asked with a surprisingly earnest attitude dominating his face.

'I don't know. Just regular like always.'

'I don't do "regular" anymore. You can have light roast, medium-light roast, medium roast, medium-dark roast, dark roast or dark-dark roast. The light roast is a Sumatran bean, the medium-dark is from Peru and the dark-dark is from . . .'

He hesitated and walked over to inspect a bag of ground coffee before returning to announce that the dark-dark was from Ethiopia.

'It's personal preference,' he continued. 'A lifestyle thing. I like a dark–dark first thing in the morning to get me fired up but then I switch to a medium-dark for the rest of the day because it's a less hectic brew.'

'You're sounding a bit pretentious, Wayne. I don't think it sits well with you,' I replied. 'What's brought all this on? The new coffee machine?'

'And you sound as ignorant as always and a bit ungrateful for the graft I'm putting in here.'

'When you say graft, you mean going down to Aldi and buying three different strengths of coffee bean?'

'What do you mean Aldi? I've got a specialist supplier.'

'I saw you checking the packet and it's from Aldi. I've got the same packet at home.'

'There's nothing wrong with Aldi, mate. Have you tried their pork luncheon meat? It literally throbs.'

Wayne's dad shouted over, interrupting our incredible conversation.

'Just give the man his coffee, Wayne, and stop prattling on like an air hostess.'

'So what blend do you want?' he asked again.

'Aldi dark–dark, please,' I replied, and then walked over to Wayne's dad and asked if I could join him.

'If you insist,' he replied as he brushed a few crumbs off the table top with his paisley handkerchief.

'Wayne's looking smart today,' I noted.

'He looks like he should be working in a laundry. He should be wearing a suit. He is the face of the business and he should be showing the world that he is serious about what he is doing.

He thinks the place is all about Wayne but it should all be about the customer.'

I felt a real connection with this man. We had the shared experience of mental torture at the hands of Detectives Peterson and Rowlett and their associates. It had been a cloud over both our lives, one that had rained on him for over fifteen years. It had been just seven or eight months for me, but we had a little window into each other's pain that we didn't peer into very often. We preferred to look to the future and take a mutual pleasure in ridiculing Wayne and his dress sense. Today was different, though.

'Are you beginning to worry about the trial? I've heard it might be starting sometime soon,' he asked out of the blue. I could see from his dark brown eyes and tightened lips that there was worry on his mind.

'A bit,' I replied. 'DS Marks phoned me the other day and told me a couple of police officers from Rowlett and Peterson's squad had been granted bail. It's made me start looking over my shoulder again.'

'I heard that too. It's got me feeling jumpy. It's taken so long to come to trial, I sometimes wonder if it will ever happen at all, that the case will be abandoned on some technicality or other. That's often how things can be when you're dealing with high and mighty people with the right connections.'

'Have they confirmed whether they want you to appear as a witness?' I asked.

'I've given them my statement and they have it on file. I'm on their list of potential witnesses but I didn't give them much.

I want nothing to do with these people, let alone have to face them in court. Strange to think they were once colleagues of mine. If they summon me to court I might just disappear, leave the country – maybe even pretend I've gone insane like my son.'

'Funny you should mention that. I've just had a bloke in the office thinking of doing the same thing. A different case, but the same line of thinking. I told him to be a good boy and turn up.'

'What if you, or someone you care about a lot, got threatened with violence? Would it really be worth it just for the sake of a "Good Boy" badge?'

'Someone like Wayne, you mean?'

'No, not that Herbert. Someone that's worth a second thought. That girlfriend of yours, or that batshit neighbour you hang around with.'

We both laughed.

'Seriously, though, Mr Gary, my legal beagle, what would you do?'

I hate the thought of physical pain being inflicted upon me by another person. I sometimes have little flashes of pain-impact moments that pass through my mind, just half a second or so of a fist smashing into my face or a boot connecting with my chin. I don't suppose anyone welcomes the prospect of pain, but for me the avoidance of it has always been something of an obsession.

When I was around ten years old I remember being followed home by a couple of lads from my estate. I didn't know them but recognized their faces. They were a couple of years older than me and their clothes and hairstyles gave me little clues that they were wrong-uns. Short shaved banana-shaped patches above their ears, highly polished ox-blood Doc Martens boots and thin, gaunt faces that suggested they lived on a diet of chicken crisps and Diet Coke. Even their movement and gait suggested slyness and malice, as did their muffled conspiratorial voices. If I sped up, then they did too. If I crossed the road, they followed me.

I knew something was going to kick off so just as I turned a street corner, I ran into what seemed to be a driveway, only to find that it was actually the entrance to a church hall car parking area from which there was no exit. They followed me in and walked silently towards me. After pinning me against a fence, one of them head-butted me on the bridge of the nose. I fell to the ground and formed myself into a ball, expecting the worst. Which is exactly what I got. Kicks rained down on my hands as they tried to damage my head and on my sides as they targeted my kidneys. Eventually the blows stopped. I was crying and pleading for them to leave me alone. One of them said that they were finished with me and told me to get up. I slowly unravelled myself from my hedgehog defence and as I did so I felt a gap in the front of my teeth and the taste of blood on my lips. Fully expecting more blows to arrive, I stood up, shaking like a leaf, and muttered, 'I think I've lost a tooth.'

One of them pointed to the floor. 'There it is, pick it up, they might be able to put it back in.'

I bent down to pick up the tooth and as my face reached a couple of feet from the ground I felt a hammer-like blow to my left eye socket. My head flew backwards with the impact of the Doc Martens toecap and left me flat on my back on the floor. I heard the lads run away laughing and whooping. I lay on the gravel with my eye rapidly swelling and closing up, convinced I was going to die. The real world suddenly seemed like a place full of evil and danger. I wanted my mum. I guess that was the day that Gary the shithouse was seeded.

I answered Wayne's dad's question: 'If I thought the threat of violence was real, then I honestly don't know what I would do. I'll give you the answer if I'm ever actually put in that situation.'

'Let's hope I never get the answer, then,' he replied.

Wayne arrived at the table with my coffee.

'One dark-dark cappuccino and a slab of Battenberg on the house,' he said as he placed them on the table in front of me.

Unfortunately, I had already consumed my morning Battenberg, so I asked Wayne's dad if he wanted it.

'If you insist,' he replied.

6

It's me again. Sorry to interrupt, but there is something I forgot to tell you that may be of importance. If you're the type of person that never forgets anything, especially tiny little details that seem of no significance at the time, then well done, get you and don't panic, the medal is in the post. I see a lot of things every minute of every day, but I don't store them all in my memory bank. I don't have the capacity. I'm an artist, not a mathematician.

There had been a lot of comings and goings at the Avocado in the months leading up to the night of the ambulance and the gurney. The first big rush of people came about three months ago. They arrived one Monday morning and spilled out of various white or grey transit vans – workmen, all dressed in vaguely sporty attire. I very much doubt, judging by the appearance of most of them, that they could run half a mile, never mind the four or five miles I walk every day. I don't wear clothes that suggest I'm anything other than what I am and I get complimented on my style every single day without fail. I put that down to the fact that I never try too hard. You may have been complimented on your appearance every now and then, but not every day, I bet. If you have then by all means treat yourself to a half-hour boat trip on me.

Anyway, within a week the hotel was covered in scaffolding and a couple of decorators were busy prepping and painting the front of the building. I took to having a sit down on the steps of the next-door Hove View Apartments so I could listen to the decorators chit chat as they painted the first-floor windows. It's not that I'm a nosy type, just that I like to keep an eye on the kinds of people that are in and around the hotel. I consider it my duty. If I don't then who will? (Not you, I expect. I mean, not that long ago you hadn't even heard of the Hotel Avocado, let alone played any part in its wellbeing.) It wasn't a memorable conversation and I think I've only recalled it because it made me think about my relationship with Gary.

The two men were both in their fifties and wore dark blue tracksuit bottoms and black hoodies. Both had beer bellies and one of them had the words 'Ha Ha Benidorm' emblazoned on the back of his top, while the other's had a printed image of a jar of mixed pickles on it.

'Have you sorted out that trouble at home?' Spanish Laughter man asked.

'Not really. It's not down to me to make a move. I haven't done nothing wrong,' replied Mr Pickles.

'So what exactly has occurred?' asked Spanish Laughter.

'Bullshit, just heaps of bullshit.'

'But not on your part?'

'No, because I don't deal in bullshit. You ask anyone about me and they will tell you that Billy the Pickle don't get involved in bullshit.'

'So why isn't she speaking to you if you've done nothing wrong?'

'Because she likes friction. Simple as that.'

'Have you asked her what the problem is?'

'No, why should I?'

'Well, maybe you have done something wrong without realizing it. She might have a genuine gripe that needs addressing.'

'The day she has a genuine gripe with me is the day I give up eating gherkins, and I tell you, Ronnie, that ain't never going to happen.'

'I think you should ask her.'

'Why don't you ask her yourself if you're so fucking interested?'

'That, Billy, is a bullshit thing to say. Are we painting all the windows?'

'Nah, we're leaving the glass see-through.'

They both laughed so hard that it seemed a thousand tiny candy canes might burst out of their lungs at any moment. I reckoned they were good friends but could be even closer if they put more effort in. One of them was looking for a deeper connection and the other was keeping their guard up, which is very much like Gary and me, if I'm being honest, and obviously Gary is the one with his guard up, while I'm an open book.

The other reason I may have remembered that conversation

between the painters was because it was later that day, when I saw them leaving in their van, that I got a feeling that something was not quite right. It started when I realized they had forgotten to remove the ladder from the lower section of the scaffolding. This meant that any Tom, Dick or other stranger could climb up and spy inside the building or even break into it. Now, you might be the type of person that would march up to the front door and inform the owner of the problem, but that's not me. I never like drawing attention to myself and I hate getting involved with any situation that's already given me an off-kilter feeling. I worry that I might affect the natural outcome of things. There was no getting away from it: I would have to hang around through the night to observe whatever was about to unfold.

Sometime around midnight, the avocado spotlights were turned off, as were the lights in the fifth-floor apartment where Emily lived. Other than a low glow coming from behind the reception desk, the hotel was in total darkness. I had never had the chance to nosey through any of the upper-floor windows so took the chance to quietly clamber up to the first-floor scaffolding deck and peer through the first large bay window. It was too dark inside for me to see anything other than the reflection of my face. I got a quick rush of my off-kilter feeling but it passed, so I continued up to the fourth-floor window adjacent to the Royal Hotel, where I noticed a very dull light coming from inside the room.

When I pressed my face against the window, I could see that a strip of light was squeezing through the little gap under the skirting board of the party wall shared with the Royal Hotel. The source of this light was a mystery. There were no lights on in any of the adjacent rooms on any floor of the Royal, and no lights on in the rooms immediately above or below. As I tried to get a better angle of view into the room, the strip of light disappeared for a second and then came back on again.

I stood back and inspected the wall about three or four feet to the right of the window at the point at which I guessed the two buildings joined. There was an old iron gutter bracket hanging by itself, no longer needed for support. I could see some light coming from a small crack around one side of the bracket and so stuck my nose right into the crack to see what I could see.

I could make out a long corridor stretching out ahead of me, the full depth of the building, and sure enough, there was a light source coming from the very far end – maybe a small reading lamp, maybe a torch, or perhaps just some stand-by light for an air-conditioning unit or some such. Then something covered the light source briefly and moved away. It was as if someone or the shadow of someone had walked in front of my spyhole. I worked away at the iron bracket to see if I could widen the crack and get a better view down the corridor. When I returned my eye to the slightly bigger crack, I could see the corridor much more clearly. It was about thirty feet long and three or four feet wide with brickwork to one side and plasterboard to the other. I focused in on the very far end of the space and could make out a man's jacket hanging from a hook above a small, school-like desk. A shadow moved across the light again and, unlike before, it didn't come back on. I felt a full-on off-kilter vibration and scarpered back down the scaffolding and out onto the street to make my way home.

And this jacket is the thing that I wanted you to know about. It was the very same jacket that the little man on the rooftop was wearing on the night of the ambulances and the hopeless gurney ride. Something tells me you should be aware of this.

You can believe what I have described or not, but I would strongly suggest that you do. If you reckon you've got a more reliable person to listen to then I'm very pleased for you, perhaps you should invite them round to share a plate of sausages, but don't come asking me for advice when your life takes a turn off-kilter, and remember: advice from a stranger like me can be a very useful tool, especially if you know how to listen to it.

7

GRACE

I just don't know what the score is with Gary since Emily moved away and stopped visiting us here in Peckham. I would hate it if he moved to Brighton full-time. It would make a big hole in my life. I don't think he's got the balls to do it, but I can sense that he's wavering and it makes me very anxious. What about me? How am I meant to cope on my own? Who's going to take me to the doctors? Who's going to pick up my prescriptions? Who's going to take Lassoo for a walk when my hip is playing up? Who's going to fetch me the occasional pie and share a bottle of lager with me when the nights draw in? And what about the work he's been doing to get me access rights to see Lizzie? If I don't get to see my granddaughter soon I doubt she will even remember me.

I keep 'encouraging' him to make the move, keep trying to prick his conscience about Emily being on her own, just to find out how strong his resolve is and thankfully he seems to be holding out on staying here with me and Lassoo. All his relationships in the past have faded and run out of steam and I doubt this one will be any different. Why give up everything he's got going on here for a gamble on a girl he's only known for six months? Only a daft bastard would do that, and I suppose that's my big worry, because that's exactly what Gary is: a daft bastard. Don't get me wrong, I love him to bits. He's like the son I never had. No, strike that, he's better than a son because there's no painful upbringing nonsense or obligations between the two of us. He's my mate – my best mate. We make each other laugh, we look after each other. That's why I want what's best for him, and I believe that to be staying right here in Peckham with me and Lassoo and getting on with sorting my visiting rights to Lizzie.

I expect you think it's selfish of me, and you're probably right. You do need to realize, though, that I have done absolutely nothing to put him off moving to Brighton. In fact, if anything, I've encouraged him to leave. Jeez, I've even pretended that I would move down there with him to stop him feeling guilty about leaving me behind on my own. All I'm saying is that I hope he stays and I think moving would be the wrong decision for him. I'm trying to look out for him. Maybe if, in a year's time or so, him and Emily are still together, I might change my mind, but not at the moment. No thank you.

Other than worrying about Gary and Lizzie, life goes on as before. The neighbours largely ignore me and if it wasn't for my television I'd have very little company in my life. Oh, on that note, I do have one nice little bit of news. I think I might have a potential new friend. An admirer even.

I was out taking Lassoo for a walk early one morning a few

weeks ago and I'd let him off his lead. He got on with his normal snuffling and running about between the beech trees that make the boundary to the play area when a fella came up and spoke to me.

'Hope you don't mind me saying, love, but that's a lovely dog you've got. He seems a bit wayward, you know, a bit of an idiot, and that's how I like my dogs.'

'I don't mind at all because he very definitely is all of those things,' I replied, meaning every word of it.

'I used to have a pug boxer mix,' he continued. 'He wasn't dozy as such but he stank to high heaven and however often I scrubbed him or changed his diet it never diluted. I got used to it so it didn't really bother me but the problem was his stench would infect quite a wide radius so it would attach to anyone in my vicinity. Couldn't take him anywhere where I would be in close proximity with people, you know, the doctors, public transport, cafés, friends and relatives.'

'Did you talk to a vet about it?' I asked.

'Yeah, he said it was something to do with his glands, probably genetic and most definitely untreatable. He gave me the option of having him put to sleep. Can you believe that?'

'Did you consider it?'

'To be honest I did, just for a moment, but then I looked into his big fat stinking face and I just couldn't do it.'

I laughed. I could tell he was just being the funny guy, trying to pass some pleasant time. 'What happened to him? Did you find a way to mask the stench?' I asked, genuinely curious.

'No, it just got worse and worse as the months passed. If I

took him on a bus he could clear the whole top deck in minutes and if I took him to the vets they would make me wait outside until it was his turn to be seen.'

'Has he passed away now?'

'Yeah, bless him.'

'What was his name?' I asked.

'Charlie.'

'Like the perfume?' I said.

We both laughed. He told me his name was Robert and he had just moved into the area. He's not from south London but I won't hold that against him until I know him a bit better. He's a bit younger than me, I think, nice-looking in a market trader kind of way. Bald head but no visible tattoos and a pleasant air of confidence about him. He says he's living off disability payments but I can't spot anything that seems to be causing him any physical trouble.

I've bumped into him a few times now when I've been out walking Lassoo. He's asked me if I would like to have lunch with him one day at the new café that's opened on the high street. I've said I'll think about it, and you know what? I probably will. Be nice to have another friend on the estate, especially given the situation with Gary.

8

GARY

A few days after my meeting with Sequence I received a blunt response from Emily to one of my texts:

'I'M BUSY! STOP BEING SO NEEDY . . . PS YOU NEED TO TALK TO GRACE AND APOLOGIZE FOR SHOUTING AT HER IN THE CAR. GOOD LUCK X'

It didn't sound as if she was upset, so I immediately felt reassured and generally encouraged. It annoyed me slightly that she had found the time to speak to Grace, but I appreciated that when Grace is trying to get in touch with you the best approach is to respond straight away (ideally within around eight minutes) to avoid upset. I was happy to give Grace her apology; there was no way she would make the first move and the stalemate would just drag on. Pride can be a formidable master, especially if you're lonely, and Grace was nearly as lonely as they come.

I bought a little gift for Grace — a savoury one of deep beauty with a thick, forgiving crust. When I returned home

47

from work she was on the walkway outside her front door, assessing a pile of old computer magazines she had stacked along her front wall.

'You having a clear-out?' I asked.

'What's it to you?'

'Do you need a hand?'

'No, I'm nearly done,' she replied, turning her back on me and facing the front wall of her flat for no reason other than to express rejection.

'I bought us a pie, steak and potato. It's still warm. Pop round if you want some. I'll do some mash?'

'Is that all you've got to offer?' she replied, still facing the wall.

'Yeah, well, I mean I've got a tin of mushy peas if you fancy them.'

Her head twitched slightly at the mention of mushy peas but it wasn't enough to turn her around to face me.

'I was thinking more along the lines of an apology,' she said, altering her posture to extremely upright.

'What am I apologizing for exactly?' I asked.

'You know very well what you did. Apologize and that will be the end of it.'

'I'm very sorry for raising my voice at you on the way back from Brighton and for anything else that may have occurred on the journey or since.'

'Apology accepted.'

'Thank you. Are you coming round or not?'

She turned around wearing a charming smile.

'Just give me ten minutes and yes, I want the mushy peas. Do you want me to bring gravy granules or is it a runny pie?' she asked.

'Best bring them just in case it's a turgid one,' I replied.

When Grace arrived at my flat (a good half-hour later and with Lassoo in tow), she was wearing her baggy yellow jumper, green neck scarf and crimson red slacks. She had tied her shoulder-length greying brown hair into a top knot and put on some red lipstick. I took this effort she had made as her visual apology to me. To accept it, all I had to do was say that she looked lovely.

'You look amazing,' I said. She smiled and told me that Lassoo was very excited about coming round to visit me.

I glanced through to the kitchen where Lassoo was fast asleep on the mat in front of the hot oven. He was twitching slightly and pushing little pipes of air through one side of his lips.

I served up the pie, mash and mushy peas. Grace lifted the lid on her half and declared the pie to be on the succulent side of sturdy and not requiring any gravy. We both attacked the meal jazz-style with spoons, as if eating a soup. I licked my plate when I'd finished, which Grace told me was disgusting and then proceeded to do the same herself. We retired to the sofa and opened a couple of bottles of lager. We were very comfortable, both with each other and with the fullness of our bellies. We didn't say much. Good friends can sustain a bit of silence. I turned on the TV. Grace grabbed the remote from my hand and turned it off.

'Why won't you move down there, Gary? What's the real

reason? I thought you loved Emily and that should be reason enough. You should want to be with her. Nothing else should matter.'

'You matter, Grace. In fact, I keep thinking that one day you might actually say you would love it if I stayed here in Peckham with you.'

Her eyes widened slightly and I'm sure I saw a happy pulse flash across her face.

'Go on, say it: say you would like me to stay here in Peckham,' I pressed.

'That's not going to happen and I don't want you worrying about me or using me as an excuse,' she replied.

Another flash of happiness crossed her face and developed into a saucy smile. She knew that I knew the game she was playing.

9

GARY

I need to tell you about Roma. A couple of months after the suicide of Tommy Briggs and the arrest of the Lewisham police officers, we were all summoned into the reception area at work by the senior partner John Blenkingstop, to meet a new employee: Roma. There were about fifteen of us cramped into the reception room and I had to peer through a couple of suited shoulders to get a view of the greeting concert.

Blenkingstop stood in the corner by the depressed and depressing cheese plant with his arm around Roma's shoulder. She didn't seem comfortable with the embrace and was holding her body with stiffness in her bones. Her eyes were tilted downwards, seemingly fascinated by the box of toys beside the desk. (The reception occasionally doubled up as a play area when a client needed that option.) I was positioned at the back of the throng, hoping to avoid eye contact with Blenkingstop. He had a habit of selecting someone for 'gentle' ridicule at these gatherings. I was a favourite victim of his because of course I never bit back or displayed any apparent hurt. (Why

51

do most people not seem to care whether I like them or not? I always have to do the heavy lifting.)

Roma was short, maybe five feet five. She was wearing black trousers, a white blouse and a grey cardigan. On her feet was a pair of casual shoes that trod the midpoint between training shoe and pensioner comfort slip-on. She had shoulder-length, strawberry-blonde hair, which was side-parted, and her face was dominated by large, round, soppy blue eyes. Her nose was standard and her lips gave no indication of meanness. She wore a good helping of foundation, which gave her a youthful appearance, and I took that into account when I assessed her to be a couple of years younger than me. Twenty-eight was my opening offer.

Blenkingstop was blarting on about what a great place this was to work and how welcome we would all make Roma feel when he suddenly called out my name.

'Gary, where are you hiding?' I held up my hand and raised my head into his view. 'Ah, there you are, come on over and introduce yourself to Roma.'

As I made my way over to cheese plant corner, the rest of the staff started ironically clapping and whooping as if I was arriving to receive a Pride of Britain award. It was their way of indicating and reinforcing the fact that I was the office runt.

'Roma, this is Gary,' said Blenkingstop. 'Don't worry, he's only half as gormless as his looks suggest.' The throng laughed dutifully and without joy. I shook Roma's hand and her face broke out into a grateful smile that suggested she really was pleased to meet me. Unusual. Blenkingstop explained that he had selected me to be Roma's mentor and first point of contact if she had any queries or questions. I was to make her feel welcome and generally show her the ropes. 'No hanky-panky, though,' he said as he gave her shoulders a final squeeze and dismissed the meeting.

I walked her round the offices, explained the various administrative forms that would become the bane of her life, made sure she had all the computer passwords and, most importantly, introduced her to the kettle and the fridge. I showed her the tin box on the shelves in my office that contained my secret stash of hot chocolate sachets for if she ever needed an afternoon pick-me-up. She was quiet and reserved and it was all a little awkward. I didn't ask her any personal questions or spout much small talk. I didn't want her thinking I was the office creep. That was more important to me than anything.

A few evenings later, straight after work, I went to watch the football at the Grove Tavern in Camberwell. It had been my local since I moved to Peckham and was a happy place for me. I hadn't made any serious connections there (other than when I met Emily, of course), but I was becoming part of the furniture and the staff would say hello and indulge me in a chat or two. On football viewing nights I would sit at the end of the bar with my football 'mate' Andy. Tonight's match was between two French teams so was full of flair, ill temper, ghost fouls and over-elaborate referee stances.

Andy was a solid sort of bloke, overweight but happy in his skin and uncompromising in his rejection of fashionable clothing. Dark blue puffa jacket, beige shirt and boot-cut jeans were his uniform. He sold various types of insurance from an office on Camberwell New Road. I knew very little about his personal life. He was single, used to own an Alsatian dog that got so tired it died, and lived in a house up Denmark Hill way. He was a bit sweaty, but pleasant company so long as you were a good listener.

'Do you like the French football?' Andy asked.

'Yeah, I'm okay with it. It's always quite lively and skilful,' I replied.

'Did you know that before the invention of paper the French used to wipe their arses with corn cobs?'

'I don't believe that.'

'It's true. Well, maybe not the actual cob,' Andy conceded, 'but the husks that you pull off to reveal the cob.'

'I don't think a corn husk would have enough absorbency. They might as well have used tree bark.'

'Well, maybe they did,' Andy mused. 'I mean, the corn is going to be seasonal, innit, so it's only going to cover them for a couple of months or so.'

'Where did you pick up this information?' I enquired.

'The internet.'

'Why were you searching this subject? What was on your mind? Had you run out of bog roll?'

'No, I'm just doing research for when the climate or artificial intelligence or fucking swift zombies bring on an apocalypse. I'm making a list for stocking my survival shelter and of course bog roll is an important but also a very bulky thing to store. I was just looking for alternatives and the corn cob stood out because it's dual-purpose: food and hygiene.'

'Why not just use a spoon?'

Andy laughed but I could tell he had made a mental note of my suggestion. He continued to tell me about his survival stock list. I remember it included:

- A periscope
- A mouse 'for company'
- Cement
- American space food
- Wadding

With one eye on the football and one ear on Andy, my eyeline and my attention drifted through into the lounge bar, where I spotted Roma sat alone against the far wall in one of the velveteen booths. My first instinct was to look away for fear that she might see me. I never liked work/leisure crossover in my life. 'Never mix business with pleasure,' my mum always said, and I had always believed her. Wayne from the café often asks me why I never come in with anyone from work. 'Never mix business with pleasure, Wayne,' I tell him. 'It will invite trouble and always end in tears.'

Truth is, there was no one at work that it would be a pleasure to share a coffee with and break the rule. I suppose my adherence to this rule was one of the reasons I was hesitant about the idea of working with Emily in the hotel.

Andy continued to talk his survivalist bullwater and was

detailing the pros and cons of having a woodburner in his underground shelter. The pros, as I remember, were:

- Heat
- Charm
- Light
- Would encourage mouse to sit with him

Cons, as I recall, included:

- Collecting firewood = exposure to e.g. fast zombies
- Might get 'stuffy'
- Flickering flames could make him yearn for romance
- Chimney would be location giveaway

I kept glancing through to where Roma was sitting. A bloke had sat down next to her and I could tell from her body language that she was uncomfortable with his attentions. He looked to be in his mid-thirties and, judging from his Herbert haircut (short on sides, brushed forward on top), was probably northern. He wore a tight cream-coloured puffa jacket and skinny blue parsnip jeans. I felt sorry for her, or rather I empathized with her. Shitty people acting shitty in pubs are a true enemy of mine.

The football match ended with the referee adopting the stance of a French archer firing an arrow at a passing pigeon and blowing the final whistle. As was his habit, Andy left for home the moment the match ended so I walked through into the lounge to try to rescue Roma from the bothering man. I strode straight in and sat down beside her like we were the oldest, closest friends on this earth.

'Hi, Roma, sorry I'm late. Can I get you a drink? Who's your mate?' I asked.

She didn't seem at all surprised to see me and flashed me a look that suggested she was already on board with my little game.

'Oh, he's not a friend. He just sat here. Yeah, just came over and sat here,' said Roma.

'We could be mates, though,' said the pub pest in a drawn-out nasal Manchester accent. 'Don't you think so, love? Don't you feel the energy between us?'

'No, I fucking don't,' said Roma, surprising me with this decent slice of attitude.

At that, he turned his attention to me: 'Alright, shorty. Fuck me, you've got a big nose. Can you actually see past it?'

'Yeah, sometimes into the distance and beyond. Can you leave us alone, please?' I asked.

'I'm a professional boxer and my brother is a loan shark, so why would I leave you alone? I want to stare at that shitty grey suit forever,' he replied as he settled back into his seat and took a sup of his beer to indicate he wasn't going anywhere soon. 'She doesn't like you, mate,' he said. 'In fact, I reckon she fucking hates you. Why don't you leave me and her alone? At least we've got a buzz going between us.'

'Come on, mate,' said Roma. 'Just leave us be.'

'Or what?' he spat, with the emphasis on the final 'T'.

'*Or I'll kick your fucking head in*' is what I wanted to say, but that's not what I did.

'Or what, what?' I said.

'As in, if I don't leave, what are you going to do?' he clarified.

'Nothing,' I replied. 'At least, nothing that you will actually be able to see or hear.'

'I bet I'll see a lot more than you do with that fucking nose blocking the view.'

'Is that a remark?' I asked.

'No, it's a comment, a comment on the size of your fucking big conk.'

Roma suddenly got up off her seat and poured her vodka drink over the bloke's head. 'Just fuck off, will you?' she said as the last drops left her glass.

Oh shit, I thought, *I'm going to pay the price for that.*

Mr Manchester jumped up out of his seat and for some reason I did exactly the same.

'Fuck's sake,' he shouted. 'Look what you've done to my fucking puffa!'

The whole of the lounge bar was now looking at the three of us.

'Take it off and wash it under a tap. It will be fine,' said Roma, seemingly unconcerned by the prospect of more trouble.

'IT'S DRY CLEAN ONLY!' he shouted.

'IT'S WORTH A GO,' I shouted back, soap-opera style. 'JUST GO EASY ON IT, GET A DAMP CLOTH FROM BEHIND THE BAR . . . AND WORK ON IT GENTLY!'

'Why did I buy it in cream? WHAT AN IDIOT!' he screamed.

'DON'T BEAT YOURSELF UP,' I shouted. 'CREAM REALLY SUITS YOU. IT'S NOT YOUR FAULT!'

He seemed torn between landing a punch on me and attempting a rescue job on his puffa jacket. The decision was made for him when a couple of barmen arrived on the scene and persuaded him that it was time that he left. As he was going, he turned back towards us and addressed a further remark to me.

'Listen up, mate, she's a wrong-un. I would proceed with caution if I was you.' Then he pointed straight at Roma's face and gave her the middle finger before waddling out of the pub.

Roma and I sat back down at her table.

'Cream jacket. Always a bad choice,' I said.

'Thanks, Gary,' beamed Roma, her eyes popping open so wide I thought one might drop out into her empty vodka glass.

'No worries. I could see he was getting on your tits. What you doing here anyway? You meeting someone?' I asked.

'No, not at all. You see, the thing is, I'm just living on a friend's floor at the moment and I feel rotten that they never get the house to themselves in the evening, so I came here, you know, just to give them a break from me.'

'You living nearby, then?' I said, immediately regretting asking such a shit and personal question.

'Yeah, well, not far. I asked Harriet on reception if she knew a decent pub and she said you always come to this one so, you know, I thought it would be a safe choice.'

'Yeah, it's a nice place. I come here a lot to watch the football on the TV in the bar. Speaking of which, I should probably go back in there with my mates. I'll see you tomorrow at work,' I said, getting up to leave.

'Do you mind if I come through and join you?' she asked slightly sheepishly and with a hint of embarrassment.

I hadn't expected that and it caught me out like a rake underfoot. Andy had gone; there were no mates for me to join.

'Oh shit,' I said, beginning to panic, 'I'm sorry. Fuck! How rude of me. I didn't think you were staying. I thought you were just waiting for that bloke to go. Shit, if you're staying then let's sit in here and have a chat. Can I get you a drink?'

So I spent the rest of the evening chatting to Roma. She told me she was from a small town in south Yorkshire near Leeds, that she'd got her Law degree at university in Huddersfield, but had lived at home with her mum and dad while studying. She was twenty-seven years old, didn't have a boyfriend, and had moved to London because her mum told her that she should live in London for at least a year of her life. In truth, she confided, she was looking forward to going back to Yorkshire as soon as her year was up. She spoke about Yorkshire a lot and occasionally put on a very thick Yorkshire accent. '*Yorkshire folk, best people in t' world*', '*Yorkshire tea, best in t' world*', '*Yorkshire detectives most thorough in t' world*', '*Yorkshire sadness, most intensive in t' world*', that sort of thing, and she obviously believed it.

She seemed very naive and a little bit lost. My sense was that she wanted to be hundreds of miles away from this place and from this job. I offered to walk her home, but she declined. We left together and before we took our separate ways, she gave me a childish hug around my waist and thanked me for keeping her company and saving her from Mr Manchester. I think she meant it, but the truth was she clearly could have looked after the situation on her own. There was a tough nut behind those big innocent eyes.

As I got back to my block of flats, my squirrel mate made a sudden dash towards me from behind a beech tree near the spot where the kids' play area used to be.

'Alright, Gary,' I asked on his behalf.

'Not too bad, boss,' I replied.

'I get the sense that you're all chuffed with yourself. Have you been talking to a lady? I always think around that scenario when I see you with a spring in your step.'

'Yeah, I was with a lass from work, just keeping her company.'

'Oh, is that all it was? Seems to me you don't even believe yourself. You want to think around who it is you're actually deceiving.'

'She's lonely. I was just trying to cheer her up, give her a new connection in a strange town.'

'And what would Emily think about you making new connections with a lady? Do you think that's something she would encourage? Have you considered having a think around that?'

'She would be fine with it. She's not the type to get a cob on over a friendly gesture.'

'You sure, mate? But have a think around this: maybe you're hedging your bets? Is that what you're up to?'

'It was one drink. I didn't even know she was going to be there. What was I meant to do? Ignore her?'

'That would have been an option. At least then we wouldn't be having this conversation. Do you like her? Are you going to invite her out again?'

'No, I am not, but I'm not going to ignore her just because it makes you get all judgemental. Goodnight.'

'Goodnight, boss. She had lovely eyes, didn't she? I expect you'll be thinking around them.'

10

GARY

I remained polite but a few per cent standoffish with Roma in the office. That was easy. More difficult was when she started turning up at the Grove a couple of nights a week under the pretence that she wanted to watch the football. She quickly became a member of the end-of-the-bar viewing club. Andy was smitten from the moment he set eyes on her and was very pleased to have her along. He stopped leaving the pub as soon as the matches finished and began wearing increasingly chirpy T-shirts as the weeks passed. It was glaringly obvious that Roma had no interest in him, but Andy wasn't picking it up. Conversations between them usually went something like this:

'Do you worry what might happen if a virus arrives and turns people into very fucking fast zombies?' Andy would ask.

'No, not really,' Roma would respond. 'Do you?'

'Yeah I do. I mean I'm not saying it's definitely going to happen but I think it's wise to prepare for the possibility.'

'And how do you prepare for something like that?' Roma would ask, her patience wearing thin.

'Well, first thing, you need a secure shelter, preferably underground, and shit loads of supplies.'

'I think I'd rather be dead. What foods would you be eating?'

'Tinned mainly – corned beef, kidney beans and peach slices.'

'Yep, I'd definitely rather be dead. Can we talk about something else? Have you got any pets?'

'No, but I would really *really* like a mouse. Very underrated companion.'

'You would rather have a mouse than a dog or a cat?'

'Every single day of the week. Far less needy and they can survive on next to nothing.'

'Shall we just watch the match?'

'Oh yeah, sorry, yes of course.'

There was no future for the two of them, which to my mind was a shame. On the other hand, I could sense that Roma had some sort of interest in me. I couldn't tell whether it was romance or companionship she wanted, but I was clearly becoming important to her. She reminded me of myself when I first arrived in London, desperately looking for a connection. I couldn't blame her for that. I decided to make more of an effort.

We became more at ease with each other at work and to be honest I enjoyed having someone to chat to as a break from the drudgery of office life. We would often have a hot chocolate break in my office mid-afternoon and have a good gossip about our colleagues. Roma was developing an aversion to Blenkingstop. She found him creepy and a bit 'touchy touchy' and hated that he smelt of 'the biscuit crumbs you find at the bottom of the jar'. I agreed he did smell a bit like he was on the turn, but thought it more like the crispy bits that stick to the baking tray after you have roast chicken. Roma didn't think it was that savoury, but accepted it had a similar depth.

During one of these afternoon chats, I asked her opinion about me packing up and moving down to Brighton. She said I would be mad to give everything up for a woman that I'd only known for such a short time and that the present arrangement of seeing her at the weekends seemed the most sensible way to proceed for the time being.

'Is she pretty?' asked Roma.

'Yes, very,' I replied.

'Then you should take even more time before doing anything drastic.'

11

EMILY

Hi again, Emily here. Hope you're good, long time no see and all that. Been some big changes since we last spoke. I am now the owner of a failing hotel on the seafront in Brighton. My father left it to me in his will when he died nine months ago.

He had been a difficult man, a prick to be honest, and always blamed me for the breakup of his marriage to my mum. This was many a long mile from the truth. She had left him because she couldn't stand the sight or sound of him, let alone his grey smell and his bullying words. He probably left the hotel to me as a last cruel punishment, or a desire to get his money's worth out of me even from beyond the grave. I could have refused and just given notice on the lease, but something inside me still wanted to prove my worth to the nasty dead bastard. I mean, it's not like I had anything else on the cards. I was living in south London at my boyfriend Gary's one-bedroom flat, working from home doing a bit of freelance graphic design and waiting for something to come along that might excite me into action. The more I thought about it the more the prospect of running a hotel got me interested in moving on in my life. If my father's approval (from beyond the grave) was one of the outcomes, then so be it. I could meet him in hell and tell him '*Told you so*', something like that.

Everyone around me, Mother included, told me that the project was far too much for me to take on. My boyfriend Gary and our friend Grace were happy to listen to my ideas, but their interest and input was limited because neither of them had actually stayed in a hotel in the past twenty years or so. '*It's a bad idea, why don't you just terminate the lease?*' was Gary's basic take. '*Because that's exactly what you would do*', was my standard and accurate response. I personally reckoned the project would be a piece of piss. The building itself didn't daunt me – it had been my family home until I ran away at seventeen, and Father had left me a lump sum to pay for any refurbishments and to cover costs and cash flow until I could turn the place to a profit. The plumbing, kitchen facilities and heating were all in great nick. What needed attention was the look and ambience of the place.

Father had relied on regular coachloads of elderly visitors during the summer and, in the winter, workmen, salesmen and courting couples looking for the cheapest rooms to rent on the seafront. Brighton had been on the up as a resort for the last fifteen years or so, but Father hadn't moved with the times. These days, Brighton attracted a much younger and cosmopolitan crowd, and there was a huge market for hotel rooms if you could get the atmosphere right. I wanted to transform it into one of Brighton's premier boutique hotels and attract the loveliest and shiniest guest available. If I got the look and the feel of the place spot on, then it could be a goldmine. If it all went tits and farts into a headwind, then nothing ventured, nothing gained. I could terminate the lease and use anything left from Father's lump sum to open a vintage clothes and cake shop. I could sell that idea to Gary in an instant – he loves to eat cake in dusty surroundings.

So that's where I am: living back in my old family apartment on the top and attic floors of the Hotel Avocado. Why Avocado? Simple really: my father hated avocados and resented their rise to prominence these last few years. It was also the name of my father's favourite restaurant in Chelsea, where I 'enjoyed' my last ever day out with him a couple of summers ago. He had treated me to lunch as an excuse to discuss the idea of me taking over the hotel when he was unable to do so himself. I now know that he had already been diagnosed with stage-four lung cancer and that the need to sort out the hotel's future was more pressing than he let on. He came straight to the point after he had tasted a couple of spoonfuls of squid ink risotto and declared it to be bullshit. I was lingering over an avocado salad, knowing the very sight of it would bubble the juices in his acidic stomach.

'What say you take over the running of the hotel when my mind goes to ruin or I'm past caring. Do you think that would be something you would be able to do?'

'I think I could do it, but that doesn't mean that I would want to,' I replied.

'You've always only done things that suit you, like stealing cosmetics to big yourself up at school or shacking up with that drug dealer Tommy Briggs because he gave you a roof over your head. You always want things easy when the truth is if you invested in something that challenged you, you might actually take pleasure in the achievement if you pulled it off. Are you scared that you might find out that your abilities are actually quite limited? That you're not the big catch that you think you are?'

'If my confidence is a bit frail then that would be entirely down to you. I was always a big lump of disappointment to you and you never missed a chance to tell me that was the case.'

'Rubbish. All I ever did was try to point you in a different direction, put you on a path to success. You simply rejected my advice because it was never the easy option.'

'You've had a shit life, Father, a shit life and a shit marriage. Why should I take advice from you? What did you get so right that I should hang on your every word? I don't want to be like you. I want to be happy.'

'Well, I think you should grant me one thing: I certainly put a fire in your belly. Even if it is fuelled by a hatred of me, at least it's there smouldering and waiting to propel you on to something greater in your life.'

'If you want me to take over the hotel when you're gone, then I will, and I'll make a fucking good job of it. Better than you could ever do.'

'That's the spirit, and do you know what? I actually believe you for once. Are you having a pudding?'

'No, I need to get out of here.'

'How's your mother doing?' he asked.

'She's very happy. I wonder why that is?'

'That's the spirit,' he replied.

I won't bore you with too many tales of the ups and downs of closing and refurbishing and rebranding the hotel, that's not what the story is here, but I should update you on a few things that are important to this tale.

You will probably remember that I was shot in the hip by my ex-boyfriend Tommy Briggs, just before he killed himself, on the back lawn of the house he had imprisoned me in. Well, after a little bit of surgery and a good few months of painkillers and physiotherapy, I'm ninety-nine per cent back to normal. I still struggle a bit going down a steep slope or set of stairs, but otherwise I'm a regular Jack Strider.

I stayed with my boyfriend Gary in Peckham for six months or so following the shooting. He was a superb carer and I think, truth be known, nursing is his true calling. He never over-fussed but always seemed able to anticipate my every need, whether it was a change of cushion angle, a pie and chips supper, or a night with the bed to myself so I could have what he would call a 'sleep bath'. When I got frustrated with the progress of my physiotherapy, he would encourage me by joining in and keeping little charts on his laptop to illustrate my progress. When he was at work, Grace would pop in at lunchtime to keep me company and sometimes share a meal. We would watch back-to-back episodes of this television show about the New Zealand customs service. Grace had a keen eye for spotting the ones that had something to hide. I wasn't so good; I always tend to believe people if they have a pleasant face. Gary has a pleasant face. I probably fell in love with him during those six months but didn't want to frighten him by telling him this on more than a couple of occasions. On those occasions he just gave me a big soft smile and told me it made him very happy before changing the subject in the blink of an eye. I don't think he believed me.

Gary and I occasionally talked about him moving down here to Brighton full-time. I would like that to happen sometime, but there's no rush. I've learnt that shithouses like Gary take a long time to come to any decision that involves big changes. In Gary's case those changes don't even have to be that serious. It took me about two months to persuade him to try a chicken madras instead of his usual chicken tikka masala.

The whole Tommy thing is fading rapidly from my mind. I have occasional flashbacks but it's largely disappeared from my list of things to worry about before I go to sleep. There is one little hangover that I can't quite shift that occurred on the day I gave evidence about the circumstances of Tommy's death at a Coroners' Court inquest.

Gary had given his evidence the day before me and actually got a snotty remark from the court clerk about his shitty grey suit, so I borrowed a black two-piece suit off Grace to wear for the hearing. It was far too big for me around the shoulders and the trousers were so heavily flared that I had to lean forward into the wind to avoid being shipwrecked. I wore my ox-blood Dr Martens boots to finish off the look. Grace said I reminded her of her daughter Mary.

'I didn't know your daughter was a clown,' I replied.

She responded by pinching my nose, making a *honk honk* sound and saying, 'All the best people are clowns deep down, darling.'

When I arrived at the Coroners' Court, a large group of Tommy's family and friends were stood outside the entrance chatting and smoking. The Briggs men were all wearing puffer jackets and white sports socks that provided a visible full stop to the legs of their skinny stretch jeans. They all had massive thighs and teenager haircuts. Gary had mentioned that Tommy's mother and father had been there the day before but he hadn't seen any others of the Briggs clan. They went silent as they saw me approaching. Tommy's mum and dad, who I had met before, both blanked me as I threw them a sympathetic smile. The others took a more aggressive stance, staring me up and down and mumbling what I assumed to be insults. Just before I reached the courthouse door, I was pulled back by my arm and confronted by a girl in her mid-twenties – maybe a friend, maybe a family member. Whatever she was, she had pure hatred etched hard into her face.

'You fucking killed him,' she said to me, her eyes bulging with anger. 'He'd still be here if it wasn't for you!'

'That's not true,' I said, pulling my arm away from her grip and turning to walk inside. She immediately grabbed my arm again to force me to face her.

'Yes it fucking is,' she spat. 'I think you or your boyfriend shot him, you stuck-up cow.'

A security guard opened the door and beckoned me inside. The woman released her grip.

'You had better watch your fucking backs,' she yelled as the doors closed behind me. It was an unexpected confrontation and left me shaking with fifty/fifty fear and anger. I turned round sharpish, intending to go back outside and confront her, but the security guard had read my intentions and blocked my path before forcibly leading me into a side room to cool myself off. This incident has lodged itself somewhere deep in my mind and won't go away however hard I try to erase it. It visits me every now and then without warning and unsettles me. If I ever saw that lady's face again I think my first instinct would be to punch it. That might be the way to cleanse myself of its grip. Truth is, I should have gone back outside the court and had it out with her there and then instead of hiding away like a Gary.

The coroner's verdict was death by accident or suicide. Apparently the Briggs family caused quite a scene and had to be forcibly escorted from the court when the verdict was announced.

12

EMILY

I should introduce you to two people who have been at my side these last months as I've worked my arse off getting the hotel ready for business: Mark McNair and Pete Forshaw. Nothing of what unfolds would have done so without their involvement.

Mark had worked at the hotel for over seven years, joining the kitchen staff straight out of school at sixteen. His father was a plumbing and heating engineer and an old friend of my dad's. He'd brought Mark to the hotel during the holidays one summer and begged Dad to give him a job. 'He's useless, a bit wayward and on the daft side of flaky. I can't have him working in my business, he could ruin its reputation and mine. If you give him a chance, I will cover any losses or repairs that he inflicts upon you' was the father's gambit. Dad took him on because his wages were cheap and he knew that his friend would owe him one. He was right: Mark's father continued to maintain the hotel's heating and plumbing at a greatly reduced rate ever since. He was one of the first people I called when I took over the hotel and he was happy to continue the reduced-fee arrangement in return for seeing his son continue in employment.

As I say, Mark started in the kitchens, and I remember well what it was like when he started (I was still living at home in the hotel at the time). He was short, really short, about five foot five inches. His hair was light brown, weak and thin, and his skin was pock-marked with acne scars. He had big carpy lips and thin eyebrows that very nearly met in the middle. His face flushed pink whenever a stranger spoke to him and in his early weeks of working, his mission seemed to be to seek out shadows and crannies that would place him out of sight and out of mind. The kitchen staff gave him the nickname 'pothole' on account of the fact that you would come across him unexpectedly behind a fridge door or around the back of the staircase, wherever it was that he had found shelter. To everyone's surprise, though, he was an incredibly efficient and hard worker. Give him any task, he would go at it like a human dynamo. He cleaned the kitchen floors with such intensity that details were revealed which had never before been seen by any current members of staff. He could wash more plates per session than had previously been deemed possible. The praise he rightly got for his work seemed to drive him on to greater things: storage cupboards would be deep-cleaned and reorganized, stair carpets would be brought back to life using his special rubber brush and secret sprays. On one occasion he scrubbed and scraped the inside of an oven to such a sparkle that one of the grill chefs swore blind that he must have had the assistance of an American ghost.

My first ever conversation with him was at the bus stop opposite the hotel. He was presumably waiting for a bus. I was on my way to the newsagent to buy my father his newspaper.

'Oh, hello there,' I said as I came to a halt, recognizing his aquatic face peeping through the tightly drawn hood of his dark blue puffer jacket. His face flushed pink as he averted his gaze away from mine. 'I'm Emily, your boss's daughter. How are you enjoying the job?' I asked.

He suffered a rush of the blinks, tapped the outside of his right trouser pocket and then slowly, ever so slowly, opened his mouth to speak. 'Yes, I agree' was his reply.

'Agree with what?' I asked.

'You, I suppose,' he said, adjusting his gaze to somewhere around my chest.

'You looking at my tits?' I said in as kindly a way as that question could be asked.

'No, no, I would never . . . it's that stain, that's all.'

His face blushed bright red as a wave of regret passed through his mind.

I looked down at the lapel of my coat and sure enough there was an ugly little stain resulting from an incident with some egg yolk.

'I could sort that for you dead easy,' he said, no longer focusing his eyes on my chest.

I declined his offer and asked him where he was headed.

'Nowhere,' he replied. 'I'm just killing time until my shift starts.'

'Do you want to walk up to the shops with me? That would kill ten minutes.'

'Why?' he asked, clearly shocked by the idea.

'I'm just being friendly,' I replied, slightly exasperated with being taken to task for such a well-intentioned offer.

'Not sure I like the sound of that. Have I done something wrong? Is that what this is about?' he asked in a monotone, looking down at the floor.

I tried to put him at ease: I didn't want him to feel awkward or to take the easy way out and reject my company.

'No, I'm just being friendly. You could tell me how things are going with your job. If you've got any complaints, I can pass them on to my dad.'

'Alright,' he said, 'but I'm not much of a talker. More of a doer. Do you get me?'

'I get you, Pothole.'

'Could you not call me that, please?'

'Of course, Mark, I apologize for presuming.'

We walked together and he told me how much he was loving his job and how much he liked the buzz he got for any task well done. He told me that cleaning and maintenance should be the number-one priority for any hospitality business. Get that right and you have a good chance of success, and that's why he approached the job with such passion. Most other jobs in the hotel looked after themselves and nobody really noticed if they were being done half-arsed. Not so with maintenance and cleaning. If a cleaner has a conscience, then they've got nowhere to hide – not even sleep can free them from the guilt of a neglected dado rail or dirty fingerplate. That was the way he saw it and who was I to disagree? I didn't mention to him that he was probably so far out on a limb in his beliefs that he was no longer actually attached to the tree.

He was a quiet one, for sure, but strong and determined as a rolling boulder when it came to hard graft. Dad had found himself a gem. Back at the bus stop, his face was no longer pinking and his blinkers were no longer blinking. He returned to his perch on the bench and looked me in the eye with a big beaming smile.

'Do you know what your dad's nickname is with the staff?'

'I have no idea.'

'You want to know?' he said, beginning to giggle.

'Yeah, why not?' I replied, starting a giggle of my own.

'You won't get mad at me?' he asked.

'Promise,' I replied.

He held his hand over his mouth to suppress a full-scale guffaw. His eyes were dancing with excitement at the thought of what he might be about to say.

'Go on, tell me!' I said.

He removed his hand from his mouth and blurted it out.

'The Wanker.'

We both laughed our heads off. It was the first time I had ever heard him spoken of without a hint of deference or respect. It felt wonderful.

'You probably shouldn't have told me that but I'm glad you did.'

'You won't tell him, will you?' he asked, suddenly returning to his worried nervous mode.

'Maybe one day, but I won't mention your name.'

'I agree,' he replied as he waddled across the road and back into the hotel to recommence his graft.

By the time I took over the hotel, he was supervising the public areas, supervising the housekeeping and single-handedly ensuring the hotel was clean and spotless. He knew every nook and cranny of the place and had cleaned or repaired every crack, blemish and creaking door. He knew the flow of the service pipes and the placements for all furnishings. If the lights ever went, just grab his coat and he would guide you to safety in no time. Sadly, the last seven years had not been easy on his hairline and it was losing the battle against its slow dissolve. He now sported a very pissy and complicated comb-over.

On my first week as his new boss, I called him into my office round the back of the kitchen and offered him a seat. He declined and explained that he would be quicker back to work from a standing start. He tapped at his right-side trouser pocket and then on the breast pocket of his white polyester shirt as if searching for a switch that might make him invisible.

'So, Mark, as you probably know, I'm going to be taking over the running of the hotel. How would you feel about staying on as my Head of Housekeeping?'

'I thoroughly agree to do that and thank you for asking, but what's with the fancy title? Does that mean my duties will change?'

'No, but you will get a wage increase, and another week's holiday every year,' I told him.

'Not so bothered about that. Like I say, I agree. Can I go now? I'm in the middle of a rust bust on a toilet seat hinge and it won't get done if we stand here talking about nothing in particular.'

I stepped out from behind my desk and gave him a hug by way of indicating a done deal. As I held him, I could sense both his arms rising slowly out to his sides and into the horizontal as if he was preparing for winged flight. Once I released him from the hug, I noticed the pinks and blinks had returned to his face. He scurried off to seek out rust and bust its balls. So that's Mark, my reliable and irreplaceable second-in-command. Every aspiring hotelier should have one or if possible two, which brings me to my old mate Pete.

13

EMILY

About a month into the refurbishment, I was sat on my favourite seafront bench on a Sunday morning, having a good old stare out to sea and trying to catalogue everything that needed to be achieved in the upcoming days. I remember I was wearing my favourite dark blue, thick-knit fisherman's jumper and a pair of baggy jeans covered in paint splashes and hard patches of dried-on wallpaper paste. The jumper had two lovely holes just above the cuff that I could stick my thumbs through and gently squeeze the cuff in the palms of my hands.

I was a mixture of happy and anxious. I wished that Gary was here with me. He wasn't visiting that weekend due to work commitments. I rang his number but it went straight to voice message. A seagull landed on the railings that marked the edge of the promenade and looked me up and down, presumably trying to assess whether I might have any chips or snacks that he could pilfer. I found a crumb or two from an old cheese cracker at the bottom of my bag and threw them on the floor in front of his perch. He jumped down, flicked a couple of the crumbs in the air, and then flew off in disgust shouting what sounded like 'Merde! Merde!' He must have popped over from France.

I rang Gary again, realizing he would worry that I hadn't left any message. I was just about to speak when somebody sat down on the other end of the bench. I didn't acknowledge the arrival in any way although, of course, internally it made me furious. I ended the call before speaking. I'm one of those people that hates to have a telephone chat in the presence of strangers. It always seems impolite, a bit cocky even. The bench squatter started to make little animal noises like a pig or an ape might make if it saw a finger of fudge being poked through a gap in their cage. It was time to leave and avoid an encounter with this unwelcome thorn. The volume and frequency of the grunts suddenly increased, which I took as my cue to get up off the bench.

'Emily, Emily Baker,' said the stranger in the style of the *Star Wars* Alec Guinness. 'I have come from Africa to tell you a thing or two, so what's not to like about that, me darling?'

The mention of my name made me turn towards him and I immediately recognized the face of my old friend Pete Forshaw. He had been my first love back in the day when I was making my first tentative steps to escape the grip of my father. In fact, our first ever date had commenced on this very bench.

'Pete Forshaw! You weird bastard! What the fuck is with the animal noises?'

'Just something I'm trying out. Did you enjoy it as an introduction?'

'No, it was fucking scary, to be honest. I thought I was about to be attacked by a nutcase.'

'That's a shame, I thought it might appeal. I'll keep working on it, try to soften its edges, make it more enticing but, you know, nothing ventured nothing gained, ooh ooh ooh ah ah aah.'

'Stop it,' I insisted.

'Okay, will do. So how are you even doing these days? I heard a rumour you've taken over your dad's hotel. Please tell me that's not true.'

Here we go, I thought, *another doubter I would have to win over* (if I could even be bothered to rise to the challenge). It was instantly lovely to see an old face from my past, a face that had no connection to garden suicides or hotel shenanigans. For some reason I'm far more trusting of a face that was a part of my formative years. It feels like you know the real, unadulterated version of the person, and that's very reassuring. Maybe because it's so much harder for them to pull off any tricks or surprises or try to rope you in with affectations and bullshit.

'It's true, it's my hotel now. Mine to do up and maybe fuck up, who knows which way it will go,' I said, feigning resilience.

'So you're a businesswoman? A high flyer? A boss woman? I have to say you don't look very businessy to me. More like a vegan cake maker or an artisan shoe maker than a hotel manager.'

'Thank you . . . Hey, that gives me an idea,' I replied. 'When the hotel is up and running, I'm going to open a little café in the half basement room at the front. Maybe I should sell cakes in the shape of shoes. You have to have a gimmick these days or you're fucked.'

'Shoe cakes. I like it. Maybe you could put a little pair of lemon drizzle Chelsea boots on the coffee table to welcome the guests to their room.'

'Nice. Or a pair of Battenberg loafers on their pillow at night.'

'Maybe. All starting to sound a bit carby, though, isn't it,' he said.

'That's often the case with treats though, innit? So, what's your low-carb suggestion for their pillows? A couple of carrots?'

'A couple of new potatoes would be better,' he said. 'When they are in season, of course. Out of season I'd suggest a nice big beef tomato.'

'Viva tomatoes,' I said.

'You've got that right,' he replied.

Pete was the same age as me but he looked older. His dark brown hair was cut short in a number-two crop and his face featured a rash of neatly tended stubble but was otherwise organized with perfect symmetry, and his teeth looked like American imports. 'Ageing boy band front man' would be a good description if the police were hunting him. The last time I had spoken to him was about three years ago when we bumped into each other at the Mexican restaurant where I was working. At the time he was studying filmmaking at the University of Bournemouth and was full of bluster and confidence in his future. The brief reunion ended badly, though, when a jealousy-fuelled Tommy Briggs arrived and beat Pete up quite badly. Pete obviously didn't bear a grudge over that incident or I doubt he would have been sat there trying to charm the pants off me.

He was wearing a vintage brown wool suit with a button-down pale yellow shirt. The trousers were held in place with wide black braces and on his feet he wore a pair of battered old brown leather steel-capped boots. He was gorgeous-looking and probably always would be. Problem with Pete was he knew this to be the case and was well aware of the advantage it often gave him. It didn't wash with me, though; I knew that beneath all the bluster he was just a daft lad who wanted to be appreciated for exactly that.

'Are you going to change the name of the hotel?' he asked. 'I noticed the old signs have all been taken down.'

'Yeah, I am, but I've not told anyone yet and I'm certainly not telling you because you'll just pick holes in it and my confidence will suffer. Sometimes it's easier being surrounded by yes men.'

'Yes, Emily. You're right.'

'What are you doing with yourself at the moment?' I asked.

'Rushed off my feet helping people around town – carpentry, tiling, painting and decorating. I'm a one-man gentrifier and I don't know if you've noticed but there's a lot of that going on round here.'

'I thought you were hell bent on being a film director?'

'I am and one day it will happen, but for the moment I'm just directing my own progress and that's invaluable experience.'

'That's just bullshit, Pete.'

'Correct, but you've got to rally around something and if it wasn't for bullshit then no movies would ever get made, you've got to believe me on that one.'

'Where are you living?'

'At my mum's mainly.'

'You got a girlfriend?'

'No, so there's an opening there if you're interested?'

'That's very tempting, Pete, but I've got a boyfriend so I'll have to pass.'

I noticed a little flash of jealousy cross his face, and I have to admit it felt nice to see it.

'What, so you're cheating on me, are you?' he asked with a little boy hurt look on his face.

I laughed. Pete had stopped talking to me, completely out of the blue and for no reason that I could fathom, when we were still in sixth form. It had broken my heart at the time but I was too proud to ask for an explanation. This seemed as good an opportunity as I was ever going to get.

'Would you care to explain why you blanked me into oblivion back in the day?'

'Self-preservation,' he replied.

'What the fuck does that mean?'

'Reciprocation of feelings.'

'What?'

'In a nutshell, I didn't think you fancied me as much as I fancied you. I was head over heels but would feign a bit of coldness now and then to test your interest. Bottom line, I didn't want to get hurt. I regret it now, of course, what with you being a hotel owner and even more beautiful than anyone could have predicted.'

'Of course I fancied you.'

'Well, you had a funny way of showing it, always bringing me down with your smart-arse comments.'

'Blimey, I thought you liked it that I wasn't a shrinking violet, at least that's the impression you gave. If I'd known you wanted to be worshipped I'd have run a mile.'

I felt a little blush of sadness over these historically crossed wires.

'So, this boyfriend, are you living together at the hotel?'

'No, he lives in London and comes and stays most weekends.'

'What's his name?' he asked.

'Gary.'

Pete feigned an incredulous laugh. 'Gary! You're going out with a Gary! What is he, a fucking optician?'

'No, he's a lawyer, and what's so amusing about the name Gary?'

'Just makes me think of Gary Barlow, that might be the problem.'

'Well, I'll raise you a Gary Oldman, how does that feel for you?'

'Gary Oldman is an actor.'

'Correct.'

'Okay, Oldman is strong, but have a think about Gary Neville. He strikes me as a lot more "Gary" than Oldman and it's easy to imagine Neville and Barlow out and about in patterned jumpers shopping for golf sticks.'

'Are you trying to suggest that Garys are boring?'
'Yes, I think I am. So, tell me, is your Gary boring?'
'Some might say so but not me. We reciprocate.'
'How do you mean?'
'We look after each other.'
'Does he want you to worship him?'
'Not in the slightest.'
'Boy, I really got it wrong, didn't I?'
'Yeah, I reckon you did.'

14

EMILY

So Pete Forshaw had dropped back into my life on my favourite bench where we first met all those years ago. He asked if he could come and have a look around the hotel and get a sense of what I was up to in there. I immediately agreed; it would be good for me to show off my plans and hopefully get a positive reaction or at least some useful feedback. He had no skin in the game and might just be the person to give me an honest appraisal of the project.

The front of the hotel was covered in the painters' scaffolding, and the entrance lobby, reception and downstairs lounge had all been emptied of furnishings and stripped back to the bare bones. Mark was on his hands and knees applying some sort of acid cleaner to the Victorian tiling that adorned the entire reception area. The air was tart with fumes from the cleaning solution, which made you gasp if you breathed it in too heartily. He took off his protective face mask as we entered and gave Pete the once-over with a slow and deliberate scan of him from his toes to his perfectly cropped hair. He didn't take his eyes off Pete as I spoke to him.

'Hey, Mark, this is my old friend Pete. I'm just showing him around so don't mind us.'

'Hello,' said Pete, chirpily as ever. 'Wow, that stuff has got quite a kick to it.'

'Not really,' replied Mark. 'But if you say so then I'm happy to pretend it does.'

'Well, it certainly seems to be doing the trick,' said Pete, slightly unnerved by Mark's attitude.

'It's not a trick,' replied Mark. 'Just chemistry and hard graft. Am I in the way here? It feels a bit like I am.'

'Not at all,' I interjected. 'It's really kind of you to come in on a Sunday. You didn't have to, you know.'

'I agree,' he replied, before replacing his mask and getting on with his scrubbing.

I gave Pete a tour of the bedrooms and explained my vision for every one of them. Each room would be themed around a different fruit – cherry, satsuma, apple, etc. The chosen fruit would dictate the colour scheme of each room and a feature wall would display a hand-painted extract from a poem about that particular fruit. The poem would be written in fancy handwriting as large as the wall would allow. We ended up on the third floor in the room earmarked as 'Peach'.

'I'm not so keen on this room,' he said.

'Why not? You got an aversion to peaches? Not manly enough for you?'

'No, it's a very strong fruit, it's just the stud wall has messed up the symmetry of the room. Why don't you take it down?'

He tapped the wall like blokes do and declared it to be 'non-supporting'.

'Mark has already investigated, says there's all sorts of pipes and old pulleys behind it. Best left alone.'

'Up to you, but it really pisses me off, especially with that terrible writing on it.'

I had already traced out a poem that Gary had written onto the stud wall. Pete read it out aloud:

> *Hairy not dairy*
> *Ripe juicy peach*
> *Perfect for a picnic*
> *Especially on the beach*
> *If you find them too spherical*
> *Just slice it with a knife*
> *Put half in your pocket*
> *And give half to your wife.*

'Did you write that?' asked Pete, unable to supress a giggle.

'No, it's one of Gary's efforts.'

'It's terrible. You're not seriously going to keep it on the wall, are you?'

'I quite like it. It's grown on me the more I read it.'

'Really?'

'Maybe,' I replied.

We made our way upstairs to my top-floor apartment. The fourth-floor landing and stairwell outside my apartment were the only part of the refurbishment that was more or less complete. The walls were decorated with wallpaper featuring a repeat pattern of dark green avocados on a turquoise and primrose striped background. I was nervous about its wider appeal but personally liked it very much.

'What's with the avocados?' asked Pete.

'Well, that's going to be the name of the hotel so, you know, it's a theme, a branding, that sort of thing. What do you think?'

'I love it. Some people might hate it but they won't forget it. Hey, I thought you weren't going to tell me the name of the hotel? So that's it: "the Avocado". It's a strong name, makes me think of somewhere fancy in France.'

He sat on the sofa and I fetched him a cup of tea and a slice of date and walnut cake.

'Very grown-up cake, that is,' said Pete, and I nodded in agreement. 'Would be a good basis for a pillow shoe or perhaps a football boot if a sporty type books the room.'

'Yeah, or a clog if the place starts to attract a Dutch following.'

We chatted for a good couple of hours. Turns out that when he had left film school, he had taken a job with a set design studio in Haywards Heath. He claimed this made him the most efficient and rapid multi-skilled decorator in the south of England and insisted that I consider employing him to help complete the refurbishment. While giving me this sales pitch, he suddenly got up from the sofa and thrust a pointing hand up towards the ceiling.

'I've just had a fucking superb idea,' said Pete.

'Oh yeah, go on.'

'I've just remembered that in the storage yard at Haywards

Heath, where I used to work, there's a fucking huge fibreglass avocado that they are desperate to get rid of. It would make a perfect sculpture to hang on the front of the hotel.'

He slowly brought his arm down from its pointing position.

'When you say huge, what do you mean?' I asked.

'It must be over five metres at least. It's very fucking impressive, impossible to ignore and very high impact. You've got to go and see it, Emily. I swear you will love it, and so will the public. I'm a fucking genius.'

I visualized a huge avocado hanging from the flagpole at the front of the hotel. I had to admit it was perfect.

'You're right, you are a fucking genius. I need that avocado.'

Pete celebrated my enthusiasm by strolling, Mick Jagger style, into the toilet. He remained in there for what seemed like an age. He then ran back into the room, leapt onto the sofa and took a large triumphant bite of his date and walnut.

'Another thing. Who put that avocado wallpaper up in the hallway?' he asked.

'Mark and me. Took us three days. Not bad going, if you ask me.'

'Not being funny, but it looks like it's been done by a child with very heavy arms and a swollen thumb. Do you intend to do any more?'

'I think it looks okay and, yes, I might have to do some more if my decorators don't get their act together. They were meant to start the inside last week but keep cuffing me off with excuses and bullshit.'

'Well, you're staring the solution in the face. When you're

building a set for TV or film you get given days not weeks to finish the job. I don't fuck about. When I'm on the brushes nobody has ever said to me, "Hey, Pete, stop fucking about, will ya." Come on, let me be your saviour. Take me on and let's get the job finished in record time. Hundred quid a day cash plus meals, drinks and a bed for the night in one of the rooms if I throw an all-nighter.'

'I don't believe what you're telling me. To be honest, your animal noises make more sense to me.'

'You nasty bastard. Come with me and I'll show you.'

Pete marched me back down to the Peach room, picking up a tin of 'Savannah Dreams' paint, a roller tray and a long-handled roller from the landing on the way.

'Do you want some overalls or something?' I asked.

'Don't insult me. I haven't spilt one single drop of paint in over two years and that was only because a Phil Collins song came on the radio mid stroke.'

He expertly manipulated the roller inside the tray, soaking up more paint into the foamy sleeve than I would have thought appropriate.

'Nice roller, this is. Nine-inch microfibre, can take a decent soak. Now, stand back and gape at me in admiration if you would be so kind.'

He had been telling the truth. He completely covered the poem wall without once returning to the tray to refill with paint. It was an incredible sight and I kid you not when I say it only took him about three minutes.

'You might have asked before you covered up the poem.'

'You'll thank me in the end. And, listen, I could do it even quicker with a spray gun rig but, to be honest, I'm a bit old-school – I prefer the brush and the roller. I see you are gaping at me. I often have that effect on the casual onlooker.'

'Fucking hell, Pete, that is amazing. I'm very impressed. Are you as incredible when it comes to preparation, because that's where the hours need to be put in. There aren't really any shortcuts when it comes to prep.'

'I can prep a room this size in two days. When do I start?'

'I thought you were busy gentrifying the whole of Brighton.'

'I am, but Brighton can wait if it means we can reconnect and be friends again.'

'You're unemployed, aren't you?'

'Absofuckinglutely.'

At this moment Mark entered the room, announcing his presence with a cough and a bang on the door with his bottle of spray.

'Everything alright in here?' he asked, pointing his spray bottle directly at Pete.

'Yeah, I've just decided to employ Pete to get going with the decoration of the bedrooms. Good news, innit?'

'If you say so,' said Mark. 'I hope he's not going to get in my way.'

'No more than any decorator would, and the bonus is that he's quick – really quick,' I said.

'More haste less speed,' said Mark before pointing at the corner of the freshly painted wall. 'He's missed a bit there and I'm sad about the poem,' he commented as he reversed himself out of the room with one eye still fixed on Pete until he went out of view.

So Pete was added to the team. He arrived at the hotel the next morning at 7am sharp. I heard the monkey grunts before I actually heard his footsteps coming up the stairs. I was a bit upset about Gary's poem being erased, but progress would surely now be made and the poem would live on in my heart until such time as it didn't need to.

15

EMILY

With the arrival of Pete, a new burst of energy came to the project. The noise of a sander working on the bedroom wood-work and walls filled the hotel for hour after hour. Electronic dance music blasted from Pete's portable speaker system and thousands of particles from the past danced around the hotel and settled on every surface that they kissed. It was two months until the first guests would book into the hotel. Pete reckoned each bedroom would take one week to complete. It was going to be touch and go.

At the end of Pete's working day, which could sometimes be as late as 7 or 8pm, he would always knock on my apart-ment door, armed with his impressive industrial-looking hoover and clean up the dust that had made its way inside through the gaps around the door. I would occasionally offer him a beer or ask him if he wanted to share my meal with me before he made his way home. He always accepted the beer but never accepted my offers of food. I wondered if he was supplementing his energy banks with some drug or other, but he always stroppily denied such indulgence whenever I asked. He seemed to be getting skinnier week by week but his spirits never waned. He was genuinely invested in both the project and me. I even grew to enjoy the monkey moments. The bedroom prep work was completed in just over two weeks, just as Pete had promised.

The other blessing in my life was of course Gary. We didn't communicate much during the week. He had his work to contend with and my head was so full of hotel shit that I was often a bit short with him if he contacted me out of the blue. I liked to get everything that needed to be done completed by Friday evening so that I could enjoy my weekends with Gary with as untroubled a mind as possible. When he arrived he would always indulge me in a quick tour of the hotel so I could show him the progress that had been made. Mark would usually still be hanging around when he arrived and would accompany us silently on the tour.

'How are you getting on?' Gary would ask him.

'Not for me to say, is it,' was always Mark's reply.

Gary was very fond of Mark's cryptic answers and would use them on me throughout the weekend.

'What do you think of the curry?' I would ask.

'Not for me to say really, is it?'

'Do you think Daniel Radcliffe is a good actor?'

'Not for me to say really, is it?'

And on one occasion, when our friend Grace came for the weekend, I asked her whether Gary had been looking after her back in Peckham.

'Not for her to say really, is it?' said Gary.

'Yes, it is,' Grace replied, 'and the answer is no, he's not.'

'What is he neglecting to do?' I asked Grace.

'That's not for me to say really, is it?' she responded, getting in on the act and leaving Gary to ponder his possible failings.

Friday evening would always be a takeaway meal and TV as we caught up with each other's lives. Saturday we would get up late and then go for a long walk along the coast or up into the South Downs. Gary hated missing the football but never complained and I always treated him to a visit to the pub of his choice at the end of our exertions. Sometimes the football would be showing in the pub and I often got the feeling Gary had contrived things so that this would be the case. He always acted surprised – 'Oh, look, they're showing the match, didn't know there was a game on today' – but I was never convinced. One Saturday we stopped at the Dun Cow, a traditional Sussex pub in Peacehaven with lots of dark wooden furniture and an open fire to warm the cockles. It was mid-afternoon after a good long walk through Kemptown, back down to the beach and then along to where the pub was situated. There was no TV in the pub so I asked Gary if he would like to go some-where else where they were showing the football.

'No, this is fine,' he replied. 'I wanted to have a chat with you about something and this place is perfect.' He went to the bar and ordered us a couple of pints. When he joined me at our table by the fire I could sense that he was flustered and slightly anxious. I was intrigued by what it was he wanted to say. It was a rare occurrence for Gary to request a serious moment. I kept my mouth shut to add to the drama of the occasion. Gary took a couple of gulps from his pint and then began to rub his hands up and down along his thighs, a sure sign that he was a bundle of nerves. It crossed my mind that he might be about to propose to me, but it was far less dramatic than that.

'Does it bother you that I haven't moved down here to be with you full-time?' he asked.

'Not really. Why do you ask? Have I done something or said something out of place?'

'No, not at all. It's just that Grace is always on my back about me neglecting you and not being as supportive as I should be if I was serious about us and I think she may have a point.'

'I wouldn't hold too much play by what Grace says. She's got her own agenda,' I assured him.

'What do you mean?'

'She's just testing the waters. She's worried sick you're going to leave, so she's trying to push you into a decision so that she can come to terms with it either way.'

'Yeah, I reckon there's a bit of that going on, but that doesn't mean what she's saying isn't true. Are you happy with the way things are?'

'Of course I am, and I would tell you if I wasn't. I look forward all week to seeing you. It's what drives me on to get all the shit done at the hotel. You're helping me more than you can imagine. I'm very happy with how things are progressing, so stop worrying about it. Do you think I'm going to finish with you or something?'

'I hope not. Can I ask you something?'

'Yes, Gary, you can ask me anything you want.'

'Do you think of me as a man? You know, an adult man. A proper, grown-up man: dependable, sturdy, reliable, that sort of thing.'

I laughed.

'Don't laugh,' he continued. 'It's just I've got it into my head that I need to grow up, stop hedging my bets, commit to something, stop living my life as if I'm a permanent student. I'm thinking that if I don't then why should anyone commit to me? Do you get what I mean?'

'Not really. I think you should just look after yourself, be happy and stop trying to guess what other people want from you. If you're feeling good then that works fine for me. Stop listening to Grace and listen to me: I'm very happy. Now, do you want to find a pub that's showing the football?'

'Yes, please.'

Without thinking, I made a short sequence of Pete-style animal noises to celebrate the end of an awkward conversation. It took us both by surprise.

'What the fuck?' said Gary. 'You trying to suggest I'm a piglet or something?'

'Pigs are my spirit animal so that wouldn't be a bad thing.'

I felt a bit guilty about the farmyard noises – you know, for bringing a private joke between Pete and myself into Gary's life. I had mentioned Pete to Gary and told him how reliable and helpful he was being, but I hadn't disclosed that he was an old flame from the past. Gary hadn't shown much interest, so I didn't feel obliged. Given the conversation we'd just had, I think my omission was probably for the best.

On Sundays we would lounge about in the apartment and then go for a long luxurious breakfast in town. Afternoons we would go shopping for tat and nonsense to fill the hotel and occasionally go to the cinema or take a walk on the beach if the weather was good. Gary would leave for home around 6pm. I was always hollow and sad for the first hour or so after he left, but then hotel matters would pour into my mind and cleanse me of my dreariness.

16

Oh hi, it's me again. I don't suppose you've missed me and if you haven't then please don't think I'm bothered by that. The reason for this interruption is that I have just remembered something that happened a couple of months before the night of the ambulances and the gurney. I think it might be important although, of course, come the crunch, you will be the judge of that.

It was early evening on a Friday. Gary was sat on the bench opposite the hotel when Pete, the nice-looking young man who was helping Emily with the decorating, joined him. Neither of them saw me keeping out of the limelight in the shadows of the bus stop, and so I listened to their conversation.

'Alright, Gary, you having a sit down? Mind if I join you?'

'Not at all. Just grabbing a bit of peace and quiet,' said Gary.

'Sorry, I'll walk on, didn't mean to interrupt.'

'No, it's fine, please have a seat. I was wrapping up anyway. Was just wondering if you can ever see France from here.'

'No, you can't unfortunately, though you can see the Isle of Wight on a clear day.'

'Did you know the French used to wipe their arses with corn cobs?' said Gary.

'No, I didn't know that.'

They both went silent for a few moments and shuffled their legs and arms in awkwardness. I sensed it was the first time that they had spoken other than in passing.

'Just thought I should say hello. Our paths never seem to cross with you only being down here on the weekend. They call you Mr Weekend round here, did you know that?' said Pete.

'I didn't know that. I suppose it makes sense and it's also very funny to boot. How's it going with the decorating? You think it will be finished in time?'

'Definitely, no doubt about it, finishing line is in sight.'

'You've been a godsend to Emily. She would have been in deep shit without you. Thank you for all your hard good work.'

'It's been a pleasure. Emily and I go back a long way. She was my first ever girlfriend back in the day.'

Another blip of silence and shuffling of arms and legs.

'Wow, that's a connection that lasts for life,' said Gary.

'Doesn't it, bro. Do you remember your first girlfriend?'

'I can remember her name but not her face. Can't have been that important to me, I suppose.'

'I could never forget Emily's face. I mean, how could you, and she's even prettier now than she was then.'

Gary shuffled forward on his seat and lowered his head so that he was facing the pavement.

'Careful, it's beginning to sound like you still fancy her.'

'I'm only human, Gary, but don't worry, she only has eyes for you. And she reckons you "reciprocate", which as I understand it is a very good thing.'

'Do you ever see each other outside of work? You know, with you being good friends,' asked Gary.

'We sometimes have a quick drink after work, just to wind down from the day.'

'That's nice.'

Silence as Pete pulled a tobacco tin out of his pocket.

'Fancy a sharing a joint? It's been a long week; I need to unwind.'

'No, I'm okay, thanks.'

'What about a quick line? Put a spring in your step, start the weekend with a bang. I can flog you a wrap if you want?'

'No, it's not my thing. Does Emily know you're on the powders?'

'Suspects it, doesn't approve, but she's not going to push it when I'm doing all the graft for her. I've earned a bit of a relax, no need to get heavy about it.'

'Well, I'd better get back inside, leave you to it. Emily's cooked us a curry.'

'She sure loves to feed a man, doesn't she? Yeah, you go back in, make some noise together.'

'See you around, then,' said Gary as he got up to leave.

'Yeah, see you around, Mr Weekend.'

Pete was left on his own. He lit up his joint and stretched out his legs. He had a big beaming smile on his face.

Something tells me this little meeting might be of importance. We will see. Don't blame me if I'm wrong, because, let's face it, you won't thank me if I'm right.

17

GARY

An epic week arrived. A week that would see me turn my life upside down. Let me take you through it.

MONDAY

At lunchtime I was walking along Camberwell New Road on my way back from an appearance at Lambeth County Court. It was beginning to rain so I held my shitty faux-leather brief-case over the top of my head with one hand and carried my plastic shopping bag containing a loaf of bread and a packet of beef mince in the other. A flashy black car pulled up beside me and the passenger door was opened by the unmistakable Mr Sequence and his bouffant hairstyle.

'You going to your office, Gary?' he asked. 'Get in, I'll give you a lift.'

I accepted his offer and got into the back seat.

'I knew it was you by that god-awful suit,' he said.

'Very kind of you to give me a lift, my suit takes on a life of its own if it gets too wet.'

'That's good to know, Gary,' he replied, turning his head to examine me from between the two front seats as he took his vaping machine out of his pocket, closed his eyes and took a deep drag. He let the vapour tumble from his mouth like dry ice over a gravestone. I coughed and the smile on his face widened. The vapour smelt of peanuts with a hint of worn trilby.

I flicked my gaze briefly to the back of the driver's head. He had short cropped reddish hair and just beneath his right ear was a tattoo of the tin man from *The Wizard of Oz* – 'If I only had a heart' and all that. On the back of his thick creamy neck was a tattoo of two butterflies in flight. I wondered what they represented – maybe a mother and her child frozen in a moment of joy? Maybe a thirst for transformation? Maybe the faces of two victims that he had bludgeoned with a frozen leg of lamb? Overall, they struck me as quite feminine in spirit, and this thought reassured me.

On the back seat beside me I noticed an extra-wide spool of white duct tape, a large pair of tailors' scissors and a crowbar. It felt like they had been deliberately placed there for the purposes of intimidation.

Sequence replaced the vape into his pocket before reaching through the gap in the seats and snatching the carrier bag off my lap.

'What you got in the bag, Gary? I love looking at people's shopping – always a nice window into their character. Oh, a nice big lump of mince. Very revealing. Very basic.'

I didn't know how to respond. I had half intended to get a gammon steak and a tin of pineapple slices but as the image of that combination passed through my mind it seemed equally basic and unimaginative. I just gave him one of my winning smiles.

We passed Camberwell Green, turned left before the Town Hall and entered my estate. The driver parked up, turned off the engine and left me alone in the car with Sequence. It took me a few seconds to realize that I had been brought home rather than to work as I'd requested. I went to open my door but it was child-locked. Sequence got out of his door and joined me on the back seat. He still had my bag of mince in his hand.

'I thought you might like to put your mince in the fridge before you got back to the grind,' he said. 'Can be a very volatile meat, mince. Might even be on the turn as we speak,' he said as he dropped the carrier bag on my lap.

'How did you know that I lived here?' I asked politely and without attitude, sensing that there was stress in the air.

'Like I told you in your office, I'm a very resourceful person, Gary. Always thinking on my feet and always one step ahead when it comes to evaluating my options. I'm also the sort of person that doesn't like to be taken for a fool.'

I was beginning to feel claustrophobic and trapped, my stomach took a hollow waffle and my mouth felt suddenly dry. The smell of his hairspray was bound to cause me a nausea if I didn't keep my breathing short, sharp and to the point. I answered him with a pathetic top note to my voice.

'Have I upset you in some way, Mr Sequence? Listen, I gave the best advice I could give but if you're not happy we could make another appointment.'

'I'm always happy, Gary, and your advice was bang on the nose professionally speaking, but better still, our little meeting gave me the opportunity to assess your character, and it was very pleasing to be able to conclude, within minutes might I add, that you are a massive shithouse. Would you agree?'

'It has been mentioned to me a few times in the past, yeah.'

'So, with that in mind, Gary, have you come to a decision regarding the little offer I made to you?'

'I'm sorry, I don't know what you mean.'

'Yes, you do. Don't fuck me about, lad. What is your decision?'

'I'm really sorry, Mr Sequence, but I honestly don't know what you mean.'

He stared me down straight into the eyes, not a flicker of emotion on his face. He licked his lips and then shut his eyes as if seeking strength from the Lord. I began to knead the mince between my fingers, and I could sense the meat warming through as my kneading became more focused. With his eyes still shut, he spelt it out for me:

'The people I represent would like to offer you ten thousand pounds if you fail to appear as a witness at their trial.'

The penny dropped. He was working on behalf of the defendants at the upcoming trial, the bent coppers from Lewisham whose influence seemed to spread throughout the south London constabulary.

'I can't do that, Mr Sequence,' I replied.

'No, of course not, because you're a good boy, aren't you. Twenty-five thousand is the highest I can go to. Ten thousand upfront and the balance after you have failed to appear.'

'I don't want the money. If I was caught, I would lose my career and, I mean, come on, I wouldn't last five minutes in prison. You're asking the wrong person.'

'To be honest, Gary, I knew that would be your initial response, but I won't take it as a final refusal. Maybe you'll have a change of heart if, for example, your circumstances should change.'

'I don't think so.'

'Oh, and don't you go running to your little friend DS Marks. We've got tabs on him, so if you do, I will one hundred per cent be informed, and in that event, believe me, your circumstances will drastically change. This is not the end of our dealings, Gary. Let's just call it a first date. I'll be in touch. Now go and get that mince in the fridge. See you soon.'

The driver opened the car door and as I raised myself up out of the seat I turned to Sequence: 'I don't want any trouble, Mr Sequence.'

'That's good to know, Gary. Now fuck off and have a good think about my offer.'

Back in my flat, I put the mince on the top shelf of the fridge alongside a couple of Babybel cheeses and half an onion. My hands were shaking. This Sequence bloke was working for Rowlett and his crew from Lewisham police station. This made it a very serious business indeed. Chances were, he was an ex-copper with deep-rooted contacts inside the police, and if

I went to DS Marks for help, Sequence would find out about it. I decided to keep things to myself for the time being in the hope that the problem might dissolve of its own accord. I would do nothing until he got in touch again. He might even give up on me – though I doubted that very much.

That evening, I lay in bed thinking about the possible consequences of giving evidence over taking the money and feigning incapacity or some such. Maybe I should decline the money but still not turn up? At least that would mean Sequence would have nothing to hold over me and likewise there would be no money trail to indicate I had succumbed to their bribery. I was already wavering from my default position of doing 'the right thing' and that felt uncomfortable. One thing I wouldn't be doing was mentioning this to Grace or Emily. No need to worry them or get them involved.

18

GARY

TUESDAY

After a standard dull day at work, I arrived back at my flat on Tuesday to find Grace hovering on the walkway outside her front door. She asked if I wanted to pop round later for a chat and a takeaway curry. I was happy to oblige. I got a text from her about ten minutes later asking me to order the curry and to get her a chicken vindaloo, plain rice, a garlic naan and a spinach bhaji for Lassoo. She thanked me for treating her. It arrived thirty minutes later and we sat in her flat, on the sofa, eating curry and watching a reality show called *Border Patrol* on the TV. It was a show following the day-to-day goings-on at various immigration and customs points in New Zealand's airports.

'Why are you watching this?' I asked as she removed the little dental plate from her mouth that provided her with one of her front teeth.

'Because it's real life with real people and I don't get to see much of that.'

'Don't get all dreary on me.'

'I'm not being dreary, it's just a fact, isn't it. I like looking at the faces of the people that the customs officers stop and trying to guess if they're wrong-uns. I'm very rarely wrong. They should employ me; I wouldn't miss a trick.'

'So now you want to move to New Zealand, do you?'

'Well, they know where I am if they fancy increasing their detection rates.'

'Problem is, Grace, if you went in with your hundred per cent "wrong-un" detection rate, the show would lose its jeopardy.'

'Good point. I withdraw my job application.'

Grace fed Lassoo a nugget of the chicken vindaloo. He took it with enthusiasm but then the taste hit him hard. His mouth opened up as wide as it would go and his eyes bulged out as if a mole was tunnelling behind them. He shook his head so vigorously that his ears rotated then ran full pelt straight into the front of the kitchen oven, before burying his face deep into his water bowl with his tail firmly lodged between his legs.

When the show finished, Grace turned off the TV and put a disc into her CD player. It was the Joni Mitchell album *Dog Eat Dog*. 'Synchronized like magic, good friends you and me,' sang Joni. I think she chose the song deliberately to give me a message she wasn't comfortable saying out loud. I first heard Joni Mitchell's music at home with my parents. Grace had re-introduced it to me.

'She's a poet and she made a difference to us girls back in the day. Everyone, especially you blokes, could be a better person

114

by listening to a bit of Joni,' she had said to me. Once the first track had finished, she replaced her front tooth, wiggled her bum deeper into the sofa cushions and took a swig from the bottle of lager I had provided.

'You know what, if I was on death row, I think a chicken vindaloo would be my request for a final meal,' she said. 'What about you?'

'I think I'd have a Sunday roast, beef with all the trimmings, and a syrup sponge pudding with custard. Pudding hot, custard cold.'

'What about a drink?'

'You know what, I think I'd have a nice pot of tea.'

'Lager for me, ice cold and freshly poured into a pint glass.'

'I've just changed my mind. I'll have one of those lagers too, please.'

I asked Lassoo what his death row meal would be. He gave me a look and a grin that indicated, without a shadow of a doubt, that his choice would be a steak and kidney suet pudding served on a warm sofa cushion.

We sat in silence for a few minutes and watched the contents of a suitcase being emptied onto a table in front of a stern-looking New Zealand customs officer. The search revealed a number of neatly taped-up plastic bags.

'Knew he was a wrong-un. Drugs, I reckon,' offered Grace.

The bags were sliced open to reveal that all of them contained dried fruits and edible insects.

'You got that one wrong, Grace,' I said.

A few beats of silence.

'I'm right about you though, Gary, aren't I?' she said in an ominous tone.

'What do you mean?' I asked, worried that she had discovered some dark secret about me.

'You've got no intention of moving to Brighton.'

It was a relief to discover that it was just this old chestnut again and I could block it off as usual.

'I'd rather not talk about that, Grace. Can we not just enjoy watching the contraband characters squirm and lie?'

'No, I'd rather watch you squirm and lie, if you don't mind.'

I felt my face give out a sequence of twitches and tics, in response to which Grace raised an eyebrow and delivered unto me the righteous knowing smile of a customs officer who has just detected the motherload.

'To be honest, Grace, at the end of the day my plans are none of your business until I've made them. You will be the first to know if and when I've made my decision.'

She stepped over to her CD player and turned it loud enough that conversation was pointless. It was her cue for me to leave. I bent down to give her a kiss on the cheek and she gave me a hug around my waist.

'If Emily gets hurt I'll bury you six foot under,' she whispered.

Lassoo had pressed his nose hard up against the CD player speakers as if trying to suck the calming musical notes directly into his stomach to ease the pain from the hot continental nugget.

19

GARY

Around mid-morning Wednesday Roma popped into my office and slumped down in the seat opposite me. She had been crying and was clearly distraught about something. In her hand was a moist and crumpled clump of paper tissues that she was kneading with her fingers and occasionally using to wipe her eyes and nose. She explained to me, through her sobs and sniffles, that she had been subjected to a 'situation' when she had been with Blenkingstop in his office that morning.

In a word, he had forced her into a hug under the guise of a greeting and then proceeded to squeeze her arse and attempt to kiss her. It had only lasted a few seconds but its impact on her was clearly going to last a lot longer. After her rejection, he told her that if she spoke to anyone about the incident, that would be the end of her employment with the firm. I asked her if anything like this had happened before and it was no surprise when she said he had been creepy and touchy-feely with her since the day she arrived. She didn't know what to do and was on the verge of packing the job in and returning to Yorkshire. I thought she should take a breath and try to calmly consider her options. We agreed to have lunch together at Wayne's café to discuss this unpleasantness. When Roma left my office I noticed Blenkingstop hanging around in the corridor. I hoped to fuck he hadn't been listening.

When we got to the café, Roma chose a seat in the corner by the window and said all she wanted was a cup of coffee – her stomach wasn't ready for feeding.

'Hey up,' said Wayne, attempting a wink but somehow managing to make his face look like a curious whelk. 'Who's the lady friend? You having a lunchtime Tinder?'

'No, she's a work colleague. Just bringing her out for lunch to try and cheer her up. She's been having a bit of a shitty day.'

'Well, the last thing she needs is your company. You'll drag her from gloom all the way down to desperation – it's what you do, it's your superpower. She should come and have a chat with me; I'm all about placing joy and laughter centre stage.'

'Well, you are dressed like a clown, so I suppose at least your intentions are clear. Have you got any wraps on today?'

'Of course, whatever you want individually made to order. I've got a choice of pitta, naan, tortilla, focaccia or chapatti, and you can choose any filling from the list behind me on the wall.'

'Which bread is the most popular?'

'I'm not willing to tell you that. You're just being lazy.'

'Fuck's sake, Wayne, which one is the softest and least chewy?'

'Can't say, mate. I'm a terrible judge of textures. It's my one culinary blind spot.'

'Okay, I'll leave it then. Just two campachoochoos, please.'

'In that case I would recommend the chicken, salsa and avocado tortilla wrap.'

'Thank you, I'll take one of those, please.'

'What blend for the coffees? Medium dark–dark? Or if you want, I'm trying out a light medium dark–dark ground that delivers quite a tart wallop on your first glug.'

'I'll just have the medium, thanks.'

Wayne looked like he was holding a bubble of upset in his throat as he turned away to make the order.

Roma and I chatted about her options for a good thirty minutes or so. It was immediately apparent that she didn't want to do anything drastic like going to the police or complaining to the other partners in the firm. She wanted to continue as normal in the hope that nothing further would happen. If something did happen, she would be better prepared for it and might well take some action against him. The job meant a lot to her and to her family back home; she didn't want to give up the ghost after the first hurdle. I think she just wanted me to agree with her approach, so that is what I did. I told her it might be worth writing down exactly what happened while it was still fresh in her mind. I offered her half of the tortilla wrap and she accepted it without hesitation.

'How's your coffee? Wayne's very proud of his new blends.'

'It's nice enough. Reminds me of the coffee I get from Aldi.'

She then did an unexpected thing and reached across the

table to grasp my hand in hers. 'Do you think maybe I could stay at your place occasionally, you know, when you're away or even just pop round occasionally if you fancy a bit of company? I would really like that. I mean, we get on great, don't you think? We could go to the Grove together and watch the football. I could cook you some decent food. Your diet is terrible, always eating pies and cakes and ready-meal rubbish.'

I pulled my hand away to grab the last bit of chicken wrap from my plate. I was shitting myself. Where had this come from?

'Erm, I don't know. Of course I'd love to help you out. I'll have a think. Let's chat again. We'd better get back to work,' is what I think I mumbled. Whatever it was I said, it was sufficient to get me out of there and back to work behind my closed office door.

I had a long telephone chat with Emily early that evening, which was a welcome surprise. She seemed in good spirits and was treating Pete and Mark to a box of Marks & Spencer's cream cakes to celebrate some milestone in the hotel's journey to being fully open. I told her all about Roma's problems with Blenkingstop. She was furious about it and told me I should stand up for her and confront Blenks (as she called him) with his behaviour. She made me promise to do something and I agreed. I, of course, instantly wished I had kept my mouth shut because a promise to Emily was something that had to be delivered.

20

GARY

THURSDAY

I spent Thursday morning in an eleventh-floor flat of a local authority tower block near the Elephant and Castle, visiting a client named Colin Driffield. He had requested a home visit on account of him suffering from a medical condition that meant he didn't leave home. He had told me over the phone that the flat was riddled with dampness and mould. He wanted to sue Southwark Council in the hope that they would offer to rehouse him on a more pleasant estate. I was there to take his statement and some photos to get the case rolling. To my surprise, when I entered the flat, it was bright, airy and clean, and on the face of it completely free from damp or condensation. Colin was in his early forties, wearing a pristine white T-shirt tucked into a pair of brown woollen trousers with a high-belted waist. He was extra clean shaven and pink-skinned with short cropped brown hair worn without a parting.

He beckoned me inside with a pleasant smile and sat us

down either side of a small dining table in the living room. I took his personal details and tenancy information and then asked if I could see the damp and the mould that was causing all the distress.

'Gosh, do you need to see it? Can't you smell the damp?' he replied. 'It's everywhere, in the furnishings, the carpets, even the walls. It's like living in a factory basement. I try to clean the mould off as soon as it appears. I don't want it in my lungs. I'm immune-complicated – I can't be having invisible spores floating around in my lungs. I think the council want me dead. Why else would they treat me this way? Oh my god, how rude of me. You must think I was brought up by a monster. Can I get you a coffee?'

'That's very kind but I think we should crack on. Is there a patch of wall or ceiling that's showing some mould? It's good to have some photographs to help build the case.'

He said that there might still be a small amount on the corner of the ceiling above the shower. I followed him through to the bathroom.

He pointed to the very top of the shower curtain at what may or may not have been two tiny specs of mould. 'It gets covered in the stuff in here if I don't keep on top of it with my bleach spray. I'm really sorry but I'm not willing to let it build up just so you can take photographs.'

I had a small damp meter in my briefcase so offered to take some moisture readings from the walls and the floors. The meter had two little sharp prongs at one end that were pushed into the wall to obtain a reading. They left two drawing-pin-sized holes in the wall after insertion. Colin inspected the little hand-held device and became worried that the making of the holes might create too much dust for his comfort.

'You must think I'm being over cautious,' he said, 'but think about it: I can't open the front door for fear of intruders and I can't use the windows for ventilation because that just lets in more London particles, and God knows what's in them. I'm a sitting duck here, I really am.'

'The thing is, without any evidence of the dampness and the mould, I can't actually start a case against the council,' I said.

'The fella in the flat three doors along took the council to court and I heard he got a few thousand pounds' compensation and he was shifted up the list for rehousing.'

'That could be true, but he will have had to show evidence of the damp. It's up to you, Colin.'

'Oh, just forget it,' he announced. 'What's the point? Do you really expect me to allow the damp and mould to overtake my home and line my lungs with gunge before they will do something about it? Well, I'm not doing that.'

It quickly dawned on me that this was one of those appointments where the client was actually seeking a bit of human interaction rather than legal advice. It was an increasingly regular occurrence since the company introduced its free initial thirty-minute consultation. He walked over to the large picture window facing south towards Greenwich and Lewisham and Crystal Palace. I joined him to take in the view for myself.

I noticed a photograph on the windowsill of Colin with his

arm around another bloke, taken in a park or out in the countryside.

'Nice photo,' I said. 'It's quite recent, isn't it? You look very different with the long hair.'

He picked up the photograph and it brought a smile out of his face.

'It was taken two years ago. That was my partner, Alec. I lost him a couple of weeks after that was taken. He liked my hair long and so when he left us I cut it all off. I didn't want anyone to see me as the same person that Alec saw every day we were together. I wanted it to be a memory that only he would have. Strange, the things you do when you lose someone you love. If I could see him again, even for just thirty seconds, I would use all that time just saying sorry for all the things I did that might have hurt him and sorry for all the things I didn't do that might have made him happy. I never did that when he was alive and that is my biggest regret.'

We talked for a short while longer. I'm sure Colin would have liked me to stay, but I had to get on with my day. He said he would take the stairs down to the lobby with me to see me out; the exercise would do him good.

As I stepped out of the building onto the paved courtyard, I immediately saw Mr Sequence walking towards me with his driver in tow. He was wearing his puffa with the bright orange hood and carrying a brown paper grocery bag. For a split second I had a flashing image of me smashing my shitty briefcase into his face, but this thought soon passed. If Emily had been there to back me up, it might have lingered longer.

'Hello, Gary, you seem surprised to see me? Am I right?'

'You're right, Mr Sequence. Am I meant to think this is purely a coincidence?'

'Not at all, Gary, because that could not be further from the truth.'

'So how did you know I was here, if you don't mind me asking?'

'Maybe I've got a tracker on your car; maybe I've implanted a chip into your skin; maybe I'm having you followed; maybe I've got a fucking crystal orb that shows me your whereabouts. It doesn't really matter, does it, Gary. The only thing you need to know is that I am never far away, that I am always looking over your shoulder.'

'Like a guardian angel?'

'No, more like a nosey fucker.'

He put his vaping unit to his mouth, shut his eyes and took a long hard suck on it. He had overreached his lung capacity on this occasion and the vapours were released in small gusts as he broke out into a fit of coughs and retching. Each gust contained the essence of a recently opened washing machine door with a side note of cherries. The driver offered up a couple of gentle taps on his back, pointless but enough to suggest 'I'm here for you, boss, if you need me.'

'Fuck off, Brian [cough]. I'm not a fucking puppy [splutter]. I'm your fucking boss [retch] and you don't start fucking patting me on the back unless [hurrgghh] I specifically ask you.'

Brian took two steps backwards, rubbed the butterflies on his neck and bowed his head slightly. Sequence recovered enough to face me, his face flushed pink and his eyes watering.

'I need your answer now, Gary, right now this very minute. What's it going to be?'

I had been caught badly off guard and my only instinct was to try to bluff out some time.

'I'm still weighing things up. Could this not wait until there's a trial date? I mean, maybe they'll plead guilty and there'll be no need for me to attend.'

'Not a chance in hell of them pleading guilty, lad.'

'I just need some thinking time and, listen, I promise I haven't spoken to the police. I haven't spoken to anyone about it—'

'Good boy,' he interrupted.

'I'm sure if we waited until a date was announced then that would focus my mind,' I pleaded.

'In that case, you can start focusing away, Gary, because a date has been fixed for the seventeenth of March, which is just two weeks away. So that is where we are: it's focus time. I've got the ten thousand pounds in cash in this bag and it's all yours if you come to the right decision. No bank records, no money trail, easy peasy. End of all the distress.'

I wanted to run, but the driver seemed to sense this as he removed his hands from his pockets and took a few steps towards me. Sequence held out the bag in front of him: 'Come on, Gary, take it. The alternative really isn't worth thinking about.'

'No, I'm not ready to do that,' I replied.

'I fucking knew it,' barked Sequence. I retreated a few steps and he moved forward to maintain the distance.

'I'm not saying I won't do it,' I continued with my hands raised defensively and a hint of mouse in my voice, 'I'm just not ready yet, and if I ever did what you're asking, it wouldn't be for money.'

'I actually thought you had more sense about you, Gary. You must realize that your refusal brings into play a whole new bag of options on my behalf, all of them deeply shit as far as you're concerned.'

'I'm sorry,' I whispered.

Before I could even think of my next move, the driver had stepped around me and forced my arms behind my back. I was too shocked to speak and my legs had turned to syrupy nonsense.

'I knew you wouldn't take the cash, Gary,' said Sequence. 'That's why I brought this.'

He reached inside the brown paper bag and pulled out a big clump of beef mince. He forced the meaty clod hard against my nose and mouth.

'*Eat it! Eat it!*' he chanted, pressing it harder and harder into my face. '*Eat the fucking beef mince.*'

It soon became difficult to breathe, especially as the driver had my head in a vice-like grip. I was making that noise that an actor might make if his mouth was duct-taped in a kidnap scenario.

'Hey, what the fuck are you doing?' It was Colin's voice. He had been watching from behind the glass doors to the tower block and was running to my assistance. The bald man threw me to the ground and turned to receive the unexpected guest.

'I've called the police,' said Colin. 'So you had better clear off out of here.'

'It's okay, Colin. I know these blokes; just keep out of it.'

He stared down at me on the floor and a look of horror spread across his face as he noticed the blood and meaty strands spread around my face.

'What have they done to you? Fucking hell, you need an ambulance.' He bent down to examine my face more closely.

'It's just minced beef,' I said as reassuringly as I could.

Sequence gave me a little kick on the side of my stomach and leant into my view.

'I am not going away, Gary. See you soon and, in the meantime, you have a good think what's best for you in the long run.'

He blew Colin a kiss and then walked away with the driver by his side.

21

GARY

FRIDAY

Blenkingstop had called me into work early on Friday for one of his face-to-face catch-ups. They were usually just another opportunity for him to gloat and bully and remind the person who the big mango was in this chutney jar. He was seated with his feet up on top of his mahogany desk when I entered and didn't look at me as he instructed me to sit down opposite him. The chair I sat in was lower to the ground than the generally acceptable height. It looked like a normal wing chair but I'm sure the legs had been cut down or some padding removed. Either way, it meant you had to look up at him as he spoke.

'Have you considered an upgrade for your suit, Gary?' he asked. 'You're beginning to look like you're selling double fucking glazing.'

'Not really, Mr Blenkingstop, unless you want to buy me a new one for all my excellent work here.'

'Do you think you're funny?' he snapped. 'Because I don't. I think you're a bore, and so does everyone else in the office, apart from you of course. I want you to buy a new suit, is that clear?'

'I'll start looking today.'

'And make it dark blue if you don't mind. Dark blue would give you a bit more clout, and my word that's something you could do with. Now, tell me, what do you think of the new girl, Roma?'

'She seems nice. Yeah, she seems a nice person.'

'Nice? Is that it? Is that as far as your vocabulary can take you? It's not much of an endorsement, is it? Puppies are nice. My shoes are nice. A piece of cake is nice.'

'A piece of cake can be very nice.'

'Has she got what it takes to be a lawyer? Is she analytical? Is she intelligent enough? How are her people skills? Is she organized in her work? That was my big worry when I took her on, that she might be a bit chaotic, a bit dipsy.'

'Yes, I think she is an excellent lawyer. Has something happened to make you worry?'

'The other day I bumped into her in the corridor after she had just left your office. She seemed upset and I thought she might have been crying. What was all that about?'

So, here was my chance to do what I had promised Emily and pull him up on his behaviour towards Roma. My mouth dried up in an instant and I felt a rush of hot worry flow up from my stomach and ride around my face. Fear. Fear of a consequence that I hadn't yet imagined and an outcome that

I probably wouldn't give a shit about come the crunch. I proceeded with caution as my guide. I guessed that Blenkingstop knew exactly why she was crying and just wanted to know how much I knew and what Roma's intentions were regarding the 'office incident'.

'You're right, she was upset. Upset because you behaved inappropriately towards her.'

Fuck. I did it, I actually said it, right into his face. Unbelievably thrilling.

'What do you mean "inappropriately"?'

'In the sexual sense. She says that you tried to kiss her and manhandled her behind.'

'Oh, do fuck off. And you believed her?'

'She seemed very truthful and genuinely upset.'

'She's lying. Nothing of the sort occurred. Why would she say that? She's a fucking liar. Do you realize how serious an accusation like that could be for me?'

'Listen, I've spoken to her about it and her attitude seems to be that she will let it pass so long as it never happens again.'

'But she's lying. Does she intend to hold it against me as leverage of some sort? Fuck. I knew she wasn't right for this firm. Do you believe me when I say there isn't an ounce of truth to what she's saying?'

'That doesn't really matter, does it? I'm just telling you the situation. I'm not the judge and jury here. If it was me, I would apologize and promise it will never happen again.'

'So you don't believe me, you little fucker, and how dare you presume to be giving me advice? Maybe it's time that this firm and you parted ways. If nothing else, I demand loyalty from my staff, and you've turned on me at the word of this girl who has barely been here ten minutes. If you think you're being employed by a pervert, maybe you should hand in your notice. The problem is, I doubt you've got the balls to do that. Go on, I dare you, quit and I won't even ask you to work your notice.'

'Maybe I will.'

'Will you fuck. Maybe I should make your life a misery here and force the issue. I would enjoy that. Yes, that's definitely an option. HOW DARE YOU NOT BELIEVE ME! Go on, fuck off out of here.'

Back in my office, I couldn't wipe the smile off my own face. *Shit, that was fun, exhilarating even, standing up against my persecutor.* I wished I could bottle up this feeling and take a sip whenever required. I imagined myself handing in my notice and just the very thought of it lifted a big old lump of weight from my shoulders; a weight that had been there so long that I hardly noticed its presence anymore. I spent the rest of the day updating all my files so that if I did leave then whoever took them over would be up to speed. By the time I had finished there was no one left in the building apart from the receptionist. I said goodbye to her as I left. She didn't even look up to acknowledge me.

Emily phoned me that evening as I was on my way to the Grove to watch the football. I told her that I had confronted Blenks about Roma and she was thrilled with me.

'How did it feel? Good, I expect?' she asked.

'Yeah, really, really good,' I replied.

She asked me if I was sure that Blenks wasn't telling the truth. I told her I was feeling about eighty/twenty in favour of Roma's version of events. Blenkingstop had actually been very convincing, but then again he was an old hand at bullshitting. Emily had to cut the call short.

'I'll miss you this weekend. Such a shame you have to do that bloody police station duty solicitor shit,' she said.

'I know. But have a lovely weekend without me,' I replied, and I meant it.

I didn't tell her that I was seriously thinking of handing in my notice. I needed to give that step a little bit more thought.

That evening I went to the Grove to watch the football. Andy was sat in his usual spot at the end of the bar. I bought us both a pint of IPA and we settled down to enjoy the match. It was a Championship game between Burnley and Millwall so featured a lot of height both in respect of the players and the general trajectory of the ball. I told Andy about Blenkingstop's suggestion that I hand in my notice or suffer the consequences.

'You won't need a job once the shit hits the fan and half the country is underwater,' he said. 'And you won't be needing a salary or any of that bollocks, because it's going to be a bartering system – survival of who's got the most valuable stuff to exchange.'

'Like corn cobs?' I suggested.

'Yep, corn cobs could well go premium, alongside fresh water and tinned food.'

'So, are you stockpiling tinned goods?'

'Too right I am. I'm concentrating on corned beef, kidney beans and sliced peaches. Did you realize that so long as the can isn't damaged, the contents can still be edible ten, even fifteen years later?'

'Jesus, don't you think you'd be better off dead than living alone in an underground bunker eating old meat and wiping your arse with corn cobs?'

'I wouldn't be alone. I'd have my mouse.'

'Nice, but you do know that mice generally only live for about two years?'

'Not if it's a dormouse. They can live for up to five years.'

'I just worry that if it died it would break your heart, and that isn't going to help with the mental side of things.'

'I'm not actually that worried about being alone. I'm well practised at that. I'll miss the football, though.'

'Will you miss sitting here with me in the pub?'

'Yes, I think I probably would.'

We both took a couple of silent sips from our pints, slightly embarrassed by the little moment of genuine friendship.

'Would you eat the mouse when it died?' I asked.

'Of course not.'

'Have you thought of a name for the mouse?'

'Yeah.'

'What is it?'

'Ron.'

'What if it's a girl?'

'Margaret.'

Andy wasn't really a viable sounding board regarding my work situation, so I put a bet on with him that at some point the camera would catch the Millwall manager Kenny Jackett either picking his nose or scratching his balls.

Just as the second half started, Roma arrived and joined us at the bar. Andy kept trying to engage her in conversation.

'I do a lot of outdoor cooking, you know. Is that something you're interested in?' he asked her.

'Not so much. I'm big on takeaways, to be honest.'

'What would you eat if there were no takeaways left standing, though?'

'Get a ready meal from the supermarket.'

'Oh, right. Do you have a good supermarket near you with decent opening hours?'

'Yes, quite a few. I like Sainsbury's, but the Tesco is a bit nearer.'

'I like Sainsbury's too. The aisles are about as wide as you can get, other than maybe a Marks & Spencer Foodhall.'

'I guess you're right.'

'Have you had a nice time recently? You know, at the cinema or in the park or something like that?'

'Nothing stands out.'

'HE JUST SCRATCHED HIS BALLS WHILE PICKING HIS NOSE!' I announced, a bit too loudly perhaps, as it briefly silenced the hubbub in the room. 'That makes us quits, Andy.'

He gave me a thumbs-up but didn't take his eyes off Roma. At the end of the match Roma had clearly had enough of

Andy and made her excuses to leave. I took the cue and joined her. We walked down Camberwell Grove together and made our way to the main road. Halfway down, we saw Mr Manchester leaning against a wall, still wearing his cream puffa jacket. He stared at us with a hint of menace as we passed him by.

'Oh, hello, big nose and the Yorkie. You owe me a tenner for the dry cleaning. You going to cough up or what?'

'You deserved it for being an arsehole. I'm not giving you a penny,' said Roma.

'I'm the arsehole?!' he replied. 'You threw a fucking drink over me!'

Roma grabbed my arm and rushed me along. 'Come on, let's just keep walking. I don't think he's got the balls to do anything.'

As we made our way down Camberwell Grove to the high street, we could sense that Mr Manchester was still following us about twenty metres behind.

My instincts told me that it might be a good idea if Roma didn't walk herself home that night. As we emerged onto the high street, a black cab was just unloading its passengers. We stepped up and got inside. As Roma shut the cab door behind her Mr Manchester appeared beside the cab. He peered in through the back window.

'I want my money,' he said in a low voice. 'I know where you live, pet. You had better watch your fucking back.'

I gave the cab driver my address and we set off. We were silent for a few minutes, both of us a bit stunned by Mr

Manchester's threatening window rant. I didn't want her to go home. What if he was telling the truth when he said he knew where Roma lived?

'You know the other day in the café when you asked if you could stay at my flat?' I said.

'Yeah,' she replied.

'Well, just wanted to say that you can sleep there anytime I'm down in Brighton. You know, to give yourself a break from sleeping on your mate's floor. In fact, I tell you what, why don't you stay tonight. I can sleep on the sofa and you can have a nice Saturday-morning lie-in.'

She agreed immediately and when we got out of the cab she linked my arm as we strolled towards the entrance stairwell. When we passed by the play area where the see-saw used to be, I heard a rustling in the leaves as my squirrel friend jumped up onto the low fence running the length of the pathway. He appeared to be shaking his head in disgust at me.

'Urghh, I fucking hate squirrels,' said Roma as she shooed him away with a flick of her foot.

Roma was thankfully not talking as we passed Grace's front door. Grace's lights were all off, so I hoped she was fast asleep. As soon as we were inside the flat, I felt uncomfortable. No female other than Emily or Grace had ever set foot inside. I would, of course, tell Emily and Grace about this visit, and I was sure they would both understand. In the event, my discomfort was eased when Roma announced that she was dog tired and wanted to go straight to bed. She declared that my sofa would be far more comfortable than the arrangement she had on her friend's floor and insisted that I take the bed. I didn't argue. Before I got off to sleep, there was a phone call from Emily. I didn't answer. It just didn't seem the right thing to do in the circumstances.

22

GARY

SATURDAY

When I woke up Saturday morning, I found Roma in bed beside me fast asleep. I nearly jumped out of skin. I couldn't say for sure, but from the sight of her bare neck and shoulders, it seemed that she was naked. I picked up my clothes, got dressed in the living room and crept out onto the walkway to reflect on what felt like a disturbing occurrence. My phone pinged. It was a message from Wayne, asking if I could come down to the café immediately. I was happy to oblige. A cup of early-morning dark–dark was just what I needed.

When I arrived outside the café, it was immediately apparent that the place had been broken into and vandalized. The glass front door had been smashed to smithereens and was in the process of being boarded up by a bloke with ginger hair and very thick thighs. I stepped over the glass and went inside. Wayne was stood at the serving counter with his father. There was a big empty space to the left of them where Wayne's state-of-the-art 'Barista' coffee machine should have been.

'What the fuck has happened, Wayne?'

'Same old Peckham shit,' he replied. 'They broke in, smashed up my machine, spray-painted the wall and fucked off back to their beds to sleep off the thrill. Fuck them.'

I peered over the counter to see the coffee machine lying defeated on the floor, smashed up and bent as if Thor had attacked it with his incredible hammer.

'Did they steal anything?' I asked.

'Not that we can tell,' said Wayne's dad. 'You mind coming outside for a chat about an insurance claim and such while Wayne gets on with the clean-up?'

'If you insist,' I replied.

We walked down to the Costa coffee shop a couple of hundred yards down the high street. It was empty apart from a bloke with his head down on a table fast asleep. He had made a thick scarf for his neck out of plastic Tesco carrier bags and was shielding the light from his eyes with a very long sports sock.

We sat down at a window table and drank our coffee. The mood was sombre and I remained silent, waiting for him to say whatever it was that was on his mind.

'What happened at the café wasn't a burglary or a prank,' he announced. 'It was a message to me. I got a visit two days ago from a couple of men claiming to represent the interests of clients involved in the upcoming trial. They claimed to have been informed that the police would be calling me as a witness, though that's the first I've heard of it.'

'What did they look like?'

'One of them was tall, thin, red-haired and haunted-looking. The other one, who did all the talking, was shorter and had the hairstyle of a lady at a 1980s disco. It was very striking.'

'I think I know them. They've been on to me as well – offered me money to fail to attend the trial. The long-haired one is called Sequence or Sequins, something like that.'

'Well, the name doesn't really matter. It's the message they've just sent that's the thing. I told them that I needed time to think about it, because I do, and then this happens. I think they want to encourage me to their way of thinking. They offered me ten thousand pounds.'

'I told them the same thing, that I needed more time, and that was two days ago. Shit, I wonder what they've got planned for me? Fuck. Do you think we should go to the police? We could go together. Let's do it now.' A part of me hoped he would get carried away by my enthusiasm, take my arm and march me down to the police station, but I knew deep down that was never going to happen.

'It's never done me any good asking for the police to help when it comes to Rowlett and his apes. Don't even think about it. That is the very last thing you should do, believe me.'

'So what are we going to do?'

'I am going to disappear off the face of this earth to somewhere I will never be found. I've been preparing for this scenario for some time. I've told Wayne to board up that café and get the hell out of London. He knows the score. He knows the danger is real. It will break his heart but at least it will still be beating.'

'Why don't you just take the money?'

'Because I will be in debt to them for the rest of my life, and as you know I've been trying to escape their clutches for fifteen years now. It has to end. I should have done this years ago, but I stayed around for Wayne, and all that has achieved is to fuck him up.'

'Jesus, it's not your fault,' I said.

'If you insist,' he replied. 'How much did they offer you?'

'Twenty-five thousand.'

'Woah, I guess you're more important to them than I am. Do they know where you live?'

'Yes, they do.'

'You need to get out of there, as soon as possible. Do the same as me and disappear. Whatever the cost, it will be good value in the long run.'

'I think you might be right.'

I popped back into the café to say goodbye to Wayne.

'Your dad says you're going to make yourself scarce for a while?'

'Yeah, it's for the best. I need to find somewhere that appreciates me more, where I'm given the appropriate respect for my entrepreneurship and physique.'

'You got somewhere in mind?'

'Maybe get myself over to Essex. I know a woman in Brentwood who'll put me up 'til I find my feet and transform the area.'

'Lucky Brentwood,' I said.

'Lucky lady,' he replied.

We said our goodbyes. There was a decent chance that we would never see each other again, so it was a bit emotional. He wrote his phone number down on a scrap of paper and told me that I must keep in touch. I told him that I definitely would and in that moment I meant it.

I left the café and went over the road to my office. Panic had set in and in the briefest of moments my 'good boy, play it by the book' approach was ditched. I spent the next few hours double-checking that all my case files were in order and I wrote a long briefing to Roma concerning Grace's child-access case. I finished it by begging her to keep me updated on its progress and apologizing for my sudden exit. I wished her luck and strength in her dealings with Blenkingstop. The final task was my notice to quit work. I kept it brief and to the point:

Dear Blenkingstop,

Please accept this letter as my notice to quit as of today's date. As per your suggestion, I will not be working out my month's notice.

You are an awful man. I hope you get what's coming.

Gary Thorn

I packed up my personal items and put them in a plastic carrier bag. As I was doing so, it suddenly struck me that Sequence might already be at my flat. Judging by what had happened to Wayne's place, he was obviously on manoeuvres at the moment. *Shit. He might even be inside the flat waiting for me or, worse still, have already set the place on fire.* I tried to calm myself and formulate a plan for the rest of the day. It went something like this:

1. Pack up the basics, leave the flat and go to Brighton.
2. Withdraw cash from a machine in London so that I don't leave a debit card trail.
3. Don't take car into Brighton in case Sequence is tracking it.
4. Once in Brighton contact DS Marks and place myself in his hands, or maybe not. (I would talk to Emily about this one.)

23

GARY

On the way back to my flat, it started to rain. I stopped at an
ATM to withdraw my daily limit. The machine stated that there
were insufficient funds in my account. I checked my balance
and it showed I only had five pounds, when there should have
been over two thousand. I had a strong suspicion that Sequence
was behind this draining.

I approached my block of flats from the rear, along a little
footpath that brought me out at the far corner so that I could
check the cars at the front for any sign of Sequence. I immediately clocked his black Mercedes parked up right by the
entrance next to the lifts and the central stairwell. Inside, I
could see the contrasting hair profiles of Sequence and his
driver. I took a few steps back to get out of sight. I took my
phone out and dialled Roma's number. Maybe she was still in
my flat and could pack up some of my stuff? I could meet her
elsewhere for a handover later in the day. The call went straight
to voicemail.

I took another peek around the front of the building.

Sequence was now stood at the side of his car, a plume of vape smoke billowing from his mouth and his phone to his ear. He glanced over to where I was standing. I ducked back behind the wall. Had he seen me? It didn't matter either way, because at that moment I felt a hand on my shoulder and turned around to see Brian the driver grinning at me. I attempted a mini scarper but he held onto my collar and grabbed me around the chest before marching me towards the Mercedes.

'Hello, Gary, what's in your bag? More mince for your dinner?'

'Just work stuff.'

'That's good to know. Get in the car, Gary.'

I did as I was told and sat centrally on the back seat. Sequence turned his head to stare at me through the gap between the front seats.

'You cold, Gary? You seem a bit damp and shivery, a little bit shaky.'

I nodded my head in agreement.

'Well, say it then. Say that you're a bit shivery and would like the heating pumped up.'

I looked at him for clarification that he really wanted me to repeat his words.

'Yes, Gary, I want you to say that you're a bit shivery and would like the heating turned up.'

I did as he asked, my voice barely louder than a whisper: 'I'm a bit shivery. Could I have the heating pumped up?'

'No, no, no, Gary. Say it a bit more angrily, like you're an impatient and very important person.'

'I'm sorry, not at the moment. I can't do that.'

'Of course you can't, Gary, because you're not important, are you?'

I shook my head in agreement.

'So why are you acting like you are and fucking me about? We need to resolve this right now. I saw you at Wayne's café this morning. I suspect that little incident has resolved things as far as Wayne senior is concerned.'

'Yes, I think you might be right.'

'That's good to know, Gary.'

Sequence took his vape machine and sucked hard on its exhaust pipe. He blew the resulting smoke slowly through his teeth and directed it towards me. It was a slightly different smell this time; less launderette and more garden centre. It seemed thicker and heavier in its impact, almost like a proper cigarette, and a lot more sticky and clingy in its attitude. The driver pressed some switch or other and hot air started to rush through the vents under the front seats and fill the rear of the car.

'Decision time, Gary: pleasure or pain – what's it going to be? I have the cash here with me now, but as I think you might have guessed, this is the last time it will be on offer.'

The only message my brain seemed to be receiving was '*Don't take the cash, don't take the cash, don't take the cash*'. It was getting hot in the back; I needed to get out. I wanted to be with Emily, out on one of our walks or sharing a pack of chips on the seafront. 'I don't want the money, Mr Sequence, but I have no intention of turning up to the trial to give evidence. I've left my job and will disappear until this thing is over.'

'Problem is, the money is kind of our guarantee of your

compliance. It gives us a bit of leverage over you until your side of the bargain is complete.'

'But I'm leaving today, it's all planned. I'm going into hiding. Nobody will be able to find me, not even you.'

'Course I could fucking find you.'

I scrolled through my phone and located the email I had sent to Blenkingstop telling him I was quitting my job. I offered it up to Sequence as proof of my genuine intent.

'I sent this an hour ago. I'm serious about this. You think I would leave my job if I wasn't serious? Honestly, you've got nothing to worry about.'

There was silence as Sequence took another big mothersuck from his vape and clouded me up with a rolling ball of peaty steam. When the fog lifted, the expression on his face suggested I might be in with a chance of striking a deal.

'Maybe I believe you, Gary. That's quite a big move for a shithouse like you. I expect your mummy will be very upset when she finds out you've quit your little lawyer job.'

He took my phone and put it in his inside coat pocket. The driver immediately handed me a replacement phone through the gap in the seats.

'I'll be keeping your phone,' Sequence continued. 'This is your new phone, Gary, and I will be using it to check in on you – maybe every hour, maybe every day or so; who knows. You must never use it for outgoing calls, you understand?'

'Yes, I do.'

'If on any occasion I can't get hold of you, then I will come and find you and bury you ten feet under. Is that understood?'

I dipped my head like a compliant army cadet as I replied, 'Yes.'

'That's good to know. Where are you going to be staying, Gary? I think I have a right to that information, given the circumstances.'

'I really don't want to say. I don't want to involve the person I'll be staying with, and surely the fewer people that know the better.'

'Well, in that case maybe we will be phoning you every hour, and, Gary, please don't think for one moment that I can't find you at the drop of a hat. Like you said before, it's very difficult to hide from a man with my connections.'

'Understood,' I replied.

'You got any close friends here on the estate, Gary?'

'No, I don't know anyone, it's not that type of place. I keep myself to myself like everyone else that lives here.'

'What about that old bird that lives next door to you? We saw her knocking on your door when we were driving into the estate. Is she a friend of yours?'

'No, she's a nutcase, always banging on people's doors and trying to get them to accept Jesus into their lives, and if not, to give her some cigarettes or money.'

'Is that right?' he said, seemingly unconvinced. I didn't want Grace anywhere near this situation and started to lay it on thick.

'She claims every bloke in the block under forty is her son and that every bloke over fifty is her ex-lover. I had to take out a restraining order against her that stops her talking to me or trying to contact me. If she took a shine to you, she might hunt you down and start bothering you for maintenance payments.'

Sequence still looked unconvinced. I took a chance on a bluff. I did not want Grace getting dragged into this.

'Here, pass me my phone back,' I said, holding out my hand. 'I'll show you the paperwork for the injunction. She should be in hospital, not living amongst us.'

'No need to do that. She did look a little odd. Reminded me of my old mum before she was dragged off into a care home. Go on, Gary, fuck off, and let's hope we never see each other again. Speak soon.'

I got out of the car and walked slowly to the lift. I was aware that Sequence was still watching me from inside the Mercedes. I managed to keep my poise as I stood outside the lift and waved towards the car as it drove out of the estate. Once inside the lift I collapsed down onto the floor, rolled into a ball and starting breathing so deeply I thought my lungs might fold in on themselves.

24

GARY

I got back into my flat and was pleased to see that Roma had already left and had thankfully missed the visits from Mr Sequence and Grace. I needed to speak to her but didn't have my phone. I started to pack a suitcase but got an instant sweat on and had to sit on the side of the bed to steady myself. My back began to dampen and I stretched the neck of my T-shirt to the limit as I yanked it off my back. Hotness continued to radiate around my body in waves.

I stood up, pulled off my jeans and socks and threw them at the wall to punish them for encouraging this clagginess. The heat continued to rise. I backed myself up against the wall, seeking relief from a cool surface. A drip of sweat made its way down the back of my thigh and tickled me as it swooped its way around my ankle and onto the wooden floor. Moving my foot to the side, I could see that the sweat drop had left a stain remarkably similar to a profile silhouette of Brian May, the guitarist from the band Queen. The image from the 'Bohemian Rhapsody' video of all the band members' faces arranged in a circle flashed through my mind, with each face replaced with that of Mr Sequence. I laughed, then felt a dizziness right behind my eyes.

I got onto my bed, laid on my back and started to breathe slowly and deeply to combat the panic. My stomach started to churn. I ran into the bathroom, discarding my onion-coloured underpants on the way and sat on the toilet rocking to and fro like a nodding dog on the back shelf of a Honda Jazz. I rolled a length of toilet roll round and round my hand until I was wearing it like a boxing glove, then pulled it off my hand and threw it into the sink. My chest hair was now damp and tangled. I rubbed at it in a circular motion with the palm of my hand, and as I did so I felt my heart pounding in my chest. The beats seemed irregular and some felt heavier and more strained than others. I closed my eyes and tried to count the spaces between the beats. This little exercise seemed to calm my body down and my breathing eventually found a more natural rhythm. I slowly got up, walked back into the living room and eased myself onto the sofa. I had the sudden realization that I was probably incapable of pulling this thing off. I couldn't even pack a case, never mind defy a witness summons from the Crown Prosecution Service.

I'm Gary. I'm a shithouse, and I'm out of my depth.

There was a knock on my front door – a very gentle one that I immediately interpreted as suspicious. My body stiffened and in the silence that followed I willed the visitor to be on their way and never return. It didn't work. There followed another knock, this time louder and more insistent. I heard the letterbox being pushed open and the words 'I know you're in there, Gary. Answer the bloody door'. It was Grace. My body relaxed and I rushed to the door to let her in.

'Jesus, Gary. Spare my eyes, you pervert,' she said and turned her back on me. I realized I was completely naked and had a large swirl of tangled hair on my chest that must have looked like the aftermath of a forest fire. I apologized to Grace and told her to come in while I leapt into the bedroom and got myself dressed. Lassoo came into the bedroom to watch, sniffed the air and then left. I joined Grace in the living room and over a cup of tea explained the situation.

'You're in the shit,' she declared after I'd blurted out the basics.

'I know that, Grace. What do you think I should do?'

'Go to Brighton, set up house in the hotel attic and don't emerge until the trial is long gone. Don't even peep out of the front door. Don't use the internet and don't use your mobile phone. Does this Sequence fella know about Emily and the hotel?'

'I can't think of any reason why he would. I mean, the people at work don't even know that I've got a girlfriend.'

'Well then, if you play it smart you should be okay. When you emerge, you can tell the police you had a mental break-down, and if you want a witness to confirm it, I will back you up to the hilt. To be honest, it wouldn't be that far from the truth.'

'You don't think I should go to the police? I trust DS Marks. Maybe he could protect me.'

'Maybe he could, but from what you've said this Sequence bloke has got his tentacles firmly planted on the inside of this case. I don't think it's worth the risk. It's up to you. If Sequence should track you down, then I reckon that's the time to go to the coppers, not now when there's a chance your plan will work.'

Even if she was wrong, I took great reassurance from her certainty. It was all I needed to galvanize me into taking the next step and getting myself down to Brighton. Making the move would gift me some distance from the situation and allow me some more thinking (prevarication) time.

'Would you like me to help you pack?' asked Grace.

'No, that's okay. Listen, Grace, I'm not saying I'm moving down there permanently. I will still come and visit if I can, and you must promise that you will come and visit us at the hotel.'

'Don't worry about me, Gary. I should be right at the very bottom of your worry list. You concentrate on yourself and Emily. I hope you do make it a permanent thing. I've lived my life. You've got the best years ahead of you and you should be spending them with Emily.'

I almost believed her. She stood up off the sofa and gave me a long and tightly grasped hug. She switched the weight between her feet as we embraced, as if remembering a dance she and a partner had enjoyed somewhere in the distant past.

'One thing, Grace,' I began as she released me from the hug. 'That bloke Sequence asked me whether you and I were good friends. I told him that you were a nutcase bible basher, a sworn enemy of mine and that I had to get a restraining order out against you.'

'Charming. Thanks for the reputation boost.'

'If he ever comes sniffing round here, you mustn't let on that we're friends. I don't want them using you to get at me.'

'Yeah, yeah, don't worry, I get it. I'll send them away none the wiser.'

'And please please please don't tell anyone where I am. I don't want this problem following me down to Brighton and engulfing Emily. I haven't even told her anything about it. Though I suppose I'll have to now. Do you promise?'

'I promise.'

As she left the flat, I bent down and gave Lassoo a great big hug and covered his forehead in kisses. They were kind of meant for Grace, but it was easier to deliver them through a third party. As I stroked him, I hit a sweet spot that made his back leg start to involuntarily twitch and swivel. His eyes looked slightly terrified, as if to say, 'I am growing a wing and if I take off I have no idea how I will land myself.'

I packed the very basics into a suitcase – casual clothes, important documents, my old lady slippers from Marks & Spencer, laptop, a few old photographs, some bits and pieces that Emily kept at the flat and my favourite coffee mug with a picture of an otter playing maracas on it. I wondered how long, if ever, it would be before I stepped into the flat again, which gave me the sudden urge to give the place a good sort out and tidy up. I often turn to cleaning as a way to divert my attention from worry, so I welcomed this urge and got stuck in. I made a nice job of it. Even cleaned the windows and the cooker and wiped down the skirting boards. It took me a couple of hours and when I was finished I sat down on my sofa and had myself a farewell cup of tea and five slightly soft gingernut biscuits.

I liked this flat. I liked that it was one-bedroomed; no second bedroom to remind me I was on my own. I liked that it was so sparsely furnished, giving it a transitory feel and helping me kid myself that I still had better things to come. I liked that living here had introduced me to Grace. I liked that it was cheap and that I wasn't responsible for repairs. I liked that I had spent so much time with Emily under its roof and that it once served as a refuge for her when she escaped her abusive relationship with Tommy Briggs. I was attached to the place, and the thought of returning was very reassuring and comforting.

When I was leaving the flat, I glanced at my shitty grey suit laid out on the mattress and got a pang of guilt about abandoning what had been a second skin for me these past years. I grabbed it and forced it into my case. As I put my suitcase into my car, I was joined by Grace, who had been walking Lassoo in the play area where the see-saw used to be.

'Skulking off without saying goodbye, was you?'

'No, Grace, I thought we had said our goodbyes, but very happy to do it again.'

I could tell by her expression and her fidgeting that something was bothering her.

'Come on, Grace, spit it out. What's on your mind? Were

you expecting me to ask you to come with me, because I'm
not going to be doing that, not when I've got these people on
my back. I want you well out of it.'

'No, don't be daft. I'm not like you. I can't just get up and
go. I'd need much more time to prepare, and I expect you'll
need me to keep an eye on the flat while you're gone, so that's
another burden you've dumped on me.'

'That's very kind of you. You're a very particular hero of
mine, no doubt about it.'

'That sounds like a remark to me.'

'I suppose it is.'

'I'll come and visit though,' added Grace. 'And you never
know, I might make the move if things pan out between you
and Emily.'

She pulled out a small package from her pocket wrapped in
greaseproof paper and handed it to me.

'Here's a little something for the journey. A nice slice of
Battenberg. It's the nub end so you've got extra marzipan. That
should keep you alert.'

I thanked her and turned to get in my car.

'There was a woman stayed with you in the flat last night,
wasn't there? I saw her leaving this morning. Are you sleeping
with her? Because if you are then Emily needs to know. And
tell me the truth; I can always tell when you're lying.'

Of course Grace would have sniffed out that Roma was here
last night. She never missed a trick.

'Don't be daft. Absolutely no way. She's a colleague from
work. We had a drink in the Grove last night and a bloke was

kind of stalking her. I didn't want her walking off on her own so I said she could stay on my sofa. She's living on a friend's floor at the moment so, stalker or not, I knew it would give her and her friend a break. That's it. Nothing more, end of story. Don't care if you believe me or not.'

She screwed up her eyes and stared at me with pensioner intensity before declaring: 'Okay, I believe you, but if I find out you've lied to me then we're finished. Not only that: I'll knock your block off with my steam iron. You hear me?'

'I hear you. She's called Roma, by the way, and she'll be looking after your access case from now on. I've briefed her to the hilt and to be honest she's more experienced in family law than I am so you'll be in good hands. She'll be in touch soon, I'm sure. I've told her it's her number-one priority.'

'Why don't you let her stay in the flat? You seem to care about her welfare, so why not let her look after it while you're away? Be nice for her to have a proper bed to herself, and I want her fully rested if she's going to be looking after my interests.'

That took me by surprise, but I realized it was actually a very good idea. It would be nice to have someone I trusted to keep an eye on Grace, and undoubtedly Grace and Lassoo would soon have her looking after their needs as well as her own.

'That's not a bad idea. Look, I'll have a word with her about it and I'll leave you my spare key in case she takes up the offer. Oh, and if she does come, don't you dare tell her where I'm staying. The less people who know the better. You promise?'

'I promise,' she said solemnly, with a tiny dip of her head in recognition of her commitment.

I handed over the key, which seemed to put a smile on Grace's face. She stood with Lassoo by the lifts and waved me away. Lassoo was staring over to the spot where the see-saw used to be. I wondered if he would ever find what he was looking for over there. As I drove out of the estate, my squirrel friend appeared on the verge. I wound my window down for a quick chat.

'So, you're leaving for good, are you, mate?' I asked on his behalf.

'Maybe, maybe not. Have to see how things pan out.'

'Seems to me you've got a good life going on here – no worries, nice and quiet, good job. A lot of people would kill for such an outcome. You want to think around that for a long moment before you give it all up.'

'I've packed in the job and, to be honest, things aren't quite as simple and pleasing as you might think.'

'Why did you pack your job in? Oh, hold on, I know, you don't trust yourself around that lass with the big daft eyes. I'm right, aren't I? And if I am, you might like to think around whether she's worth the upset.'

'You've got that wrong. I'm in a bit of bother and I need to get away for a while – keep myself out of harm's way.'

'And what about the old lady? Have you thought around how she must be feeling about you abandoning her at the drop of your clown's hat?'

'Of course I have. She's going to be okay, I promise.'

'Don't want your promises, mate. They're not worth a rotten nut to me. Anyway, hope you can live with yourself. I know I couldn't.'

'Will you miss me?' I asked.

'That's a daft question, mate. You'll be back soon enough. Shithouse is as shithouse was and will always be. Think around that.'

He skipped off towards the play area and disappeared behind a beech tree. I took a deep breath, hoping this would be the end of all excitement for this particularly fraught Saturday. Unfortunately, however, that wasn't to be the case.

25

GARY

SATURDAY WHAT A DAY

After bidding a silent farewell to my squirrel friend, I drove
along Peckham Road and turned up Camberwell Grove to
make my way towards the A23 and my escape to Brighton. I
decided to park up outside the Grove pub and give the journey
a little more thought. I didn't want Sequence to know where
I would be hiding out, after all.

The other day he had told me that he could always find me,
and he seemed very confident in that belief. Could he be
tracking my car? Could he be somehow tracking the telephone
he had given me? The possibility couldn't be ignored; he was,
after all, working on behalf of a gang of bent coppers. Perhaps
I would be better off making the journey by train. Denmark
Hill Station was just around the corner and would take me to
Victoria where I could catch a direct train to Brighton. The
problem was, I only had about ten pounds on me and had no
idea if my debit card would work given the lack of funds in

my account. I popped into the Grove to buy a snack and test out my card. I ordered an orange juice and a bacon roll and the card payment was accepted.

The bacon roll was a good one – thick back bacon, soft bread and plenty of butter. I relaxed ever so slightly for the first time that day and opened up my laptop to check for any emails or messages. There was nothing of importance. Next I logged on to my banking app to see what my financial state of play was. To my instant shock and surprise, my current account was showing a credit balance of ten thousand pounds. The money had been deposited in cash this very morning at a branch of Barclays Bank in London Bridge. There were no details of the payee; it was simply listed as a 'cash deposit'. Obviously it had been made by Sequence to potentially incrim- inate me at a later date, and perhaps also to encourage me to provide him with my location details via the use of my debit card. It also successfully sent me a message that, in truth, Sequence was playing me like a little baby's glockenspiel.

The phone Sequence had given me rang. My stomach wallowed and my throat tightened. I knew it had to be answered, my escape hadn't even started.

'Hello, Gary. I see you've made a move. Not gone very far, have you?'

'I'm just at my local, having a pint. Is there something in particular you want?'

'No, Gary, just checking in, making sure you're being a good boy.'

'Yes, of course I am, don't worry about me.'

'That's good to know. Bon voyage, Gary.'

The call induced a brief sweat on. I needed some actual cash to fund my escape and my prayers were answered when Andy strolled into the bar, bought himself a pint and joined me at my table.

'That bacon roll looks nice. I might get one myself,' he said. 'Bacon and beer, a very underrated combination.'

I was instantly envious of the very ordinary day he was obviously having. I would have swapped shoes in an instant even if just for a couple of hours to experience life in his untroubled mind.

I explained to him that I was leaving London and going back up north in a big hurry due to urgent family business. I told him that for some reason or other my debit card had been stopped and I urgently needed some cash to pay my train fare. I didn't trust my car to make the long journey up north. Before I even asked him, he took out a large wad of notes from his back pocket and asked me how much I needed.

'Jesus, Andy,' I said. 'What are you doing carrying that amount of cash around? Are you dealing drugs on the side or something? Growing skunk in your shelter?'

'Cash is king, mate,' he replied. 'Especially when the big adjustment arrives – which, my friend, could be sooner than you think. How much do you want?'

I tapped him for fifty quid then sat and had a pint with him out of respect for his kindness. It was the first time I had sat with him when we weren't watching a football match on the big-screen TV. It felt different – very agreeable, in fact. We should have done this months before now, not on the cusp of my great escape. Who knows, we might have become proper friends.

'You're really serious about this survival shelter thing, aren't you? Do you honestly see yourself living in it one day?'

'Yes, I do, and in fact I look forward to it. There's not much in this world that I would really miss. I hate my job and I only get out of the house to watch the football down here. The rest of the time I just spend building and kitting out my shelter and researching all the dos and don'ts of bunker survival. There's a lot of good stuff on YouTube – likeminded people who know what's coming.'

'Has it got a good lock on it? Those slow zombies are really strong, you know,' I said.

'No need to take the piss. You simply don't know what you will be facing – could be AI units, could be virus-infected lads with boosted strength. I tell you, mate, it's me that will be having the last laugh.'

'Fair enough. So, like I say, have you got an intimidating lock system? You know, with levers and a keyboard, like in a bank?'

'Yep, don't you worry about that. Code 196651 – as in the World Cup and Area 51.'

'Good choice. Is it nearly finished?'

'Not far off. I've done all the sound and heat insulation. I just need to get it hooked up to mains electricity and to install a decent generator for emergency use – you've got to have electric for heat and light if you're going to cope after the big event. The shelter's made from an old metal shipping container

that I've buried under my garden and I kid you not when I say it is fucking freezing – as cold as the moon's tits.'

'Have you got yourself a mouse yet?'

'No, I'm still looking at the options, taking my time. I've seen the type I want – white with a pink nose and ears. They seem like the best laugh, but it's a big decision and I'm not going to rush it.'

'Sounds sensible. A pet is for life, not just the duration of an apocalypse.'

I asked Andy if I could borrow his mobile and left a message on Roma's office phone, telling her that I was leaving my job as of today and wouldn't be needing my flat for at least the next couple of months. I told her she was more than welcome to stay there while I was away and that I had left a spare front-door key with the neighbour, Grace. I asked her to take care of Grace if she moved in and warned her that she was a grumpy old bugger but lovely to boot. I told her if she ever needed to butter Grace up, just take Lassoo for a walk or buy her a pie. I wished her good luck with Grace's access case. I didn't mention where I was going; there was no need for her to know.

Pint finished, I said my goodbyes to Andy. He gave me a little business card with his telephone number and address written on the back and asked me to keep in touch. I said I would and in that moment I meant it. I left the pub and fetched my suitcase from the car. I put the keys in the ignition, put Sequence's phone in the glove compartment and left the doors unlocked. My hope was that the car would inevitably be stolen and, at least for a short time, put Sequence off my trail, if indeed he was tracking the car or the phone. The car was only worth a few hundred quid, so it was no great sacrifice. I walked off towards Denmark Hill Station feeling like an escaped POW with counterfeit papers and a backstory nobody would believe.

26

It's me again. I want to fill you in on something that I was told a few days before the night of the ambulances and the gurney. I'm not going to tell you who told me, because I don't think it's important. If, come the crunch, you wish I had told you, then I'm sorry for your pain. Just remember that time is a great healer, as is tramadol if you wash it down with a plate of sausages. The information I have concerns Gary's 'football friend' Andy, and I'll tell it to you as it was told to me. Please remember that I WASN'T ACTUALLY THERE TO WITNESS THESE EVENTS, so if you want verification, then I am not your man.

(I've added some notes of my own that I hope you will find helpful, but you can skip them if you want. All they do is offer a bit of insight and comment, though if that's not your sort of thing then why not go and paint an exterior wall instead.)

Apparently, Gary and Andy had been having a drink together on the day that Gary set off on his escape to Brighton. After they'd said their goodbyes, Andy set off home for a session watching YouTube. Outside the pub, he noticed Gary's car parked up and spotted that the keys were still in the ignition. Being a good football friend and a decent bloke to boot, he took the decision to drive the car back to his house and park it up in his driveway for safekeeping. He lived half a mile away in an end-of-terrace Victorian house on Herne Hill Road. He then got stuck into watching videos about doomsday bunker building and survival food storage. As always, he had changed into his comfy camouflage-pattern tracksuit to focus his mind and enrich the fantasy.

(Two things here. Firstly, regarding the moving of the car: I, person-ally, would never touch another person's property without their permission. You might be the sort that can't keep your sweaty paws off other people's stuff, but believe me: deep down it's never appreciated and can cause short- to medium-term resentment. Just ask first – 'Hey, is it okay if I handle your hairbrushes, mate?' 'Yes, that's fine, thank you for asking.' Easy.

Second thing is the camouflage tracksuit. I've told you before I don't like tracksuits. You might think it's okay to wear one in your own home, to which I would say, as Andy found out, you never know when a stranger might visit and end up being insulted by your appearance. After 9pm? Maybe, but not before. If you disagree, please feel free to write down your feelings and post them to the Chief of Police, Twin Falls, Idaho.)

He had only been home for half an hour or so when there was a knock on the door. Andy answered it and was faced with the sight of a tall, red-headed man in a Crombie overcoat and a smaller bloke wearing a black and orange puffa jacket with a hairstyle so bouffant that it made him look like an owl peering through a hedge. It was the owl that spoke first.

'Hi there, sorry to bother you, sir, I'm Detective Coulson and this is my colleague Detective Parker. We're making some enquiries about a gentleman named Gary Thorn and wondered if you might know anything about his current whereabouts?'

Andy immediately requested they present him with proof of identity and both men flashed what appeared to be genuine Metropolitan Police ID cards.

'Why do you want him for?' asked Andy. 'Has he done something wrong? I very much doubt it. He's a good boy, is Gary.'

'That's good to know,' replied Owl Man. 'We just need to speak to him. Don't concern yourself with the reason, sir. Is he staying here with you?'

'No, what makes you think that?'

'Well, his car is parked in your driveway. I think you would agree that might indicate that he is on the premises. Can we come in and look, please?'

'No, you can't, because he's not here and I don't see a warrant to search these premises, so might I politely request that you fuck off.'

(You should never tell a stranger to fuck off unless you're at least a foot taller and two stone heavier than them. It's a useful rule of thumb, but don't come running to me if some little bloke you insult turns out to be some sort of bare-fist-fighting whippet.)

Andy went to shut the door in their faces, but as he did so Tall Man stepped forward and pushed him hard in the chest, sending him flat onto his arse in the hallway. He then grabbed him around the neck, dragged him through to the living room and dumped him onto the sofa. Owl Man walked through to the back kitchen while Tall Man stood guard at the living room door.

(Told you the 'fuck off' was a bad idea.)

Andy was scared. He no longer believed them to be policemen and doubted they were really searching for a prime shithouse like Gary. Maybe they were from the government. Maybe they were here to requisition his bunker for their own purposes or, worse still, dismantle it. This was just the sort of thing he had been warned about by the online doomsday prepper community. He made the decision to cooperate but say as little as possible. He would even try to get away with saying 'no comment' to any questions they asked.

(I've been scared – very scared – on more than one occasion. It's a feeling that I don't mind that much, because things generally turn out to be okay and if they don't it won't be the fear that's caused the problem. From the sound of things, it seems the fear helped Andy focus his thoughts. That might not be the case with you, but next time you're afraid, please try to be more like Andy: look beyond the fear and concentrate on what lies ahead. Like I've told you before: fear can be a terrible thing if you choose not to trust it.)

Owl Man returned to the room. He sat next to Andy on the sofa, placed a hand on his thigh and gave it a little squeeze of encouragement.

'Let's get this over and done with,' he said. 'What's your name, by the way?'

'Can I say no comment?' Andy replied.

'Of course you can, but you will suffer the consequences if that's how you want to play this.'

Tall Man picked up a small brown onyx mantle clock off the sideboard and assessed its heft by tossing it lightly from one hand to the other.

'Is it a nice clock?' asked Owl Man of his tall colleague.

'Not my cup of tea, boss, but it's a functional piece.'

'That's good to know,' said Owl Man. 'So, I'll ask again: what's your name, lad?'

'Andrew Duff.'

'What a shit name. Really fucking dreary.' He turned to Tall Man. 'What do you think?'

'It's deeply shit. Surprisingly so, and very depressing. Almost wintry. Can't have been easy as a kid.'

Owl Man put a hand on Andy's shoulder and almost whispered into his ear: 'Is Gary here in this house, yes or no?'

'No comment.'

Owl Man released his hand from Andy's shoulder just as Tall Man took a step forward, raised the clock in the air and brought it down with a sharp strike to Andy's temple, causing his head to drop down onto the arm of the sofa. Andy moaned with pain and upset, but the attack had clearly been intended as a warning rather than a knockout blow. Owl Man pulled him upright again and then took his vape machine out of the pocket of his puffer jacket. He sucked hard on its outlet then blew the smoke directly at the small cut that had opened up on the side of Andy's head. He asked him again if Gary was in the house while Tall Man continued to toss the clock between his hands.

'No, he isn't. I haven't seen him since we were in the pub earlier today,' said Andy meekly but defiantly, staring Owl Man directly in the eye.

'Well, you won't mind if we have a quick search around, then, will you?'

'Be my guest.'

Tall Man took the cue and left the room to carry out the search.

'Why have you got his car on your drive?'

'He left it outside the pub with the keys in the ignition, so I brought it home for safekeeping.'

'How thoughtful of you. So, did Gary tell you where he was going?'

'He said he was going up north to see his family. Some sort of emergency; he didn't say what.'

'Did he give you a contact number, or any way of getting in touch with him?'

'No, we're not really friends, just acquaintances.'

'Does Gary have any other friends that you know of? Anyone who might let him stay with them for a while?'

'Not that I know of. There's a woman from his work he's friendly with called Roma, but she lives on a friend's floor so he's not going to be staying with her. He's a bit of a loner; he's never mentioned anyone else to me.'

(I often wish that I could have been in Peckham with Gary so that I could have been a good friend to him. He doesn't have many friends.

You might be one of those people that judge the success of your life by the number of friends you claim to have. For me, that's a dangerous game, spreading yourself too thin, treating friendship as a hobby. Believe me, you only need one, maybe two good friends in your life; that will give you time to nurture those friendships and make them deep and lasting, like me and Gary. If you disagree, then off you go and repeat the same old gossip and bullshit to as many pipsqueaks as you can, then try to draw them into your little obligation circle. Good luck with that. I for one would rather be a Gary.)

'Does he have a girlfriend?' asked Owl Man.

'I'm not sure. He was seeing a girl called Emily, but she moved away. I honestly don't know him that well; we just sit together and watch the football in the pub, that's it. Truth is you couldn't really call us friends. Why are you so desperate to contact him?'

At that moment, Tall Man returned from his search.

'He's not in here, boss, but there's a storage container sunk into the ground in the back garden. It's got some really fancy locks on it. We should check it out. The locks need a code and a key so better bring him through with us.'

Tall Man made his way to the back door as Owl Man picked himself up off the sofa and offered his hand to Andy to help him get up.

As he did so, Andy reached under the cushion of the sofa and pulled out a handheld stun gun, presumably purchased off the dark net, and forced it point first into Owl Man's thigh. Owl Man screamed out in pain as he grabbed onto the front of Andy's tracksuit and gripped it like a vice with both hands.

However much Andy shoved and pushed and forced his way to the front door, Owl Man just wouldn't let go. His screams continued and Andy had barely dragged himself out of the lounge when Tall Man appeared in the hallway, took a gun out of his coat pocket and pointed it directly at Andy's face. The escape attempt was over.

Andy was pushed back onto the sofa and struck around the head a number of times with the onyx clock. He handed over the key and the codes to the bunker – a moment that broke his heart. Once Tall Man had checked the bunker for any signs of Gary, he threw Andy inside the bunker and locked the doors behind him. It was dark, cold, and there was no way for Andy to contact the outside world. In many ways it was his dream come true. He had a spare set of keys inside the bunker but decided not to use them for the time being.

27

GARY

About an hour after leaving the Grove I got on a train from Victoria Station to Brighton. I sat in the third coach from the rear, because in my experience that carriage always has the fewest passengers. I love having a whole train coach to myself, and that is exactly what happened until it made its first stop at East Croydon. A new passenger got onto 'my' coach and sat down directly opposite me. I don't know why people do that. There was a whole empty coach for him to choose a seat, but he parked his arse straight across from me. I wanted to get up and move seats, but just couldn't find the strength to overcome the guilt I would experience. No idea why I would give a fuck about this stranger's feelings, but there you are.

I glanced at his face, like you do, just to check for any danger and to place the face in a broad category of 'type'. He was in his mid-forties and was staring straight at me with a big, broad '*hello there*' expression on his face. Judging by his light grey woollen suit jacket and Disney baseball cap, I concluded he was a harmless soul but might be inclined to try to strike up a conversation. I stared out of the window with the intensity of a Belgium sniper but it didn't swerve him off.

'You going to Gatwick Airport, are you? Getting off on your holidays?' he said in a deep, raspy, posh–sounding accent.

'No, just going to Brighton for the day,' I replied with the briefest of smiles in his direction, and then conducted a sharp return to my intense window stare.

There followed some moments of silence; maybe I'd discouraged him with my brief, disinterested reply.

'Bit late to be setting off for a day by the seaside, isn't it?' said Disney man.

He was right, of course. I'd messed up. I couldn't think of a satisfactory backtrack so just gave him a nod of my head and another weak smile. Who was this bloke? Why the interest in me? Fuck, what if he was something to do with Sequence? *Of course he isn't*, I told myself. *Stop getting paranoid. He's just a train guy doing his thing.* I desperately wanted to move seats, but the invisible force of good manners kept me where I was. I wished I had my phone with me so that I could pretend to be absorbed with a video clip of some nonsense such as a man being sick into a Koi Carp pond or a monkey trying its hand at bricklaying but, alas, I was phoneless. I intensified my window stare.

'That's a big old suitcase to take for a day by the seaside,' he said, nodding his head in the direction of my suitcase in the aisle next to me.

He was right again. I didn't think a smile would cut it as

a response, so I blurted the first thing that came into my head.

'It's not a suitcase as such. I'm a salesman; it's how I carry my samples.'

'Why would you take a train and not a car if you're a travelling salesman?'

'I'm not a *travelling* salesman. It's just a one-off pitch at a hotel near the station. Thought this would be the easiest way.'

'What do you sell? Anything interesting?'

'No, not interesting at all.' I replied, returning my gaze to the window. A few moments of silence followed, maybe he had lost interest in me.

'So, what is it?' asked the train detective.

'What is what?' I replied, pretending I'd forgotten the gist of the conversation while rapidly trying to come up with a plausible answer.

'What is it that you sell?'

'Putty,' I blurted. 'A new type of putty. It never cracks or taints and its drying time is five times quicker than traditional putties.'

'I like the sound of that putty,' he said, then leant forward towards me and placed a hand on my knee. 'Well done, son. Hope it all works out well for you.' Then he got up, picked up my suitcase and placed it in the luggage gap between the seats. 'Best keep them samples out of harm's way,' he said, before walking off and sitting himself down at the far end of the carriage.

We both got off at Brighton Station, but the last I saw of

him was as he walked through the ticket barriers. I held back and watched him disappear into the distance and out of sight. The whole encounter had got me worried. I bent down and inspected my suitcase, thinking that he might have placed some tracking chip or homing device onto it. I was getting very twitchy. This hiding away was not going to be easy on the mental health. I couldn't wait to be holed up in Emily's apartment just passing time until the whole situation had concluded. That thought reminded me that I hadn't actually informed Emily of my imminent arrival. As far as she knew, I was staying in Peckham this weekend to cover the duty solicitor rota at Peckham Police Station. I could have messaged her when I had Andy's phone in the pub. Never mind, I thought, hopefully it would be a nice surprise for her.

I decided against getting a taxi and having to interact with another person, so walked the mile or so down Queens Road and Kings Road to the seafront and the Hotel Avocado. There were still no guests staying there, but the front door was open. Mark, Emily's right-hand man, was busy fitting some new shelving behind reception.

'Hi, Mark. Are you working Saturdays now?' I asked.

'Yep,' he replied.

I made my way up the stairs to Emily's apartment. It would be such a relief to see her and to have her support. Everything had turned on its head in the last couple of days and I really needed a loved one's advice.

I walked into the apartment and there she was, sat on the sofa in her leggings and a crop top. Her face instantly dropped when she saw me. It was as if she had been suddenly exposed to the ghost of a person who had murdered her in a previous life.

My stomach wallowed and a wave of dread rippled through me. Something was wrong. Something had changed. I shouldn't have come.

28

GRACE

The day Gary abandoned me was a terrible day. It had come completely out of the blue, which gave me no chance to mentally prepare for it. I'd given him a slice of Battenburg to send him on his way then sat down on my sofa and wept for what seemed like a couple of hours. He was in trouble again with those bent policemen, so I understood the need for a swift exit, but, blimey, it was a shock when it happened. I didn't think he would ever be coming back, and let's face it he would be impossible to replace.

I felt physically lonely and, for the first time since meeting Gary, hopeless and unwanted. This feeling was an old familiar foe and I knew I didn't have the resolve to banish it without the help of a friend. Trouble was, I didn't have any; my own fault, I know, but the truth nevertheless.

I went through to my bedroom, followed closely by Lassoo. He always sensed when I was upset and he pawed at my knees as if trying to scrape away the sadness.

'Gary's left us, Lassoo. It's just me and you again,' I whispered.

Just saying those words brought on the tears again. Lassoo jumped onto the bed and sat by my side. 'We're both getting old, sunshine, old and useless, good for no one except each other.' Lassoo gave me his *I need a walk, right now, this minute* face and I was happy to oblige. I needed to get out of the flat myself, so I put on a coat and scarf and off we went. As I stood watching Lassoo mess about in the play area where the see-saw used to be, I saw Robert, the bloke whose sweaty dog had died, approaching. I turned my back in the hope that he wouldn't see me, but to no avail.

'Is that dog of yours looking for its brain?' He added a laugh so that I would know he was having a joke.

'Something like that,' I replied.

'You still up for a visit to that café on the high street? I'm not busy now if you're inclined to give it a go?'

'No, you've caught me on a bad day, to be honest. Some other time though, for sure.'

I turned away and beckoned Lassoo, half hoping this would discourage Robert from talking any further.

'Is something the matter? he asked. 'You look a bit upset with yourself. Is there anything I can do to help?'

'No, I'm fine, just had some bad news. I'll soon be over it. Life's a long song and I'm still singing,' I replied, not believing a word of it.

I began to walk away towards Lassoo, who was refusing to respond to my calls. Robert stepped alongside me.

'I find having a chat is the best way to get through these things. Come on, tell me what's happened. If it's too personal then of course I understand, but if not then, believe me, unloading on a stranger is the best possible medicine. I'm a gift horse looking you straight in the face – no skin in the game, as it were.'

I knew he was right and, to be blunt, if I didn't talk to him, then who was I going to talk to? Lassoo was a good listener but his feedback was a bit samey. There was no harm having a chinwag. I stopped in my tracks and faced him.

'I lost a good friend today – my only friend really. I suppose I'm a bit in shock. Feels like my life has been turned upside down.'

I could feel the tears welling up inside me again, so I dipped my head to avoid his gaze.

'I'm really sorry to hear that. I hope they passed peacefully on their way.'

'Oh, nobody has died, sorry if I gave that impression. I'm being a bit overdramatic really. It's just one of my neighbours. He's moved away and, like I say, he was my best – if not my only – friend around here.'

'So you can still keep in touch, then – you know, by phone, on the internet. You can do those live chats now on your computer. Has he moved far away?'

'No, not so far, but I don't drive and to be honest he's starting a new life with his girlfriend. I'll be just a distant memory soon enough. I'm happy for him really, just have to get over it and stop feeling sorry for myself.'

'I can't believe you haven't got any other friends, a lovely funny lady like you.'

'It's the truth. It's my own fault. I don't let people into my life very easily. Gary says I should trust people a bit more but I'm not sure about that. All the evidence I have is that people are best kept at a distance, and it's hard to change your outlook at my age. Gary was the exception. Got a kind heart. It's written all over his face.'

'I know where you're coming from. I lost my wife a couple of years ago. We were a tight unit, relied on each other for everything. When she went, I realized the world had moved on while we had been living in our own little bubble. I was pretty much on my own, had to start from scratch and try and build something new. It will never be the same, but I'm making progress as the years pass; a little chat here, a night out every now and then. I've just joined the darts team down the pub and there're a couple of blokes that I've got friendly with. Early days, but it's a chink of light. It's easy to hide behind closed doors, but I made a terrible prisoner. Don't let that happen to you.'

'I think I would make a very good prisoner. I wouldn't be no trouble to anyone and hopefully no one would trouble me. I don't play darts, by the way.'

'I could teach you,' he said with a childish smile on his face. 'So, tell me this,' he continued. 'If you're so unappealing like you say, then why did this Gary want to spend his time with you?'

'You'd have to ask him. He's a lot younger than me and when he moved into the flats he was fresh to London and all alone in the big city. I sometimes think he saw me as a substitute mum or just someone to keep him company until he found his feet. Looks like I was right in that respect.'

'I doubt it. It sounds as if you were very close. Why can't you accept that he just enjoyed your company and wanted to spend time with you? I think you're very wrong to think that way. You need to snap out of that thinking before it drags you down.'

'Give me a chance – he's only just left. I'm in a right old state and as far as I can tell you haven't got a magic wand that's going to set me straight. Don't mean to be rude, but I've heard all these words before and I'm a bit too long in the tooth to take them on board. Are you going to tell me to "pull myself together" now?'

'Pull yourself together,' he said. 'And while you're at it wipe that bubble from the end of your nose – you look like you've got a frog living up there.'

I forced a little smile onto my face. He obviously meant well and seemed a decent type. His face showed no obvious signs of unkindness, and I liked the way his bald head glistened a bit in the sunlight. Lassoo arrived at my feet and directed a little bark towards my new friend. I used the moment to peel off towards the flats.

'Thanks for the chat. I'd better get back inside.'

'No problem, I'm happy to chat anytime.'

He handed me a blank card with a telephone number scribbled on it.

'Give me a ring if you ever feel the need. And what about that trip to the café – are we still on?'

'Yeah, of course, maybe when I'm feeling more myself, I'll give you a ring.'

I took a few steps towards the flats and he quickly caught me up again.

'I've got wheels, you know,' he said. 'If you ever want a lift to visit your friend, all you have to do is ask.'

And that was that. I doubted very much that I would get in touch with him, but it was an option of sorts if I ever needed it. I still felt shit, but was glad of the chat. My tears felt a little bit further down my gullet than they had been when I left the flat.

A couple of days later, around midday, I was still in bed with Lassoo beside me resting his head on my thigh. I'd just finished a bowl of tomato soup and had spilt a big gloop down the front of my pyjama top. I dragged myself into the bathroom and worked at the stain with a lump of damp toilet paper. It was just making it worse. I was caught sharp by my reflection in the mirror above the sink. I looked old – really old. My hair was beginning to look ragged and was in need of a cut and some love and attention.

I stretched the skin of my forehead with both hands to try to make the frown lines disappear, but three or four of them remained stubbornly obvious. I had been a smoker for maybe forty years, only packing it in when my granddaughter Lizzie was born. Her mother had made it perfectly clear that Lizzie would not be visiting me at home while I was still puffing on the smokes. Those years had left a parade of creases across my top lip that were highlighted rather than concealed by the wispy white hair growing around them. The same downy hairs were beginning to taint my cheeks and my neck. They looked worse in the harsh light of the bathroom, but this would be the image of my face I would be stuck with for the rest of the day.

My eyes had always been my best feature – loads of blokes had told me that in the past – grey-green with lovely long lashes. Now the brightness was gone and the sparkle replaced with a watery film of dishwater. I didn't even dare look at my neck; the sight of the folds and creases might have pushed me over the edge – not that I would have needed much of a shove.

I gave up on the pyjama stain and put on my blue-and-white-striped towelling dressing gown. I had a sudden urge for a glass of vodka and tonic and followed Lassoo out of the bedroom to fetch the bottle from the fridge. Then I heard a knock on my front door.

Who on earth could that be when I'm about to grab a bit of me time? I thought. It crossed my mind that it might be that Robert bloke sniffing around, so I stood stock still, hoping whoever it was would go away. Then there was another knock, this time with a bit more clout applied. I kept still. Lassoo ran to the door and started to bark.

'Shut up, you daft bastard,' I whispered angrily through gritted teeth. I didn't think whoever was outside would have heard it, but covered my mouth with my hand to stop me from a repeat.

'I can hear you, Grace. It's Roma, Gary's friend from the solicitors. Can we have a chat?'

I had given the game away but nevertheless kept stock still

and silent. I didn't want to see anyone or have anyone see me
in the state I was in.

'Grace, I really need to speak to you. I've got some good
news. It's about your granddaughter Lizzie.'

The mention of good news and Lizzie in the same sentence
propelled me, without a second's hesitation, to the door.

'What is it? What's happened?' I asked without even consid-
ering a greeting or a smile.

She hesitated before answering and I noticed her eyes glance
down to the vodka bottle in my hand. In return I took a glance
down to her side and noticed that she was lugging a huge
black suitcase.

'Sorry, I was in the middle of tidying up,' I said, opening my
eyes up wide to give the impression I was telling the truth.

'Can I come in, Grace? Like I say, I've got some really good
news.'

I ushered her in and sat her on the chair by my desk while
I parked myself on the sofa.

'Do you mind if I eat my sandwich?' she asked. 'I've come
in my lunch hour so it's my only chance.'

'No, you carry on, love.'

'Well, the good news is, and I'm sorry that this is such short
notice—'

'What sort of sandwich is it?' I asked. I couldn't help myself:
when it came to an unopened sandwich, I need to know what
lurks between the bread or I can't concentrate on anything
else. I had to know what was inside, right that moment; nothing
else mattered. I think Lassoo felt the same because he was sat

at her feet with his head to one side, giving his '*She never feeds me, you know, I'm wasting away*' look directly up at her face.

'Bacon, lettuce and tomato,' she replied.

'Decent. I personally could do without the greenery but that is a very strong choice. Suggests you might be a solid character. You can tell a lot about a person by their sandwich choice. If you ever meet a bloke who chooses corned beef and onion, start running immediately, don't look back and if need be change your identity. I should know – my ex-husband was a corned beefer and you'd never meet a bigger arsehole in your life. Sorry, you didn't need to know any of that. Come on, the news about Lizzie, let's have it.'

'Well, keeping it simple, do you remember that the court ordered—'

'Would you like a cuppa with your sandwich?'

'Yes, that would be great.'

'How do you take it?'

'Milk and two sugars, the stronger the better.'

'Thatta girl! Pissy tea, pissy pants, that's what I always say, and don't get me on to that herbal stuff – you might as well drink the hot water from your radiators; it would probably have more taste and would be a lot cheaper.'

'No need to do it now, Grace, it can wait until I've finished the sandwich.'

'I insist. You carry on. I can hear you from the kitchen.'

As I waited for the kettle to boil, I listened to her explain that a social worker called Hannah Lewis had been appointed to arrange a supervised visit between myself and Lizzie to 'assess the nature and extent of the relationship'. It was to take place at a family centre in Lewes the following week. It sounded like progress; it sounded positive. I closed my eyes and thanked the Lord. I think bad news about Lizzie would have finished me off.

I gave Roma her tea and listened as she explained the ins and outs of the meeting. When I had no more questions to ask, she took a good long gulp from her tea and handed Lassoo a piece of bacon she had saved for him. Bacon wasn't something I ever gave him and the taste of it hit him like a mallet. He started to furiously lick his lips at such speed he was in danger of rubbing out his entire face.

Roma reached for her bag and I wondered if she had more bacon to offer Lassoo. He obviously thought the same, as his licking suddenly stopped and he went full on cross-eyed for a moment. It wasn't another bacon sandwich, it was a shortcrust pie from Matthews Bakers on the high street – a quality pie with very few weak points. Lassoo couldn't hide his disappointment, dropping his head to stare at the floor, hoping he might spot a stray molecule of bacon rind.

'I got you a steak and kidney pie, Grace. Gary said you were a sucker for a pie.'

'That's very kind of you; I shall have it for my tea with some sprouts. What's in your suitcase? Not more food, is it?'

'No, it's all my clothes and bits and pieces. I got a message from Gary saying he wouldn't be home for a few months and that I was more than welcome to stay in his flat until he got back. He said I should pick the key up from you so I thought

I'd get that done in my lunch hour and move myself in. Shit, he did mention it to you, didn't he?'

'Yeah, he said something about it. So, he reckons he's coming back, does he?'

'That's what he said. Has he been in touch with you? Is he getting on okay?' she asked.

'No, I haven't heard a word from him. I expect he's got other things on his mind. Did he tell you why he packed in his job and didn't just ask for some time off?'

'Rumour in the office is that he had a big argument with the boss and told him where he could stick his job.'

'Doesn't sound like Gary. I always think of him as being a shithouse – you know, a yes man. Do you think he's a shithouse?'

'I wouldn't like to say. He's always stuck up for me at work and looked after me if I was struggling.'

'That's because he fancies you.'

'I doubt that very much. He's got a girlfriend, hasn't he, and seems very happy with how it's going. Have you ever met her?'

'Yeah, Emily, she lived with him next door for six months or so after her operation. Lovely girl, absolute diamond, far too good for him.'

'You don't mean that.'

'I bloody well do, and if you met her you'd feel exactly the same. Hold on and I'll get you the key.'

'Did Gary tell you where he was going to be staying?'

'Up north somewhere to deal with some family business. I expect he'll get in touch with you if he wants you to know. Got to respect a man's privacy.'

'I've tried phoning him a few times,' she said, 'but his phone seems to be switched off. I don't think he would mind you telling me. I know he wants me to keep him updated about your case.'

'I'm sure you're right, but I want to be good to my word. I hope you don't think I'm being rude – just loyal, that's all. I like to be loyal to my friends.'

I felt a bit guilty about blocking her, but a promise is a promise.

'Of course,' she replied, looking slightly disappointed in me. 'Hey, and I hope you and me can become friends. Gary always spoke of you as a "livewire" and that sounds right up my street.'

'I hope so too. Listen, why don't you come over after work and we can share this pie for our tea. It's far too big for one person. Be nice to have a chat when you haven't got your lawyer's hat on.'

'I'd love to,' she replied. 'But I don't want any sprouts. Can't stand them.'

'Me neither,' I replied. 'I just blurted that out so you'd think I was the healthy type. I'll be having it with baked beans and mash. Seven o'clock suits me.'

'Perfect, see you later.'

Lassoo showed her to the door and off she went, my new neighbour. I wasn't quite sure what to make of her. She came over very naive and innocent but there was a steely resolve about her. Why would she have any interest in me? Maybe she didn't. Maybe once she was safely installed in the flat she would shun me, just like the rest of them on this poxy estate.

Alternatively, perhaps I should stop being so hesitant and suspicious of people. It took me months to say hello to Gary when he first moved in and even then I was rude to him. I can't believe he persevered with me, but he did, and I'm very grateful for that. She was right: I did used to be a bit of a lively one, and quite popular too. On the day I left work at the Department of Education, over fifty people came to my leaving do. We went to a karaoke bar just off Tottenham Court Road. I sang 'Hot Legs', the Rod Stewart song, and took my skirt off while singing to emphasize the strength of Rod's lyrics.

I could trace my journey from lively to lonely back to the accident on the see-saw when Lizzie got badly hurt. It didn't take a genius to work that one out. The pain of losing contact with Lizzie and my daughter had changed me, made me trust people less, overthink things too much and shut people out before I even gave them a chance. I needed to stop that nonsense. I was going to make an effort with Roma, and to hell with it if it turned around and bit me on the arse.

29

EMILY

It was around six weeks before the hotel was due to open its doors that things started to go wrong. Nothing catastrophic, but a definite decline in the smooth progress I had being enjoying since taking over the hotel. It was just little things at first – contractors not showing up, the new IT system failing (on what sometimes seemed an hourly basis), beds and bedding turning up in the wrong size, old plumbing having to be replaced in the en suites, fire certificates being refused, the alcohol licence running out . . . blah blah blah. All stuff that I half expected and that I won't bore you with any further.

The first slightly unexpected hiccup came about because of the big fibreglass avocado I purchased to hang from the old flagpole at the front of the hotel. I applied for planning permission and a couple of weeks later a planning officer called Ralph Bollocks or similar arrived to 'evaluate' the site and assess the 'impact' of the proposal. He was a short, skinny man with a large Adam's apple and massive hands and feet. He was wearing a brown corduroy jacket and black slacks. His hair was light brown, greasy and side-parted and his voice sharp and nasally. He looked the type that might be vulnerable to female charms so I adopted a gushing but naive approach – think Marilyn Monroe on a tour of NASA headquarters.

The avocado had already been delivered and was resting upright on the basement patio at the front of the hotel. Mark and I had removed the plastic sheet that was protecting it in anticipation of the visit. Ralph himself was most impressed when he first clocked his eyes on the thing and even asked me to take a photo of him next to it, 'for the wife'.

'It's a very unusual application,' he said. 'I don't think there would be a problem if it was a temporary structure, but I understand you want it to be displayed permanently. Am I right?'

'You are, Ralph. The Avocado is the name of the hotel, so it's basically the hotel sign – you know, the means by which people will know that this building is the Hotel Avocado. It's something a bit different and I reckon it's a lot prettier than just having big letters plastered on the front of the building.'

'It's a cute idea.'

'Thank you, Ralph.'

'But, like I say, very unusual. I don't think I've ever dealt with an application involving a large vegetable. My wife is going to think the world has gone nuts.'

'It's a fruit, a large fruit. Does that make it more acceptable to the powers that be?'

'I'm pretty sure it's a vegetable. Hold on, let me check that. I suppose it could have a bearing somewhere down the line.'

Ralph got out his phone to investigate. It had a photograph of a lady set as its background. She had a large, round face, big brassy blonde hair and was wearing a very low-cut dress. It looked as if she might be severely cross-eyed but Ralph's middle finger was covering the left eye so it was impossible to make the required comparison. Ralph's tongue was flicking around the side opening of his mouth as he stared at the phone screen.

'Well, blow me,' he said. 'Never in a million years would I have thought the avocado was a fruit. I've got to message the wife. She really is going to think the world's going mad when I tell her.'

'Is that a picture of your wife on your background?'

'No,' he replied without looking up from his phone.

He took some photos of the place and then got into his car to fill in a form on his laptop. I waited outside the car, giving him the occasional smile whenever he glanced over to me. Eventually he finished and got out of the car.

'Well, Miss Baker, this is going to be an interesting one.'

My heart sank. I didn't want it to be interesting; I wanted it to be as dull and ordinary as brown slippers.

'As I'm sure you are aware, your property is in a Conservation Area, and special rules apply. You can find further information about Conservation Areas on our website. Given the sensitive nature of the location and the size of the proposed structure, I am legally bound to refer the matter to the Planning Committee.'

'It's just a sign,' I said. 'I'm not asking to build a car park or open a homeless hostel. Surely you can just sign it off? I mean, come on, it's going to look great.'

'Well, it's certainly going to look unusual, and to my mind that's a good indication that people might want to object. It doesn't actually matter what I think. Like I say, I'm legally obliged to refer it to committee level.'

'So what do I do now?'

'You will receive a letter containing full details of the procedure and explaining your rights and obligations. If anything is unclear, you can always contact me or of course consult your legal advisers. When were you hoping to open the hotel?'

'In six weeks' time.'

'You're cutting it very tight,' he replied.

I didn't respond and a little hole developed in the conversation. He turned away to get into his car and then turned back again.

'I might come and stay here when it opens – you know, for a naughty weekend.'

'It's not going to be that sort of place, thank you.'

'Oh, they all turn out that way in the end. This is Brighton, not the Cotswolds. Cheerio.'

I had a meeting with my builder immediately afterwards. He had nearly completed the refurbishment of the half basement into a coffee bar with outdoor seating accessed down some steps off the promenade. I had to choose the paving stones. I chose some large grey porcelain slabs from his grubby, dirty-fingered catalogue. I explained to him what had happened with the planning officer.

'You've got to work the system, love. It's not what you're asking for, it's who you know. The system is well bent – if you don't play their game you'll get turned over like a doughnut in a deep fryer. This neck of the woods is legendary for it. It's all bungs and sweeteners — been that way for years. Grease the right palms and you'll slip through the pipework nice and easy.'

'Really? I thought that sort of thing went out in the seventies and eighties.'

'Nah, you need to get Councillor Jordan on your side, chairman of the Planning Committee. He can swing anything in your favour if he thinks there's something in it for him. Up to you, but without him on board I don't fancy your chances of getting permission.'

'And how the fuck do I go about getting this Jordan bloke on my side?'

'I don't know, buy him a meal, butter him up, tell him his mates can have rooms here on the cheap? Best of all, give him a big wad of cash — it will be cheaper than fighting the case and getting lawyers involved.'

This all really threw me. I was hoping the big fat hanging avocado would gift me all the furore I needed to launch the hotel. I knew it would divide opinion and in doing so stir up publicity and hype. Pete reckoned it might even go viral on social media and become a local attraction in itself. In short, I'd hung a lot of my PR hopes in the hanging fruit basket. I had a chat with Gary about the situation, and he reckoned I should just go through the process and see what happened. Worst comes to worst, I could put it in the reception as a striking centrepiece. I told him that was a shit idea, mainly, but not only, because it wouldn't actually fit through the front doors. Pete reckoned I should just put the thing up and reap all the publicity it would attract if the council demanded I take it down. I liked his take; that would be my fallback solution. In the meantime, I became hell bent on getting this Councillor Jordan on my side. I was vaguely aware of him as a local character and had some distant memory of him being a friend or acquaintance of my father. I looked him up on the internet and concluded that he had the look and feel of a bloke I might be able to persuade to my way of thinking without costing myself a fortune. I didn't tell Gary about my plans; he would have nipped them in the bud and told me to behave myself.

30

GRACE

Roma arrived at my flat at 7pm sharp as I had suggested and brought two bottles of IPA with her. I hoped they were both for me but I was wrong. Gary had briefed her well, but not quite well enough. One bottle is a hello, two bottles is a conversation. We sat at the table by the window overlooking the trees and the high street beyond. She was very down to earth and very proud of her Yorkshire roots: '*Most beautiful county in t' UK*', '*Yorkshire tea towels, most absorbent you can get*', '*Yorkshire hospitality, most generous in t' world*'. I'm exaggerating, but you probably know what I mean. You could tell she didn't think much of London; she hadn't even bothered to have a trip down to Blackheath or Greenwich, and worst of all, she had yet to set foot in a pie and mash shop.

'Why did you move down here if you like it so much up north?' I asked her.

'For me mum. She's got it in her head that London is where the opportunities are, that that's where your fortune is to be made. I've half an inkling that she thinks I might meet a rich banker or a TV presenter while I'm down here. She has this idea that the streets of London are paved with wealthy single blokes looking for love. Her dream would be for me to nab one and bring him back up north where she could parade him around town to piss off her friends and neighbours.'

'Oh, so it's her dream, not yours. Have you not got a mind of your own?'

'Well, it's only for a year, and hey, I wouldn't have met you if she hadn't sent me down here. This, by the way, is a very nice pie, and being from Yorkshire I know about good pies.'

Pie demolished, I asked her if she fancied tinned peaches and evaporated milk for pudding.

'Could I just have the juice from the can with a bit of the evaporated milk mixed in and served in a glass so I can have it as a pudding drink?'

'Is that a Yorkshire thing? It sounds bloody harrowing.'

'Have you ever tried it?'

'No, I haven't, I'm not a scavenger.'

'Well, don't knock it until you have.'

I prepared her pudding liquid for her and took a little sip for myself before taking it through to her. It was really tasty. I poured half of it out into another glass for myself.

'I did one for myself. Like you say, don't spout out an opinion unless you've been there and done it.'

We both took a mouthful at the same time.

'Hmm, not too bad,' I said. 'Doubt I'll have it again though.'

I made a mental note to buy some more tinned peaches and

evaporated milk on my next shop and then asked Roma if she fancied watching a bit of TV before she left.

'I'd rather have a chat about next week's meeting with Lizzie and the social worker, to be honest, and this time it would be great if you didn't disappear off into the kitchen when I'm talking.'

'Okay, Miss, but then can we watch a bit of *New Zealand Border Patrol*? It's such a good show, I bet you'd love it. Be great not to have to watch it on my own.'

'Yes, we can do that.'

'So, what do you want to ask me, or is it best if I just keep my trap shut?'

'Well, I'll start off and you can chip in as and when you fancy it or when I tell you to.'

'Fire away, my darling.'

'The social worker is going to want to ask you exactly what happened that evening.'

'She already knows.'

'It won't help you if you take that attitude when you speak to her.'

'Am I meant to treat her like she's my boss, lick her arse and pretend I'm ever so grateful for her time and expertise? It's not like she's the judge in the case, is it?'

'Well, I'm afraid in these cases she more or less is. You need her to like you, or at least feel a bit of sympathy and warmth towards you.'

'That's Gary's thing. It's never really been my forte.'

'Do you want to see Lizzie again?'

'Yes, of course I do.'

'Then drop the grumpy old bastard routine and put on the charm. I know it's buried deep inside you just waiting to be tapped.'

'It's buried very deep.'

'Then use a very big spade or the meeting is not going to go as you might hope.'

She took me through the practical details of the appointment. I would arrive at 1:30pm, an hour before Lizzie was due to attend with her mother. I would be interviewed by the social worker, Hannah Lewis, before seeing Lizzie, so she could satisfy herself that a face-to-face meeting was still appropriate.

'Checking that I'm not a nutcase?' I said.

'No, I've already told her you're nuts so that she doesn't get taken by surprise,' said Roma.

'You think of everything,' I replied with a regal smile.

Roma would not be allowed in with me at the interview, but would be permitted to observe the visit with Lizzie if it went ahead. I would have to make my own way down to Lewes, and Roma suggested I indulge in a taxi. I remembered the card in my handbag that Robert had given me. Perhaps I would be giving him a ring after all.

Once she had finished her little lecture, we both supped on our beers for a few moments.

'Grace,' she said. 'There's something I wanted to ask you, unrelated to your case.'

'Let me guess, you want to know why I'm not on HRT because it would make me a more balanced and pleasant person.'

'Grace, I couldn't care less whether you're on HRT or not. That's absolutely none of my business. Where did that idea come from?'

'Yeah, sorry, that was a strange thing to accuse you of. It's just that there's a lot of chat about HRT on the television and on the internet at the moment so I suppose it's a question I've been asking of myself recently.'

'Well, why not go and see a doctor about it?'

'Because I can't be bothered. Now, what was it you were wanting to ask me?'

'Last week I spent a night at Gary's flat, and I think you know that. I heard your door shut just after I walked by. I want you to know that nothing happened between Gary and me. He only let me stay because a bloke from the pub was bothering me and Gary didn't want him following me home.'

I took on a calming attitude to stop her from getting into a fidget.

'Yes, I know all this, Roma. Gary explained it to me. It's not an issue – no need to mention it again. He didn't try it on with you, did he?'

'No, he went to bed the moment we got into the flat.'

'Yeah, that sounds like Gary.'

We both laughed but I don't think either of us knew why.

I turned the TV on and Roma sat beside me on the sofa. The channel was showing a ghost-hunting show and a Geordie bloke was in the cellar of some old pub in Nottinghamshire, trying to make contact with something from the past.

'Is thu unyone in here that means uny harm to wah? Uny spooks,

spirits, ghosts, plasmas, orbs or owt like that? If so giv us a sign and I'll gan oot of here pronto, no hard feelings or nowt.'

We laughed again. I liked this Roma lady.

31

EMILY

James Jordan was fifty years old and the elected local councillor for the Central Hove Ward. He had held the seat for the last eleven years running as an independent candidate. He was a short, skinny man with thinning grey hair that he wore in a weak side parting. His face was small and bird-like with dark brown eyes and a sharp, abrupt nose. In nearly every photograph I could find of him he was dressed scruffily in a tired grey suit jacket with slightly lighter grey trousers. The shirts he wore had a polyester easy-iron look to them and the collar was always buttoned, despite the absence of a tie. There was nothing in the articles I read about him to suggest that he had any form of employment outside of his work as a councillor. He had resigned from his job as a planning officer a year or so before he first stood for election to the council. I couldn't find any controversy surrounding him in the local news and nor could I find any mention of a family life. I assumed him to be single. He looked lonely. Maybe he had dedicated his life to public service at the expense of the personal, though I doubted this to be the case, largely due to what my contractor had told me about him being susceptible to sweeteners, bribes and favours. We would have to see.

As a resident of the Central Hove Ward, it would have been easy for me to make an appointment to meet him in person at one of his twice-monthly surgeries held at Hove Town Hall. I didn't want to approach him that way, however; I wanted to meet him in a more social environment so that I could see the real person behind the grift. A few enquiries revealed that he could be found most weekday lunchtimes dining and drinking in The Albany, a private members' club on Fourth Avenue in Hove, only half a mile or so from the Avocado. A few days after the planning officer had visited, I booked a table for one for lunch in the downstairs non-members' dining room. It was a sunny Tuesday as I recall, and I was dressed up smartly in my grey trouser suit, white blouse and black Doc Martens.

I arrived at midday and stepped out of the light into the sombre dark mahogany panelled reception. The walls were adorned with framed oil paintings of what I presumed were the founder members or alumni of the club. Needless to say, they were all male, with stern expressions and eyes that seemed to follow my every step. A man wearing a white shirt, black tie and grey waistcoat ushered me from the reception into the dining room. He had massive ears, a small head and a gaunt, pock-marked face. I could sense that he didn't really approve of my presence in the building. The Albany had been a male-only institution in the past and I sensed his attitude was part of an unwritten policy to discourage the presence of women.

I sat down at the long wood and brass bar counter that ran along one side of the dining room. The red leather-topped barstool was tall and awkward to clamber onto. There was no footrest, so my legs were left to dangle self-consciously a foot or so above the floor. Big Ears tossed a menu onto the counter in front of me and asked if I wanted anything to drink.

'Ten pints of beer, please,' I replied, thinking that such a ridiculous order for a 'lady' might amuse him and soften his attitude. It didn't.

'We don't serve beer at our lunchtime service.'

'I was only joking. Do you sell wine by the pint?'

'No, we serve wine by the glass only, large or small measure. The small measure is 125 millilitres and the large measure is 250.'

'Okay, I'll have a Virgin Mary, then, please.'

'Do you mean a Bloody Mary, madam?'

'No, a Virgin Mary. It's the same as a Bloody Mary but without the vodka.'

He stared sternly at me as if I was an unwelcome advert for panty pads in the middle of a YouTube cat antics compilation and then passed me the cocktail menu.

'If it is not on the cocktail menu, then we do not serve it. Club rules. The Albany is a private members' club. Maybe you were not aware of that. We have these rules so that standards are maintained for our members.'

'How thrilling for you all. Maybe I should become a member and work to get the rules changed.'

'For that to happen you would need to be proposed by an existing member.'

'I don't know any existing members.'

'Ah, that is a shame, but at least it means standards will be maintained for a little while longer. I'm joking, of course. Will madam be ordering a drink or not?'

'I'll just have a cranberry juice if that's not too upsetting for your members.'

'Excellent choice, madam. I can show you to your table as soon as you are ready.'

'Can I have the table in the alcove by the window, please?'

'I'll see what I can do, madam.'

I had wanted the window table so that I could keep a lookout for Councillor Jordan arriving. As Big Ears handed me my cranberry juice (mainly ice), he rushed out from behind the bar to greet an elderly man who had just entered the dining room. He showed him straight to the window alcove seat, took his drinks order, then walked back past me with a huge grin on his face. I needn't have worried about losing out on the window seat, however, as a few minutes later I heard Big Ears give a loud 'Good afternoon, Mr Jordan' from his perch next to the dining room door. I didn't hear any response from Jordan and assumed that to be the standard practice of the members in a place such as this.

Big Ears eventually seated me at a table behind a column at the far end of the room next to the fire exit. I ordered a starter of mushroom soup and fish and chips for my main. As soon as I had finished my soup, I walked out into the reception and headed upstairs to the private members' dining room. I chose a walking style that suggested not only did I actually own the building, but also held riparian rights over the whole neighbourhood. I entered the dining room and strode confidently over to the table by the grand fireplace where Jordan was sat on his own eating a bowl of mushroom soup. He was wearing a pinky grey polyester shirt with the cuffs folded halfway up his forearm, just as my father used to do. He didn't notice me until I was stood right beside him offering up my hand for it to be shaken. His pointy nose had a little lump at the end and his lips were surprisingly plump and fresh. He was clean shaven apart from a little copse of stubble around his protruding Adam's apple and I noticed a tattoo on his forearm that at first glance appeared to be a skull sinking into a pond of baked beans.

'Hello, Councillor Jordan. I'm Emily Baker, the new owner of the old Honeymoon Hotel on Kingsway. Lovely to meet you.'

'The fuck it is. Can't you see I'm in the middle of my lunch? Fuck off,' he said, fixing his stare directly into my eyes, as if daring me not to follow his instruction.

This really took me by surprise. I had expected a slightly meek, polite and shy man; a man who manipulates by the absence of any obvious malice or threat. Instead, I appeared to have stepped into the lair of a honey badger who had just received his latest gas bill.

'Don't be like that, Councillor,' I said, struggling to hide the fact that his intimidation had thrown me off course. 'I think you knew my father, Keith Baker. He ran the hotel until he passed away last year. He always spoke very highly of you.'

'Liar. Nobody I have ever had dealings with speaks highly of me. That is something that simply never happens. Do I have to get a member of staff to throw you out? Is that what you want? Fuck's sake.'

I always found older blokes who swore a lot quite amusing. I would immediately imagine them as little boys chancing their first swear words and being delighted when it was greeted with laughter by their fathers or having little sweary tantrums as teenagers when they were asked to tidy their bedroom. This thought helped me to keep my composure.

'Please don't do that. I just wanted to say a quick hello, ask you a simple question and then I will be on my way like a good little girl.'

'Did you say Keith Baker?'

'Yes, I did. I'm his daughter, Emily.'

'And he's popped his clogs, has he?'

'Yes, and I've taken over the hotel.'

'I'm sorry to hear that. My condolences.'

'We weren't that close, to be honest.'

'No, I meant with regard to taking over the hotel. You poor fucker.'

'It's the hotel that I wanted to talk to you about.'

At that moment Big Ears appeared at my side and gently grabbed me by the elbow.

'I'm afraid you are not allowed in the private members' area, madam,' said Ears. 'I'm sorry, Mr Jordan, this lady has been making a nuisance of herself since she arrived.'

I tugged my arm away from him. 'I'm just having a chat

with Mr Jordan, who happens to be an old family friend. Please don't grab at me like that.'

I looked pleadingly into Jordan's eyes, hoping that he might pity me and grant me a stay of execution. I noticed an insipid smile spread across his face, followed by a little greedy glint in his eye. He realized I was desperate; he realized that there might be something he could gain from continuing our conversation.

'It's okay, Kevin, this place doesn't need any more women trouble. Leave this to me.'

'But, Mr Jordan, this lady is eating downstairs in the *non-members' room*. For Christ's sake, I have just put her fish and chips on her table.'

'Well, bring them up here, why don't you? Ms Baker will be joining me. Take a seat, Emily.'

At that, Big Ears skulked off with a slight shaking of his head. As he reached the dining room door, he turned his head to take one last look at the scene of his defeat. A beam of sunlight caught him from behind, making his ears glow like little beacons of anger. If he could have got me alone at that moment, I think he might well have ripped my ears off with his bare teeth.

'So, what's this about you making a nuisance of yourself?' asked Jordan, sucking at some mushroom residue on his teeth.

'I ordered ten pints of beer.'

'For yourself?'

'Yes, I was very thirsty.'

'I get thirsty from time to time. Very thirsty. But not for drink, if you know what I mean.'

'No, I don't. I was just being light-hearted, trying to break the ice with Big Ears.'

He smiled at the reference, placed his spoon into the soup bowl and leant back in his chair.

'You've made me very curious, sweetheart – thirsty, even, as you might say. So, what is it that you want from me?'

32

GRACE

The day of my visit with Lizzie arrived. I'll be honest, ever since Roma gave me the news that I might get to see her, I had been a nervous wreck. What was I going to wear? How was I going to do my hair? These two questions dominated my thoughts. Thinking about anything else that might occur on the day was just too much for my brain and my nerves to handle.

My first choice was the old grey tweed jacket and skirt that I wore most days at the Department for Education. I reckoned it might make me look respectable, dependable and serious – all the things that the social worker would be looking for. I could wear it with a pale pink button-down blouse and the amethyst and gold brooch I had been gifted as a leaving present from the department. If I paired it with socks and a pair of brown brogues, it would give me that 'granny' look that often warms a sentimental person's heart.

The previous weekend, Roma had kindly helped me dye my hair to take out most of the grey. It made me look slightly less haggard. I would wear it in a bun to complete the granny look. I put the outfit on and stood in front of the full-length bedroom mirror. Lassoo, who was sat on the bed dribbling slightly, stared at my reflection in the mirror and cowed slightly into the sheets. I'm sure it wasn't genuine fear or anything (he probably thought I was going back to work), but in that moment I became convinced that the outfit made me look severe, temperamental and dangerous – all things that a social worker might hold against me. I untied the bun and let my hair fall into its natural shape. I turned towards Lassoo for his opinion. He jumped off the bed and ran off into the hallway. He was right; I looked like a mad woman.

Next up I tried a long flowing cotton dress I had bought from Laura Ashley about twenty years ago. It was lilac with a turquoise flower print, round neck and short, baggy sleeves. I tied my hair back into a pony tail and checked myself out in the mirror. I thought it made me look gentle, kind even, and gave me a bit of an old hippie vibe. I reckoned that most social workers would be of a liberal persuasion and this outfit might just tempt her into thinking I was a wise and elderly member of her tribe. That would surely be a plus mark for me – you know, first impressions and all that. The only problem was that the dress was now about two sizes too small for me and revealed a great big woggle of fat around my waist. It looked as if a big fat anaconda had wrapped itself around my tummy and had settled in for a kip. My confidence in the dress washed away in an instant. I didn't want to look like a lazy, overweight sofa dweller and, worse than that, I didn't want her to think I was a feeder. The authorities are big on diet these days. It was a no.

I tried a few more outfits and hair arrangements but nothing seemed to fit the bill. I put my big yellow wool jumper and baggy blue jeans back on and flopped onto my bed and began to cry. It was a huge effort to keep my emotions at bay and my outfit dilemma had broken my defences. Lassoo crept back into the bedroom, jumped onto the bed and lay down beside me with his head resting on my stomach. He had a keen eye for the softest, warmest places to rest his chin. Surely it shouldn't matter what I fucking looked like? Wouldn't it be enough for them to know that I loved Lizzie more than anything in the world? I would have no problem in convincing them of that. At the end of the day, that's all I had to give, and in my book that should be enough to see me through. I didn't need to pretend to be someone I wasn't; I would wear my yellow jumper and jeans and be dammed if it didn't do the trick. I had been wearing that jumper forever and it felt very 'me'. Also, with a bit of luck, Lizzie might still have a memory of me wearing it when we were out and about having fun together. It could actually be my secret weapon.

I had bitten the bullet and asked my new friend Robert to give me a lift down to the Family Centre in Lewes. He was over the moon that I had got in touch and declared that it would be like our first date. I told him not to get ahead of himself. He apologized for sounding a tad creepy and offered me the option of sitting in the back seat if I wanted to create a safe space.

When he arrived to pick me up, he was wearing a dark blue woollen overcoat, black cap, white shirt with black tie and the shiniest pair of black leather shoes I had seen this side of *Strictly Come Dancing*. He opened the back passenger door for me.

'Hello, madam. I'm Robert and I will be your chauffeur for the day.'

I wasn't in the mood for nonsense.

'I'll sit in the front, thanks, and drop the chauffeur patter – I'm not in the mood for it today. A bit of peace and quiet would be nice; I need to gather my thoughts and get prepared for the interrogation.'

'As you wish, madam.'

'Stop it or I'll walk.'

'Sorry, Grace, I was just trying to lighten the day.'

As we drove out of the estate we got stuck behind a dustbin wagon. A grey squirrel jumped up on the low wall beside the car and stared at me like I was an elaborate wedding hat. I smiled back at him and gave him a little wave. I thought it might bring me good luck for the day if I had him on my side. He gave me a little sequence of blinks and then scratched his whiskers with his paws.

Hey, little guy, do you think it's going to go okay today? I asked myself. He froze solid, with his arms suspended in front of him as if casting a spell. *Is that a yes?* I said to myself. He raised his tail up to the back of his head and jumped off the wall. I didn't know which way to take that response. Fifty/fifty either way was my conclusion. Not too bad.

We had got as far as Crystal Palace before a word was said

between Robert and me. I apologized for being a bit stroppy and told him how much I appreciated his help. I could have got the train from Peckham Rye but it involved two or three changes and the last time I got on a train a bloke in my carriage was spitting onto the seat in front of him while eating a burger that smelt of a tooth infection. I promised myself that day I would never travel by train again.

I asked him if he had any children. He told me he had a son that lived in Blackburn and ran a business involved with hard landscaping. His son was in his late thirties now (he didn't seem to know his exact age) and they hadn't seen each other since his wife's funeral.

'We never really got on,' he said. 'A very quiet boy, almost secretive. I tried my best to bring him out of himself but I never made any progress. I just seemed to make him go further into his shell. We text each other occasionally, on birthdays, that sort of thing, but he's got his own life now. One of us should make the effort but I don't know which one of us that is going to be. I've got a feeling that he will probably breathe a sigh of relief when I'm gone; it will put an end to any guilt he feels. It makes me sad from time to time when I remember the days we went fishing together or to the football when he was a kid. We'll always have that invisible bond we built in the past. It's a shame to waste it really, because you don't make many of those connections in your life.'

'You should go and see him, you prick, instead of feeling sorry for yourself. Fuck knows where Blackburn is but it can't be that far.'

'You're right and I know it, and I know I shouldn't do the self-pity thing, but that's my age speaking. Hey, do you fancy a trip to Blackburn?'

'It's never entered my thinking before and I don't see any reason for that to change now. I'm sure Blackburn will get on fine without me.'

We arrived at the Family Centre about fifteen minutes early. It was part of a large one-storey brick-built building on the outskirts of the town that also served as a Health Centre. The car park was freshly tarmacked, which for some reason gave me a little ping of hope for the day. Robert reached into the back seat and fetched a small bag containing a flask and some sandwiches wrapped in greaseproof paper.

'I thought you might like a cuppa and a sarnie,' he said.

'In principle I would,' I replied. 'But my stomach is turning over something rotten and I reckon anything that passes my lips would reappear pronto. You haven't got anything a bit stronger, have you?' I asked with what I hoped was an impish look on my face.

He pulled a small hip flask out of his inside jacket pocket.

'I've got this,' he announced with a look that was definitely copied from an actual living and breathing imp.

I took a swig and it hit my chest and stomach in unison, warming me through and for a brief moment settling my nerves.

'That's better,' I said.

'No, that's brandy,' he replied.

As I left the car I felt my legs give way slightly with what my mother would have called the collywobbles. I took a deep breath and off I went to my destiny. I heard the car door open behind me and then a shout of *'good luck'* from Robert. I desperately wanted to turn back and re-join him in the car, but I didn't. I pushed the door to the centre open and stood upright before the reception desk.

'Hello, my name is Grace Dawson and I'm here to see my granddaughter Lizzie.'

33

EMILY

'So, what can I do for you, Emily?' asked Councillor Jordan.

'It's to do with the hotel,' I replied.

'Of course it is. Let me guess: you want me, with my influence and contacts, to find somebody to take the hotel off your hands, take over the lease and get you out of the hole you've dug for yourself?'

'Nope. You couldn't be more wrong.'

'Of course I could, but come on, I've seen that you've been putting a lick of paint on the place, and you're probably putting in some new carpets and budget wallpapers, but it's just a sticking plaster. The place is a shithole. It's fallen behind the times and will cost a small fortune to update. I admire your pluck, but it's bound to fail.'

'That's what most people say.'

'Of course they do, because it's the truth. Come on then, spill the beans. What is this ambush all about?'

'I may have a problem with a planning application.'

'Of course you have, you poor thing.'

I wanted to throw the bowl of mushroom soup right at the centre of his grinning face, but kept my composure. I was well practised at this game from years of sitting at the dining table with my father.

'I am poor but not so much of a "thing" as I might appear.'

'Listen,' he said, leaning forward to rest his elbows on the table. 'You obviously know that I am the chair of the local Planning Committee and therefore must realize that I cannot discuss any application directly with you; that would be entirely inappropriate and, if you don't mind me saying, probably prejudicial to any planning application you might wish to make. Are you sure you want to carry on with this conversation?'

'Yes, I think I am.'

'Now, let me guess,' he said. 'You want to convert the hotel into a bloody nightclub, am I right?'

'Nope. I live on the top floor, so I can't see that working for me.'

'Okay, in that case, I'm going to guess that you want to knock out a few walls and open a large Anglo-Asian fucking restaurant on the ground floor. Well, that's not going to happen. It's a Conservation Area and we don't need any more eateries blighting up the place.'

'No, that's not it. I'm keeping the dining room as it is, just for serving breakfast and dinner to the hotel guests.'

'Of course you are. How wonderfully nostalgic of you.'

At that moment Kevin returned with my plate of fish and chips.

'Ha ha ha,' burped Jordan unconvincingly. 'I was just saying I'm all ears — a bit like you, Kevin.'

'Oh, sir, what an excellent comment,' replied Kevin, turning away quickly but allowing himself a moment to give me a blameful look.

I decided to put my cards on the table, right next to his soup, and get the meeting moving.

'It's about a giant avocado that I want to use as the hotel sign.'

'Giant avocado? I don't like the sound of that one bit. How big exactly?'

'Fucking massive.'

He spat out a laugh and I glimpsed a tiny speck of mushroom land on my fish batter.

'It's about five metres high and nearly three metres at its widest point near the base of the bulb. I want to hang it from the flagpole on the second floor to serve as the signage for the hotel.'

'In a Conservation Area? You must be fucking joking. And how does it even make any sense as a hotel sign?'

'The hotel is going to be called "The Avocado".'

'You're going to name the hotel after a vegetable?'

'It's a fruit.'

'The fuck it is. Ridiculous idea. Are you sure you're cut out for the hospitality business? I'm not convinced that you are. Well – unless you want to be a waitress! Sorry, that's unfair. But I do kind of mean it.'

'I've applied for planning permission and I really need it to go through. I was wondering if you could help?'

'Of course you were.'

'Can you?'

'Well, see, now you have crossed a line. I'm sure you must know that it's highly irregular to personally approach a member of the Planning Committee about an application. All submissions must be made in writing either on the website or by letter. You have a right to speak at the application hearing but coming here and ambushing me, well, that, young lady, is a real no-no. I'm even tempted to call you a cheeky fucker.'

'That's not what I've heard,' I said. 'I've heard that wheels can be greased, doors can be opened, miracles can happen.'

A knowing smile spread across his face as he picked up his spoon and began slurping away at his mushroom soup.

'Eat your fish and chips,' he said. 'And then let's have a little stroll down to your hotel – an informal site visit, if you like. Maybe I can do you a massive service and persuade you to sell up. Wouldn't that be something?'

We finished our meals and strode out of the club entrance. Jordan made a small fuss of placing a ten-pound note into Kevin's pocket as he passed him in the doorway. I turned around and blew Kevin a kiss, which he pretended to catch in his right hand before rubbing it onto the arse of his trousers.

We walked along Church Street and then turned onto Sackville Street heading towards the seafront. Halfway down, Jordan stopped and announced that we were outside his flat and that he would like me to pop inside with him. He wanted to show me something relating to my father. He lived in the front first-floor flat of a large, late Georgian, four-storey terraced house. He showed me into his front living room.

The room had been very grand back in its heyday but was now faded and neglected. The high plaster ceiling was beginning to crack and peel and the huge bay window overlooking the street was misted with dirt and framed by sun-blemished browny-yellow velvet drapes. The room was full of ill-matched and random pieces of furniture, a floral-patterned sofa, various pink and red easy chairs, a large trestle table piled high with files and papers, table lamps that at one time might have been considered erotic and a red and blue geometrical design carpet that might have come from the head office of a skip hire company.

The room shouted single man in its untidiness but old lady in its design. I wondered if he had inherited it from his mother. There were no obvious signs of wealth on display, which surprised me. The only hints of indulgence I spotted were a couple of Rolex watches on a side table and a huge flat-screen television in one corner.

'Do you live here on your own?'

'Of course I do. That way I can keep it exactly as I like it and use it exactly as I please.'

'Do you not get lonely?'

'Not so much as to make changing my lifestyle worthwhile. What about you? Are you married, or shacked up as they say?'

'My boyfriend comes and stays most weekends. He works in London and doesn't fancy commuting. Seems to work for us both.'

'Sounds like there's a lack of commitment going on from one end – probably yours is my guess. Good for you.'

'So, what was it you wanted to show me?' I asked.

'Ah, right, yes. You see that painting over the fireplace?' he said, pointing at a large gilt-framed oil painting of a ship in choppy waters that had the look of a jigsaw puzzle about it. 'Your father gave that to me three or four years ago. Lovely, isn't it? And worth a few bob, I can tell you.'

'Why would he give you a gift like that? I don't remember you two being particularly close.'

'Let's just say I did him a favour and he wanted to show his appreciation.'

'Was it a planning matter?'

'Do you know, I really can't remember now. He must have been feeling generous towards me though. I just wanted you to see it – you know, for old times' sake. I hope you didn't mind the diversion.'

'Of course not,' I replied.

I had got the message: he could be 'bought'.

When we arrived outside the hotel, the Avocado was still stood upright on the paved area in front of the basement, covered with white plastic sheeting secured with a web of old rope.

'Jesus, it's massive,' he declared.

'Well, I did say so.'

'But that's ridiculous. How could it ever be anything but an eyesore? It's hard to believe that you're actually serious about this.'

'Would you like me to take the sheeting off so you can see it in its full glory?'

'If you think it might make any difference, but I haven't got all day.'

I ran inside and mustered up Pete and Mark to do the deed. They didn't say a word to each other as they unwrapped the beast. Mark disappeared back into the hotel as soon as the job was complete. Pete hung around and joined Jordan and me on the hotel steps. We stood looking down upon the huge fruity green teardrop.

'It's awesome, isn't it?' Pete said to Jordan.

'Where on earth did you get it from?' Jordan asked by way of reply. 'Nicolas Cage's fun fair?'

'No,' said Pete. 'But funnily enough it *was* made for a movie set — a movie about some allotment owners who take on an American corporation that wanted to develop their land.'

'What was the movie called?' asked Jordan. 'It rings a bell.'

'It was never made,' said Pete. 'It was cancelled just before filming was about to start when some bright spark pointed out that the script was shit.'

'Well, that doesn't usually stop them from filming these days, more's the pity,' said Jordan, allowing himself a nasally laugh that didn't require him to open his mouth or display a smile.

I took Jordan inside and Pete disappeared to get on with decorating the bedrooms. We walked through to my office behind the reception and sat down either side of my father's old leather-topped colonial desk.

'You've certainly brightened the place up,' said Jordan, 'but like I say, it's just a sticking plaster. You would need at least a quarter of a million pounds to bring it up to standard.'

'Maybe you're right,' I replied. 'But I'm going to try and prove all you doubters wrong, make you eat humble pie.'

'That's something I've never tried. Is it sweet or savoury?'

'Definitely be sweet for me if I'm serving it.'

'I see you've kept your father's old desk. Is that for old times' sake or because you can't afford a replacement?'

'A bit of both. So, tell me, Councillor Jordan, what are your thoughts regarding the avocado?'

'I actually think that it's a very good idea, but you'll never get it through planning. I can tell you now that all the Brighton conservation groups will object, as will a number of your competitors and plenty of residents who have nothing better to do. I mean, it's not like a fucking huge avocado is going to slip under the radar.'

'The objections are rolling in as we speak,' I said. 'And obviously you will do your duty and listen to them all, but the ultimate decision rests with the Planning Committee, and you are the boss of that committee, so I'm asking if you might be able to sway them in my favour.'

'Of course you are, but why on earth would I put my head on the block for you? I have a lot of interests to balance in my work – people to keep happy, people to keep off my back, people to avoid – and I'm afraid you don't even register as a party that's of interest or of potential use to me.'

'What about for old times' sake, for the friendship between you and my father?'

'Your father wasn't a friend of mine. We had a purely business relationship. As I'm sure you are at least partially aware, the man was a miserable arsehole. I doubt he had any friends other than those he paid for.'

'Well, what about *we* start up a business relationship? I mean, just you coming here today has been a big help. Maybe I could buy you a painting in return for your advice and support. No one need ever know.'

'You're beginning to sound desperate.'

'Well, I'm sorry if that's how I sound. I don't mean to. I'm just asking the question.'

'No need to apologize. I like dealing with desperate people. I like holding a ladder into the well and holding it out of reach until I decide the person's fate. It's a wonderful game.'

'I'm not desperate.'

'Yes, you are. A nice young lady like you doesn't come offering bribes unless they're desperate.'

'Alright, yes, I'm desperate.'

'Say it again.' He smiled.

'I'm desperate,' I said, through gritted teeth.

'One more time,' he leaned forward as his smile broadened.

'I am desperate,' I said, leaning forward myself and staring straight into his eyes.

'In that case, maybe I can help you.'

'Thank you,' I replied with a bit more sarcasm in my voice than intended. 'You're a life saver.'

'We will see about that. First up, you're going to have to buy me a ladder – a rather expensive one.' He smiled and leant back in his chair with folded arms.

34

It's me again. If you think my timing is a bit off then that's something you're just going to have to live with – put a warm jumper on or pop a toffee in your mouth if that helps. If you think that I'm interrupting the flow slightly, then you're wrong. You might be the sort of person that interrupts or hijacks conversations when your input is not required, but that isn't something that I would do. Ninety-nine per cent of the time I wait until a person has finished speaking before I pipe up and, what's more, I actually listen to what they're saying rather than simply looking for an opportunity to play sniper and kill the conversation dead. You should be interes*ted*, not interes*ting* has always been my motto.

The other one per cent of the time I am willing to utilize an interruption if I think it important to do so beyond even a shadow of a doubt. This is one of those occasions. You see, I know of this Councillor Jordan, and in fact I was hanging around the bus stop opposite the hotel on the day that he came to look at the big avocado with Emily. (She looked really fancy that day, like a lady on the up.)

I've seen him a lot over the last year or so going in and out of the apartments and the hotel next to the Avocado. He's often with people that I don't like the look of and I don't like the look of Jordan. I reckon he's a right wrong-un. Every time I see him I get my off-kilter feeling and, as you know, that should never be ignored. I've been worried about Emily ever since I saw them together and, now you know he activates my early-warning system, I think you should be worried too.

35

EMILY

By the end of my meeting with Jordan, the situation was clear. To cut to the chase, he wanted an envelope containing five thousand pounds in cash delivered to his flat anonymously in return for smoothing the path of my planning application through the committee. He wanted no further contact between us until such time as he deemed it acceptable. I was not to attend the planning hearing and there were to be no phone calls, no messages and no emails between us and, above all, no more uninvited visits to his private members' club. That last requirement was a shame; I knew that Kevin would miss me terribly.

I had been mulling over Jordan's proposal for nearly a week. The more I thought about it the more I became convinced that the big avocado was the key to a successful launch of the hotel. Unfortunately, with all the objections to my application, I didn't fancy my chances of getting planning permission without Jordan's help. What's more, I was worried that if I didn't pay up Jordan would make sure that the application was refused out of spite or just for his own amusement.

The money was a problem. I had about seventeen thousand pounds left from the refurbishment fund that my father had provided for me. It was all accounted for in my budget with no wriggle room. The solution might be to halt the upgrades to two of the en suites and open the hotel with just the eight bedrooms, or alternatively to abandon the kitting out of the coffee shop on the semi basement floor. I wasn't averse to either of these options as a short-term fix.

The legality of it all didn't worry me unduly. I sensed this sort of scheming had been going on for years and had obviously been utilized by my father. He was the last person that would take any unnecessary risk and I was very reassured by his previous participation. Nevertheless, I didn't want to discuss the proposal with Gary just in case it somehow kicked back on him and put his legal career in jeopardy. I would tell him when the dust had settled. If he got mad with me, I knew it wouldn't be for long.

The only person I could talk this over with was Pete. I knew he wouldn't judge me and would put a positive spin on the situation, which was just what I needed at the time. It was a Saturday when I asked him to come up to my apartment after work for a chat. Both him and Mark had been working all day. Time was getting tight; the first guests would be arriving soon and the planning hearing was next week. Everything was coming to fruition – apart, of course, from my glorious epic avocado that was still sulking under its plastic sheeting outside the basement.

Pete came round earlier than I was expecting and I was still wearing leggings and a crop top from the rehab exercises I did every evening. I was aware that a bit of tummy podge was dripping over the waistband, but no matter – it was only Pete. I put a bit of lippy on to make me look less shagged out. As soon as he arrived he asked if he could take a shower, claiming he was 'sweatier than a pig in a chip shop'. I showed him through to my bedroom shower and left him to it. I cooked steak for us both with grilled tomatoes and oven chips. When he emerged he was wearing a T-shirt that Gary had bought me with a photograph of a chimp using a telephone on the front.

'I hope you don't mind me wearing this,' he said. 'Do you know who the chimp is on the phone to?'

'His broadband provider, I assume, because he's been on that call since I first set eyes on him over a year ago.'

He laughed, which put a smile on my face. He wasn't an easy man to make laugh. It sometimes seemed that it was a personal insult to him if you delivered a line that he hadn't already thought of. I placed his steak and chips on the table and poured a capful of brandy on top of the meat before igniting it with a lighter. A low, weak blue flame lapped across the surface of the meat.

'There you go,' I said. 'I know you like a bit of theatre in your life.'

'It's a very pissy flame,' he replied. 'I don't know if it's accurate to compare it to live theatre.'

'I think it is.'

'You think it is.'

'Yes, I fucking do.'

'So, you reckon that if you were sat centre stalls in the Theatre Royal Drury Lane, and when the show started it turned out to be just a steak with a feeble flame on top of it, you would be happy to have paid the price of admission?'

'I've seen shows less entertaining than a steak with a flame on top and not walked out.'

'I doubt that very much. I think within five minutes of the flame being ignited someone in the audience would shout out, "Boo! This is just a steak with a small flame licking its surface! Boo! I wish I'd stayed at home and cleaned out the rabbit hutch," and then other people would join in and before you know it you'd have a riot on your hands.'

I laughed, knowing that in doing so I would make him happy. We opened a couple of lagers and tucked into the meal. He gave me an update on the work completed and confirmed that all bedrooms would be ready in time for the opening week. He seemed nearly as excited as me that everything was coming together. He asked me about any progress with the giant avocado, which gave me the chance to discuss the shenanigans with Jordan.

'I had a meeting with Councillor Jordan about it at his private members' club.'

'What's he doing being a member of a private club? I thought he was unemployed? I'm sure you can't afford that sort of thing on your councillor expenses.'

'I think he's got other sources of income. You know, back-handers, retainers, sweeteners, that sort of thing.'

'Wouldn't surprise me. The whole world is bent at the moment.'

'He offered to help me with the planning application.'

'Oh yeah, and what's the catch? Or should I ask: how much does he want paying?'

'A lot.'

'Tell him to fuck off. Let's do what I suggested and just put the avocado up, permission or no permission. Like I said, the fuss it will all cause is worth a fortune in publicity. Worst comes to the worst, we have to take it down, by which time it will have done its job for us. We could take it down to the beach and set fire to it. Now that really would be theatre, and another big piece of publicity to boot.'

'I can afford to pay him if I halt work on two of the bedrooms and maybe the basement café.'

'Up to you. It's your cash, your project. I've told you what I think you should do.'

'I think I'm going to pay him.'

'Well good luck, and I confirm that my lips will remain forever sealed.'

'Are you disappointed with me?'

'None of my business really and, if it all goes to plan with Jordan, then I can see the sense in going that way. It's probably a good investment. If you're going to play the game then you've got to be a player, no good just watching from the sidelines.'

'I agree. So, Pete, there's one favour I need to ask of you: would you be willing to deliver the dirty envelope to Jordan's flat? He doesn't want me involved in the transaction.'

'Yes, I am happy to do that for you, my darling.'

I went into the kitchen and took the envelope containing the crooked money out of the microwave where it was hiding. The address was written on the front of the envelope. Pete barely glanced at it before folding it and forcing it into the front pocket of his jeans.

'Can you deliver it first thing in the morning?'

'Yep, and you just want me to put it through the letter box?'

'Well, see if he's in and, if so, hand it over – if not just post it. He lives on his own, so that shouldn't be a problem.'

There was a knock on the apartment door and in walked Mark. He stood by the table and started to blink and tap his hand on his hip, which I took to mean he was surprised and confused by the scene before him.

'Am I meant to ask if this is a bad time to call, or am I not meant to do that?' he asked.

'It's not a bad time at all,' replied Pete. 'But if you had got here a bit earlier you would have witnessed a weak flame on top of some meat. It was like being at the theatre.'

'I agree,' said Mark.

He stood in silence for a few moments, staring at Pete's freshly scrubbed face. He pushed both hands deep into the pockets of his jeans and started to clench and unclench his buttocks.

'Is this some sort of meeting or a social thing?' asked Mark. 'Because if it's a meeting about hotel business than perhaps I should be involved, but if it's a social thing then I suppose I'm not needed.'

'We're just having a chat and a bite to eat before Pete goes home,' I said. 'Was there something you wanted?' I asked.

'No, just wanted to say hello. That's always a nice thing to do. Oh and to ask if you wanted me to stay here tonight what with Gary not being down to visit.'

I avoided his question. The mention of Gary gave me a little blast of guilt for the fact that I was sat here eating steak and sharing a beer with another bloke. I didn't want Mark to think anything untoward was going on.

'Why don't you join us, have a beer, Mark?' I asked.

'We hardly ever see you having a relax,' Pete chimed in.

'I don't drink beer,' said Mark.

'What do you drink?' asked Pete. 'Hey, I've always thought that lemon cleaning spray you use might be refreshing.'

'I don't agree,' Mark replied, 'but, talking of cleaning, you look very clean and refreshed. That must be nice for you.'

'Yeah, Emily let me have a shower.'

'Can't argue with that,' said Mark. 'So, I guess he's staying the night is he? To look after security? Guess I'll be on my way, then.'

I didn't reply. He turned on his heels and walked hurriedly out of the flat without saying another word.

'He's on a different planet, isn't he?' said Pete as soon as he was sure Mark had left the vicinity.

'Maybe, but he's an absolute gem and I'd be lost without him,' I replied.

36

GRACE

I was shown into a small waiting room with bare painted walls and blue plastic chairs around two of its sides. A window opposite the door allowed a view outside over a patch of lawn that divided the building from the car park. I could see the back end of Robert's car stood idling with a whisper of grey smoke coming from its exhaust. It was nice of him to bring me here. I felt a bit rotten for being sharp with him. He had shown me nothing but kindness since I met him and it really was time that I took my barriers down a little.

A few other cars were parked up and I wondered if any of them had been used to bring Lizzie here. My stomach churned. I wished I had someone here with me to hold my hand. Failing that, I wished I could have another glug of brandy from Robert's flask. It was nearly four years since I had seen Lizzie. She would be ten years old now. I used to think that she looked a lot like me when I was her age. Her mum always said that Lizzie looked the spit of her, which I always hated hearing because she was the spit of her father. What on earth would I say to

Lizzie if and when we met? '*Hello, darling, give us a hug*' is what I used to say, and it felt as natural as taking a breath, but I wondered if the words would even come out in the emotion of a first meeting.

What if she started crying or got all scared when she saw this old witch walk through the door? What if *I* started crying and got her all upset? Would her mum be there? And, if she was, what would she be like with me? The last time we spoke at any length was in the hospital after Lizzie's operation when she threw me out and told me I would never see Lizzie or her ever again. Surely she can't still be as angry as that? She had agreed to today's meeting, after all, so she must have softened up her attitude a bit. I love my daughter as much as I love Lizzie. If they could both be back in my life then I could die a very happy lady indeed. I would give anything for the chance to die happy.

The waiting room door opened and there stood Hannah Lewis, the allocated social worker. She looked young, around forty years old, with curly light brown hair and a large, round, friendly face. She was wearing tight denim jeans that strained against her thick, heavy thighs and a grey hoodie sweatshirt with a loaf of brown bread printed on the chest. In an apron she would have looked like a butcher or a baker. She shook my hand with quite a heavy grip and introduced herself.

'I'm Hannah Lewis. Lovely to meet you, Grace. If you could follow me that would be just great.'

She was posh and well spoken, which always made me feel a bit inferior. I warned myself to mind my language and not to lose my temper. Roma had told me that the most important thing was that the social worker liked and trusted me. Some people get right put off by a bad-tempered, sweary old lady.

'Don't fuck it up, Grace,' I whispered to myself as I followed her down the corridor to her office. We sat down and did a bit of small talk.

'Have you been to Lewes before?' she asked while taking a form out of her desk drawer.

'No, never had any reason to come here. It's a lot different from Peckham – quieter and nicer to look at.'

'I love it here,' she gushed. 'If you get the chance, you should have a stroll down the high street. There's a deli next to the old court house that sells the best lemon drizzle cake in the whole of Sussex – and believe me, I know my cake.'

'I'm not that keen on lemon drizzle; I find it a bit dreary on the eye. I prefer a Battenberg – that's a cake that adds a bit of sparkle to your plate.'

I reminded myself to keep things cordial.

'But, yeah, if I get the chance I'll go to the deli,' I added. 'That lemon drizzle cake sounds epic.'

'Oh wow, Battenberg. I used to love that when I was a child. I don't think they sell it at the deli – a bit too post-war and depressing if you know what I mean.' She made a noise that represented her laughing; it sounded like a trumpet being played inside a mattress. 'Mental note to seek out a slab of Battenberg for a nostalgia hit ASAP,' she said, followed by another muffled trumpet sound that ended very suddenly as her face gave way to a look of concern and sympathy.

'So, how are you feeling about today, Grace? Excited? Nervous? A bit of both maybe?'

'Yeah, that about sums it up. I'll be okay though once I see Lizzie.'

I thought I smelt a whiff of Robert's brandy on my breath so I asked if we could have the window open. As Hannah got up to attend to the window, I adjusted the position of my shoulders slightly so that the breeze would catch my words and cleanse them of their brandy fumes. Good job I did, as the next thing I knew she was asking me to sign a form confirming that I was not under the influence of any drink or drugs. Finally, she got down to the nitty gritty.

'So, Grace, I've read all the reports and interviews with both yourself, Lizzie and her mum, but I would still like you to tell me, in your own words, about the incident that led to your estrangement from Lizzie and your daughter. If you could do that for me, that would be great.'

She leant her head to the side and gave a half smile that suggested her empathy was overflowing and spilling onto her lap. I took a deep breath and once again blurted out the story that had haunted me for all these years.

'It was about three and a half years ago. Lizzie was staying with me for the weekend, just like she often did – you know, to give her mum a break. On the Saturday evening, when she was already in her pink pyjamas and her dressing gown, she asked if she could have some spaghetti hoops for her supper. I didn't have any in the cupboards, but Lizzie started making quite a fuss, so I caved in and went to the shop to get some for her. The corner shop was only two minutes away so she would only be alone for five minutes. I told her to give my dog Lassoo a cuddle and a tickle and that I would be back in no time. When I got back, the front door was open and Lizzie wasn't in the flat. I went outside and I could see Lassoo running around in the play area near the swings and the see-saw. I ran over to fetch him, shouting Lizzie's name with every other step, but she was nowhere to be seen. As I got nearer to the swings, I saw Lizzie lying face down on the mud beneath one of the arms of the see-saw. I turned her over and could see that her little jaw had been smashed to smithereens by the paddle on the end of the see-saw and there was blood streaming from her nose and mouth. We never found out how it had happened. Lizzie told me afterwards in the hospital that some boys had been playing and she got in the way of the see-saw. They had run off and were never identified. I don't really remember much after finding her until the ambulance arrived and I went in the back with her to the hospital. She had to have her jaw wired back together and an operation on her tongue. When her mum came to the hospital, she threw me out, and to be honest I can't blame her. I miss them both so much, I would never let anything happen to Lizzie. I've learnt my lesson the hard way and that's the way that lasts forever.'

I was crying. She offered me a hankie and I blew my nose into it then patted my eyes dry. I sensed that I might have spread some residue from the nose blow around my eyes so used the sleeve of my yellow jumper to wipe it off. I glanced at my cuff on its way down and saw that it was stained with mascara. I guessed my eyes would also be covered in the stuff. I really was going to look like a witch.

'We can all make mistakes, Grace,' said Hannah. 'You can't punish yourself forever or start thinking that you are a uniquely bad person. That's a very negative way of thinking.'

'I'll never forgive myself,' I replied. 'I would understand if Lizzie and my daughter felt the same.'

'They don't, Grace. I've spoken to Lizzie and her mum this last month and both of them have indicated a desire to rekindle their relationships with you.'

It was the first hard confirmation of this development and I swallowed two or three times, trying to hold back more tears.

'Lizzie mentioned something about a story you used to read to her about a cat called Billy. Do you remember that?'

'Of course I do. The story is called *Billy's Bus*. It's about a fat black and white cat that drives a bus around town so that cats can go and visit each other. I had a little hand bell on my bedside table that Lizzie would ring every time the word "bus" was mentioned in the story. I know it might seem daft, but I brought the book and the bell here with me today just in case she remembered and wanted to hear the story again. Stupid, I know, now that she's all grown up.'

'Not at all. That's a lovely idea. It's obviously something she remembers very fondly. Can I ask you, Grace, why did you wait so long to try and get access to Lizzie?'

'Well, at first I was just too shell-shocked and embarrassed to do anything. I kind of hoped that my daughter Mary would get in touch with me but it just never happened. Given the circumstances, I didn't feel like I had any right to make a fuss. I used to take the bus over to where they lived a few times, just on the off chance of getting a glimpse of them both. I thought that if Mary saw me, she might at least talk to me so that I would know where I stood. I did bump into her once outside Lizzie's school and she threatened me with the police and solicitors and all sorts of horrible stuff. Then she moved out of London to down here and I suppose I gave up. I've no idea where they're even living or if Lizzie is doing well or anything. I didn't know that I could apply for access until about a year ago when my new neighbour Gary, who is a lawyer, told me that I could. I took a bit of persuading – you know, thinking that I didn't want to cause any more upset – but eventually I thought there's no harm and if it didn't work out then at least I tried. So that's how I come to be here really.'

'Well, Grace, as has probably been explained to you by your lawyers, every decision in these cases is taken on the basis of what is in the best interests of the child. Lizzie is a very bright little girl and it is very important that her wishes come right at the top of the list. I've spoken to her on a couple of occasions now and she seems very keen to re-establish contact with her "Nana". I don't think it's my job to stand in the way of her wishes as long as everything is handled safely and correctly.

'Is she doing well at school, then?' I asked, desperate to know more about how she was doing. 'You said she was a bright little girl.'

'I suggest you ask her that question when you see her,' Hannah smiled.

The penny dropped: I was going to be allowed my visit with Lizzie. I started to blubber like a baby as I got off my chair, walked round the desk and gave Hannah a massive hug and a kiss on the top of her head. I was giddy with joy and excitement. I hadn't had a moment like this for years and had given up thinking I ever would. I had forgotten what happiness felt like and that made its reappearance all the more thrilling and overpowering.

'Oh thank you thank you thank you. I can't believe that I'm actually going to see her . . .'

'I know it's all very emotional, Grace, but if you could just return to your seat and try to calm down that would be great.'

I did as I was told apart from the calming-down bit.

'Do you think she might be able to come and stay with me again? Not right away, I realize, but, you know, if things go well and everyone agrees? Do you think that could happen? I would love it if—'

'Let's take it one step at a time, Grace,' she interrupted. 'Is there anyone else living in your home?'

'No, just my dozy dog Lassoo, but he barely knows up from down and he always loved Lizzie and she loved him. I bet she remembers him.'

'Yes, she mentioned "Nana's dog" to me quite a lot, said he likes eating pies and sleeping with his nose in a slipper,' Hannah said with a muffled trumpet trill.

'He does – or a dishcloth if it's fallen on the floor.'

'Are you in any kind of relationship at the moment?' Hannah continued.

'You mean have I got a fella? No, don't be daft. My friend Robert brought me here today but that's all he is, just a friend. He's never even been in my flat.'

'Well, if the possibility of Lizzie staying at your place ever raises its head, then we would want to know about any adult person she is likely to come into contact with during that visit.'

'It would just be me, I promise.'

'Well, that sounds just great but, as I say, let's not get ahead of ourselves. Let's just get through today first.'

She got up from behind her desk and I found myself staring at the loaf of brown bread on the front of her hoodie top.

'Why have you got a loaf of bread on the front of your top? Does it mean something? Is it like a logo for a particular brand of bread?'

'No chance, I'm not someone who goes around giving free advertising to big business. It's just a pleasant, simple image that I hope says something about me as a person.'

'What, that you like baking?'

'No, that I've got good morals, wholesome, if you like.'

'Or wholemeal even.'

She laughed again, this time with an open mouth so that the trumpet playing had a hint of donkey about it. She reached into her desk drawer and pulled out a packet of wet wipes.

'If you could give your eyes a wipe and clean off the mascara that would be just great. We don't want to frighten Lizzie, do we?'

I took a wipe and gently cleaned around my eyes. Hannah watched me do this as if proudly watching her child clean their own face for the very first time.

'Have I got it all?' I asked.

'Yes, you have. Come on, let's go through to the playroom and meet Lizzie and your daughter.'

Roma was waiting in the corridor outside; she was there to observe the meeting and have an informal chat with Hannah afterwards. As the three of us approached the door to the playroom, I felt my legs turning to jelly, so grabbed hold of Roma's arm for support. We entered the playroom in silence. Lizzie and my daughter Mary were sat opposite the door. They both looked directly at me. Mary gave a reassuring smile that said, *'Don't worry, this is all fine by me.'* Lizzie turned her face towards her mum, as if looking for permission to get up from her seat. They were both silent; we were all still silent. I looked towards Hannah and then Roma, hoping they might break the silence, but they both just smiled at me. Lizzie was now staring at Hannah, looking for some sort of guidance, but again received only a smile in return. Nobody had actually prepared something to say. We were all tongue-tied by the enormity of the situation. *Fuck it*, I thought as I held my arms out in front of me and took a few steps towards Lizzie.

'Hello, my darling, give us a hug!'

Lizzie jumped off her seat and ran into my arms. I couldn't lift her up like I used to; she was far too big for that now. She jumped up and down, hugging me around my hips, and looked up at me with her gorgeous eyes sparkling with what I took to be love.

'Nana, Nana, did you bring *Billy's Bus*? Did you bring it, Nana?'

'Of course I did, and your little bell.'

'Hurray! Will you read it for me?'

'You bet I will.'

The visit lasted forty minutes but it felt like only ten had passed when Lizzie and her mum left the room and waved me goodbye. I, of course, started to cry as soon as they were out of sight, but for the fifth or sixth time that day the tears contained a big helping of happiness.

After she had met with Hannah, Roma and I walked back out to the car. I was still on cloud nine and wanted to know when I could have my next visit. Roma explained that Hannah and my daughter would be making that decision, not me and not her; Roma had asked for another visit and we would just have to wait and see.

Robert was waiting by the car, stood to attention and giving me the double thumbs-up sign. I asked Roma to take a selfie of the three of us to help remember this wonderful day.

37

EMILY

After we had finished our steaks, Pete and I went through to the living room, plonked ourselves down on the sofa and started watching some TV. I put on the QVC shopping channel. A man in a tight pink shirt and slacks and a woman in a tight light blue blouse were trying to flog various items of bedding. It was one of my and Gary's favourite pastimes, watching the shopping channels. We would shout out 'LIAR!' every time the presenters made an outrageous claim for the product they were flogging and 'Oh, matron!' every time the presenters accidentally spoke over each other. Wanky, I know, but one of those little things that couples indulge in to keep themselves in tune.

It was strange to be without Gary on a Saturday evening. On the last couple of occasions Gary hadn't come for the weekend, I'd asked Mark to stay over in the hotel at night so that I didn't feel too vulnerable. I'm not normally worried about being alone, but the hotel was a big old empty place and it was nice to have someone else under the roof. I was okay during the week; it was just something about the weekends that got me feeling a bit exposed. Mark would arrive around 10pm and sleep on a camp bed in the unfinished Peach bedroom a floor down from the apartment. You would barely know he was in the building apart from the light shining from beneath the bedroom door. I always told him to pop up if he wanted a bit of company, but he never did. It was strange that he had popped in earlier, bold as brass without knocking. He had never done that before.

I'd never asked Pete to stay and be my security guard. I always presumed that he would have better things to do – nightclubs to prowl or dates arranged with one of Brighton's pretty young things. I was imposing on his life enough as it was. As we sat there, relaxed and with him seemingly happy to watch the shopping shit, I did wonder if I should ask him to stay – you know, if he had nothing better to do. He could sleep in my old room and we could drink late into the night if that was how the evening progressed. I needed some fun amongst all the chaos of the refurbishment.

I fetched some more beers from the kitchen and returned to the lounge to find him bent over the coffee table snorting some white powder, presumably cocaine, through a rolled-up banknote. He looked up and saw the disapproval on my face.

'You don't mind, do you?' he asked, with his face shaped into an apology. 'I mean, have a toot yourself if you're feeling in the mood. You need to turn off from this place sometimes, have a relax, pick up the Pete vibe. You've earned it and you deserve it.'

'No thanks, Pete, and, to be honest, I'd rather you didn't

either. I'd have thought you would have grown out of that nonsense.'

'You're never too old to treat yourself to a bit of euphoria, and since when did you get so judgemental? I've heard that back in the day you used to love to rip it up on the owl powder, *hoot hoot*.'

'Christ's sake, don't add owl noises to your repertoire, and at the very least please don't do that stuff in front of me. I'll be honest with you, it brings back some very bad memories.'

'You mean from your time with Tommy Briggs, the bloke who killed himself before your presumably innocent eyes.'

'What do you mean "presumably"? You think I shot him or something?'

'Maybe. I bet you've got it in you, especially after the way Briggs abused you. I certainly wouldn't judge you if you'd contributed to his termination. I would have probably done the same.'

'Fuck off, Pete, what a thing to say.'

'Well, there are rumours, you know, amongst Tommy's old gang. After all, the only witnesses are you and Gary. Maybe the two of you cooked up the suicide story to avoid a murder charge.'

'Are you being serious or is this just the owl talking?'

'You know, I sometimes think you would have been well advised to steer away from Brighton. His old mates are proper little tin gangsters. They might organize a hit on you.'

'Tell me you're joking before I throw you out of here on your arse,' I said, meaning every word.

He stared at me for a few beats and then exploded with hysterical laughter, rolling back into the sofa and kicking his legs, bicycle style, over the coffee table. He looked about ten years old. I couldn't help but join in with his laughter.

'Of course I'm joking. Your face, though, it was a picture. Emily the murderer! How could you have thought I was being serious? *Hoot hoot hoot!*'

I jumped on top of him and started slapping him around his dozy head.

'Get off me, get off me, you freak!' he shouted as his laughter continued in little spasms.

'Make me!' I replied.

He grabbed me around my waist in a bear hug and started to squeeze. My anger had subsided and I gave up on the assault. We were now face to face and suddenly embarrassed at the position we had got ourselves into. He stopped laughing.

'Say you're sorry,' I said.

'I'm sorry.'

'And that you won't mention that bullshit again.'

'I promise. Do you forgive me?' he asked.

'Yes, I do.'

I gave him a little peck on the cheek and clambered off the sofa. Pete got up and went upstairs to the bedroom, claiming he needed to use the toilet. I think he was as embarrassed as me. I sat back on the sofa, knowing I had just made a terrible mistake. I looked down and noticed that my crop top had ridden up above my bra. Perhaps I should have had some drugs. At least then I would have an excuse for my behaviour. Ten minutes passed and he had still not returned when the front door of the apartment opened and somebody entered. I presumed it was another surprise appearance from Mark, but I was wrong.

38

GARY

As I said earlier, the moment I entered Emily's lounge, I knew that something was badly wrong. Her face told me she was shocked and flustered by my unexpected arrival. My immediate thought was that she had found someone else, that I was interrupting a new life she had found for herself. It might seem a bit of a dramatic conclusion for me to have drawn, but the look on her face suggested just that. All I could think to say was 'I'm sorry' as I turned on my heels to walk straight back out of the door. Emily followed me out onto the landing.

'Hold on, where do you think you're going?'

'You don't want me here; it's written all over your face.'

Her eyes were avoiding mine and she took a few glances towards the apartment behind her.

'Is there somebody in there?' I asked.

I noticed a little quiver of uncertainty pass through her body that was expelled with a tiny shiver in her shoulders.

'Something's wrong. I can tell,' I said.

Her eyes widened slightly and she nodded her head as if to

suggest everything wasn't as it should be. I'd fucked up. I had lost Emily. My mouth dried up and my stomach lurched and rolled with abandon. Without thinking, I reached out and hugged her as tightly as I dared. She felt tiny in my arms. I wanted to absorb her, reclaim her and somehow repair us. Emily was silent. I knew I had to speak or regret it for the rest of my life.

'I'm sorry I've taken you for granted. I'm sorry I haven't supported you.'

Emily placed her hands on the front of my hips and gently pushed to try to unlock herself from the hug.

'Gary—' she said, but I ploughed on:

'I'm sorry for being so selfish. I'm sorry I can never work things out on my own. I'm sorry I didn't move down here with you . . .'

She pushed a little harder: 'Gary—'

I ploughed on.

'I'm sorry you had to do all this on your own. I'm sorry I've neglected you. I'm sorry I'm such a shithouse. I'm sorry I didn't tell you I was coming here today. I'm sorry I've wasted your time.'

I sensed some movement in the apartment doorway and lifted my head off Emily's shoulder. A man was stood in the doorway grinning at me.

'You seem upset, Gary. I hope it's nothing to do with me?'

It was Sequence.

What the fuck was he doing in Emily's apartment?

'What the fuck are you doing here?' I asked.

'Looking after business, taking care of my client's interests, making sure I don't get fucked about, that sort of thing.'

'Can we do this somewhere else? This has nothing to do with Emily. She knows nothing about our arrangement. I don't want her involved.'

'That's good to know, Gary, really good. Perhaps you should have thought about that before you came here.'

He was right and I knew it, instantly.

He took a big suck on his vape, expelling the smoke from one side of his mouth so that he could maintain his lopsided grin. 'No, this place is perfect for me,' he continued. 'Come on inside so that we can have a little chat.'

I did as I was asked. He told us both to take a seat on the sofa while he stood by the coffee table, clearly revelling in the distress he was causing. I put my arm around Emily. It was difficult to organize my emotions at that moment. I was elated to know that Emily wasn't with a new fella and that my outpouring of self-pity was as misguided as it was pathetic, but frightened by the fact that Sequence was here. I was confused as to how he had arrived before me, was worried that he would drag Emily into his plans and spooked by not knowing what those plans were. I sensed a speech or a lecture coming from Sequence, so made an attempt to try to set the agenda myself.

'How did you know I was coming here?' I asked.

'Because I'm good at my job – the best, in fact – and like I've told you many times before, Gary, you can't hide from the police.'

'But you're not the police.'

'As good as, Gary. I have all their resources at my command with just a phone call or two. Truth is, I didn't need them on this occasion. I got all the information I needed from your friend Andy. As soon as he mentioned you had a girlfriend called Emily, I knew exactly where you'd be. Anyone involved in this business would recognize that name immediately.'

'Well, if you can find me, then so can the actual police, so that's a bit of a twin-edged sword, isn't it?'

'Yes, but they're not looking for you yet, are they, Gary? So I'm always going to be one step ahead of them. Why were you crying, Gary? Is it because you love her and you missed her? Does this love for her make you cry? Do you love her, Gary?'

'None of your business but yes I do.'

'That's good to know. It should make my life a lot easier, increase your vulnerability, and give me an extra bargaining tool. Does she love you?'

I looked at Emily to see her reaction.

'Fuck off' was the reply she gave on my behalf.

'I was in love once,' he continued. 'With a dog. A big fat mongrel that could eat a whole loaf of bread in a couple of bites. He was called Doner Kebab – you know, after the Turkish meat column – and I loved him to bits, but he never made me cry, not even when he was run over by a Renault Scenic. I made the driver cry quite heavily though.'

Just then I noticed something crawling on the shoulder of his blue woollen overcoat. It seemed to have come out from under his ridiculous 1980s bouffant hair.

'There's a spider or something on your shoulder,' I said.

He brushed his hand over his coat without taking his eyes off mine.

'I'm not interested in spiders, Gary. I'm only interested in sobriety. And please don't interrupt me again or I might have to give your face another mince bath.'

'That's good to know,' I replied, mimicking his catchphrase, then held up my hands by way of an apology.

'I've been having a nice chat with your lady, and it seems she had no idea you were on your way here. Or, on the other hand, perhaps she's just a very good actress.'

At that Emily was jolted into action.

'FUCK OFF OUT OF MY APARTMENT!' she screamed. I had to hold her back from jumping off the sofa in case she was going to attempt to deliver one of her tomato kicks to Sequence's face.

'Keep her under control, Gary, or she will get a slap. I'm not gender specific come the crunch.'

I tightened my grip on Emily's shoulder and offered her a reassuring smile that incorporated a hint of sternness.

'So, what's the problem here?' I asked. 'You told me to disappear and that's what I've done. I've packed in my job, I've left my flat and I've ditched my car. What more could you want?'

'You've left your flat and packed in your job?! Fucking hell – what is going on here, Gary?' asked Emily.

'Well, well, well,' said Sequence. 'It seems young Emily was telling the truth. You haven't put her in the loop, as it were. Perhaps you're not as close as you're making out.'

Emily untangled herself from my arm and pointed her finger at Sequence.

'This arsehole barged in here, five minutes ago, claimed he was an old friend of yours, took my phone off me and said that if I didn't tell him where you were he would burn the fucking hotel down.'

'That is all true,' interrupted Sequence. 'And I assure you that Gary and I are friends, just not the type of friends that like each other. It's more of a working relationship. You could call us colleagues if that takes your fancy. Oh, and don't point at me like that, young lady. I find it very triggering.'

I put my arm back around Emily's shoulder in the hope it would discourage her aggression.

'What the fuck is with your hair?' asked Emily, unhelpfully and out of the blue.

'That's a very brave and forward question, sweetheart. I'll tell you what's with it: potency, vigour and a lot of sway. It's a kind of branding, if you like, a visual indication of authority. Now shut the fuck up or I promise you will get that slap.'

I noticed that the skin on Emily's face had broken out into hives. She was beginning to realize that Sequence was a real and genuine threat.

'Let me explain,' he continued, speaking directly to Emily. 'Gary, the man who claims to be in love with you, has obviously failed to inform you of his predicament, so let me do that on his behalf. In a nutshell, I work on behalf of clients who are anxious that Gary fails to turn up at their upcoming criminal trial. Gary has seen sense and agreed to make himself scarce until the trial is over and it would seem he has chosen your place as his little hidey hole. It's as simple and glorious as that, and we must all work together to ensure that his plan succeeds. I have to say that, by leaving his job and his flat, Gary has shown a commitment to the cause that reassures me greatly. My one worry is you, though, my love. I need to know if you are on board and that you can be trusted. What do you say to that?'

'Is it the Briggs family you're working for?' asked Emily.

'No, it is not,' said Sequence. 'That side of the matter is nothing to do with the upcoming trial and of no interest to me.'

'So, you're working for Rowlett and all the other bent coppers?' she asked.

'If you say so, sweetheart.'

He walked over to the sideboard, picked up the land line trimphone and ripped the cord out of the wall.

'I don't think telecommunications will be your friend these next few weeks. Talking of which, where is the fucking phone I gave you, Gary, that you promised to keep by your side twenty-four hours a day?'

'I'm sorry, I left it in my car by mistake.'

Sequence took two long strides back towards the sofa and struck me dead on the temple with the trimphone.

'Sorry, Gary, that was a mistake.'

It didn't hurt that much and I answered the blow with a defiant stare. I desperately wanted to rub at the point of impact but refused to give myself permission.

He tossed me another cheap phone, the sort that might be labelled a 'burner' phone and favoured by those who deal drugs or sell counterfeit designer clothing.

'I thought you were using the phone to track my movements. I just didn't want you to know where I had chosen to hide. I didn't want Emily to be involved. I'll keep this phone safe and that's a promise. You can contact me any time you want, day or night.'

'My advice to you, Gary, is to not think too hard about your circumstances. Just keep your head down, keep the phone by your side and enjoy some quality time with your girlfriend. I think she might well have a lot of questions for you, and I'm glad I'm not in your shoes. I'm afraid the fairer sex can be very persistent and aggressive when it comes to being left out of the loop.'

'First sensible thing you have said,' remarked Emily, looking me straight in the eyes.

Sequence took a few steps towards the sofa, bent down, grabbed Emily by the chin and turned her head round to face him.

'I'm beginning to think you might be trouble, sweetheart,' said Sequence. 'Do you intend to cause me trouble? Because if you do, it is a fight you will lose. I've never lost a fight in my life.'

Emily forced his hand off her chin with a swipe of her arm. Sequence immediately grabbed her arm and twisted it slightly in its socket, enough to make her cry out in pain.

'That's your one free strike used up,' he said. 'Next time, you will get a back-hander right on your pretty face.'

At that moment, Sequence's driver entered the room.

'I've swept the place, boss. There's nobody else in the building,' he said. 'I did find this in the downstairs kitchen, though.' He held up a thin polythene butcher's bag containing half a kilo of mince and then stood in the doorway like a bouncer at a Peterborough nightclub.

'So, what happens now?' I asked.

'That's largely up to you, Gary. If you keep your head down, don't do anything stupid like contacting your policeman friend, then very little actually needs to happen. Just enjoy yourself and pass the time until this whole thing goes away.'

'Are you going to leave now?'

'Yes, I am, Gary, but my good friend Brian will be staying here to make sure that you stay put and don't go all cracker barrel on me. It's a hotel, after all, so I'm sure you can make his stay a comfortable one.'

'There's a camp bed in a room on the floor below I can use,' said Brian.

'That sounds very pleasant,' said Sequence. 'I thank you in advance and on my colleagues' behalf for the hospitality that I know you will afford him.'

'Are you saying that we're not allowed to leave the hotel?' I asked.

'You can leave with Brian's permission, and if he agrees he might accompany you or he might not. You will just have to wait and see. It's not for long, Gary. The trial starts the week after next. Don't get a pancake on over it. And remember: I'm always watching, so just be a good boy. I'll leave you to it.

Don't be too hard on him, love. I need this arrangement to work, and a lovers' tiff might not be conducive.'

Sequence and his driver left the apartment. I listened at the door to check that they had descended the stairs. Emily was now stood defiantly with arms crossed in the middle of the room.

'Well, off you go, then. Put me in the loop,' she said.

39

GARY

I explained what had come to pass since I first met Sequence, what it was that he wanted from me and why, and how I had packed in my job. I apologized again for assuming she would be okay with my hiding up in the hotel and for getting her involved in the farce that my life had become.

'Do you really think he would burn down the hotel?' she asked.

'Yes, I do. He's already smashed up Wayne's café and forced him to shut up shop. The bloke's a total nutcase. Same as Tommy Briggs' old boss, same as Rowlett and Peterson. Bad people, really bad people. Psychopaths if you ask me.'

'Fuck's sake, Gary, I'm due to open the hotel in a couple of weeks. I don't know if I can handle taking this shit on board as well.'

'I'm sorry. Look, I can just get on the phone to Sequence right now and tell him I'm not staying here and he'll have to sort out somewhere for me to stay.'

As she listened, I couldn't tell from her expression whether

her mind was moving for me or against me. I knew I was asking a lot, and I could see in her eyes that she was judging me.

'So, you really have decided not to give evidence. You think that's a risk worth taking when you might end up losing your career or, worse still, putting you in prison?'

'I'm fifty/fifty. I wanted to talk it over with you. I'm scared of Sequence and what he might do to me, or both of us now that I've fucked up and brought him to your door.'

'Fuck Sequence. You need to get in touch with DS Marks and put an end to this before it's too late.'

'The thing is, Emily, I don't think my evidence is make-or-break for the case. I don't reckon the police will be that bothered if they can't get me to court. They might not even summons me; it might at least be worth waiting it out to see what happens.'

'I think you're dead wrong,' she said. 'If you weren't a key witness, they wouldn't be going to such great lengths to make sure you're a no-show. How do you get in touch with Marks? Do you have his telephone number?'

'No, it's on the phone that Sequence took from me. I have it on my computer at work. I could phone Roma and ask her to get it for me.'

'I don't think you should be using the phone that he gave you. He's probably monitoring it somehow. Could you not just email Marks, ask him to get in touch?'

'All I have is his work email and that would be too risky. If Sequence finds out from his police mates that I've contacted Marks, then everything will go to shit.'

'What about you just run out of here at the first opportunity and hand yourself in at the police station?'

'I think you know why I can't do that.'

'No, you tell me.'

'Because then Sequence will come after you, and if not you, the hotel. Shit, he was even asking me about Grace. I'd never forgive myself if anything happened to either of you two.'

We went silent. The enormity of the situation was beginning to bear down upon us.

'What did he mean when he said he would give your face another mince bath?'

'He had a bag of mince with him last week, when he attacked me outside a client's block of flats. He started forcing it into my face whilst his mate held my hands behind my back. I wouldn't have minded – I mean, you know how much I love mince – but this was cheap mince, you know, the sort that Lassoo eats, and I could hardly breathe. I thought I was going to suffocate. Death by budget mince.'

Emily laughed.

'Sorry, I don't mean to make light, that must have been horrific.'

'I've really fucking missed you,' I said as we allowed each other a hug in the hope it would grant us a bit of strength and a blink of peace. As I rested my head on her shoulders, I noticed a figure enter from the stairs leading up to the attic floor by the kitchen entrance. It was her friend Pete, the decorator and handyman.

He was wearing an old monkey image T-shirt that I bought for Emily ages ago. He looked freshly showered and very athletic, a lot better put together than me without a shadow of a doubt. My eyes focused in on a patch of lipstick just to the left-hand side of his lips. What was he doing here on a Saturday night? Why was he wearing Emily's T-shirt? Why did the look on his face suggest that it was perfectly normal for him to be creeping down the attic stairs with lipstick on his face? I turned to Emily, expecting some sort of instant explanation. It didn't come. It was Pete who spoke first.

'Hi, Gary, how's it going?' he said, then turned to Emily and asked in a slightly hushed voice: 'Is it safe for me to come out now?'

'What is he doing here?' I asked, thinking that I probably knew exactly what he was doing here.

'Fuck's sake, Gary,' she replied, 'it's just Pete. I cooked him steak and chips as a thank-you for all the work he's been doing and for putting in a day's graft on a Saturday.'

'Why is he wearing your T-shirt?'

'Because he had a shower and needed something clean to put on.'

'All sounds very cosy. I feel as if I might be interrupting something here.'

'Hey, chill out, Gary,' said Pete. 'It's like Emily said: I've been grafting all day and she was kind enough to let me have a shower and give me something to eat, that's all. Nothing more to it.'

'Is that lipstick on your face?' I asked.

He seemed caught out for the briefest of moments before wiping the mark off his cheek with his hand.

'It's just a tiny cut, Gary. You get them, you know, when you're on the tools all day,' he said with a half sliver of sarcasm before turning to Emily: 'So, is it safe or not? Have those monkey men gone?'

Why was he acting so normal? There didn't seem to be even a hint of guilt in his words. How come he didn't realize the awkwardness of the situation? Should I go over and punch him? Was Emily sleeping with him? Should I just pick up my suitcase and walk out of the hotel?

'So, you moving in, then?' said Pete, pointing at the suitcase. 'About time.'

'Maybe,' I replied.

Emily walked over to the front door and out onto the landing. She returned and informed us that Brian was set up on the landing with a chair, a small table from reception, a can of beer and a laptop. He was watching *Mrs Doubtfire* with a face like thunder. She doubted he could hear us and guessed that he was going to be posting himself there for the foreseeable.

'What do they want and who the fuck are they? They looked like a pair of nasty bastards. Do you owe them money or something?' asked Pete.

'So you weren't listening?' asked Emily.

'No chance. I hid in the upstairs bedroom closet. I don't want anything to do with people like that and I don't want to know any of their business. If I'd barged in it could have aggravated everything. Probably be all right if it was Gary – you know, no threat or anything.'

'Shithouse,' I said, and enjoyed doing so very much.

'No, that's not fair,' bleated Pete. 'The first hint of any trouble I would have been down here in a flash.'

'I thought you weren't listening,' I said.

'I wasn't, not to individual words, but I was definitely keeping an ear open for the ambience, the mood, the atmosphere, if you know what I mean.'

'No, I don't. What are you, a fucking dolphin or something?' I said.

'Hey, mate, don't get all cocky. I don't get the sense that you exactly waded in and shifted their arses.'

'Stop it, you two,' said Emily. 'Get your stuff, Pete, and go home. I'll see you on Monday.'

'So did you sort it out with those blokes?'

'Everything is fine, Pete. It's just a bit of extra security. There's a lot of stuff worth nicking now the rooms are done up and an empty hotel feels like an easy target. Just ignore him and stop asking questions. Go home, enjoy the rest of your weekend.'

Pete went back up the stairs to fetch his stuff.

'Is there something going on between you and Pete?' I asked.

'No, there is not, and don't you dare ask me again, ever. You're the one who needs to start answering questions, not me.'

Pete passed us by, gave a cheerful goodbye, walked out of the front door and then, almost immediately, walked back in.

'The bloke outside took my phone off me and told me I can't leave. You do realize my mother is expecting me home later and I can't have her worrying.'

The phone that Sequence had given me rang. He told me to go into another room so we could speak privately.

'Hello, Gary. Brian tells me there was a bloke in your flat. Who the fuck is he?'

'It's Emily's painter and decorator. He's called Pete.'

'What the fuck is he doing there?'

'I've asked myself the same question.'

'Oh, I see, maybe her little bit on the side. Wouldn't that be a shame.'

'What do you want?

'Did he overhear anything of our conversation? Did I mistakenly put him in the loop, as it were?'

'Nah, he's a shithouse, hid in a closet upstairs. Didn't hear a thing, hasn't got a clue, and that's a promise.'

'That's good to know. I'm choosing to believe you. Keep behaving yourself, Gary, and this thing will be over before you know it. This Pete bloke, is he a druggie? My colleague sensed that he might be.'

'Might be. I don't really know him.'

'We need to keep him in ignorance, Gary, and I'm going to allocate that job to you.'

'Fair enough. I don't want to drag anyone else into this.'

'What, not even if they're shagging your missus? I could warn him off if you like?'

'That's okay. I don't want to stack up any debts with you. Can he leave now?'

'Yeah, just give it a few minutes. I'll tell Brian to let him pass.'

'Can he have his phone back? He wants to call his mum.'

'Yes, he can, for now. She's very pretty, your little lady, isn't she? I was thinking to myself what a shame it would be if anything untoward happened to her.'

'It won't.'

I ended the call and went back in to the lounge to tell Pete the good news.

40

It's me again. I think you should know that I was sat on the wall by the bench opposite the hotel on the Saturday when the bloke with the daft hair and the bald bloke arrived. They both marched inside the building as if they owned the place; that's what drew my attention to them. Personally, I would never enter an establishment with such a flourish or air of importance. Not even my own home. Not even if I had just won a million pounds on the lottery and not even if I had a bag of fresh sausages under my arm. You never know who might be watching and think the less of you because of your highfalutin attitude. Keep your demeanour humble when you're out and about, it's just good manners really, and bear this in mind: you get to see and hear a lot more when other people don't notice you.

About ten minutes after the two men arrived, I got a pleasant surprise when Gary turned up. He looked a bit flustered, dragging a large suitcase on wheels behind him and huffing and puffing like a pensioner on an uphill jog. I was actually about to go home but decided to stick around a while to see if anything developed.

Anyway, the man with the big hair came back out of the hotel about thirty minutes later and sat down on the bench just along from me. He barely noticed my presence, just had a quick glance over towards me for assessment purposes. I instantly looked away in a gesture of subservience and humility. From that moment I might as well have been invisible. He took a phone out of his pocket and began to scroll through its contents. It was Emily's phone. I recognized it from the photograph of Gary on the screen. It was a close-up portrait taken from a side angle so that his magnificent nose looked even bigger than it was in real life. Well, obviously, this man having Emily's phone piqued my interest. It didn't give me a skew-whiff feeling but, like I say, it put me on high alert, made me tune in.

He was a difficult one to get a handle on. He obviously thought a lot of himself. His hair was unique and well groomed, lacked a bit of sheen but fair play to him – when you've reached your fifties it's an achievement just having hair, never mind maintaining a healthy lustre. I myself have a deep sheen, and I put that down to the natural spray from the sea. Whenever I'm down on the beach I always turn my head towards the shore and receive a good old misting. You should try this method. You might be worth it.

If I was to label him a poundshop gangster, that would probably be unfair. More likely he fancied himself as one, hence the black and orange hooded puffer jacket and the black slacks and shoes, the gold sovereign rings and the twitchy, agitated attitude.

He dialled his own phone and spoke the name Gary during the conversation. I instantly wished I had Gary's phone number. Imagine being able to speak to him any time of the day whenever the need arose? Wow!

Not long after the phone call, he crossed the road and stood at the bottom of the hotel steps. Moments later, Emily's friend Pete emerged. The man grabbed him by the arm and marched him back over to the bench. Pete didn't seem inclined to put up any resistance to this manhandling.

They had a conversation. It was very one-sided. I don't remember the decorator saying more than the odd word or two. The hairstyle man took a small bag of what I thought might be drugs from his pocket and gave it to the painter. The man told the painter he would be grateful if he refrained from talking to Emily and Gary for the next week or so and assured him that they would understand. He told him he must not venture up into Emily's apartment until he was told otherwise. The painter objected to this instruction and the man grabbed him around the neck and started to choke him. The painter apologized profusely and bowed his head in defeat. At that moment the hairstyle man looked at me and seemed to take offence at my presence. He got up and took a few steps towards me, telling me to 'Fuck off' as he did so. I did as I was told. (I always do when faced with aggression.) The two of them chatted for a while longer, then hairstyle man attacked him again. When the attack was over, Pete walked away slowly, clearly shaken and definitely stirred. I wish I could have heard what was being said but I was too far away.

It was then that I got a full-on off-kilter feeling. Something was not right, and it was going to impact Gary. It was only a week or so before the night with the ambulance and the gurney. Once again, my kilter radar was working to full effect.

P.S. I hope you don't think I was being judgemental about the man's hairstyle. I would never do that; live and let live is my motto. I admire individuality. I myself occasionally indulge in a very unique walking style that utilizes a circular limp in the left leg. It's not much, not showy or anything, but enough to make me stand out from the crowd if that's what I want to do. So, go for it, big-hair man! Don't listen to the doubters out there.

41

EMILY

We stayed up late into the night, going over our options and their possible consequences. Gary started the conversation veering on the side of cooperating with Sequence. He reckoned that it was the only course of action that guaranteed the safety of everyone involved. He seemed strangely ambivalent towards the possibility of him being caught and prosecuted for perverting the course of justice. I put this down to a bit of self-pity caused by the presence of Pete in the flat last night. Above all, though, in typical Gary fashion, he kept saying, '*I want to do what's best for you*' and '*You should decide; it's me that got you into this*' or '*I'll do whatever you think's best*'. Typical bloke, typical shithouse.

In my mind, we had three options:

1. Contact the only policeman associated with the case that Gary could trust: DS Marks.
2. Cooperate with Sequence. Gary had not yet received his official summons to appear at court, so, as long as the case wasn't adjourned, he would probably get

away with pleading ignorance of the date. If the case was adjourned because of his failure to appear, then that would be a whole new ball game; he might have to leave the country and find a job picking limpets off boats somewhere on the East Africa coast. This option didn't sit well with me. Rowlett and Peterson should be in prison for all the people they had harmed. I wasn't willing to shift in this belief, at least for the time being.

3. To save my bacon completely, he could leave the hotel and ask Sequence to hide him up somewhere else. Sequence might agree, but I had a terrible feeling that he would insist upon me coming along as well. I wasn't prepared to do that and jeopardize the opening of the hotel.

I chose option one, to contact DS Marks. He would know how to handle things; he could protect us and he knew how dangerous the people were that we were dealing with. Gary was very concerned about the guilty implications of the ten thousand pounds in his bank account, but to me that seemed a minor problem compared to the possibility of Gary being harmed or the hotel being burnt down, both of which seemed likely eventualities from where we were sitting. The only way to eradicate those possibilities was to get Sequence and his mates arrested. Gary worried that getting rid of Sequence would not be enough. He could easily be replaced. Round and round we went without coming to a decision. We decided to sleep on it.

I didn't sleep well and nor did Gary. We both had a lot of worries to silently ponder. I could sense a tension within the silence that I was quick to blame on Gary. In truth, I was at least partially responsible. Surely he didn't think there was something going on between Pete and me? Did *I* think there was something going on between Pete and me? I wasn't one hundred per cent sure of the answer to that. I had a nagging desire to pack in my efforts to sleep, pull him out of bed and demand to know why the fuck he had landed me in this hot nonsense and why on earth he would ever think I was into something with Pete. I resisted the urge and eventually sleep arrived.

During the night, we both thought we heard someone creeping around in the apartment. I thought it was probably Brian doing a security sweep or just having a nose around to relieve his boredom. Gary sarcastically suggested it was Pete looking for his underpants. I ignored him and got out of bed.

I made myself a cup of coffee in the kitchen and when I returned to the bedroom Gary was holding a pair of dark blue socks in his hand.

'These were on the floor by the bed. Are they yours?'

They didn't belong to me. Pete must have left them in the room after he had his shower. But I wasn't going to get into that conversation.

'Yes,' I replied. 'Are you trying to suggest they belong to someone else? Pete, for example?'

'It's just I've never seen them before.'

I went over to my sock drawer and started pulling out different pairs of socks one by one and throwing them at Gary.

'And have you seen these? Or these? Or these? How about this pair? Do you recognize them? Fuck's sake, Gary, stop acting like a prick. If this is how you're going to be then maybe you *should* leave.'

'Look,' he said. 'If they're Pete's, just tell me.'

'I would tell you and they are not.'

'Okay, I'm sorry, I'll shut up. I was just on a wind-up.'

He smiled as if to confirm that he was just having a joke. He wasn't; he was being an arse. I couldn't be bothered with it. I left the bedroom and went through to the front door of the apartment to see what was occurring on the other side. Brian was sat at a little table on the landing still watching *Mrs Doubtfire* on his laptop. Maybe he had it on a loop. His face didn't suggest he was getting much pleasure from the viewing. My mobile phone was plugged into the laptop via a USB cable.

'Oh, good morning, Brian,' I said cheerfully, so as to suggest his presence wasn't getting to me.

'Huh,' he grunted. 'What do you want?' His voice was deep and his words spoken slowly and deliberately.

'Just saying good morning,' I said with a fixed smile on my face.

'I did notice that,' he replied. 'But do you actually want something?'

'Well,' I continued as if talking to a sensitive child. 'I was just wondering what the arrangement is here. You see, I've got work to get on with and a hotel to get ready for opening, so I don't need any inconvenience or bother. Does that make sense?'

'I'm not stopping you, just keeping an eye on you, checking

no funny business is occurring. Just think of me as a friendly observer. It's Sunday today, so what's the panic? I'm sure this arrangement is very much a temporary one.'

'But you've turned off the internet and taken both our phones. I can't run a business like that, it's impossible.'

'My boss is aware of that and doesn't want to cause you or your boyfriend any hardship.'

He unplugged my mobile phone and returned it to me.

'Oh, that's great, how kind of you. So, am I free to move around the hotel to get on with shit?'

'Absolutely, but if either of you want to leave the hotel, I would be grateful if you would ask my permission. No funny business, no problems. That seems workable to me, do you agree?'

'No, I don't. And are you going to be out here every night like a prison guard?'

'Here or hereabouts. You see, the boss believes that the night time is when creepers choose to creep, when instabilities rear their head and when lovers choose to elope. I think he's got a point. Do you?'

'Maybe, but then again you seem a bit of a creeper, so maybe we should be keeping an eye on you?'

He delivered a weak smile in my direction. Mrs Doubtfire took a tumble on his laptop screen. It didn't amuse him.

I went back through into my kitchen, where Gary joined me a few minutes later.

'Brian is outside on the landing,' I explained. 'I presume he's been there all night. He had my phone plugged into his laptop but he gave me it back.'

'Well, that's a result. Why was it plugged into his laptop, do you think?'

'I don't know, probably having a nose around, checking that I really didn't know you were coming here. We had a quick chat and he's obviously going to follow us around and watch our every move. It's not going to work, Gary. Maybe I should just jump on him while you run outside onto the street, get yourself arrested, smash some windows or something and put yourself in the hands of the police.'

'If I do that, Sequence will come for you.'

'Not if the police arrest him.'

'He'll get to you long before I would be able to convince the police to make a move on him. Even if they did arrest him, he would just be replaced by another gangster. South London is full of them. Maybe we should just cooperate with Sequence. Better the devil you know and all that. If the shit hits the fan then I'll take the fall. You and Pete will be fine. You haven't broken any laws.'

We stood in silence, both having a good think. I sensed from the Pete reference that Gary was still fermenting a sulk.

'I asked you to drop the attitude. Are you going to do that, because it really isn't helping,' I said.

'What attitude?'

'The one that's written all over your face, suggesting that I've betrayed you in some way by having Pete round the flat for steak and chips.'

'I'm sorry, it was a shock. Give me some time for it to wear off. I think I'm entitled to that.'

'No, you're not. Just snap out of it. You're getting on my tits.'

He took a couple of steps towards me, folded his arms and tipped his head over to one side.

'Did you pour brandy on his steak?' he asked.

'Yes, I did. I always do. Have you got a problem with that?'

'I thought maybe that was something you only did for me.'

'God's sake, Gary, stop being such an arse. I've got a hotel to open and I don't need you sucking my spirit away like, like, I don't know . . . a fucking dinghy limpet.'

He spluttered out a genuine laugh.

'A dinghy limpet?!' he repeated, still laughing at the thought of it. 'Where the fuck did that come from?'

'From frustration, you idiot.'

'I'm sorry, I know you like to set steaks alight whenever you get the chance. So, was it a good display? Any decent flames?' he asked.

'No, very weak, just a hint of blue. They faded away in seconds, like mouse piss on a griddle pan.'

He laughed again. 'I'm glad about that,' he said. 'Could I have a coffee, please?'

'Do limpets drink coffee?' I asked.

'Yes, *dinghy* limpets do, by the boatful.'

It felt like the jealousy thing was on hold and on its way towards repair. We chatted over our coffee and came up with a plan. The trial was listed to start a week tomorrow. We would go along with Sequence and keep him sweet until Thursday. We would try to arrange to meet DS Marks on the Thursday or the Friday. Hopefully he could protect us, arrest Sequence and there would be too little time left for Sequence's employees to replace him.

'So, are we all agreed?' I asked.

He didn't respond. It was as if my words had had no more impact than the gentle hum that was coming from the coffee maker as it heated the water. He had a look of realization on his face.

'Why did they give you your phone back? It doesn't really make sense,' he said.

'Because they're convinced we're going to cooperate. They think that we're so shit scared we wouldn't dream of calling the police.'

'I don't think Sequence would take that risk,' he said. 'What if they've done something with your phone so they can use it as a trap to catch us out? To see if we try to contact anyone that we shouldn't?'

'Do you really think that Sequence can monitor calls? Seems a bit far-fetched to me,' I replied.

'Yes, I do. In fact, I'm certain of it. The bloke has got resources, police resources, quality ones.'

'Well, if that's the case, we can't use my phone to get in touch with DS Marks.'

'I don't think we can, not until we find out if either of our phones are safe to use. I'm going to have a shower. I have strong ideas in the shower – it's the heightened speed of the water, brings out the best in me.'

When Gary reappeared, he had re-jigged the plan and seemed very pleased with himself. The plan went something like this:

Firstly, he would phone his friend Andy using the *burner* phone that Sequence gave him. Sequence had spoken to Andy yesterday when he was looking for Gary, and so a phone call to him might provoke a response from Sequence. This would confirm whether the burner phone was being monitored. If not, then it could be used to contact Roma.

Secondly, and in the event that the burner phone was a no-no, he would phone his friend Wayne using *my phone*. Wayne had also had recent dealings with Sequence's people and contact with him would likely raise a query from Sequence's end. If a query came, then my phone was useless. If not, then we would take a chance and use my phone to contact Gary's work friend Roma. If that phone call to Roma did not raise a response from Sequence then we would ask Roma to arrange a meeting with Marks down here in Brighton and hope that he could get us out of this mess.

It all seemed a bit convoluted and unscientific to me but I accepted that it was crucial to have a safe phone in our possession. I could tell that he was chuffed with himself and I didn't want to burst his bubble. For my part, I thought the inevitable end game would be DS Marks coming to the hotel and forcing Gary to attend the trial. It wouldn't take Marks long to guess that Gary was probably down here in Brighton with his girl-friend. I wondered why Sequence hadn't come to the same conclusion; perhaps he just wanted to keep a close eye on Gary before choosing a moment to move him elsewhere. I don't know how these things work. I'm just a waitress turned hotel owner, not a criminologist.

I agreed with the plan. I had an incredibly busy week ahead of me, which included the Planning Committee meeting about the giant avocado. The plan would at least give Gary something to latch onto and help stop him falling apart. It would only take a couple of days to find out if it had worked. If Sequence was monitoring both phones, then we were fucked, but no worse off than we were now. Sequence would be annoyed and Gary might get a kicking, but then again, I thought, maybe he deserves one – nothing serious, of course, just a slap on his daft nose. Second thoughts, maybe I should just do that myself. Second thoughts part two, I don't want him hurt; he's a good lad and none of this is his fault. I've got to stand by him and help him find a way out of this bullshit.

Gary phoned Andy around 11am using the burner phone. It went straight to answerphone. He didn't leave a message. He phoned again at 11:30; same thing. At 11:35, the burner phone rang. Gary answered. It was Sequence.

42

GARY

I answered the call.

'Hello, Gary, how's it going?'

'Fine. A bit like being in prison but we're okay, thanks for asking.'

'That's good to know. Just checking up on you. Have you made peace with the lovely Emily?'

'More or less.'

'Well, why don't you go the extra mile and complete the reconciliation process? I reckon she's worth it.'

'That's wonderful advice. Anything else?'

'Just to say if you need anything, don't hesitate to ask my man Brian. I think you'll find him very accommodating provided you keep on his good side. Did you know that he once kept a man in the boot of his car for five days just to make sure he didn't go all canary on a client of mine?'

'Boot camp?'

'Very funny, Gary, I'm glad you're keeping your spirits up. Listen, I know it's a pain being holed up, but just think of it as honeymoon practice.'

'Emily hasn't got time for honeymooning; she's got a hotel to get up and running.'

'And I'm sure she will do just fine. I promise we will keep disruption to a minimum.'

'Oh, well, that's alright, then. I should be thanking you really.'

'No need to get all balsamic with me, Gary. It was you who chose to squat in the hotel, not me. Speak soon.'

He ended the call. He hadn't mentioned my calls to Andy. I couldn't decide whether that was a good or a bad thing. In the moment, I was actually disappointed. It felt as if my bluff had been called. The outcome was inconclusive. I was no further forward. I needed to get at least a foothold of control over the situation, try to get myself one little sliver of advantage. My instincts told me he was on a bluff; I needed to put a bit more pressure on him. At 3pm I called Andy again and this time I left a message:

'Hi, Andy, Gary here. Could you contact me urgently? I need another favour. Would really appreciate it. Cheers.'

I waited a couple of hours but there was no response from either Andy or Sequence. I phoned again and left another message:

'Hi, Andy, it's me, Gary. Sorry to bother you again but I really need an urgent chat. Please can you call me ASAP?'

Ten minutes later my phone rang. It was Sequence.

'Are you misbehaving, Gary?'

'What do you mean?'

'I thought I made it clear to you that your phone is for incoming calls only?'

'You did.'

'So, why have you been phoning your friend Andy?'

Gotcha, I thought, and a tiny squirt of adrenaline entered my stomach and watered my mouth. A victory at last – tiny, but satisfying.

'Sorry, I just needed to speak to him urgently,' I said.

'What about?'

'I wanted him to check if my car was still parked up and if so to ask if he would maybe move it to his driveway.'

'Ah, right, you were worried about that old banger being nicked.'

'Yeah, I'm very attached to it – had it a long time, sweet memories and all that.'

'So why did you leave the keys in the ignition?'

'I wasn't feeling so warm towards it at the time. You know, it was a difficult day.'

'Every day could become difficult if you fuck me about, Gary.'

'I won't be doing that.'

'That's good to know. There's no need for you to worry about the car. It's already parked up at your mate's house.'

'That's great, thank you, big relief. So, why aren't you staying here with us? I thought you might want to be hands on.'

'I've got standards. I'm up the road at The Grand, much more up my street. It's the hotel where Norman Cook blew himself up.'

'I think you mean the politician Norman Tebbit.'

'Sorry, yeah, that's the one.'

'He didn't blow himself up. Someone planted a bomb and he got hurt in the explosion.'

'Oh, yeah, that's right. Same outcome though. The place is lovely now, you would never know that it'd been bombed – lovely refurbishment. I might treat you to a night here when this is all over.'

'I might take you up on that,' I lied.

'I'm good to you, aren't I, Gary?'

'Yes,' I said, thinking that's what he'd want to hear.

'Well say it, then, so I can tell that you mean it.'

'You are very good to me, Mr Sequence. I mean it,' I said with soap-opera sincerity.

'Good boy. Now, listen, if you use that phone again, things will escalate, the situation will change and jeopardy will envelop you. Do you understand?'

'I do.'

'That's good to know. Cheerio, speak to you soon.'

So, the burner phone was a no-no and my little plan was looking like it had legs.

43

GARY

Not much sleep that evening and I awoke to my first week of unemployment in nearly ten years. If it wasn't for the Sequence situation, I would have had a smile on my face as long as a toothbrush. I resented him deeply for stealing that little moment of joy away from me. I walked down to the hotel reception to look for Emily, who had woken up a good hour or so before me and left the apartment to get on with her day.

On my way down the stairs, I passed a first-floor bedroom where Pete was attaching a white porcelain tile to the door with the image of a single pear in the centre. He looked a bit sheepish when he saw me approaching, a bit apologetic in his stance.

'Nice pear,' I said, pointing at his balls so as to invite laughter into the moment. He didn't even smile, just flashed a disappointing look across his face. I had backfooted myself, which is not unusual.

'Look, Gary, I'm sorry about last night. I could tell it made you feel awkward. Emily and me work here together nearly every day, we're good friends, but that's all – just friends.'

I feigned surprise at his need to apologize and made light of the situation.

'It wasn't awkward, Pete, just a bit unexpected, that's all. I'd had a really strange day already. No need to apologize at all. Emily told me she did a brandy fire on your steak. She always does that, it's her "thing".'

'Yeah, "a bit of theatre" is what she said.'

'And was it?' I asked. 'Was it like going to the theatre?'

'I didn't think so.'

'Did you tell her that?'

'Yeah.'

'She'll never forgive you.'

No response.

'See you around,' I said before turning away and walking on down the hallway.

'Gary,' he said, stopping me in my tracks. 'I didn't hear a word that those two blokes said last night. Just want you to know that. I don't want you thinking otherwise.'

'Okay, understood. No problem,' I replied. 'Oh, I saw you painted over the poem in the Peach room. Did Emily ask you to do that?'

'Yeah, I think she wanted to go in a different direction.'

'No worries. Like I say, nice pear,' this time pointing at the porcelain tile on the door.

I walked on down the stairs, disappointed that, even when it came to a bloke who I suspected might have designs on Emily, I still wanted him to like me. I was beginning to acknowledge I had an illness.

Emily was in the hotel office at her computer screen. I popped my head around the door to see Brian sat behind her looking over her shoulder. I could tell by her expression and demeanour that she was infuriated by his presence. I said a quick good morning but got no response from either of them. I walked out of the hotel and onto the promenade, fascinated to see if Brian would try to stop me or follow me out. In the event he did neither. I crossed the road and sat on the bench by the bus stop and looked out towards the sea. I half expected Brian to join me at any moment but he never came. It was a relief to take my thoughts and worries outside rather than have them infecting the hotel and Emily.

The sky was grey and the sea was even greyer. The wind was blowing in little gusts around me and rainfall seemed inevitable.

I had sat on this bench many times over the past six months. It was the place I always escaped to when I wanted a bit of solitude. I sometimes brought a bit of cake or a slice of bread out with me and fed some crumbs to the seagulls and the pigeons. I wasn't so keen on the seagulls – most of them seemed to be bullies and their voices sounded angry and accusing. I think they spoke mainly in lies: '*Give us some cake, I haven't eaten for months, mate*', '*I've got ten kids to feed*', '*Why did you throw it to that manky pigeon?*', '*Jesus, not more crust! I'll report you to the RSPB*'. That sort of thing.

I would just ignore them and eventually they would move on to find another victim. I preferred the pigeons; they had better manners and a more agreeable attitude. I had made friends with a pretty plump one that occasionally walked with a limp. He reminded me of my squirrel mate back in Peckham. He was a good listener and had helped me solve many a dilemma and complication.

I know it sounds daft, but I think he looked forward to seeing me. Sometimes he would appear a few minutes after me as if he's been on a perch somewhere waiting for my arrival.

That morning, he approached me from the direction of the bus stop, walking, at quite a lick, without a limp.

'Alright, mate,' I said.

'Alright, Gary,' I replied on his behalf.

'No limp today, then.'

'Ah, shit, I forgot. How are you doing, Gary? You look a bit dreary.'

'Not dreary, just scared. Scared stiff actually. I've got myself in a scary situation and the fear has taken me over.'

'Fear's a terrible thing, especially if you don't trust it, mate. You need to embrace it and use it to sharpen your focus, that's what I would do. At the end of the day, fear is just a thought. You generated it, so either turn off the tap or run with it.'

'Easier said than done. Tell me, have you ever been cheated on?' I asked.

'I'm a sole trader, mate, don't get involved in relationships, so no, I haven't. Why do you ask?'

'I think Emily might have cheated on me.'

'Woah, that's a sidewinder, but now you've said it, I've got to ask: can you blame her? You've been farting about, prevaricating like a pipsqueak and burying your head in the mud.

293

Think of things from her point of view. Doesn't she deserve a bit of commitment from you? Do you know what people call you round here? "Mr Weekends", that's what they call you.'

'I've packed my bags and moved here. Can't do more than that, can I?'

'Might be too little too late. You might like to think around that. What makes you think she's cheated on you?'

'There was a fella in her apartment last night when I arrived. They'd been eating steak and chips, he was wearing one of Emily's T-shirts and I'm sure I saw a patch of lipstick on his mouth before he wiped it off when I pointed it out.'

'Sounds bad. Have you asked Emily about it?'

'Yeah, she told me I was being a prick and to never bring the matter up again.'

'Have you spoken to the fella?'

'Yeah, he said they're just friends.'

'Do you believe them?'

'I want to but I can't quite get there.'

'Has Emily ever lied to you before?'

'Never.'

'Then why would she start now? Strikes me you don't really think she's cheated on you at all. Maybe you're looking for a way out of the relationship, which would be typical of you. Maybe you're just a prick like Emily said. Have you thought around that?'

'I'm not looking for a way out. I'm looking for a new beginning.'

'Then that's settled: you're being a prick by not believing

Emily, nothing new there. So, tell me about what's causing you the fear.'

'I've got a gangster on my back and if I don't do what he's asking he's going to hurt me, or Emily, or possibly both of us. He's even made some sort of threat to burn the hotel down. It's complicated.'

'Strikes me you need to do what he wants.'

'Emily wants to go to the police.'

'Then you should do what she wants. She's got your best interests at heart and that's a fact worth thinking around.'

'But if he finds out we intend to go to the police then we will definitely be in the deepest of shit.'

'Well, don't do it, then. Keep your head in the mud, ride it out.'

'But Emily isn't going to change her mind.'

'Then do what Emily wants, show some loyalty towards her.'

'But if she's wrong then she might lose everything.'

'Then that's a risk you can't take – you need to persuade her to get her head down in the mud with yours.'

'I've got a little plan I'm running with.'

'Don't tell me: it involves hedging your bets and putting a decision off until someone else makes it for you.'

'I suppose there is a bit of that involved.'

'You shithouse.'

'Is that a remark?'

'I guess.'

The conversation hadn't helped. I threw him a handful of crumbs from my pocket as I turned around towards the hotel.

Brian was stood on the top step of the entrance staring at me. I got up and walked back to the hotel.

'Don't stray too far without asking first, lad. No nonsense, no pain,' said Brian as I passed him by.

'No oven, no pie,' I replied and popped back into the office. Emily wasn't there. I found her on the first floor, talking to Pete about the pear door plaque.

'Nice pear,' I said.

'Not now, Gary, I'm working,' she replied.

44

GARY

Back in the flat, it was time to phone Wayne from the café and find out if Emily's phone was safe to use. It struck me as odd that Brian hadn't insisted that Emily's phone was in his presence. Maybe it meant that he was monitoring it from his laptop so it was of no concern to him. Maybe he had just forgotten. I took my shitty grey suit out of the suitcase and found the contact details that Wayne had given me. He answered the phone after a couple of rings.

'Whassup, bro. Wayne speaking.'

'Fucking hell, Wayne, grow up.'

'Who is this?'

'It's me, Gary. You know, your favourite customer at the café.'

'Oh right, shit suit Gary the big-nosed lawyer.'

'Yeah, how's it going?'

'Sweet, man, and by the way: you weren't my favourite customer. I gave that impression because I'm good at my job, helps create loyalty to the brand.'

'Brand *Wayne*?'

'Innit. So, what can I do for you, Gary?'

'Just catching up really. You still wearing that safari suit?'

'Nah, dungarees and a tweed jacket with Timberland boots. I intend to dominate the urban catwalk. You know me, I'm a lion not a sheep.'

'Sounds fucking awful, like a kids' TV presenter.'

'Says shitty suit guy.'

'So, where are you living, Wayne? In your dad's spare bedroom?'

'No, I'm in Brentwood, Essex, the carnival county. Got a pad above a nail bar. I've got my eyes on the lady that runs it, and I reckon it's just a matter of time before she's living very near to work.'

'Have you actually spoken to her yet?'

'No, you don't need to when you've got a body and the swag that I have. It will just happen naturally.'

'Well, you sound in good spirits. You not missing the coffee shop?'

'No way, I'm a new man already.'

'But it's only been a few days.'

'Yeah, but I've got more time on my hands and a lot less worries, and best of all I don't have to arse-lick idiots like you.'

'You wouldn't say that if you didn't love me. So, what's your plan?'

'I'm on it already, bro. I'm starting a vlog channel on YouTube, all about street food and street fashion – going to propel me right to the forefront. I've already edited the first one and it's a pip, a game changer.'

'Will you send it to me?'

'I fucking will.'

We chatted for a while more. I mentioned that if the vlog-
ging didn't take off ('No chance,' he insisted) I could put a
word in with Emily about him running the coffee shop at the
hotel. He thanked me but doubted that option would be needed.
The phone call cheered me up a degree or two. He hadn't
asked after me, so I assumed he still thought I was plodding
away as a lawyer in my shitty suit. It was best that he didn't
know otherwise.

I watched a bit of daytime TV and at lunchtime went downstairs to find Emily and see if she wanted me to cook her some
lunch. I found her and Mark on their hands and knees in the
dining room, applying some sort of sealant or varnish to the
wooden floor. They were both wearing face masks and protective gloves. The fumes were strong; it was obviously a very
serious bit of product.

'Hi, boss,' I said. 'You want me to put some lunch on?'

She pulled down her mask.

'I don't have the time. Could you just get me a sandwich
or something from the deli on Fourth Avenue? I can't stop
what we're doing 'til it's finished and then I'm helping Pete
with the last of the painting in the Blackcurrant room.'

'Would you like me to help?'

'No, that's okay, too many cooks and all that.'

Mark had chosen not to acknowledge my presence, but I
asked him if he wanted something fetching from the deli. He
looked up at me: 'Could you get me a banana?'

299

'Sure. Do you like them ripe or undercooked?'

He started to blink and tap his hand against his thigh.

'Just yellow, please. Would you agree?'

I nodded my head.

'Did you phone Wayne?' asked Emily.

'Yeah.'

'Any response from Sequence?'

'Nothing yet.'

Brian stopped me on my way out and asked where I was going. He seemed satisfied but stated again that he might follow me and he might not. I told him I was fine either way.

On my way to the deli, I tried to conjure up a daydream that would lift my spirits.

I imagined that I was wearing a large woven gold hat that drooped down to the small of my back. I was walking with a magnificent lion on the end of a golden lead and it was behaving impeccably in acknowledgement of my authority.

As I strode victorious down the street, startled onlookers gasped and waved. Children ran for their lives and passing cars slowed down to observe the wonder, pulling down their windows to laud me.

'Wow, Gary, that lion certainly knows who's boss!'

'What a remarkable man you are, Gary!'

'That's not a hat, it's a way of life!'

'I couldn't believe my eyes and then I saw it was you, Gary. It made perfect sense immediately.'

'That's more like a dwelling than a hat!'

'Brighton has never felt a safer place to live. Thank you, Gary.'

'Now that's what I call a tableau! Well done, son!'

It put a smile on my face for a moment and made me feel a bit brighter regarding my prospects. I would treat myself to a slice of cake in the deli. I ordered a campachoochoo and a slice of lemon drizzle then sat at a window table to watch the world go by. There was no sign of Brian. It was the first time since I'd arrived in Brighton that I actually felt content to be here. I accompanied each bite of drizzle cake with a mouthful of coffee and then kept the inside of my mouth static so that the cake dissolved into the coffee like a sinking ship. You can't really use this technique with a Battenberg – it's the one advantage that the drizzle has over the pink and yellow. The coffee had a hint of the ash tray and wasn't a patch on Wayne's Aldi dark-dark. I missed Wayne. It would be great if he took over Emily's coffee shop and brought a little bit of Peckham to the neighbourhood.

A man joined me at my table. Didn't ask for permission, just sat down and stared me dead in the face.

'Aren't you something to do with Emily and the hotel?'

'Err, yes, who's asking?'

'My name is Councillor James Jordan. I've been helping Emily with her application for planning permission for the massive avocado.'

'Oh, right, I see. Thank you for that.'

'Are you her boyfriend? Fiancé? Something like that?' he asked. 'I've seen you around the place from time to time. I have an interest in the buildings either side of the hotel so I'm often sniffing around. I've seen you sat on the bench with her and

I've seen you walking along hand in hand like you're in a fucking wet wipe advert.'

That made me laugh. He was about fifty, with a small face and greasy side-parted hair, and he was wearing a well-worn grey suit, which warmed me to him. His eyes were on the beady side of birdlike and his nose was as sharp as a nose could be without collapsing in on itself. He was unapologetically rude in his manner but interesting enough to indulge in a chat.

'I'm her boyfriend. I've just moved in with her, so I guess you'll be seeing a lot more of me when you're sniffing around.'

'Of course I will. Anyway, the thing is, the Planning Committee meets the day after tomorrow and I'm fifty/fifty which way the decision is going to go. I can't perform miracles.'

'I'm sure she understands that.'

'Do you know about that business with Tommy Briggs last year?'

'Yes, I do. In fact, I was there.'

'Well, then you must know that Briggs had some very strong connections here in Brighton with some very influential people.'

'I didn't, but carry on.'

'Well, it's come to my attention that these associates of Briggs don't want Emily to succeed in her new venture. They would rather she went bankrupt and suffered along the way. I suspect that they want to purchase the hotel and develop it themselves. They don't want her here in Brighton. They want some sort of revenge. I'm pretty sure they have a couple of councillors in their pockets and that could make the meeting on Wednesday very tricky. I thought she should know.'

'Why don't you tell her yourself?'

'Emily and I have agreed to remain discreet about our business arrangements and, anyway, it's probably better coming from you. You look the type who'll try to put a positive spin on the news.'

At that, he got up out of his seat and walked out of the deli. I probably should have chased after him and insisted on more information, but I didn't. I just sat there, blindsided, and let another lump of drizzle melt in my mouth.

On my way back to the hotel, I dialled Wayne's number two more times, ending both calls as soon as they rung at the other end. Even before I arrived at the hotel, Wayne phoned me back. I didn't answer. It was a nice bit of activity to draw Sequence in if he was monitoring the calls.

I decided not to tell Emily about my meeting with Jordan. I couldn't think of any way that it would be helpful for her to know what he had said. There was nothing she could do with the information. It would just be another slab of worry and stress on top of everything else.

Early evening, I phoned Wayne again.

'Hi, Wayne. I saw you called earlier. You want to follow up about running the coffee shop for Emily?'

'What you on about? You called *me*.'

'I didn't call you.'

'Yes, you did, and I've got the receipts here on my phone.'

'Shit, sorry, must have been a pocket dial or something.'

'Look, I've got to disengage. I've got a new handheld tripod for my phone and I can't get it vertical. It's doing my head in – how can I winfluence with a tripod that's on the wobble? See ya, bro.'

Another nice bit of telephone activity that might draw Sequence out into the open, I thought.

45

EMILY

Wednesday was a big day. Pete and I had finished the last two bedrooms and Mark had given his final approval to the ground-floor refurbishment. I had just over a week to arrange the final details. It was a scary time wrapped in a cloak of excitement. The Planning Committee was meeting this morning and it felt like the final piece of the jigsaw. The moment the giant avocado was raised onto its perch, I would know that the project had fruited and that it had a decent chance of success. At lunchtime I sat in the office with Brian looking over my shoulder, waiting for the email from the planning department telling me the decision. Eventually it dropped into my inbox.

Dear Ms Baker,

I regret to inform you that your planning application no. TP10447-9 has been refused. Full details of the decision will be available on the planning portal from 9:00am tomorrow and will be posted to you directly in due course.

Etc., etc., etc.

Brian read the email and offered me his condolences. I asked if I could leave the hotel to take the matter up directly with the planning officer at the Town Hall, to which he agreed.

'I understand the gravity of the situation,' he said.

He didn't understand the half of it, but I appreciated the gesture.

I shouted out for Mark and Pete to join me in reception and told them to get on immediately with hoisting the avocado into position. The pulley was already in position and a last bit of scaffolding had been left in place to provide a platform for the job.

'You got your permission, then?' said Pete. 'That's amazing news,' he said, holding his hand up to me for a high-five. I left it hanging and ran out of the hotel.

I didn't go to the Town Hall, of course. I marched myself straight round to the Albany Club to confront Jordan. He was bound to be there after his hard morning's work sat on his arse pissing on our agreement.

When I arrived, Kevin was at the reception. He stepped out from behind his desk to stop me in my tracks.

'Good afternoon, madam. Do you have a table reservation?'

'No, I do not. I'm here to see Councillor Jordan.'

I made a step towards the stairs to the first-floor dining room but Kevin blocked my path.

'Mr Jordan did not mention that a guest would be joining him today. I will need to check with him that that is in fact the case. You must wait here – patiently, if possible. No funny business like last time. Please take a seat. I will return shortly.'

'I'll come with you.'

'No, you won't.'

'Why not?'

'Because I am ferocious when it comes to application of the rules. I am your match, lady. Don't mess with me.'

He had a look in his eye that suggested he would relish the chance to manhandle my person, like he had a special move that he wanted to unleash on me. I sat down and festered as he disappeared upstairs. After he had been gone about five minutes, my patience ran out. I ran up the stairs and into the dining room. It was absolutely packed with diners, and their presence drained some of my courage. I felt myself shrink and deflate. The vast majority of the diners were men, and a percentage of them were already looking me up and down as if I was a magician's assistant. Jordan was nowhere to be seen.

To the left was a large open doorway with 'LIBRARY' written overhead on the architrave in gold lettering. I walked through, trying to adopt the gait of someone whose natural habitat was a shelved area. Jordan was sat on a winged chair to one side of a huge marble fireplace with a plate of lamb chops on a side table next to the chair. Kevin was stood beside him. Kevin saw me first and approached me at a pace and with great importance.

'Mr Jordan will see you for five minutes only. He agrees with me that this is all very irregular and that you are a signif-icant nuisance. I am to remain in the library to ensure things remain civil and that you are removed when the five minutes is expired.'

He pressed the start button on his phone stopwatch and

swished his arm to indicate I was free to approach Jordan. I sat on the winged chair to the other side of the fireplace. I was wearing my hiking anorak and the heat from the fire was instantly unbearable. I took the coat off to reveal the paint-tainted tracksuit bottoms and old 'meat is murder' T-shirt that I was wearing underneath. Jordan picked up a chop and poked it towards me as a means of emphasizing his words.

'I know you're disappointed, but that doesn't give you the right to march in here demanding my attention. Say your piece then fuck off.'

'I thought we had a deal,' I said, surprised at my composure.

'We did, but you didn't hold up your end.'

'Yes, I did. You got what you wanted on Monday – hand-delivered. Don't you dare say you didn't.'

'I will and I must. I didn't receive what I was due so I'm afraid I took a back seat at the meeting. It became an issue that didn't really interest me.'

'You're lying. I know you got what you wanted. I trust the person who delivered it one hundred per cent.'

'Who was it? Your boyfriend Gary?'

'No, it wasn't, and how the hell do you know my boyfriend's name?'

'We had a little chat on Monday. I tried to impress on him that the matter was still up in the air. I told him to inform you of my concern.'

I didn't know whether to believe him.

'I don't believe you,' I said.

'Seems he didn't pass on my concerns. Probably too worried

that he might upset you. That would make sense – he struck me as a bit of a shithouse. Probably didn't want to stick that big nose of his into a delicate situation.'

I started to believe him.

'I want my money back.'

'I never got your money so I have nothing to return. It's time for you to leave. You don't want to make an enemy of me, darling. Sounds like your real enemies are closer to home. I would have a chat with Gary if I were you. Goodbye.'

He began to bite into his chop as Kevin arrived by my side and put a hand on my shoulder.

'Come with me, please. Time is up.'

'Take your hands off me.'

He tightened his grip and pulled my coat off the chair behind me with his other hand. I jumped out of the chair to confront him and before I could blink an eye he had grabbed my head in his arms and trapped my neck in a chokehold. He was squeezing so tightly that I couldn't speak and could barely breathe. I was facing Jordan, who stared at me with amusement on his lips as he continued to suck away on his lamb chop. Kevin wasn't letting go or easing the pressure. I wondered if I should pretend to faint and hope that would stop him.

'Put her down, NOW!'

I glanced over to the doorway, which was filled by the frame of Brian brandishing some sort of telescopic cosh in his hand. Kevin didn't immediately let go of me, which caused Brian to stride towards us with the cosh raised above his head. Kevin released his grip and I fell to the floor, gasping for breath.

'Who the fuck are you?' shouted Kevin.

'I'm Brian and I'm a fucking nightmare. Pleased to meet you, squire. Are you alright, Emily?'

'Yes, I'm fine,' I replied, slowly recovering my faculties.

'Do you want me to teach him a lesson?'

'No, that's okay, I've got this.'

I turned my back on Kevin and delivered a donkey kick to his privates. It hit the sweet spot. I could feel the slight 'give' beneath my foot as it impacted. He doubled up and fell onto the library carpet.

'Oh my god! You terrible woman. Such a spiteful crunch.'

Jordan put down the lamb chop and applauded. Brian retracted his cosh and out we walked.

'Good luck!' shouted Jordan as we left the room.

'Why did you follow me?' I asked Brian on our way back to the hotel. 'You said you were happy for me to go out.'

'You had a look in your eye that said you were up to something. It's my job to spot these things and I'm good at my job. Are you okay?'

'Not really. I think someone has been lying to me and I don't deal very well with that sort of thing.'

46

GRACE

The weekend after my visit with Lizzie I invited Robert over for afternoon tea as a thank-you for taking me down to Lewes. When he arrived he had obviously made a bit of an effort. He was wearing a beige sports jacket, blue shirt, red cravat and freshly ironed blue jeans. He had a small bunch of flowers in his hand, which I thanked him for as best as I could.

'Thank you, Robert, how thoughtful of you. It's a lovely garage, isn't it? They sometimes do donuts half price on a Sunday.'

'Yes, they do,' he said, handing me a white paper bag with three jam donuts inside. We both laughed and I allowed him a little peck on my cheek by way of a greeting.

I sat him down on the sofa and went over to the little dining table under the window, where I had set out my display of sandwiches and cake.

'I've got pastrami and pickle [Lassoo barked twice], sliced ham and mustard [Lassoo barked once] and egg and cress [Lassoo stayed silent]. Which do you fancy?'

'That's quite a spread. You needn't have gone to so much bother on my account,' he replied.

'Don't you worry about that. I'll be eating anything that's left over. My appetite has gone through the roof since I saw Lizzie. It's like there was a balloon stuck in my stomach and she has popped it.'

'That's good news. Pastrami and pickle. Haven't had that for ages. I'll take a plate of those, please, Grace.'

'Good lad. It's my favourite – the only sandwich that gets near to being a meal in itself. It could almost be a flattened pie.'

'Or a keema naan.'

'Never heard of that. What is it?'

'It's a flat Indian bread with mince in the middle.'

'Well I never.' I said, admiringly. 'My friend Gary, the neighbour I told you about, he loved his pies and his cakes.'

'Has he been in touch?'

'Nah, busy time for him, I reckon. I'll speak to him as soon as things slow down for him.'

'You really miss him, don't you? Did you say he's a lot younger than you?'

'Yeah, he's only thirty. But it didn't seem to get in the way. We always had a laugh and that's what it's all about, isn't it?'

'I reckon it is. Not being rude or anything, but that's quite an age difference. You wouldn't think he would want to hang around with an oldie. He must have had his own set of friends.'

'Not really; a bloke that he watched the football with down

the pub and his girlfriend Emily. I reckon I'm probably his best friend, we could be mother and son and ain't that strange but lovely.'

'My son's lost interest in me really – brought it home to me when you saw Lizzie. I'm pretty much on my own. I need to get myself a Gary.'

'Hey, hands off – he's mine. Now eat your sandwiches; I want to see if you're a muncher or a gnawer.'

We chatted about our pasts for a while and gave each other a snapshot of our lives. He seemed a bit lost, but not desperate, and there was a calmness about him that I liked. I wished he wasn't bald, but hey, I'm nothing much to look at and he didn't seem to mind. We finished all the sandwiches apart from a couple of egg and cress. I put them on the floor for Lassoo. He took a sniff and looked up at me as if to say 'Do you really hate me that much?'

It was time to find out if he liked to watch the TV. There was no future for our friendship if he was one of those snobs that hated the television. I took a chance and sat by him on the sofa as I turned it on and tuned into *New Zealand Border Patrol*. I awaited his response and it was pretty instant.

'*Border Patrol*. I absolutely love this show.'

We watched three episodes back to back. He didn't get a single case wrong, nailed every one of them in what Gary and I used to call 'a doubler', i.e., he guessed their guilt and he guessed the contraband they were carrying. He was a natural. Maybe there was a future for this budding friendship.

He left early evening and I was sad when he was gone. He

invited me out the following Friday for a meal and a drink at a restaurant near to where he lived. I accepted the invitation on the condition that he didn't wear a cravat. He agreed but insisted that I left Lassoo at home. I said I would think about it.

47

EMILY

I returned to the hotel to find the avocado already in position above the front entrance between the windows of the two first-floor front rooms. Mark and Pete were just fiddling with the fixings at the base of the flagpole. It looked magnificent – not quite as huge as I had expected now it was in position, and dwarfed slightly by the frontage of the building, but still magnificent. There was no doubting it would cause an instant furore, and that was all I required from it. I bet it would take months for them to force me to remove it, and by that time its job would be done. Pete shouted down a greeting that I ignored with the utmost sincerity. He had some explaining to do, and the rest.

I went straight up to the apartment and found Gary sat at the dining table eating tinned tomatoes on toast.

'Have you seen the avocado?' I asked.

'What do you mean?'

'The avocado – it's up and in position.'

'I didn't know. When did that happen?'

'It's just gone up. They're just finishing off the fixings. Did you not hear them or think to give them a hand?'

'I didn't think you wanted me getting involved – too many cooks an' that. Would you like some tinned tomatoes on toast? It's a great celebratory snack.'

'No, I wouldn't, but I would like an explanation from you.'

'About what?'

'Why didn't you tell me that you spoke to Councillor Jordan on Monday and that he told you he hadn't received the payment from me?'

'Hold on, he never mentioned anything about a payment. What payment? What are you on about?'

I could tell instantly that he was telling the truth; I always know with Gary. It's one reason we get on so well: he's more or less incapable of lying without giving himself away with a tick or a slide in his voice.

'So, what *did* you talk about?'

'He just told me that there were other councillors on the committee that didn't want to grant the permission. Apparently some of them have connections to Tommy Briggs' old gang and would rather you didn't succeed with the hotel. That's it. I couldn't think of a single reason why that information would be helpful to you. I wanted to protect you from such bullshit; it's not like it's something you can have any control over.'

I had heard these rumours before, that some influential people in the town wanted me to fail. But I had never heard that these people were connected to Tommy Briggs. I wished for a fleeting moment that my father could return for a week or so to deal with these people and guide me through this mess. All I had was Gary and his big daft nose and I wasn't confident that he would be the one to see me through.

'So, tell me about this payment,' said Gary. 'I'm thinking it sounds a bit dodgy. What have you been up to?'

I explained to him about the 'gift' and how it was just the continuation of an arrangement between my father and Jordan. I told him I had asked Pete to deliver the money but it would appear that he had failed to do that. I could tell he was disappointed in me but he made no comment.

'Shall we go and confront him?' he asked.

'I'd rather do it myself, thanks. I think you being there would confuse the situation.'

'What about the tinned tomatoes on toast?'

'Fuck tomatoes on toast; it's a kid's meal. I'll go and find him now. Wish me luck.'

I found Pete outside the hotel on a stepladder, making adjustments to a spotlight so that it shone the full length of the avocado's flank. Once he was done, I asked if we could have a chat on the bench over the road by the bus stop. His face dropped; he knew he was in trouble. Before sitting down, we both turned to look back at the freshly hung fruit. It looked extraordinary, beautiful even. Whatever Pete was about to tell me, I would always be grateful to him for suggesting the avocado display. Brian had positioned himself at the top of the steps to keep an eye on us.

'So, you got permission. That's a miracle.'

'No, I didn't, Pete, and I'm surprised that you think I might have.'

'Why do you say that?'

'Because you didn't give the money to Jordan, did you? And don't lie to me, Pete. This is far too important for any of your bullshit. I'm feeling on the ropes here.'

He hunched over, stared at his knees, rose upright again and started to rub his thighs. He didn't answer me.

'Come on, Pete, tell me what you've done.'

He got up, walked to the railings at the edge of the prom and again dipped his head towards the floor.

'I fucked up,' he said without turning to face me. His head shook as if he was crying. I told him to come and sit on the bench.

'Come on, spill the beans, Pete. Let's get this over and done with.'

'That night when the fancy-haired bloke came to the flat. Well, when I left, he was waiting for me outside. He made me sit on this bench with him. He's a nasty bastard, so I did what I was told. He went on at me for a while about whether I had overheard anything in the flat. He took a bit of persuading but eventually he seemed to believe me.'

'*Did* you overhear anything?'

'No, absolutely not.'

'Okay. Go on,' I prompted.

'Then he started to ask me questions about you and Gary, how close you were, how serious your relationship was. I told him you were pretty solid as far as I could tell. He asked me if I had any intentions towards you and I said something flippant like, "Chance would be a fine thing". He didn't like that.

He said that if he ever found out I was trying to bother you he would kick my head in every day for the following month. He's evil, Emily. How the fuck did you get involved with him?'

'Well, that's complicated. Carry on.'

'He told me that I mustn't ask you or Gary about his visit or about his mate staying at the hotel. He said that would be "too upsetting for everyone involved". I asked him why his friend was staying and he said they were doing a favour for you and making sure that everything ran smoothly up until the hotel opening. I didn't have a clue what that meant. I half wondered if you had hired him because one of Tommy Briggs' old mates was making trouble for you or handing out threats.'

I shrugged my shoulders. 'So, the money, Pete. What happened with it?'

'He suddenly changed his tune and got all pally with me, asked me if I wanted any drugs. He had a massive bag of coke, the most I've ever seen in my life, and I've been around a lot of the stuff. I suppose you've probably guessed, it's the way I get through the days. This work is so soul-destroying.'

'I didn't know you were on it all day. Bloody hell, Pete, that's crazy.'

'I know, it's fucked up. I'm so sorry.'

'Sorry for what?'

'He offered me the bag for five hundred pounds, which was about half of what it was worth. I paid him out of your envelope. I'm so sorry, Emily, I was going to replace the money the next day . . .'

'Why didn't you, then?'

319

'He grabbed the envelope and saw the name Councillor Jordan on it. He asked me what the money was for and I said it was just a debt I was repaying. He didn't believe me. And you won't believe what happened next.'

'Try me.'

'He pulled a polythene bag out of his coat pocket and it was full of mince – beef mince. I kid you not, a bag of fucking mince! He grabbed the back of my head and forced the meat into my face. I couldn't breathe; I thought I was going to die if he didn't stop. I was suffocating, proper suffocating. "*Eat the mince, eat the beef,*" he kept saying. I had to tell him or I was a goner.'

'I believe you. And then what?'

'He told me that I should never have got involved in such a scam and that he would do me a favour and deliver the money himself. He said it was just the kind of work that you had asked him to carry out for you. I wasn't to tell you about the change of plan and I could keep the drugs. I don't know why but I believed him when he said he was working for you.'

'You mean you *chose* to believe him so you could scamper off with your little bag of drugs. Sorry, Pete, but you have let me down really badly.'

'But, Emily, the avocado is up, the rooms are finished; we've been a good team. I want to be around for the opening. Please don't be like this.'

'You've messed everything up, Pete. Look, I'm grateful for all your help, and as you say the job is more or less done. Let's leave it at that and call it a day. I don't want you around anymore.'

I got up and walked back into the hotel. Gary wasn't in the

apartment so I went into my bedroom and poured myself onto the bed. I'd lost a good friend and it hurt. I tried to drift off to sleep but my heart was pounding loudly in my chest and ears. I had no real anger towards Pete, but my brain was filled with hatred for Sequence and Jordan. I imagined the revenge I would take if the chance came along. Jordan was easy; I would strip him naked in front of all the members of the Albany Club and feed lamb chops up his arse until he collapsed with a heart attack. Sequence I would like to poison; I would lock him in a room with a live camera feed and watch him writhe and contort in agony as the poison began to dissolve his body. Hopefully all that would be left of him would be a pool of blood and guts with his ridiculous hairstyle floating on the top. I could mount the hair onto a pole and display it on the roof of the hotel. That would feel like proper revenge.

My fantasy was interrupted when Gary popped his head around the door and asked if I was okay. I told him that I'd sacked Pete off and that he wouldn't be around anymore. Gary didn't smile or acknowledge the moment in any way at all. I expect he didn't dare. He changed the subject in a millisecond and said he wanted me to come and see something that would cheer me right up. He took my hand, helped me off the bed and walked me down to the front bedroom on the second floor. I had named this room 'Kiwi' and filled it with various items of 'hairy' green furnishings; a green shag-pile rug, a darker green sheepskin throw on the bed, a lime-green fun-fur easy chair by the window and dark green curtains made out of a highly tufted material the manufacturer described as 'tactile and compelling'. The curtains were hung on a long old-fashioned wood and bristle broom. A big map of New Zealand hung above the mantelpiece with a hundred or so nails standing proud on its frame, all lovingly hammered in place by Mark. Gary hated the room; said it looked more like a display in a garden centre than a bedroom. It was my favourite.

'I love this room,' I said, full of pride at what I had achieved.

'I still think you should have put some lawn care products and some buckets in here – you know, to complete the hardware shop theme.'

He beckoned me over to the window.

'Look outside,' he said with schoolboy excitement. 'You're not going to believe it.'

I looked out down to the promenade. There was a crowd of people staring up at the giant avocado. And the number kept growing as nearly every passerby stopped in their tracks to stare at the massive fruity beast. People were taking photographs and manoeuvring themselves so that the avocado would be in the background of their selfies.

'It's incredible,' gushed Gary. 'I reckon that only about one person in twenty can resist stopping and having a gawp. The traffic even keeps stopping while the drivers have a good old stare. It's worked, Emily, you're on the map. In fact, as far as Brighton is concerned, you're on the front page.'

Then he seemed to have a thought and took my phone out of his pocket.

'Fucking hell, Emily, you're trending. Well, at least the massive avocado is. Look at all these tweets! Just look at them.'

I took the phone and scrolled down through the seemingly endless stream of photos of my hotel. The avocado was a news story. It had already been picked up by the local newspaper and regurgitated by the *Daily Mail*. I could have cried with happiness. *See that, Dad, that's your daughter, that is*, I said to myself, and then the tears came. Gary picked me up and hugged me.

I looked over his shoulder at the bus stop opposite. Councillor Jordan was stood on his own, staring up at the fruit with a face like a constipated fox. Then he suddenly jerked his head and shoulders, looked up to the sky and stared at the shoulder of his jacket. He appeared to have been shat on by a pigeon.

48

GARY

Wednesday was always going to be fraught. For Emily, it was the day of the Planning Committee meeting, and for me it was the day when I would have to decide whether Emily's phone was safe for us to use to contact DS Marks. When I woke up, Emily had already left the apartment to get on with her business. She had left her phone by the kettle for me. We would just have to hope that Brian didn't question her about not having it on her person.

I still hadn't had any response from Sequence regarding the phone calls to and from Wayne. That was a positive. It was time to make contact with Roma. First up, I telephoned my old office and left a message for Roma to contact me on Emily's number. The receptionist didn't recognize my voice or name until I reminded her. She didn't make any enquiry as to how I was faring, or express any desire to know. Roma phoned an hour or so later.

'Hi, Gary, I'm in my car but I got your message to ring. How's it going? You with your family still?'

'Yeah, what's left of it. How are you getting on without me?'

'Doing good. I'm glad you phoned – gives me a chance to update you on Grace.'

I felt a pang of guilt. I hadn't given Grace a moment's thought since we said goodbye. I remembered the slice of Battenberg she'd given me and wondered what I had done with it. Probably left it in the car.

'Yeah,' I replied, 'that's one of the reasons I'm phoning. How is she? What's been going on?'

'She's better than ever. Claims she's got a new lease of life since she had her access visit with her daughter and Lizzie.'

'Shit, she's been to see her? When did it happen?'

'Last week. She was with Lizzie for forty minutes or so. She loved it. Never seen her so happy. I took a photo straight after; I'll send it to you.'

'That's brilliant. Give her my love, won't you?'

'Yes, I will. She misses you, Gary. You should give her a call, so she can tell you all about it.'

'I will. How's Blenkingstop treating you?'

'He just ignores me. It's like I don't exist, which is fine by me. He probably thinks I miss his attention.'

'Yeah, you must miss the gropings and the humour.'

'Oh, yeah, it's a big hole in my life. So, what is it you wanted?'

'Wanted to ask you a favour, but it's best if you're in the office. Just want a phone number off my old computer.'

'Yeah, sure, no problem. I won't be back 'til this afternoon. I'll ring you then.'

'Thanks, Roma.'

A few minutes later a message came through from Roma. 'Look at her face!' it said, and attached was a photograph of Grace and Roma beaming into the camera as if they'd just watched the release of a beloved hedgehog back into the wild. There was a man's arm around her shoulder, which intrigued me. I messaged back asking who the arm belonged to.

THAT'S GRACE'S NEW FRIEND ROBERT. HE GAVE HER A LIFT TO THE MEETING. NICE BLOKE . . . I THINK GRACE MIGHT FANCY HIM!

That made me smile. Trust Grace to be the one that cheered me up. Poor bloke didn't know what he was getting into. I was glad she had made a connection with someone, though I would definitely be vetting him when I got the chance.

By mid-afternoon there had been no response from Sequence to my calls with Roma — a good sign. I was in the bedroom called Kiwi, idly watching people walking up and down the promenade, when Roma phoned me back as promised. I decided to take a chance and go ahead and ask her for the favour. It was shit or bust.

'I wondered if you would be willing to help me set up a meeting with a policeman called DS Marks. I can't do it myself because of what I can only call reasons. It's nothing dodgy, I just need to speak to him in confidence about a private matter. As soon as he knows it's me asking, he'll be fine. We go back a long way.'

'Yeah, sure, have you got his number?'

'No, I've lost it. It's listed in my contacts as his personal mobile.'

'So, when and where do you want to meet him?'

'There's a pub in Peacehaven called the Dun Cow. Sometime around midday on Friday would be perfect.'

'Where on earth is Peacehaven? Sounds like an old folks' home.'

'It's just outside of Brighton.'

'That's a big ask, isn't it?'

'I'm pretty sure he'll do it for me. If he agrees, just text me a smiley face or a thumbs-up or something.'

'Okay then, I'll try and arrange it. Talking of coppers, I've had a visit from one earlier this week trying to serve a witness summons on you. I told him you weren't living here at the moment and that I didn't have a forwarding address. Is that something to do with why you're wanting this meeting?'

'Yeah, something like that. Thanks for doing this, Roma. See you soon, I hope.'

So, the police were aware that I might need tracking down. It wouldn't take them long to start sniffing around Emily and the hotel. If they did, then it could make things awkward. They would serve the summons on me, Sequence would undoubtedly find out about it and then take some drastic action against Emily and me. I needed it to be DS Marks dealing with the case. The fact that the summons had not been served might just help encourage him to take the meeting with me.

The phone call made me nervous and I instantly regretted making it. I would find out soon enough if Sequence had been listening in and if it had been a dangerous mistake. I stared through the bedroom window and out to the sea, hoping for a calming effect. It was then I began to notice a small crowd gathering opposite the hotel, and that nearly every person that passed by was looking up at it and taking photographs on their phones. The giant avocado was causing something of a local sensation. I went up to the apartment and fetched Emily down to the Kiwi room so that she could witness the furore herself.

To say she was chuffed would be an understatement, and when I showed her the fuss it was causing on Twitter she nearly burst with excitement. We hugged on account of the success of the green beast. It was a glimmer of hope for a future where Sequence was out of our lives. Hopefully that would be very soon, provided Roma came good with DS Marks. That thought brought on the fear again along with another rush of doubt about the wisdom of using Emily's phone.

That fear was all but confirmed when Brian entered the room and took the phone out of my hands.

'You been using Emily's phone, Gary?'

'Yes, just to phone an old friend and the solicitors I worked for until last Friday.'

'And do you think that is something my boss would approve of? Because my instant answer would be a very plump *no.*'

'Brian, I phoned up my old mate Wayne, who your boss knows, to ask if he would be interested in running the café that Emily is going to open downstairs. Nothing dodgy at all. And I phoned up my old office to ask a colleague to take some things I'd left there and drop them off at my flat. I presumed you would be listening in on the calls so I'm not going to do anything stupid.'

'I know who you've phoned, Gary, and I'm sure those calls were innocent. You're too much of a shithouse to stir the pot but, having said that, I think maybe you should give the phone to me for safe keeping. If Emily needs to make a call, she can do it in my presence. Does that work for you, Emily?'

'Not like I've got a choice, is it?'

'Correct.'

So, I reasoned to myself, *they could see who I was phoning, but not the contents of the call.* Big moment.

49

GARY

THE DAY BEFORE THE MEETING

On Thursday, the day before the possible meeting with DS Marks, I woke up before Emily and went through to the kitchen to make us both some breakfast. I kept expecting Sequence to ring any moment and interrogate me about my telephone chats with Roma. My nerves were bagged and the toast burnt without me noticing. I hated the phone being in Brian's possession. What if Roma sent a message and gave the game away? Worse still, what if she ignored my instructions and actually rang Emily's phone? Brian might answer and take a message or perhaps start chatting and get the truth out of her. I should have been clearer and more insistent with my instructions to Roma. I had fucked up. I had wanted today to be a pleasant day, a diverting one to see if me and Emily could still enjoy each other's company amongst all the bullwater, but that didn't seem possible in my current state of unease. Best thing I could do was pretend to be on top of things and not pass my needles on to Emily.

Emily joined me in the kitchen already dressed for the day and with springs in her step.

'We need to get your phone off Brian,' I said.

'Good morning to you as well, in case you're interested.'

'Sorry. Hello, Emily, did you have a good sleep?'

'Best I've had since you arrived. What's your big panic about the phone?'

'I'm worried Roma might message or call and give the game away to Brian.'

'I thought you told her just to send a happy face or something if the meeting was on?'

'I did, but I've got a bad feeling about it. I don't know if Roma realizes the shit that we're in. I had to be a bit cryptic on the phone and she's a bit scatty – you know, a bit light-hearted about things.'

Emily put her business face on, which I was pleased to see. If it had been her angry face, then it might have indicated an incoming tomato kick.

'How would you describe these next few days, Gary?'

'Err, important? Scary? I don't know – *the be-all and end-all*?' I ventured.

'They are *pivotal*, Gary, that's what they are: pivotal to my future, your future and the future of the hotel. You need to get calm, get focused and get a serious head on. I had better get down to the office and sit there with the phone in front of me, which means you will have to get off your arse and put up all the paintings that I've laid out in the halls and landings. Do you know how nails work?'

'Yes, you hit them on the head with a hammer.'

'Well, off you go, then. You never know, the practice might come in useful if your little plan backfires. Do you feel me?'

'I do. Thanks for supporting me and . . . well, yeah, just thanks for supporting me and everything.'

'Pop down to the office every hour or so. Brian lets me have the phone when I'm with him. I'll give you a "Viva tomatoes" if Roma's confirmed the meeting. And keep your burner phone with you in case Sequence calls to tell you he's on to you. You might need to do a runner. If that's the case, try to say goodbye before you go.'

And off she went to reclaim and coddle the phone and hopefully save my bacon. So much for the pleasant day I had been hoping for.

I borrowed Mark's toolkit and set about hanging the pictures. It proved a good way of taking my mind off things. By lunch-time I had hung ten pictures, some with nails and some with screws and wall plugs. I began to consider myself a tradesman and even caught myself whistling as I stepped back to admire my work. I had popped down to the office a couple of times but received no 'Viva tomatoes' from Emily. I made a tray of sandwiches and a pot of tea for Emily and Brian and took them down to the office.

'Lunchtime,' I announced as I backed in through the office door.

'Here he comes. Mister Jittery Thoughtful, the King of Woe.'

It was Sequence. I immediately assumed he was here because I was busted. He must have found out about the meeting. He had bluffed me a good 'un with the phone. He had probably listened to every word. I began to shake, and the tea pot lid started to rattle. I looked at Emily, and she looked up from the computer screen.

'Hi, Gary, look who's here. Great news, isn't it?' said Emily.

'Wye aye,' I said, hoping that the pretence of being a Geordie might in some way endear me to Sequence and persuade him to go easy on me. It did cross my mind to just put the tray down, say goodbye to Emily and walk out of the office straight into the sea and let my lungs fill with cold salty water, but the expression on Emily's face suggested there was no need to do a Lucan.

'You would not believe the amount of bookings that have come through this morning,' said Emily with excitement jogging along with her voice. 'I've got some rooms with reservations right through to September. Can you believe it?'

'Wye aye,' I said.

'It's that fucking bulky avocado out front,' said Sequence. 'It's drawing them in just like that "World's Biggest Ball of Twine" they've got in America. Have you heard about that, Gary?'

'Wye aye.'

'I'm very surprised that you got planning permission for that monstrosity,' said Sequence.

'I didn't,' said Emily.

'Woman after my own heart,' replied Sequence.

I put the tray down on the table. I was still shaking a bit; not too bad, but Sequence noticed.

'Are you shaking, Gary? Have you done something that you shouldn't? Or are you just scared of me?'

'I'm just worried about the whole situation and you make me nervous. Can't help it.'

'That's good to know. That's how it should be. Have you ever thought about how I'm feeling, Gary? Do you not think that I've got worries to deal with? If I don't pull this off and keep you away from next week's trial, you cannot begin to imagine what my clients would do to me.'

'Would they stuff lamb chops up your arse?' said Emily with a fixed grin aimed directly at Sequence's face.

Sequence laughed. 'They might well do that. In fact, that wouldn't be a bad way to go. I shall mention it to them if it ever comes to pass.'

'I reckon they might scalp you,' I suggested. 'Put your scalp on display at the end of the pier. "World's Biggest Hairstyle." Could be a bigger draw than the ball of twine.'

'Shut up, Gary,' said Sequence, 'And leave the jokes to Emily. She's the funny one here – well, her and me. Brian's a bit dreary like you, Gary. Aren't you, Brian?'

'Yeah, I reckon,' said Brian. 'What's in the sandwiches?' he asked me.

'Corned beef and onion, cheese and—' I started to say.

'I hate onions,' interrupted Brian.

'Hold on, I'm not finished yet.' I continued: 'Cheese and onion . . .'

'He just told you,' said Sequence, 'he doesn't like onions. Come to think, I'm not that fussed either. And anyway, what's with the onions? It's not the 1970s anymore; you'll be offering me tinned potato salad next.'

'Hold your horses. There's still another option.' I continued: 'Cheese and onion or ham and—'

Brian interrupted again. 'Don't tell me, ham and fucking onion.'

'Can you let me finish, please?' I asked.

'You had better not be about to say onion,' said Sequence.

'To be honest,' I said, 'you shouldn't interrupt a bloke when he's reading out a list. It messes up the rhythm, sucks all the energy. You know what, I'm tempted to start at the top of the list again.'

'Don't you dare fucking do that, son,' said Sequence. 'I accept it was rude to interrupt, but I've already noted the first two onion options and I'm ready for the next reveal.'

Brian leant forward slightly menacingly. 'I should warn you that this next option better not include onion. In fact, I don't want to hear the word onion spoken again. It's beginning to turn my stomach.'

I noticed Emily glance down at the screen of her phone that was nestled tight in front of her on the desk.

'Well, thanks for the apology. I'll carry on, then. Ham and tomato . . .'

'Viva tomato!' shouted Emily.

'Really?' I asked her.

'Yes, really,' she replied, her eyes widening as she said it to confirm that it was the 'Viva tomato' I had been praying for.

'If she has the ham and tomato, then I don't have a non-onion option. That is a fucking nightmare,' said Brian.

'Agreed,' said Sequence. 'A literal fucking nightmare.'

In my sudden euphoria I told them I would take the onion options back up to the apartment and make them whatever sandwiches they fancied.

'What bread have you got?' asked Sequence.

'White sliced.'

'Have you got any tinned tomatoes?' asked Brian.

'Yes, four cans of them at my last count.'

'Do you have a toaster?' asked Sequence.

'Yes, a four-slicer.'

'Can I have tomatoes on toast, please?' said Brian.

'I'll jump on that too please, Gary, and thank you,' said Sequence.

'Of course you can. Viva tomatoes!' I said.

'Viva tomatoes!' said Brian with a thumbs–up and a schoolboy grin on his face.

'Viva fucking tomatoes!' shouted Sequence, running a hand through his luscious hair and taking a great big draw on his vape. 'Now, get them onion–tainted ones out of here before Brian is sick.'

I glanced at Emily before leaving the room. She was turning off her phone. No more calls. No more worry on that front. The meeting was on. DS Marks to the rescue. Viva tomatoes indeed.

50

GRACE

A couple of hours after Robert left following the *Border Patrol* viewing session, Roma arrived at the flat and plonked herself down on my sofa for a chat. She had a cheeky grin on her face.

'What?' I asked.

'What?' she said, refusing to give up on the grin.

'What you smiling at?'

'You,' she replied.

'Why?'

'No reason. You just look happy, and that makes me smile.'

'Don't be so daft. You want a cup of tea? I'm going to have a lager if you'd prefer something stronger.'

'Lager, please. Been a long day.'

I went through to the kitchen.

'So, how did it go with Robert?' shouted Roma. 'I see most of the spread has gone. He must have a good appetite. I like that in a bloke.'

'Yeah, he's got a decent stomach on him and likes a bit of pastrami, which is a big plus in this gaff.'

'So, you like him, then?'

'Stop prying. What's it to you anyway?'

'Like I just said, I like seeing you happy, and maybe this Robert can play a part in that.'

'I wouldn't get ahead of yourself if I was you. He wears cravats.'

'Oh shit, that's bad.'

'Isn't it. He's taking me out for a meal on Friday and I've told him if he's wearing a cravat I'm doing a runner.'

'So, you're having another date. Sounds very promising.'

'Maybe. Can we shut up about him, please?'

Lassoo jumped up on the sofa and lay between us as if he wanted to join in with the chat.

'So, when do you reckon I can see Lizzie again?' I asked.

'I'm trying to arrange another meet down in Lewes at the end of the month. Haven't heard back yet. I won't be coming with you this time. Waste of your money to have me there, to be honest.'

'I'll be okay with Robert.'

She started grinning again.

'What?' I asked.

'You know fine well.'

'No, I don't.'

'Yes, you do.'

'Oh fuck off and drink your drink,' I said.

We had a lovely night in, watching telly and getting a little bit pissed. She was a lot happier now that she had her own place to live but she hadn't made any new connections here in London apart from me and I suppose Gary. She missed having Gary at work; he was apparently the only one who gave her the time of day. She reckoned that her boss was leaning on the other staff to ostracize her. It wasn't any fun, but she was determined to see her year through to please her mum back home.

Before she left, she asked me if I would read her a bit of the *Billy's Bus* story. I agreed and gave her the bell to ring whenever the word bus was mentioned.

'Billy was eating a sardine as he drove the *bus* . . .'

Roma rang her bell: *Ding.*

Lassoo barked: *Rrughhh.*

'. . . to the next *bus stop* . . .'

Roma: *Ding.*

Lassoo: *Rrugghhh.*

'. . . outside the park gates. It was an unusual *bus stop* . . .'

Roma: *Ding.*

Lassoo: *Rrugghhh.*

'. . . because it had a carving of a monkey on its pole. "Why is there a monkey on that *bus stop*?" asked Buttery Ken.'

Roma: *Ding.*

Lassoo: *Rrugghhh.*

'Buttery Ken had never been on the *bus* before . . .'

Roma: *DING.*

Lassoo: *RRUGGHHH.*

We laughed like drains. I liked Roma very much and I hoped that she liked me. She would be leaving in eight months' time and I would miss her when she went. Another parting of ways, but I wasn't going to let that eventuality get in the way this time. I had promised Gary I would stop keeping people at arm's length and engage more with the world. Just try and enjoy what's left of my life. Roma and Robert were a small step in the right direction. I was well chuffed with myself.

51

GARY

THE NIGHT BEFORE THE MEETING

'Do you think we're going to be alright?' I asked Emily as we lay in bed on Thursday night, both waiting for sleep to arrive in any of its forms.

'Maybe, maybe not. I keep wondering if Brian might just set fire to the hotel tonight and be done with us.'

'That's not going to happen. Far too messy and there's absolutely no need for them to do it. As far as Sequence is concerned, we're going along with his plan, and victory and payment will soon be his.'

'What you think DS Marks will do?' asked Emily.

'I think he will offer to take me somewhere safe, arrest Sequence and his mate and make sure they aren't granted bail until after the trial is over.'

'What about me?'

'Probably offer you a safe place as well, if I insist, but my guess is that when Sequence is out of the picture you would rather just stay at the hotel and get everything ready for the opening. I mean, once I'm in DS Marks' arms it's over for Sequence really.'

Silence followed as we both willed that to be true.

'I didn't tell you,' said Emily, breaking the pause, 'but it was Sequence that took the cash that was meant for Councillor Jordan. He took it off Pete before he could deliver it. Very clever of him, really, putting more pressure on me like that. I hope I never ever see him or his hairstyle again.'

'I'm sure you won't. He'll be in prison or moved on to a different victim, told to mess up someone else's life. I doubt he feels anything personal. This is all just a job to him. There's no way I can get to sleep. You don't fancy a walk, do you?'

'Do you know what, I *would* like that,' she replied.

We got dressed and walked down to the reception. Brian was in the office, watching something on his laptop.

'Hi, Brian,' said Emily. 'We're just popping out for a walk along the beach. Does that meet with your approval?'

'Bit late for that, isn't it?'

'We can't sleep,' she said.

'Guilty conscience, is it?'

'No, Brian, more likely just the moon and the tides and the presence of you and your boss in our lives.'

'You give me too much credit. I'm here to help, I really am.'

'Oh, and could I take my phone, please? I want to take some photos of the avocado from the promenade and check my messages.'

'You haven't had any messages,' he replied.

'Well, to take some photos, then.'

'Yeah, go on. But no outgoing calls, okay?'

'Agreed. I suppose you'll be coming with us?' asked Emily.

'Yes, I will. Got to make sure you don't do a midnight run together. I'll keep my distance. You won't even notice me.'

'What are you watching?' I asked.

'*Ace Ventura: Pet Detective*. I don't get it. I just don't get the idea of it,' replied Brian.

'Yeah, it's a tricky one. You need to watch it a few times really.'

'Really? That's a pain.'

'I think it would be for the best, Brian – you know, if you want to really understand it.'

'I do. I really do,' he concluded.

We walked up the promenade towards the Palace Pier. Brian was true to his word and kept a good twenty yards behind us. It was approaching midnight and there were only a few people around, a few drunks outside the conference centre and a gaggle of lasses outside the Grand Hotel.

'That's where Sequence is staying,' I said, pointing up towards The Grand.

'Hey, should we go up to his room and do him in?' said Emily.

'I haven't got any lamb chops with me, sorry,' I replied.

'Shame,' said Emily as we walked down some steps onto the beach and sat on the dry pebbles under the pier. Brian stayed up on the promenade, staring down at us from the railings, but well out of earshot.

'Do you think I'm doing the right thing?' I asked.

'Yep. DS Marks is the only option.'

'No, I mean, coming down here and moving in with you.'

'Why are you asking me that?' she asked.

'Because I feel that since I arrived my presence has been nothing but a pain in the arse for you.'

'That's not right,' she replied. 'It's not *you* that's the problem; it's the situation you've found yourself in. We're in this together, mate, come rain come shine, good times bad times, viva tomatoes or tinned tomatoes.'

She turned to face me. The lights from the pier above us shone through the slits in the boardwalk and danced on her face. She looked absolutely beautiful. It was the actual moment that I fell in love with her forever. She was, and would always be, the love of my life. I had made the right decision.

'Did I thank you for putting up with everything?' I asked.

'Yes, too many times. It's beginning to get on my nerves,' she replied with a beaming smile.

I asked for her phone so I could take a photo to remember this moment. It was a nice shot. We both looked very happy. I checked Twitter to see if the avocado was still making a splash. It was; a whole new raft of photos and comments had appeared of the spotlit beast in the evening light. I showed Emily.

'Love it,' she said proudly. 'That's my hotel, that is.'

I checked the messages screen for any activity. There was nothing new. The last message from Roma was the one with the photograph of her and Grace after the meeting with Lizzie.

'Did you see the photo of Grace that Roma sent?' I asked.

She shook her head, so I showed her the screen. She smiled at first and then her face went all curious.

'I know that woman,' she said.

'That's Roma from work,' I replied. 'I didn't think you'd ever met.'

Emily's eyes widened and her face indicated sudden worry.

'No, I didn't think we had either, but whoever that woman is with Grace is the woman I saw at the Coroners' Court on the day I gave evidence about Tommy's death. I'm sure of it. She attacked me. She's something to do with the Briggs family. She said that Tommy would still be here if it wasn't for me. If it hadn't been for the security guard that stepped in, I think she would've ripped my head off and kicked it over the moon. Why the fuck would she be in Peckham working at your office? Jesus, she's actually living in your flat. Something is not right here, Gary.'

I asked her if she was one hundred per cent sure. She enlarged Roma's face on the screen and had a good long thoughtful stare at it.

'Shit, it's hard to be certain. Hair seems a bit longer and maybe darker than I remember, but the eyes – shit, it looks like her. I'm going to say eighty-five per cent sure – no, seventy-five per cent. That is so weird. It can't just be a coincidence, can it?'

'I think it probably can. If you think she might be working with Sequence I reckon you are way off the mark. She's been a big help to us. I would put that line of thought in the bread bin to rot.'

'No, you're right, I don't think she can be. It was her you asked to arrange the meeting with DS Marks. If she was working with Sequence, we would already be locked up in some basement somewhere or have been drowned in a bath of minced beef. I just think it's very odd – a bit spooky.'

She looked at the photograph again.

'Oh, I don't know. I can't be sure. Maybe I'm just going a bit bonkers with all the nonsense that's going on.'

'I think we both are,' I replied, putting my arm around her.

She shivered slightly, vibrated her head and chatted her teeth deliberately so that she, effectively, appeared to be moronic.

'Shall we get back now?' she asked. 'We really should try to get some sleep.'

I agreed.

52

GARY

On the day of the meeting, Emily and Mark spent the morning cleaning windows and giving the hotel kitchen a final deep clean. Deliveries were being made every half-hour or so and the place felt busy, as if it was finally coming to life. In five days' time it would be receiving its first paying guests – two days after the trial of Rowlett and Peterson was due to commence. I could tell I was just getting in the way and so went up to the apartment to sweat and fester and worry about the meeting.

I had an hour and a half to fill before I was due to set off for Peacehaven. I filled the dishwasher, arranged the spice rack in height order, didn't like what I had achieved so replaced the spices in a random order. One of the little jars was labelled 'Italian mix' and was nearly empty, so I poured what was left of it into the one labelled 'Mexican' and hoped that those two great cultures could find agreement on a way forward. I cleaned the chrome sink taps with one of those sponges that has a green rough side and a thicker light yellow spongy side, then dried the taps off with some blue checked kitchen towel. I

347

cleaned the top of the washing-up liquid bottle, was pleased with the outcome, so cleaned the spout of the hand soap bottle on the windowsill above the sink.

I opened every wall cupboard and peered inside. In the third one, I found a bag of sultanas that was a month past its use-by date. Beside it was a dead wasp. I guessed that the wasp had been lured into the cupboard by the scent of the once succulent sultanas. It had been a deadly attraction. I popped the wasp in with the sultanas and threw them in the bin. As the top of the swing bin caught the light, I noticed an amount of grime on its surface, so I wiped it clean with a product called 'Ron Waller's Magic Drops'. It had a decent amount of clout and cut through the residues just as it promised on the bottle. I noted that it was manufactured in Northampton, which was a place I had been to in the past to pick up a rubber door seal for a washing machine.

I went into the bedroom to pick an outfit for the meeting, and when I opened the wardrobe the first thing I noticed was my shitty grey suit. It struck me that it would help provide a good cover story for my trip out of the hotel. I would tell Brian that I was going to register with an executive recruitment office in town and that he was welcome to join me if he was looking for a change of job himself. He would never think that the suit was an escape outfit. It should do the trick and also remind DS Marks that I was an educated bloke with the fashion sense to prove it. Surely Brian was bound to want to stay with Emily in the office rather than take a trip out with me. He knew that I would never do a runner on my own and leave Emily behind and in his clutches. I would wear an open-neck blue shirt and my brown suede desert boots. It was an outfit that would attract very little criticism or attention and I was pleased with the choice.

I got a sudden sweaty worry on and decided to take a quick bath. I find a bath a good way to introduce a calming lull in times of panic. When I was young, the bathroom was the only room in the family house that had a lock on the door and the only place that I could withdraw to for a dose of peace and solitude. That was probably the root of my keen interest in bathing therapy.

It was an old avocado-green bath that was probably installed sometime in the 1980s by Emily's father. Once in the water, I ducked my head beneath its surface and expelled all the air from my lungs. I held my breath as the water above me settled and could feel the tension slacken in my stomach and chest. I repeated this three times then raised myself up so that my head was resting against the rim of the bath. The rim was cold on my neck and that was something I felt able to enjoy.

I noticed that the sealant between the bath and the wall was coming loose at the end nearest my head and picked at it to assess the extent of the damage. The last couple of inches came away from the gap into my hands, so I tugged on them and the whole length of sealant began to lift away, inch by inch, as I tugged. I knew I was making a terrible mistake but couldn't stop myself. It was an urge that I didn't have the strength or intelligence to resist. Once the whole strip of sealant was lifted, it fell into the water and dispersed a little trail of ancient dark filth. I feared its provenance so exited the bath sharpish. I was no cleaner, but I had, for the time being at least, averted the sweats.

I sprayed myself with deodorant and got into my suit. It was still half an hour before I had intended to leave but I was hit with an overpowering need to get out of the hotel and get on with the mission. I went downstairs to the office, where Emily was unpacking boxes of crockery with Brian watching on like a curious owl in a Crombie coat. I told him I needed to pop out for a couple of hours if that was okay by him.

'What for?' he asked.

I told him I was going to register at an executive employment agency and then do some shopping, that I might even buy some cakes for us all if I could find anything decent.

'Maybe I'll come with you, Gary,' he said.

'Up to you,' I replied. 'Do you like shopping for cakes?'

'Not as a rule, but I could make an exception for you. Come on, let's go.'

'Could you not help me unpack these boxes instead?' asked Emily, slightly too quickly to hide the panic in her voice.

'No, I'm here to observe, not to get involved, and I could do with some fresh air,' Brian replied.

He got up and walked me out of the office. Emily was staring at me open-mouthed with her hands outstretched in consternation. There was nothing I could say. It seemed that Brian was going to scupper everything.

Was it just by chance that he was coming, or did he know the real intention of my trip? A trip that I would have to abandon if he was by my side.

It was a hot, sunny day. Brian deposited his coat on the back seat of his car, outside the hotel.

'I've never seen you without your coat on,' I commented.

'It's a rare sight,' he replied. 'It's like a second skin for me.'

'I know what you mean,' I replied. 'I'm a bit the same with this suit I'm wearing. It's apologetic, non-threatening, helps people relax around me. It's been a good friend over the years.'

'I'm very pleased for you son, having a garment as a friend, but let's not get too chatty. I'm still sore with you over those onions.'

We walked along the promenade towards the town centre.

'So, where is this executive recruitment agency?' he asked.

'Churchill Square, right in the centre of town.'

'And what's it called?'

'Executive Recruitments,' I replied, almost choking on my words as they revealed how shit they were.

'Sounds like the right sort of place for an executive seeking work.'

'That's what I thought. I was drawn to it by the name.'

'Don't blame you. These people are very clever when it comes to branding, you have to hand it to them.'

'I agree, Brian. Big time. They certainly know how to cast a spell.'

I could not for the life of me think of a way out of the situation. I was fucked. I wanted to weep with frustration and then I was saved. Saved by Sequence. As we approached The Grand's entrance, he was exiting the hotel through its revolving glass doors.

'Brian, Gary, what a lovely surprise. I saw you walking up from my seat in the restaurant. Where you going?'

'I've got an interview with an executive recruitment agency in Churchill Square,' I replied.

'I thought I'd keep an eye on him for you, boss.'

'Nah, no need for that, Brian. He's got his shitty suit on; we don't need to follow him. Trust me, he's not up to anything. You're a good boy, aren't you, Gary?'

'I try.'

'Of course you do, and I'm glad to hear you're seeking employment and putting some roots down. I sense that all is good between you and Emily, am I right?'

'Yep, all good, no worries. Just keeping our heads down.'

'That's good to know,' said Sequence. 'Come inside with me, Brian. Join me for some brunch.'

'I've already had my breakfast. Emily made me an egg and bacon sandwich.'

'Lucky you, but this is brunch, not breakfast.'

'I've heard of it, boss, but I don't know what it involves.'

'It's whatever you want it to be, Brian. You could have a pastry, a crab salad, a burger — you could even have ice cream if you're feeling a bit coastal.'

'Sounds very liberating. Thanks, boss.'

'Off you go, Gary,' said Sequence. 'Maybe see you later.'

'I'll look forward to it.'

'That's good to know.'

They walked into The Grand. My legs felt as if they were made of hair gel. I couldn't believe my luck. Someone must be looking down on me with favour in their heart. I thought of Grace for a fleeting moment and thanked her out loud. I walked the hundred or so yards up to the pier and took a seat on a bench to try to recover my composure and my bearings. Doubled over, with my head in my hands and breathing as heavily as a pug in a greenhouse, my limping pigeon friend arrived at my feet.

'I see you remembered your limp today,' I said.

'Never mind that, you look like you've had a hell of a fright – found a ghost in your pocket or something. You want to tell me about it so I can think around it and sort you out?'

'I've got a meeting with a bloke that will decide my future and even perhaps whether I live or die or Emily loses her hotel.'

'Shit! That is one hell of a meeting. Have you prepared for it properly? Have you visualized it in your mind so that nothing takes you by surprise? When it comes to meetings, preparation is ninety per cent of the game. Have you thought around that?'

'It's not really a meeting that I can prepare for. All I can do is explain my situation and ask for his help.'

'Sounds like a sales job to me. I'm glad you wore a suit – gives you the look of a carpet salesman, which is low-ranking sales wise but at least indicates you're in the sales game. This bloke you're meeting – is he reliable? Is he solid? Is he on your side?'

'Yes, he is. I have no doubt of that.'

'Careful, sunshine. You should always have a bit of doubt when it comes to your judgement of people. Keeps you on your toes. Might end up keeping you safe from harm. Have you thought around that as a caution?'

'Yeah, okay, point taken. I'll keep my wits about me.'

Pigeon spotted a crumb of something at the base of the railing and dashed off with a flap of his wings to investigate it. It was just a bit of plastic and he returned disappointed.

'You forgot your limp again,' I commented.

'And you forgot to bring any grub, so let's say we're even in the overall failings register. So, a mate of mine saw you and Emily having a chat under the pier late last night. What was all that about?'

'Couldn't sleep with the worry, so we came out for a walk.'

'My mate said the two of you had a romantic air about you. Didn't mention anything about you looking panicky or dreadful.'

'We had a nice time, a bit of peace in the storm. She said we were in this thing together, rain or shine, tinned tomatoes or no tomatoes.'

'You should have asked her to marry you, that's what I would have done.'

'Do you know what, I think you're right. It would have been perfect. Then again, she's under a lot of pressure at the moment. Probably best I didn't.'

'Fuck's sake, Gary, just go for it. For once in your life, take a chance, go with your gut, be spontaneous, leave the worry in your haversack and – to be honest, mate – be a grown-up. Good luck with your meeting.'

And off he went to peck around the feet of a man enjoying a pack of fish and chips by the pier entrance. Halfway there he remembered his limp and on arrival immediately received a nice chunk of batter.

53

GARY

I walked over the road to the Royal Albion Hotel and used the payphone by the reception to ring Emily's office landline. I knew she would be in a panic and didn't want her to do anything hasty or risky. I gave her the joyous news that I had shaken off Brian and was free to go to the meeting. She wished me luck and ended the call with *I love you*. Nice.

I walked on along the promenade up towards the marina, regularly checking behind to see if Brian or Sequence were following. There was no sign of them, but I still thought it wise to take a bus some of the way to Peacehaven as another means of ensuring that I wasn't being followed. I sat on the downstairs back row of seats so that I would have a good discreet view of anyone getting on the bus, and got off a couple of stops before Peacehaven to give me another chance to scan around and look for anyone on my trail. Satisfied that I was on my own, I turned off the coast road and walked along the bungalow-lined street that led to the Dun Cow Pub.

So, this was it, my salvation awaited me, and yet again DS Marks was to be my saviour. I must have only been ten feet from the side entrance of the pub when a black car pulled up beside me and blocked my way. It gave me quite a start and I backed away as a figure jumped out of the driver's side, ran around the front of the car and grabbed me by the throat. It was Sequence. He pushed me around to the back of the car, his fingers clasped so tightly around my neck that I couldn't speak or breathe. He opened the boot of the car.

'Fucking get inside,' he said through gritted teeth, his eyes full of anger and loathing.

He pushed me towards the boot opening and I clambered inside as instructed. Fear overtook me as the car was quickly reversed a hundred yards or so back down the road. The boot lid was opened again.

'Where the fuck were you going, Gary?'

'Just to the pub. It's a place Emily and I go. I just wanted a break from the hotel and from you and your mate.'

He slammed the lid down again and I returned to the darkness. The engine of the car was turned off and the world went silent for a couple of minutes before I heard the driver's door open, the engine start up again and the car drive away. About ten minutes later, the car parked up and the boot lid opened again.

'Get out,' shouted Sequence. My exit was too slow for his liking so he grabbed me mid-manoeuvre and threw me onto the floor. It was a layby in the middle of nowhere. Nobody else was around; just me and him and a bin overflowing with litter. I stumbled up onto my feet, my lower back throbbing from its impact with the floor.

'I was just going to the pub,' I pleaded. 'I know I should have told you but . . .'

Sequence punched me right on the jaw and I fell to the floor like a sack of horseshoes. I don't think I was knocked out, but the next thing I knew I was stood up, face to face with Sequence, and he was slapping my cheek with the palm of his hand.

'This could have been so fucking easy [slap], so fucking trouble-free [slap]. All you had to do was keep your head down and do as you were told [slap], but instead you've fucked up and now it's got complicated. You fucking moron! [slap]'

'What have I done?' I asked, knowing the answer but unsure as to whether he did.

'Don't treat me like a pancake, Gary. I went into the pub and who do I see in the corner but your old friend DS Marks. You think running to him is going to save you and Emily? Because if you do you are well off the money. I can't fucking believe you would be so stupid. It's a whole different ball game now. Marks is going to get queasy when you don't turn up and soon enough he'll put two and two together and head for the hotel. Only question is whether I bother to move you somewhere else or just fucking get rid of you now. Get in the car, and if you try to deny what you were up to again I will set fire to you and that's a promise.'

We drove back to the hotel. How had Sequence known where I was headed? He always seemed to know my every move. I remembered what Emily had said about Roma and the answer seemed suddenly obvious: she was working with Sequence.

She had been in my flat alone the morning after she stayed over; maybe she had taken my bank details so that the ten thousand pounds could be paid into my account.

On the day that Sequence attacked me with the bag of mince outside one of my clients' block of flats, only someone with access to the office diary could have known I would be there.

Most damning of all, it was Roma who'd arranged today's meeting, and only her, DS Marks, Emily and myself knew of the meeting. It had to be her. The only doubt in my mind was the fact that she had actually arranged the meeting. Why wouldn't she have just told Sequence that we had asked to meet Marks? That seemed odd. Maybe Sequence just wanted to see if I would actually go ahead with it? It was hard to think straight and ask myself the right questions, but, nevertheless, the answer always seemed to be Roma. If I was right, she had played her part superbly; I hadn't suspected her for a moment. I had even let her live in my flat and introduced her to Grace. As soon as I had that thought, I wondered if Grace herself was in danger. Surely not. What benefit could she possibly be to Sequence when he already had Emily in his clutches?

When we arrived at the hotel, Brian was waiting for us in reception.

'Take care of him until I get back in touch,' shouted Sequence. 'Check the place is empty and lock it up. I'll update you in a couple of hours. Can you handle that?'

'Yes, boss,' said Brian, holding me firmly in a headlock.

'What about the other one?' asked Sequence.

'Already sorted,' said Brian.

Sequence ran out of the hotel. Brian dragged me with him as he locked and bolted the front door shut. He then hauled me into the office, where he switched off the broadband and unplugged the telephones. He marched me up to the Kiwi room, zip-tied me to the radiator beneath the window, sat himself down on the bed, opened up his laptop and settled down to re-watch *Ace Ventura: Pet Detective*.

'Where's Emily?' I asked, not managing to hide my panic.

'Like I said, she is sorted.'

'What does that even mean?'

'It means she is none of your concern.'

'Of course she is. Where the fuck is she?'

He turned his head towards me.

'You ask one more time and I guarantee you will never see her again.'

I believed him; he was the tin man and had no heart. I shut my mouth and tried to imagine Emily's fate. Every scenario made me want to weep. I felt helpless and entirely useless. This was all of my making. Why hadn't I just done as Sequence asked instead of acting the good boy? Why hadn't I told Emily that I loved her last night under the pier? I would have willingly given a thousand delightful stars away to see her face right now, this moment, and kiss her beautiful cheeks.

54

EMILY

When Gary left the office with Brian, I assumed the meeting with DS Marks would not be happening. I was briefly tempted to telephone Roma so that she could alert Marks to the cancellation and perhaps even ask Marks to come and rescue us. Something stopped me, though. I couldn't get the thought that she was connected to the Briggs clan out of my mind. It didn't feel right to put her in the picture and put our eggs in her basket. Then Gary rang me from a payphone and told me that he had shaken off Brian and was on his way to the meeting. Panic over. Although my nerves didn't seem to want to recognize that fact.

Mark came into the office. He could sense that I was flustered.

'What's the matter, Emily?'

'Nothing, Mark.'

'I agree, but you seem on edge.'

'Yeah, a bit. It's only five days until we open, got the new staff starting on Monday and I can't get rid of the nagging feeling that I've forgotten something crucial.'

'You haven't; everything is in place,' he said. 'I've gone through it in my mind a thousand times. We're ready. It's going to be amazing.'

I got up from behind the desk and gave him a big hug. His arms slowly lifted to horizontal and I could feel his eyes blinking through the back of his neck. He was giving those lids quite a workout.

Over Mark's shoulder I saw Brian running towards the office. He was flushed in the face and angry. I released Mark and jumped back behind the desk. He entered the room and shouted to Mark: 'You, fetch your stuff and get the fuck out of here.'

Mark looked at me for guidance. I nodded my head to indicate he should do as he was being told.

'It's all fine, Mark. Just take the day off. I'll be in touch,' I reassured him.

'NOW!' bellowed Brian. 'And don't come back until you're told to.' Mark scuttled off to collect his bits and pieces. Once he was gone, Brian turned around to face me again. 'Get up.'

'No, not until you tell me what the problem is.'

'Gary is the problem. Now, get up or I will pick you up and drag you out of here on your arse.'

He took a step towards the desk so I got out of my seat and approached him. He grabbed me by the arm and pulled me out of the room and up the stairs to the apartment. I didn't struggle but he rag-dolled me all the way as if to emphasize that things were about to be taken to the next level.

Once inside, he took me into my parents' old bedroom and threw me on the bed. He instructed me to sit upright and then tied my hands behind my back and fixed the zip ties to the iron frame of the bed. He disappeared for a few moments and then returned with a roll of extra-wide white duct tape that he used to gag my mouth.

'Your bloke has messed up. This isn't going to end well for either of you. Keep fucking peaceful and *you* might just survive it.'

He left the bedroom and I could hear him banging away at the apartment door, presumably taking off the inside handles and locks so that there was no means of escaping. Eventually it went quiet. The jabbing pain from the zip ties became my immediate focus. They were pulled incredibly tightly against my wrists and even the smallest movement would dig them into my flesh. The ties weren't going to come off with my efforts, so I tried to find a comfortable position to rest my head. There was no such position available.

I hated this room with its pink-and-red-striped wallpaper, chintzy light fittings and dark wooden furniture. It was more or less as my father had left it, aside from a few piles of storage boxes filled with nonsense from the apartment that I couldn't bear to throw away. I had caught my mum crying on this very bed on many occasions when I was a child. I could never be in this room without thinking of her and the sadness of her marriage. If I were to rot in this room, then it would connect me and Mum in a way that I could never have imagined would happen. My fluids would seep into the very sheets that had absorbed her tears.

All I could do was sit it out on the pale yellow nylon bedding and wait to see how things panned out. The glue on the back of the tape was beginning to burn my lips and I was desperate for a drink of water. I began to wonder how long I could actually last without falling apart. Maybe Gary was working on a plan. Perhaps he would agree to Sequence's every demand and then my internment would become unnecessary. All my eggs in the Gary basket; it didn't fill me with hope.

Three or four hours passed. Brian had popped his head around the door a couple of times but didn't speak. I tried to stare at him defiantly but it must have read as fear. He just smiled back at me, as satisfied in his work as a man can be.

I guessed it was about 5pm when I heard the slightly muffled sound of maintenance being carried out in one of the Royal Hotel rooms on the other side of the bedroom wall. It was frustrating that someone was so near to me but I had no way of alerting them to my situation. I shook the bed frame a bit in a pointless attempt to attract attention, but all this did was hit home how dire my predicament had become. *Please, Gary. Please, Gary, do something. I'm begging you.* All I wanted was to be with him, sat back under the pier, hand in hand, planning our future.

The noise from next door suddenly sounded slightly less distant. It seemed to be coming from beyond the en-suite bathroom. If only I could get in there and bang on the walls to attract attention. I couldn't scream for help; the tacky tape around my mouth and face was stubborn and unmoveable.

The work stopped and the room fell silent. The door to the en suite opened slightly, then a bit more, and then a bit more until it was half open. My heart pounded and my guts wallowed like a drain as a face appeared around the door and blinked at me. It was Mark. He raised a finger to his mouth to indicate I should remain silent, not realizing that I didn't have a choice in the matter.

He slowly approached the bed and sat down next to me. He began to speak softly and assuredly, without a hint of a blink. It was not a version of Mark I had ever encountered before.

'Emily, I have an apology to make. Please don't be mad at me. I've been hiding in the space between the apartment below and the hotel next door where the workings of the old lift used to be. It's not the first time. Sometimes I make myself a bed for the night in the void because I prefer being here than being at home. You will never let me stay overnight on the weekends Gary isn't here, but sometimes I do stay just in case something happens. When I untie you, we could get into the space and drop down into the Peach room through the service panel in the wall. That Brian man is with Gary in the Kiwi room. I have no idea whether it's a good idea, but I'm not leaving you here on your own. I think that man intends to do you harm and I will not have that happen on my watch. I'm going to untie you now. Please don't be mad at me.'

Mark pulled the tape away from my face and I sucked in the air like a newborn. I couldn't speak. He went through into the kitchen and fetched a knife to cut through the ties.

'Thank you, thank you, thank you,' I whispered, holding his face in my hands as his blinks kicked in again.

'You should call the police,' said Mark.

'Shit, I'm not sure. Let me think.'

The lock to the apartment door rattled. Brian was doing his rounds. Without thinking I jumped back onto the bed and assumed my captured position. Mark ran off towards the kitchen. Moments later, Brian came to the bedroom doorway and stared at me with contempt. It took him a second or two to notice that the tape had been removed from my mouth. He stepped into the room and as he did so Mark appeared behind him and brought the full force of my marble rolling pin down onto the back of his neck. He fell to his knees and Mark struck him again on the side of his head. He crumpled onto the floor. He wasn't moving and he wasn't making a sound. As far as my knowledge could inform me, he was stone-cold knocked out.

'Fuck,' I said.

'I agree,' said Mark before he fainted and dropped to the floor next to Brian.

55

GARY

Ace Ventura had finished and he was now watching the movie *Daddy Day Care*. He didn't appear to be enjoying it but never took his eyes off the screen. When the film had finished, he got up to leave the room.

'You want anything to eat?' he asked.

'No, I'm alright, thanks.'

'What about tomatoes on toast?'

For the first time in my life the thought of tinned tomatoes turned my stomach.

'No, but could I have a cup of tea?'

'You can, my friend. I shall go up to the apartment and make you one. Where will I find the tea bags?'

'They are on the windowsill in a white jar with "sugar" written on it.'

'Is that some sort of practical joke?'

'No, it's just that we threw out the one with "tea" written on it because it had a strange smell that was tainting the tea bags.'

'What kind of smell?'

'Like a dead mouse?'

'How curious. Do you know if a mouse did actually die in the jar?'

'We couldn't find any record of that happening.'

'Interesting. I like a mystery.'

He left the room and I had one of my occasional tugs at the zip tie around my wrist. It was never going to shift. I wondered what Sequence had planned. He now knew that I had intended to give evidence at the trial, so I guessed he was busy finding somewhere that he could imprison Emily and me until the trial was over. What his intentions for us were after that was the bigger worry. No doubt about it, we would be better dead than alive from his point of view. Would he really, actually kill us? It seemed far-fetched, but his clients had murdered before to save their skins. As I stood helpless, tied to a radiator and obsessing over Emily's fate, I would have gladly killed Sequence at the drop of a hat.

'Gary! Gary!'

It was Emily running down the hall.

'Gary!' she shouted as she ran into the room with a kitchen knife in her hand. 'Oh fuck, Gary. Mark has knocked Brian out. He's on the floor in the apartment and then Mark fainted and what the fuck are we going to do?'

Emily cut the zip ties and as we left the room I picked up Brian's telescopic cosh thing from the bed. Inside the apartment, Brian was still on the floor and Mark was sat beside him, looking fully confused and thoroughly uncertain.

'Shall we just run?' said Emily.

'I don't think so.'

'What should we do?'

'I don't know.'

'Shall we phone the police?'

'Probably but I'm not sure.'

Brian began to groan and his arms moved and stretched out.

'Tie him up!' shouted Emily.

'What with?' I replied.

His legs moved and his arse started to raise off the floor.

'HIT HIM!' shouted Emily.

I pressed the little button on the side of the cosh and it extended itself to about two feet. I raised it to shoulder height, closed my eyes and took a swipe at his head.

'You missed! Do it again!'

I raised the cosh again, this time with my eyes wide open. I couldn't do it. I couldn't bring it down on this defenceless bloke, no matter what he had done to us. I heard my stomach telling me I was about to be sick. Brian pulled his arms back so that he could use his elbows to lever himself up.

Emily kicked him in the kidneys a couple of times but it didn't stop him continuing his rise off the floor.

'HIT HIM!' she shouted again, almost hysterical in her fear.

I raised the cosh above my head this time, took aim, closed my eyes and struck. My grip on the cosh failed halfway down and it flew out of my hand, bounced on the bed and cracked one of the windowpanes.

'Fuck's sake,' said Emily as she took the rolling pin out of

Mark's hand and smacked Brian on the junction of the head and the neck. A big red bump appeared almost immediately. Brian went still and silent. Maybe he was dead. We needed to phone an ambulance.

The phone in Brian's pocket began to ring. I took it from his pocket. Sequence's name came up on the screen. I didn't answer. Emily checked Brian for a pulse; he was still alive and might come round any moment. His phone rang again. I didn't answer. I turned Brian's phone to silent and put it in my suit pocket. Emily's phone dinged a notification. I took it out of Brian's pocket. It was a message from Sequence with a photograph attached.

FACETIME ME RIGHT NOW OR YOU WILL REGRET IT FOREVER

My face dropped and my legs nearly gave way again.

'We can't phone the police,' I said.

'What? Why not?' asked Emily as she grabbed her phone off me and looked at the message.

'Oh fuck,' she said, sitting herself on the bed and holding her head tightly in her hands.

56

GRACE

Robert was due to pick me up for our Friday dinner date at 6:30pm. I asked Roma to come over at five o'clock so that she could help me get ready, have herself a bite to eat and generally calm my nerves over my first actual date for over ten years. She arrived carrying a bottle of prosecco and a quilted bag full of makeup on her shoulder. Lassoo welcomed her with a bark and a swift hundred-and-eighty-degree rotation then ran into the lounge to stare at the steak pie that was hot and ready on the table. I took a baking tray of chips out of the oven and poured them onto her plate.

'There you go, it's all yours.'

She got stuck in to the comfort platter. 'This is an excellent pie, Grace.'

'What about the chips?' I asked.

'Well, chips is chips,' she replied, hinting that they were nothing special.

'They are twice-fried-in-beef-dripping chips,' I said. 'They should have a good crunch, and a nice beefy aftertaste. If you don't think they're anything special then I won't be buying them again. They cost twice the price of the normal ones.'

'They're oven chips, Grace, nothing less nothing more. They do a job and they do it well. I'm very grateful for them.'

'Leave them if you want. I'm sure Lassoo will have them, or maybe not if they are as bad as you say.'

'Pack it in, Grace. The pie is fine, the chips are fine and you're going to have a fine time tonight. Just relax.'

'I'm thinking of calling it off. I don't feel right. I don't know if I can be bothered. I don't know what I was thinking agreeing to this stupid date. We could just stop in and watch *Border Patrol* or *Married at First Sight.*'

'No chance. You're going on this date even if I have to drag you into the car. Robert has been very kind to you and I can tell that you get on well. Take a deep breath and pour us both a glass of that prosecco I brought with me.'

I poured the prosecco and took a first sip.

'Did you get this from the garage?'

'Yes, I did, is there something wrong with it?'

'Well, you know, plonk is plonk, isn't it, nothing less and nothing more, does a job, I suppose.'

Roma gave me a little insincere round of applause, as if she had just watched a child she hated reciting a poem.

I would have preferred lager, that nice American one that Gary used to bring round, but Roma had insisted that we commence this momentous evening with some sparkles. I would pretend to enjoy it for her sake. After she had eaten, she sat me down at the dining table by the window to try to sort my hair out. She brushed it through, seemingly hitting a new tangle with every stroke. My hair still had a few streaks of grey at the front and sides but was thick and strong. Roma had brought some hair products and curlers and asked if a fancied a fuller, wavy look for the evening.

'Why not?' I replied. 'It might soften my haggard face, knock a few years off me.'

Roma began to back-comb my hair as I stared at myself in the makeup mirror she had placed on the table in front of me. My face looked so old. I could see the younger, pretty me hiding in there somewhere, but it was getting ever further from view.

'I bet you were a bit of a stunner in your youth, weren't you, Grace?' said Roma, as if reading my thoughts. 'I bet you had the boys slavering over you.'

'I had my admirers. My mum used to say that I was a work of art. That's a long time ago now. I prefer not to look at myself too often these days so I can kid myself I've still got a bit of something worth looking at. Ignorance is bliss and all that.'

'Well, Robert clearly thinks so,' said Roma.

'Thinks what?'

'That you've got something worth looking at.'

'Yeah, well, Robert is a very plain bald man with a flaky scalp and fat fingers. Of course he sees something in me; he's desperate.'

My hair looked good after its wave and back-comb. It reminded me of how I used to wear it in my teens when I was trying to look like a dark-haired Debbie Harry. I put on my grey trouser suit and a white blouse with long pointy collars. Roma said I looked 'classy'. Lassoo made a face as if to suggest 'brassy'. I agreed with Lassoo and changed out of the suit and into my yellow jumper and jeans. We were only going for a bloody pub meal – no need to pretend otherwise. I felt good in my jumper and new hairstyle; I didn't look like I did when I was twenty, but I didn't look awful, just different. I was going to stick with that thought for the evening. *'Just different.'* It would keep me cheerful with a bit of luck.

We sat on the sofa, I poured Roma another glass of prosecco and fetched myself a lager from the fridge.

'Oh, I heard from Gary, by the way. He wanted me to arrange a meeting for him with a policeman, something to do with that trial that's coming up, next week I think. Did he ever speak to you about that case?'

'Yeah, he never shut up about it for a while.'

'Did he tell you what happened in the garden? You know, when that fella Tommy Briggs got shot?'

'Yeah, I've spoken to him and Emily many times about that afternoon. He didn't get shot. He shot himself; it was a suicide. He tried to kill Emily, shot her in the hip. Probably thought he'd killed her, so he shot himself to avoid the consequences.'

'I've heard that some people think it was Gary that shot Tommy or maybe even Emily.'

'Gary? Gary?!' I laughed. 'You have got to be kidding. He's the biggest shithouse on this planet, you must know that. And as for Emily, I don't know why but she adored that Tommy bloke. She was pretty upset about him passing for a long time afterwards. Women are funny buggers. He used to slap her about and bully her up but she still loved him to the end. I'd have ripped his head off in the night first time he ever laid a finger on me.'

'I believe you,' she replied.

'Did he ask after me?' I said.

'Yes, of course. I sent him that photo we took after the meeting with Lizzie.'

Robert arrived on time and without a cravat. He was wearing a pair of brown leather driving gloves which, if the truth be known, I hated more than the cravat. I kept my mouth shut though and accepted a peck on the cheek from him as we entered the lift. Roma was stood watching on the walkway and I waved her a goodbye as the lift doors closed. Robert had parked his car about a hundred yards away at the entrance to the estate. It was a chilly, crisp evening and I wished I had worn a coat. Robert sensed my regret and offered me his to wear.

'You look lovely,' he said as he helped me into his coat.

'No, I look different,' I replied.

We hadn't been in the car much longer than five minutes when he pulled over and parked up on a street I didn't recognize.

'Why are we stopping?' I asked.

'This is my house, Grace. I hope you don't mind but I've forgotten my stomach pills and I need to change these shoes – they're ripping my heels a fresh one. Why don't you come

in with me and have a quick nose about or a little tipple?
We've got plenty of time.'

Permission to 'have a nose about' is like a red rag to a curious
bull with me, and I was out of that car before you could say
boo to a goose. He offered me his arm as we crossed the street.
I linked my forearm through the loop and it felt nice. It was
something I hadn't done for a long time. We seemed to fit
nicely; he was probably an inch or two taller than me, which
worked well for the arm coupling. I was carrying more girth
around the stomach and had the more thunderous thighs (bloody
cakes and pies), but overall we were a good physical match.

He left me alone in the living room while he went about
his pill hunt and shoe change. The house was freezing, as if it
hadn't had the heating turned on for weeks. I kept the coat
on and had a nose around the room. It was completely devoid
of any character, as if everything had been boxed up and only
the very essentials remained. Bare shelves, empty cupboards,
drawn curtains and underlay on the floor rather than carpeting.
There was a large smart TV still mounted on the wall above
the fireplace. A brown leather settee was facing the television.
It was the ultimate stripped-down bachelor pad.

Robert returned and asked me to come out with him into
the garden. Using a torch to guide us, he took me down a set
of steps that had been carved into the lawn. At the bottom of
the steps was a pair of large metal doors, like you would see
on the end of a shipping container.

'Come on in. There's something I want to show you.'

He seemed like an excited child, and so I followed him

inside to make him happy. He sat me down on a chair and then turned off his torch. It was pitch black. I felt very uncomfortable.

'What the fuck is going on, Robert?'

'I've got a nice surprise for you, Grace. How do you fancy a little chat with Gary?'

57

GARY

I FaceTimed Sequence's number and his bony face filled the screen. He was in a room without light, total darkness, and all I could see was his face, washed out and bright white like a ghost in the glow of the phone. He obviously didn't want to give me any clue about where he was located.

'Hello, Gary, very surprised to see you up and about. Where is Brian?'

'He's on the floor. We've knocked him out.'

'Show me.'

I tilted the phone down towards the floor so that he could view his fallen comrade.

'Nice work, Gary, I'm very impressed. Is he actually still alive? I don't want to be forced into a tooth-for-a-tooth situation here.'

'Yeah, we think he's okay. We're going to call an ambulance.'

'That's up to you. I'm not bothered either way.'

'So, what's with the photograph of Grace?' I said. 'What's going on?'

'Oh, she's here with me now. Would you like to say hello?'

'He turned his phone to his side and the light shone into Grace's face. She seemed to be wearing a new makeup regime and looked slightly confused. I waved at Grace.

'Hi, Gary,' she said, giving me a little smile and a wave.

Sequence turned his camera back on himself. The light on his face made it impossible to judge his mood. It was like staring at an owl up a drainpipe with a torch.

'I'm thinking that you're thinking that you had better do as you're told.'

I looked at Emily and she nodded her agreement.

'Correct,' I confirmed

'That's good to know. I want you to go to the Grand Hotel and check in to the room that I have booked for you in my name. Do it immediately and wait for my instructions. I think I might have found a place to store you away. I'll come and pick you up from the Grand.'

'What about Emily?'

'I don't care about Emily. I've got Grace now and that's enough to keep you both quiet. Hurry up, Gary, I want you out of there pronto.'

Just before he ended the call, I heard Grace shout: 'Tell him to eff off, don't you dare—' And then they were gone.

We both quickly agreed that it was time to forget Marks and do whatever Sequence asked. Grace was the priority and I would have to take whatever shit was coming in order to keep her safe. And then it hit me; I knew exactly where Sequence was phoning me from. When he had turned the phone towards

Grace, behind her, in the darkness, there was a bank of tinned corned beef, tinned kidney beans and tinned peaches. On top of the tins was a pile of corn cob husks. He was in Andy's bunker. That was where he was planning to take me.

'I'm going to drive up there,' I announced. 'I might be able to rescue her. Sequence is on his way down here to Brighton so that gives me a chance. I'll take your car; you stay here.'

'I'm not staying here, mate. I'm coming with you. I'm not sitting here on my own out on a limb, like a sitting duck.'

'Yes, of course. What was I thinking? Come on, let's go. Have you got your car keys?'

'I haven't got a car, Gary, haven't had one since I moved down here.'

'I thought your dad left you his Nissan Micra?'

'He did but I sold it to a bloke from Watford, don't you remember?'

'Yeah, yeah, I remember the sale itself but not the Watford part. So how the fuck do we get up to Peckham?'

Emily was already ahead of me as she pulled Brian's car keys from his pocket and held them up in front of her face. 'Let's take the Mercedes.'

I wanted to tell Mark to phone an ambulance, but he had rushed out of the apartment, unable to bear the sight of Brian's unconscious body. Emily could phone once we had got away from the hotel. We had reached the first-floor landing at the top of the grand stairs when we heard a roar behind us and turned to see Brian running at us like a bull with an arse full of ants. We moved to the side of the landing so that his impact wouldn't send us hurtling down the stairs. He stopped himself just before the lip of the stairs and raised his cosh in the air. I stood in front of Emily, awaiting the impact of the steel rod. It never came. Mark emerged from the other end of the landing, leapt at Brian rugby-style and sent him hurtling down the stairs. We all froze for a moment and then rushed to the bottom to see what had happened to him. He looked very nearly dead. Blood was pooling under his head, his eyes were empty and his body was twitching and convulsing like a fish out of water.

I told Mark to phone an ambulance and then get out of the hotel and go home. I picked Brian's cosh up from the floor then ran with Emily around to the side of the hotel. We got into Brian's black Mercedes and set off for Andy's house.

We were barely half a mile from the hotel when we passed an ambulance with its lights flashing heading the way of the hotel. Soon there would be a gurney wheeling Brian down the steps of the hotel. I prayed that Brian might still be alive.

58

GARY

It struck me as strange that Sequence didn't phone once during the drive up to Peckham. I wondered if we might have passed each other on the road as we drove the same journey in different directions. When he found out that Emily and I had bolted, it would hopefully be too late for him to do anything about it. Grace would be rescued and we could, at last, contact DS Marks without fear of repercussions.

I turned off the car headlights and then the engine as we approached Andy's house. My old car was on the drive and there were a few other cars parked in the road. I didn't recognize any of them. There was a light on inside the front living room of Andy's house. Everything seemed normal, the street was quiet and well lit by the street lamps, and the only thing moving was a fluffy grey-and-white cat wandering up the road as if he was the local bobby.

'What's the plan?' asked Emily.

'Don't really have one. I'm going to have a sniff about. Maybe Andy is home and he can let me in to the bunker. If not, then

I'll go round to the bunker and smash the lock off or something. If I'm right and that's where he's holding Grace, then fuck it, we can call the fire brigade if need be. Sequence can't do anything about it, he must be in Brighton by now.'

'Do you want me to come with you?'

'No, you stay here. If you haven't heard from me in, say, ten minutes, give me a ring to check everything is okay.'

'Have you got a phone?'

'Yeah, I've got Brian's phone. I thought it might come in useful. I'll text you the number.'

Emily took off her seat belt and leaned over to give me a hug. I think we were both quite relaxed and calm. We were out in the open and in control of our own movements for the first time in a week. It started to rain and the drops pitter-pattered on the roof of the car. The car was warm and cosy. Emily was by my side. I closed my eyes and drank in every single inch of her hug until it dissolved; it was time to carry out my incredible rescue attempt.

I grabbed Brian's cosh from the back footwell, walked the pavement to a spot opposite the house and watched for any movement inside. The living room had a large bay window to the front and a smaller window to the side. The curtains to both windows were drawn shut and there was nothing to be seen. I looked back towards Emily; I think she was giving me a thumbs-up, though it was difficult to tell in the darkness. I gave a thumbs-up back to her anyway, just for completeness. I bent over and crept across the road, stopping in the drive at the back of my old car from where I could peep over the bonnet and get a good view of the side and the front of the house. I noticed that the front door was slightly ajar. Maybe Sequence had left in a hurry.

I kept the car between the house and myself as I made a dash down the side path and into the back garden. The rear kitchen light was on but, again, I couldn't see anyone moving around inside. I crept around the edge of the garden until I was adjacent to the steps down to the bunker entrance. I ran down them and tried the door. As I expected, it was locked solid. I had the code (196651) but not the key. I tapped the door with Brian's cosh as hard as I dared, then pressed my ear against the door to listen for any sound. Nothing could be heard. Andy had soundproofed the unit to within an inch of its life, so I hoped that Grace was still inside and just hadn't heard my knocking. I needed to see if Andy was home so he could open the door, or, failing that, if I could find the key inside the house.

I ran back along the side of the house, being careful to keep my head beneath the window line. I wanted to check the front room again for any sign of movement. I reached the side window and slowly raised my head up to peer through the tiny gap between the overlapping curtains. There was somebody sitting on the sofa. The gap I was viewing through was about half a centimetre, and I could only see the back of their head and a bit of shoulder, but I immediately recognized to whom they belonged. It was Sequence, with his unmistakeable flouncy hair and his black and orange puffa jacket. I ducked down beneath the window and backed away from the house towards my car, where I took shelter.

Once again Sequence had got the better of me. He wasn't on his way down to Brighton; he was waiting for me in Andy's house. How the fuck could he have known that was where I was headed?

I reckoned I had two possible courses of action:

1. With Emily safe in the car and Grace in the bunker,
   I could phone the police and put an end to this.
   Only problem was that it would be the south
   London police that would respond and they were the
   people that Sequence was working for.
2. Have a go at taking Sequence by surprise and knock
   the fucker out with his mate's cosh.

You will no doubt find this hard to believe, but I chose the latter option.

I crouched right down again and slowly made my way under the side window, round to the front, beneath the front bay window and into the small entrance porch. I stood myself up and pressed the little button on the cosh to extend its threat. It made a sudden 'click'. I froze stock still as I listened to judge whether the click had alerted Sequence. I heard nothing from inside the house and so presumed it safe to proceed.

As I slowly, ever so slowly pushed the door open, I got a waft of Sequence's launderette smoke and then heard him speaking as if finishing off a telephone call. Silence. I took my first step into the house, stopped and then took another step until I was adjacent to the door in to the living room. This was it. I glanced back towards the open front door. It was very tempting to just run back out of it, regroup with Emily and come up with another plan that wouldn't involve me going head to head with Sequence. I remembered the words he had said to Emily back in the apartment: *'I've never lost a fight in my life.'* He was probably telling the truth and would undoubtedly have fought many people with higher-level fighting skills than me. My legs were weak, my heart was pounding and a fat eel was somersaulting in my stomach.

I thought of Grace, all alone in the bunker, scared and confused.

I thought of Lassoo, sat alone on the bed, waiting for Grace's return.

I thought back to Emily cowering on the sofa as Sequence bullied and threatened her.

I thought of Sequence nearly suffocating me with his meat bag.

I thought about the destruction of Wayne's café and the dream that evaporated on that day.

I thought about the Hotel Avocado and the future that Emily and I could have within its walls.

It was time to drop the shithousery, time to try and take control, try and be the bloke that I had always wanted to be and take a chance. I grasped the cosh tightly in my hand, raised it above my head and ran into the room.

'Aaaghhh!' screamed the person on the sofa.

I stopped myself just as the cosh was about to commence its downwards strike.

'What the fuck are you doing, Gary?!'

It was Grace, not Sequence, sat on the sofa. She was wearing his black-and-orange hooded coat and had her hair all bouffant and fancy like Sequence.

'Jesus, Grace! What's with the hair and the coat? I thought you were Sequence. I was just about to attack you. Are you okay?'

'Get out, Gary!' shouted Grace. 'You shouldn't have come here!'

'She's right, Gary, you shouldn't have come.'

I turned around to see a bald man in the doorway with Sequence's features but without the hair. On the crown of his head was a wide strip of toupee tape, the same tape I had seen in his car and that Brian had used to gag Emily. It took a few seconds to be sure that this was definitely Sequence and not some twin or look-a-like. He was pointing a gun at me, a real gun – there was no doubt about that. I dropped the cosh and held my hands in the air. He took a big, satisfied suck on his vape and told me to sit down on the sofa next to Grace. I did as I was told.

'Did you really think that Grace was me?' he asked.

'Easy mistake. She's wearing your jacket and her hair is all bouffant like yours.'

'I suppose you're right,' he said. 'Seems I got lucky by showing her a bit of kindness and storing her in here rather than the bunker. An accidental decoy I shall call her and be pleased with myself for doing so.'

'Hit him,' said Grace. 'I bet that's not a real gun.'

'Oh, it is, Grace. Do you want me to prove it?'

He pointed the gun at my forehead and closed one eye as if taking aim.

'Don't you dare!' said Grace.

'Then I suggest you shut your mouth,' said Sequence, adjusting his aim to the centre of Grace's face. She sat back in the sofa, silent but furious.

'You knew I was coming, didn't you?' I said.

'Of course I did, Gary. Like I've told you many times, I'm always watching.'

'It's Roma, isn't it? You're working with her, aren't you? She got you my bank details from my flat and told you what my movements at work would be. She told you about the meeting with DS Marks and I bet she helped you grab Grace.'

'What? Grace's neighbour? Have you lost your mind?'

'No, I haven't. She's something to do with the Briggs family, isn't she? You're working together, aren't you?'

Grace let out a little yelp. 'What you on about, Gary? Roma would never have anything to do with this little piece of shit.'

'Thank you for the compliment, Grace, and please pipe down or I'll have to shut you up. I am not working with that Roma woman. I think you must be having a turn, Gary, which is sad for you given that your mental health is all that you've really got going for yourself at the moment.'

'So, go on, then, put me out of my misery. How the fuck did you know I was on my way here?'

'You are wearing the answer, Gary.'

'What do you mean?'

'That shitty grey suit. I put a little GPS tracker in the lining that very first time I met you in the office. You were very obliging. Went out and made me a cup of tea so I could make the job a good 'un. Do you feel a chump now, lad? I hope you do and I think you should.'

I traced my fingers along the bottom seam of my jacket and in the corner of the vent I could feel some sort of device. It was small and insubstantial, like one of those flat circular batteries you put in the back of a clock.

'I told you it wouldn't be Roma,' said Grace.

I felt deflated, defeated and helpless. I had nearly been the hero that I wanted to be. Nearly, but not quite.

'You haven't seen me without my wig before, have you, Gary? What do you think? Sometimes it's useful to be two people; it can double your chances of success.'

'I've never seen him in a wig. I bet he looks like a little horse,' said Grace.

'Do you think I look handsome, Gary? Grace certainly does. We were out on a date tonight, weren't we, darling, and then it all went to shit for you, didn't it, Grace? All because of your precious Gary. If it wasn't for him, then you would be back at home dreaming of your next visit with little Lizzie.'

'How does he know about Lizzie?' I asked Grace.

'He's been buttering me up these last few weeks and I agreed to let him give me a lift down to Lewes when I had my first visit. He's a sneaky bastard. I had no idea he just wanted to get his paws on me so that he could use me to get to you. He had me hook, line and sinker, and you know how suspicious I am of all men, bald ones especially.'

'You don't have many connections, do you, Gary? And this old lady was the only back-up plan I could find when it came to gaining leverage. And this place with its bunker is perfect to hide you all away, or dispose of you if that becomes the plan.'

'What about Andy? What have you done with him? Is he locked up in the bunker, or have you done away with him?'

'He was very obliging actually. Seemed to think I was from some powerful government organization and was very happy to disappear for the time being while we used his facility for our work. I've paid him handsomely so don't shed any tears for him.'

'Are you going to let Grace go now that you've got me?' I asked.

'I don't think I can do that, Gary. I'm waiting for instructions but I doubt that is going to happen.'

'Well, I think you should make it happen.'

'Why is that, Gary? Why would I want her running to the police and causing problems? Probably better I just leave you to rot in the bunker, or better still, just get rid of the both of you. Like I say, I'm waiting for instructions. I'm not bothered either way.'

'Emily is still in Brighton and she is going to telephone me any moment now. If she doesn't get any reply, she is going to go straight to DS Marks.'

'We'll see about that, Gary. In the meantime, get up and let's go for a little walk into the garden.'

I stood up.

'I fucking hate you,' I said.

'Not as much as I do,' said Grace.

'That's good to know,' he replied. 'And a very healthy attitude, if you don't mind me saying.'

'I'm not going back in that bunker,' said Grace. 'Go on, I dare you to shoot me. Go on, shoot me.' She stood up with her chest puffed out towards him, seemingly happy to receive a bullet.

Sequence laughed and raised the gun upwards again. 'Let's go,' he said.

'Don't worry, Grace, it will be okay,' I said, not believing a single word of it.

He pushed us out of the back door and marched us down into the bunker. The door clanged shut behind us and we found ourselves in total darkness. Grace grasped my hand and held it tightly.

59

EMILY

I watched Gary cross the road from opposite Andy's house and disappear into the driveway. I wished him good luck under my breath and checked the time on my phone so that I would know when the ten minutes was up. I didn't like being alone again; it filled my head with negative thoughts. Ten minutes wasn't long. I checked my phone; only nine minutes to go.

It was getting cold, but I couldn't turn on the ignition for fear of alerting anyone to my presence. Brian had left his big dark blue woollen coat on the back seat, so I stepped out of the car, grabbed it and put it on. It drowned me with its size but felt instantly cosy. Back in the car, I turned the ignition key one click and the dashboard came to life; the glow of the light felt reassuring. I checked inside the storage space beneath the armrest. Inside was a little silver puppet of the Tin Man from the yellow brick road movie. I picked it up and looked into its dead eyes. It seemed to be telling me that I should leave this place immediately and never return. Six minutes to go.

Surely if everything was okay Gary would have emerged with Grace by now? I tried to imagine a reason for the delay. Perhaps Gary was having trouble with the locks on the bunker? Perhaps Grace was having a cuppa to calm her nerves? Perhaps Andy was at home and him and Gary were having a quick catchup? I wasn't convinced. It felt as if something was going wrong. I pictured Gary dead on the lawn. *Where did that thought come from?* I pictured Grace dead inside the bunker. *Stop it, everything is going to be fine.* I started rocking gently in the seat and gripping and pumping the steering wheel as if trying to bring it to life. Three minutes to go.

The grey fluffy cat that seemed to own this particular stretch of the road stopped to stare at me from the opposite pavement. I wound my window down and made that sucky noise that seems to attract a cat's attention. He slowly walked over and sat in the middle of the road, having a good old stare at my predicament.

Hello, Mr Pussy, you doing your rounds?

He licked his lips and blinked.

Come on. Come on over and say hello.

He sat on his arse and lifted one back leg high in the air as if playing a cello.

What's your name, little fella? PC Woodruff?

He started to lick and clean the underneath of his thigh before lying down and rubbing his back against the surface of the road.

Ooh I bet that feels good!

Something gave the cat a sudden fright and he jumped back

up on all-fours and sprinted into the nearest garden. I looked all around to see what it might have been but all seemed quiet and dead. One minute to go. *Fuck it, let's phone Gary.*

Gary answered after just a couple of rings.

'What's happening? Are you alright? Have you got Grace?' I asked with panic clothing every single word.

'Sequence was here,' said Gary without any emotion. 'I'm with Grace; he's locked us both in the bunker.'

'What shall I do? Shall I phone the police?'

'Yes, do it now.'

The door beside me opened and the phone was grabbed out of my hand. I looked up to see a bald man with a thick stripe of bright white tape across the centre of his dome staring down on me. I screamed as he dragged me out of the car with his hand pressed tightly against my mouth. Fear engulfed me as I was frogmarched down the road and into the driveway of Andy's house.

'You don't recognize me, do you, darling?' said the man.

It was true, but I did recognize the voice. It was Sequence, which meant everything had backfired and turned to shit.

60

GARY

I activated the torch on Brian's phone and shone it at Grace. 'Emily is outside. She's going to call any minute. I'll tell her to phone the police and then this will all be over.'

'Can you get that thing out of my face, please?' said Grace.

I turned the light away from her and shone it around the bunker. There was an old leather chesterfield sofa along one side, a work station at the far end, floor-to-ceiling shelves stacked with equipment and two large columns of tinned food on the side opposite the sofa. I told Grace to sit down on the sofa while I scanned around with the torch, trying to find a light switch.

'Don't bother looking for a light switch,' said Grace. 'There's no power in here. He brought me in here earlier when we had that phone call.'

I examined the shelving and came across a box with five or six different battery torches inside. I took one for myself, gave one to Grace and placed the others on various shelves to fill the bunker with cross-beams of light.

'That's better,' said Grace. 'Now we can actually see each other shitting ourselves.'

I sat down beside Grace on the sofa.

'Are you okay, Grace? Did he hurt you at all?'

'Nah, just my pride. My own fault really – should never have trusted him. He was far too pushy from the start. More fool me for thinking he might be interested in an old trumpet like me that's lost its parp.'

'I'm so sorry, Grace.'

'What's his real name?' she asked.

'He told me his name was Clive Sequence but I doubt that's his real name.'

'Why didn't you just go to the police? Look at all the trouble you've caused. Lassoo will be expecting me back soon and if I don't appear he will rip the flat apart looking for me.'

'It's not as simple as you think, Grace. The problem is that Robert, as you call him, kind of *is* the police. I've been trying to hedge my bets and it's looking like it was the wrong thing to do.'

My phone rang. Emily. I picked it up immediately. She asked me what was going on and I quickly filled her in and told her to phone the police. Her phone went dead. Maybe the battery had gone? Maybe Sequence had got her? It was probably the latter. I rang her again but there was no reply. It was definitely the latter.

A minute later the door to the bunker opened and Sequence threw Emily inside and onto the floor. She stayed down on the deck with her head resting on her outstretched arm. She looked up at me and gave me a smile. It felt like a goodbye.

Sequence shut the door behind him, stepped over Emily, lifted up his gun and fired directly into the stack of tinned goods. Grace and I both screamed with the shock of it and the sheer volume of the firing.

'I DON'T WANT TO HEAR A FUCKING WORD OUT OF ANY OF YOU!' shouted Sequence before stepping back out of the bunker door to make a telephone call. He stared directly at me from the doorway as he spoke to whoever was on the other end.

'Yep . . . Yeah . . . I understand. . . . I agree . . . Of course. Consider it done.' He ended the call, stepped back inside and closed the door behind him. He picked Emily up by the shoulder of the coat she was wearing and dragged her over to the base of the shelves opposite the sofa. She didn't resist. She just slumped onto the floor, still wearing her farewell smile.

'I'm sorry, Gary, but this is it. You can have a second or two to say your goodbyes.'

Grace got up off the sofa and stood directly between myself and Sequence.

'Don't you dare,' she said.

'Good idea, Grace, I can take you both out with one shot, save me a bullet.'

I stood up and placed myself between Grace and Sequence.

'Fair enough,' he said. 'I don't mind which of you goes first.'

'Why can't you just leave us here until the trial is over?' I pleaded. 'None of us are going to tell the police about you.'

'That's good to know, Gary,' he replied.

'There's no need for this,' I said.

'You might be right, Gary, but I'm just following instructions. Now shut the fuck up.'

He lowered his gun so that it was pointing at the centre of my chest. Grace grabbed me around my middle and held me tightly in a hug. I turned around to throw her off me so that she wouldn't be in the line of fire and then ... *BANG!* I shuddered and froze, waiting for the pain of the impact, but it didn't arrive. I turned around to see Sequence jerking and wriggling on the floor. I looked towards Emily, who was now sitting up backlit by the two torches on the shelves behind her. She had a gun in her hand pointing directly down at Sequence. I ran over to him and kicked the gun out of his hand.

Emily started to shake as she lowered the gun to her side. 'What the fuck have I done?' she said. 'It was in the coat, Brian's coat. The gun, it was in his pocket.'

I grabbed her just as she was about to collapse onto the floor and walked her over to the sofa. 'Is he dead? Please tell me he's not dead,' she said.

Grace was now leaning over Sequence. 'Nah, he's okay. Won't be getting up for a while, though,' she said. 'His thigh is shot to shit. Now can someone please phone the police?'

Grace handed me her phone, took off the puffa jacket and used it to help stem the flow of blood from Sequence's thigh.

Sequence started to catch his breath and moan with the pain of it all. 'Aaghh! Oh my god, please fucking do something, please! It hurts so fucking bad, I can't take it!' he said, the agony etched on his face.

'That's good to know,' I said.

I dialled 999, then hesitated and ended the call.

I asked Grace if she had Roma's number and she told me it was the last number she had dialled. I rang Roma and got the number of DS Marks from her. I phoned Marks and blurted out the basics of what had just happened.

'Stay where you are,' he replied. 'You've done all you can. Just look after each other until we arrive.'

'Will do.'

I sat down next to Emily and took her in my arms.

'Are you okay?' I asked.

'I think so. I've never shot anyone before so I'm not really sure how I should feel.'

'He was going to shoot me. You saved my life and probably yours and Grace's too.'

'Is this over now? Is this the end?' she asked.

'Yeah, I reckon. I love you, Emily Baker.'

'I love you too.'

There was silence apart from the dripping of some juices from a can of kidney beans, the occasional moan from Sequence and Grace's swear-filled mutterings as she tended to him. Maybe it was the torchlight, maybe the euphoria of the victory, but whatever it was, the moment seemed right.

'Shall we get married?' I asked.

'I think we should,' said Emily.

'Viva tomatoes.'

'Viva tomatoes.'

POSTSCRIPT

As it turned out, Rowley and Peterson and their crew of bent coppers all pleaded guilty on the first day of their trial and so I wasn't required to attend court and give my evidence. DS Marks reckoned that if Sequence had succeeded in stopping me from attending then they would have pleaded not guilty and would have had a good chance of being acquitted. The USB stick containing the evidence against them would not have been admissible in court without me in the witness box to confirm how it had come into my possession in the first place. The case would have collapsed. I had been a good boy – a very good boy.

Brian and Sequence both survived their injuries and were remanded in custody, awaiting a trial of their own for kidnapping, false imprisonment and perverting the course of justice. Some sort of thug pride or code ensured that Brian never mentioned a word to the police about Mark pushing him down the stairs. He stuck to his story that he had simply fallen down due to queasiness brought on by a particularly turgid brunch.

The Hotel Avocado opened on time and seemed to be hitting the mark that Emily had intended. This review on TripAdvisor probably sums things up better than I ever could:

The first thing that hits you when you arrive is obviously the huge avocado that hangs on the front of the hotel. Me and the husband got the obligatory selfie (attached)!

Apparently the local council are trying to get the avocado taken down, but the owners are fighting tooth and nail for it to remain. There's a petition in the lobby and when we signed it there was quite a queue of locals waiting to do the same.

The hotel is immaculately clean and well run. From the moment we checked in we knew we were in good hands. The Assistant Manager, Gary Thorn, had clearly spent years in the hospitality business as he seemed able to predict our every need, often even before we had thought it ourselves. We requested 'The Kiwi Room' as it's been my husband Ken's favourite fruit ever since he was advised that it would help his insomnia. Breakfast was served in the beautiful tiled lounge overlooking the seafront. Our server, Mark, was a tad nervous but absolutely charming. He recommended the fried bread, which was dry fried in the oven and absolutely delicious with a poached egg on top. The hotel was fully booked during our stay and had a very lively buzz about it. The owner, Emily, is a wonderful host and keeps everything ticking over effortlessly. We were lucky enough to be staying on the first weekend that the coffee shop in the front basement opened. It's managed by a young man called Wayne who was charming if a bit overly informative when it came to serving up the coffee. We tried his dark-dark roast, which was nice but not very different to the Aldi coffee that we have at home. Gary recommended we try the Battenberg cake and he was bang on the nose. We had a slice every day with our afternoon tea.

All in all, we would say it's the best little seaside boutique hotel we have stayed in for some time. We have already booked our next stay and can't wait to return.

Two months after the bunker incident, Grace and Lassoo came to visit us in Brighton. Before she left, we all sat down together on our favourite seafront bench opposite the hotel and shared a bag of chips.

'You still angry with Sequence for getting you to fall for him?' I asked Grace.

'No, I never give him a second's thought. Hardly knew the bloke, hope he rots in hell.'

Grace picked a large chip out of the bag and chewed on it ferociously as if it were her sworn enemy. Maybe I shouldn't have asked.

'Hope it hasn't put you off men forever, Grace. That would be a shame,' said Emily.

'Wouldn't be a shame at all,' said Grace. 'I'm absolutely fine with just my daughter Mary, Lizzie, Roma, you two and Lassoo. I consider myself to be blessed. I'm finished with all blokes apart from you, Gary, though you're not really a bloke, and Lassoo, who isn't either, in the strictest sense. Can't see the point of them, to be honest.'

We both laughed; Grace joined in eventually.

'You've done amazing with the hotel, Emily,' said Grace. 'No thanks to him, of course.'

'Excuse me, Grace, but it was me that hung all the pictures up on the second-floor landing.'

'Funny that,' said Grace. 'That was the only part of the hotel that didn't work for me. Spacing was all wrong.'

'Bit like your teeth,' I said.

'Do you know what I would really love?' Grace continued, ignoring my excellent remark. 'If Lizzie and Mary could come and stay here together with me one weekend. That would be just wonderful.'

'Well, get it sorted,' said Emily. 'Maybe you could come on the weekend we get married.'

'You really going to marry this chump? You must be a sucker for punishment. Just look at all the trouble he's caused you already.'

'He's been unlucky, Grace, that's all. Stop being so hard on him.'

'Never.'

We all laughed and Lassoo wagged his tail so hard in agreement that it seemed he was trying to disperse a thousand magical stars into the happiness of it all.

PIGEON POST

It's me again. I thought I should sign off and clear up a couple of things before I go. If you're the sort of person that likes to leave a few loose ends hanging about, then that's your choice. Truth is, you probably have an untidy mind and an untidy house and that's only going to cause your loved ones distress and irritation come your last supper.

Firstly, you might remember that on the night of the blue lights and the gurney I saw a little fellow standing on the roof line as if he might be about to jump off into oblivion. Well, it turns out he didn't jump. Gary told me he was up there hiding a marble rolling pin that could have got him into trouble. I didn't ask for any more details because I could sense that none were forthcoming. Like I've told you before, I'm not in the slightest bit nosey. If you think I am then I hope you fall arse first onto a plate of sausages at your next gossip party.

Secondly, you will have heard talk about a lady called Roma. Both Emily and Gary were worried that she might have some connection to Sequence or a family called Briggs that had bad intentions towards Emily and the hotel. Well, here's the thing; she had nothing to do with Sequence and was in fact very pleased that he failed in his plans. It did, however, turn out that she was a niece of this Briggs fella. Apparently she was on a mission to find out the truth about what happened in that garden when Tommy died. She had got the job at Gary's old firm of solicitors so that she could be as close to the case as possible. What she hadn't expected was that she would find a good friend in Gary (though she never got as close to him as I did) and a willing talker in Grace, who convinced her beyond doubt that Emily and Gary were just innocent bystanders to his suicide. Her and Grace are best buddies now and Gary tells me they are talking about taking a trip to New Zealand together to see if they can smuggle some nuts and seeds through customs.

I have to admit to one loose end, but I promise I will try to tie it up at some future date. I still see Councillor Jordan sniffing around the Avocado and the two buildings either side. Every time I see him I get an off-kilter feeling and, as you know, that's as good an indication of trouble ahead as you can get. I'll keep an eye on him, don't you worry about that.

So, sorry, but yeah, there is a loose end, and if that upsets you then post your complaint to your nearest harbourmaster and include a fiver so they can have a small coffee and a slice of Battenberg on me.

Must fly.

ACKNOWLEDGEMENTS

Thanks to Holly Harris, Lisa Clark and Caroline Chignell for their advice, encouragement and support throughout this process.

And thank you to my son Tom, who would play a game of darts with me whenever my eyes went bent and my mind wandered due to the writing and the worry.